Praise for *TOPANGA CANYON*

"Mother-daughter relationships are fraught with expectations, disappointments, and love. This story's warm, real, and true. The characters will resonate with you beyond the last poignant page."

—Laura Drake
Author of *The Road to Me*

"... a cast of captivating characters, who embrace the openness and honesty that lead to glorious truths and much-needed forgiveness."

—Maggie Giles
Author of *The Things We Lost*

"... the charming tale of a multi-generational family and their complicated and ofttimes sticky relationships ... the women of Topanga Canyon will have you crying and laughing through their struggles and triumphs ... a warm, multi-layered novel to love."

—Rita Woods
Author of *Remembrance*

"Wafler's prose is as rich and lyrical as the timeless songs she weaves through Dare and Caroline's days as they tumble toward healing and forgiveness. A smart, tender, uplifting story about the power of compassion, forgiveness, and found family."

—Christine Adler
Author of *Undressing the Heart*

"An evocative, authentic, and sanguine saga that women's fiction lovers will devour. Wafler explores the importance of the mother-daughter bond and how patterns set forth by previous generations can impact a family's future."

—Kristina Parro
Author of *Lucky*

TOPANGA CANYON

ALSO BY ELIZABETH SUMNER WAFLER

Georgie Girl
In Robin's Nest

To Suzanne

TOPANGA CANYON

A Novel

Elizabeth Sumner Wafler

*XO,
Elizabeth Sumner Wafler*

EVOCATIVE PUBLISHING LLC

ELIZABETHSUMNERWAFLER.COM

Copyright © 2022 by Elizabeth Sumner Wafler

All rights reserved. No part of this book may be reproduced, distributed or transmitted, in any form or by any means, without prior written permission.

TOPANGA CANYON is a work of fiction. Names, characters, places, and incidents are a product of the author's imagination. Locales and public names are sometimes used for atmospheric purposes. Any resemblance to persons, living or dead, are coincidental. Any mistakes are the author's alone.

Cover Design: Kristina Parro

Formatting: Julie Klein

First U.S. Edition: May 2022

ISBN: 9798449774910

evocativepublishing@elizabethsumnerwafler.com

For Porter Wafler: my hero and the love of my life.
Every woman deserves to be so cherished.

Chapter One

Dare O'Day
2021

Caroline is on my mind. Through the kitchen window, the sky is such an unsullied blue miracle that I almost believe my life's most enduring wrong might somehow be made right. My Colombian housekeeper, Seraphina Perez, and I sit on stools at the marble island, decorating boiled eggs for the hunt the Episcopal church hosts for the children of Foxfield, Virginia. Easter's late this year. Just weeks before Caroline's birthday. It's the season of new life, of hope.

This afternoon, the alumnae association at our women's college is hosting a gathering in my garden for the senior class. Seraphina and I are waiting for the caterers to arrive. Three months ago, Holland Hutton, the new president contacted me at the *Journal* where, after a decade, a peek at the masthead with my name DARE MARSTON O'DAY next to the title of FEATURES EDITOR still makes me smile. *Your garden is the perfect setting for the event, Dare. And you won't have to lift a pinkie.* Now, when the caterers arrive, I step out to greet them and to let my one-eared rescue dog Lucie tinkle beneath a flowering crab apple. As the team unloads their van, I brush a pop-up shower of pink blossoms from Lucie's coat before leading her back inside. Still at the island, Seraphina wriggles on her stool and uncaps a paint pen. "Let's stay here and watch."

"Like with a bucket of popcorn and a box of Junior Mints?"

She grins. "If we keep the lights out, they won't be able to see inside."

"Well," I say, taking a seat again, "I'll stay 'til we get the eggs finished."

The caterers drape round tables with white cloth and plant the legs of gilded chairs in the tender spring grass. A tiny woman laboring under an enormous empty crystal punch bowl is crossing the terrace. Seraphina gasps and crosses herself until the woman sets the bowl safely on the end of a long table. At the whoosh of luxury cars nosing into the driveway behind my ten-year-old Toyota, Lucie lets fly a shrill bark.

"Hush, whistle britches. The alumnae are here." On teetering heels, the women help the caterers carry plastic-wrapped silver trays from the van.

Seraphina touches the paint on the last of the eggs and, satisfied, begins nesting them into the cartons we'd saved. "Thank goodness I remembered to put a pair of crossed spoons on the grass," she mutters, "or else it would've rained." The roots of Seraphina's superstitions are deep and many branched, covering every human circumstance. I help her bag up pens, remembering the first time we met, when she was my mother's caretaker. She reminded me of tiny, rawboned Carla from TV's *Cheers*. But when she opened her mouth and Sophia Vergara came out larger than life, I knew I'd met a friend. My mother, the indomitable Taft "Taffy" Marston of Marston Candies, was weary of big city life. She up and left D.C. for northern Virginia and the hamlet of Foxfield. Here she hired Seraphina. Years later, when Taffy died and I moved from D.C. and into her home, neither Seraphina nor I had a reason for her not to stay. She even coerced me into raising her already prodigious salary.

Someone slams the back doors of the catering van, and we both look toward the sound. Lucie lifts her head from her dog bed beneath the table and looks at me before letting go a menacing growl. Hopping out, she trots to her water bowl. "You know that's like a crime van," Seraphina—a devotee of *Law and Order: Special Victims Unit*—says, giving me a confidential side-eye.

I stare at her. "What *in the world* are you talking about?"

"A kidnapping van." She flips a palm indicating the immaculate white van with the fancy script on the side. "No windows to see the evil happening inside."

"You've lost your mind. The only crime going on in there is

highway robbery, the prices they charge." We're laughing as the living room clock chimes four and the thunk of car doors out front announces the students' arrivals. "We better get those eggs in the fridge. I can't smell them anymore, but if somebody comes in, they might think . . . you know."

Seraphina grins. "What? That you farted?"

"Seraphina! *Me?* And don't use that tacky word." I open the refrigerator and push the cartons inside. She's still cackling as we watch the girls float into the garden in pastels and sunglasses, cellphones in hands, their hair gleaming black, chestnut, and blonde in the sunshine. The alums greet the students with professional handshakes and direct them to a wrought iron table to fill out nametags with Sharpie markers.

"I wish I could hear what they're saying," Seraphina says, fussy faced. I'd forgotten that Holland is not only the president of the alumnae association but also has a daughter at the college. I watch them now, chatting and laughing at the edge of the terrace, as alike in appearance as a pair of dangly earrings. The daughter moves behind Holland for a moment and gives her mom's shoulders a little massage. When another student appears, bouncing up and down in an I'm-next posture, Holland steps aside and rolls her shoulders as though in relief. I read her bold pink lips: *Thank you, sweetheart.*

I reel with wistfulness. This is one of the times I long to text my daughter and know she'll ping me right back, maybe even engage in a brief dialogue about our days. *You should see what's going on here. Seraphina's having a field day.* Even though Caroline's an adult now, we haven't reached the point where we've become friends like many of the mothers and daughters I know. I wonder how often she thinks of me where she lives in California. Probably about as often as she cleans her rain barrel. It stings that we're not close, though I own my share of the estrangement that lies like a bottomless canyon between us.

I sigh and turn my attention to the girls filling their plates, forcing myself to focus on a sweeter topic: a tray of petit fours on the dessert table.

"Why don't you make coffee?" I ask Seraphina. "Maybe they'll leave a few of those cakes behind."

"You make it," she says, her eyes glued to the window. "I wouldn't miss this for a date with *the* Andy Garcia." She makes a humph in her throat. "Those fancy caterers. If they got a taste of my tres leches cake, they'd be begging for the recipe."

"True that," I say, smiling again as I measure the Colombian coffee she insists we order online into the machine. Well-mannered and subdued, the girls seat themselves on the gilded chairs. Maybe they're nervous or just making their best impressions before taking part in a discussion on the rollout of a slick new alumnae magazine. The great glass bowl is full of what appears to be pineapple punch. A caterer ladles it into a dozen or so cut-glass cups and then moves on to help tend to the food. The washing machine signal burrs. Seraphina hops up to put the load in the dryer, muttering about the cheap-ass new detergent I bought that makes her itch. A pregnant alum hauls herself to her feet and brushes crumbs from her ship's prow of a belly. She takes a microphone and thumps it a couple of times to check the sound. Looking out through a low pane of glass in the back door, Lucie cocks her head.

"Good back there?" the alum asks the students at the farthest table nearest the refreshments. The girls offer her brisk thumbs-ups, and a discussion begins.

"Let there be sound!" Seraphina says, hurrying back into the room. The alum asks the seniors what content they think should be included in the publication based on their years at the college. I sip coffee and listen as a cordless mic is passed from hand to hand. "Check out the fake Kate Spade tote," Seraphina says.

"Where?"

"At the back table, on the chair of the chica with her hair dyed silver like an old lady. Why the hell do they do that anyway?"

"It's just fashion. How do you know the tote's a fake?"

Seraphina sniffs. "I read *In Style* magazine." I grin and raise an eyebrow at her Lamar Jackson, Raven's football jersey and purple stretch pants. She ignores me and pours herself a cup of coffee, then sits, her elbows on the island. From time to time, girls rise to go back for seconds on punch and refreshments. I check the petit fours: still half a tray left. "Miss Kate Spade sure has been back to the punch bowl enough times," Seraphina says, twisting her lips to one side. "I knew we should have put a porta potty in the yard."

I hoot. "That would have gone over really big with the association."

Before long, the microphone is passed to the girl with the fake bag. She stands, the skinny heels of her shoes miring into the grass. Maybe all the heels will help aerate my lawn. The girl struggles to steady herself.

"What's your name, please?" the pregnant alum asks her.

"Oh," she answers, slapping a hand over the name tag on her chest. "I'm Allie Ahern." Then she hiccup-burps loud enough to be heard in Baltimore. Right into the microphone. Her face turns the color of the lone raspberry on the fruit tray. "Please excuse me!" But as the girls at her table dissolve into giggles, Allie joins them and plops back into her gilded chair. She shakes her head and waves her hand in a come-back-to-me-later gesture. Seraphina swings her head toward the alum at the microphone. I follow her gaze to the woman's waxen face.

"Perhaps someone else has an idea for the student life pages," the alum says through tick-tight lips. Then "Yes," she says with a grateful smile, calling on a tall black girl who has raised her hand from a table up front.

As the student begins speaking, Seraphina elbows me and indicates with her chin the students at Allie Ahern's table, where a quieter flurry of commotion has ensued. "Joseph, Mary, and Jesus," she says, pronouncing the Lord's name Haysoos.

"Well, they probably just have a touch of senioritis," I say but with an unexamined sense of unease.

When the shadows have lengthened across the terrace, the party wraps and the young women troop to their cars, no doubt to get ready for big Saturday nights. As the caterers began their dismantling, the alums come inside, the chill spring night rushing past them.

Holland rubs briskly at her arms. "It sure feels good in here! What a cute dog," she says, though I see the double take she gives Lucie's missing ear. The pregnant one asks to use the powder room and toddles down the hall. A caterer makes a platter of leftovers to leave with Seraphina and me, including a packet of *five* petit fours. Woot! As the last of the alumnae cars pulls from the driveway, Lucie clips over to her food bowl as she does every afternoon promptly at 5:25. I feed her and pour myself a glass of wine to kick off another thrilling Saturday night. Is spending so much time with a cheeky sixty-five-year-old woman making me old? I'm only forty-five, but sometimes I feel like I'm living a season of *The Golden Girls*.

Taking my glass of wine with me, I walk Lucie down the block and back, waving to neighbors and stopping as our newest one meets me at her picket fence to return an empty casserole dish from the welcome meal I'd made her. Then Seraphina and I make our dinner from the leftovers, including two petit fours apiece. We're in the living room and midway through a movie featuring *the* Andy Garcia when my cell chimes. I reach around Lucie, who's snoring on a sofa cushion, and collect the phone. Carmen DiMora from the paper. In ten years, my boss has only called me once on a weekend, when the college was under financial stress and about to shutter, which would have pretty much closed down the town *and* the paper. This couldn't be good. Seraphina is mouthing something about arm wrestling me for the last petit four. I place a finger over my lips to shush her and, with a prickle of foreboding, take Carmen's call.

"Dare," he says, his typically affable voice grim. "Can you come in? There's been a car crash." In an area where a women's and men's college are separated by a twisty two-lane stretch of road, there are often accidents on Saturday nights. What's different about this one that Carmen had called me? He draws a breath. "A student, a Miss Allie Ahern, struck a pedestrian with her car tonight. Her blood alcohol was 1.6. The man's critical at Foxfield Memorial."

"Oh, my Lord," I whisper as it sinks in that Allie Ahern was the girl acting like a kindergartener in my garden today. I slump boneless into the corner of the sofa, my mind a Rube Goldberg machine. Carmen wants *me* to come in. But our news editor is the one who writes pieces of this nature. I search for a tactful response, one that proves my loyalty to the team. "Do you . . . uh, want me to come down and work up a piece?"

His next words are like a punch to my petit four-filled gut.

Chapter Two

Caroline O'Day
2021

I chance a peek at my computer clock. 4:10! I spring to my feet and pull my stand-up desk to its highest position. The document I'm translating from English to French for an export company client is due in fifty minutes. I collect the empty Anthropologie coffee cup my mother sent for my birthday last year and hurry from my room, hoping another shot of caffeine will keep my head in the game.

Gifts are one of Mom's love languages. And I get that. I like giving friends little happies myself. Mom was a creative, even awe-inspiring Easter Bunny, Santa Claus, and Tooth Fairy. Though I have everything I need, the cup *is* beautiful—blue floral and delicate, but the flowers remind me more of my grandmother Taffy than my mother, which would disappoint Mom. And the fancy gift is yet another reminder that my mother didn't give me more of *herself*. It wasn't a magical fantasy figure I needed but a mom: when I was twelve and trying to make sense of the directions on the box of tampons she'd simply left on my vanity; or when I was sixteen and Tom Smithwick had broken my heart; or when I was eighteen and needed one really good reason not to attend college clear on the other side of the country. I think by the time my mother realized I wasn't the type of girl she envisioned—a University of Virginia sorority sister, a debutante, a tulle-swathed bride—she poured her efforts into her editorial career. Though I could always count on my best friend Peach to drop everything for me, Mom's priority was the *Washington Times*.

I have my Crewtopia family now, but I sometimes wish Mom and I had a chill relationship. When I visit her in Virginia, it's like we're both afraid of saying the wrong things. So we tread lightly within the boundaries we've set along the way and keep our ears pricked for lane-departure alerts.

In the hall, the heady aroma of fresh coffee clears my cobwebs. Rebekah Jackson has made another pot before setting up her quilting frame on the porch. Everyone in our intentional community works hard, but we strive to balance it with play. In the sun-dashed kitchen, I refill my cup and add a splash of raw milk. Quilting is Rebekah's side hustle from teaching music to homeschooled kids in town. I can't help but pause at the screen door and admire my friend: the way her nimble brown fingers work as well with a needle as they do along the keys of her flute; her slender bare feet; her loose black braid an undulating waterfall over one shoulder. Padding promptly back to my room, I call out to her, "Thanks so much for the coffee, 'Bekah."

"No problem, boo," she says.

Back at my desk, the clock flashes an accusatory 4:20. I blow across the surface of my coffee and take a big sip. I've got this. I translate the last page, then double-check my markings against the cheat sheet I've taped to my desk. Outside the open window, Parker Randall, whose life was first wrecked and then resurrected by baseball, has galvanized batting practice on our baseball diamond.

One of Rebekah's twin sons' shrieks "Foul ball!" at the top of his six-year-old lungs. Living in Topanga Canyon with three other adults and two kids has a butt-ton of merits. But Parker's field can leap from low-key to rowdy in no time.

I stick my head out the window to see if my boyfriend Griffin's Jeep is in the drive. It isn't. Shutting the window on the whooping and capering, I wonder why he's so late getting back from Santa Monica, where he was meeting with the printer of his magazine, *Quiver*, named for the collection of boards a surfer keeps. *Griffin*. Who makes me quiver. Whose kisses make me feel like he's sliding his fingers into me even when he's not. My glance falls on our bed, the canopy I created with sheer fabric, the bright boho pillows, the beeswax candles, the slick-sided massage oil bottle on Griff's bedside table. A ripple of want makes its way through my core.

The clock whispers, *thirty minutes*. If I miss my deadline, I could risk losing my highest-paying client. I twist my auburn hair into a practiced topknot and plant my fingers on my black ergonomic keyboard. By the time I've proofed the document one last time and pushed the Send button, I've beaten my deadline by only seven minutes.

I toe my Crocs out from under my desk. It's time for some vitamin D and quality time with the crew. On the porch, Rebekah's still quilting. With our long canyon winters, people clamor to buy her vividly patterned textiles. I give her shoulders a little kneading.

"Oh, that's perfection," she says, smiling up at me. "Why are you so good to me?"

"Because you're a mousekin. And I'm expecting you to hit Griff and me up with a new quilt for Christmas."

Rebekah laughs. "All our gifts this year may be homemade—not that there's anything wrong with that—with the economy taking a hit."

"Right?" I do a couple of yoga stretches to unwind, then sit on the top step of our bungalow, built by a film star in the 1930s as a retreat. Topanga rumor has it that it was Jean Harlow or Bette Davis. The property is situated so far from town, its first owner was either a recluse or someone who planned on having some *pre*-tty wild parties. We'd gotten a pinch-me deal on the property and made the long-needed repairs ourselves.

"Those colors are so pretty, Rebekah. They remind me of this poufy comforter I had on a canopy bed when I was nine or ten."

Rebekah teases me. "You mean while living the life of a candy heiress's daughter in the District of Columbia?"

I blow an amused puff through my lips. "Pretty much."

"Tell me about your grandmother."

I clear my throat and recite my grandmother's bio in my private-girls-school tone: "Taft (Taffy) Kendall Marston, CEO Marston Candies—though phobic about anything sticky or messy and didn't allow sweets in the house; major backer for the National Archives;

and finally, a reclusive Virginia gardener and *Jeopardy* aficionado."

Lifting her head from her work, Rebekah frowns as though I've spoken in an obscure Arabic dialect. "Who owns a candy company and doesn't allow sweets in the house?"

I grin. "Her caretaker Seraphina used to sneak it in and drive her meteorically crazy."

Rebekah chuckles. Even though we met with her several times before she committed to the crew, I think of the risk she took handing over a five-thousand-dollar nest egg to cover her share of the down payment on the mortgage. To live and raise her children here when she didn't know us from the Manson clan. But Jimi and Miles are the picture of truly happy, well-adjusted kids. And Rebekah's happy here. Though sometimes the way she looks at Griff and me, I feel like she yearns for a love of her own.

Shading my eyes, I survey Crewtopia with satisfaction. It is a peculiar lot, triangular-shaped, broadest west and east and tapering to a point to the south where our gravel driveway begins. The bungalow sits smack in the middle of the triangle. To its east, the baseball field—which fit neatly into that corner of the parcel—is still alive with sound. To the house's west on a slight rise abounds our garden. Downwind from the garden hulks our composting bin under a piney wood at the edge of the property. *The Taffy I came to know would probably love our iteration of communal living. But what would Mom think of the cadre of chickens in the wire coop on the side of the house? The jungle of food and flowering-bearing vines that go crazy after the winter rains? The double-rowed clothesline that in her quaint Virginia town would have hillbilly stamped all over it? But whenever I gather our sun-dried sheets in my arms—crisply scented with the nectar of sagebrush and woolly blue curls drifting in the canyon air—I'm intoxicated. The linens in the fine town house my mother maintained in D.C. smelled of fabric softener and starch. Our linens smell like home. Like love.*

"Sometimes I feel guilty about never inviting my mom here," I say to Rebekah.

"Why?"

I retrieve an errant quilter's pin from the porch—lest it end up in somebody's foot—and use it to pick at a scrim of dirt under my thumbnail. "Well, she *is* my mother. And I feel like she's lonely. But if she didn't approve of the choices I made when I lived at home, she probably wouldn't give them a standing ovation now."

"Like what choices?"

"She just didn't like who I was very much. She wanted me to be a preppy girl and all that implies."

"Well, if you ever want to invite her, it would be cool with me."

"You're a sweetie."

She gazes over the quilting frame at her fraternal twins, now hooting to each other through a found length of PVC pipe. "The boys would probably like having her here, you know, like a grandma to spoil them."

"Dare O'Day a doting grandmother? That would be about as likely as her army crawling under the chicken coop to rescue a trapped hen."

"OMG, army crawling!" I join Rebekah when she cracks up, her tittering, me cackling at my imagery. "Do not make me wet my pants."

Finally, she looks at me with soft eyes. "If you and Griff *did* have a baby, you don't think your mom would rise to the occasion?"

"First of all, you know Griff and I agreed we didn't want children—"

She puts a hand on my arm, stilling my tongue and commanding my eyes. "But you've said your mother loves *you*. And that just might be enough."

I choose my words carefully. "She does. And I think she *wanted* to be a good mother, but she had a pretty poor way of showing it sometimes. I just didn't feel... nurtured." The boys chase each other around Rebekah's little yellow Subaru. She glances at them, but then pivots slowly toward me on her stool.

"Poor Caroline," she says, the prevailing polite padding around her voice falling away. "You didn't feel *nurtured*?" She crosses her legs. "I was raised by two parents. But they were extremely authoritarian and religious. I had nightmares about going to hell when I was six. Not only did they not nurture me, but in the end, they committed a much greater sin." Rebekah's eyes are so dark, the pupil so indistinct, I can see my shrinking reflection in them. "I told you I got pregnant by a new boyfriend, Denzel, just after graduating college, that we broke up and I came here."

I take a deep breath. "You did."

"He hoped I'd choose abortion. I didn't tell him there was no way I'd do that, but I dragged him with me to a pregnancy center, hoping an ultrasound would make the baby real for him, stir his heart." She closes her eyes. "I can still smell that room: disinfectant wipes beneath the ultrasound tech's perfume and breath mints, the stink of Denzel's disapproval, his fear. I was on the table, Denzel slumped in a chair across the close room, his head in his hands. Then the tech flipped on a TV monitor on the wall. It was like *ta-da*, there are *two* squiggly shapes. I froze, absolutely stunned, as the tech confirmed twins and pointed out the glowing white blips of their heartbeats. I thought *my heart* would explode, this *rapture* racing through me from head to toe. I dragged my eyes from the screen to look at Denzel, who hadn't made a peep." Rebekah gives a big sniff. "His eyes were dull, just void. He stood slowly, looked from the screen to me and then the tech, like, apologetically. He held up his hands, gave his head this slow silent shake, and . . . just walked out of there. I never saw him again."

A moan escapes me. *Oh, Rebekah.*

She gazes down the drive. "I spent a tortured week in my apartment, inside my head, missing two promising teaching interviews. Then completely bewildered, I called my parents. My father answered the phone. Five minutes into the conversation, he called me a harlot and a disgrace. 'I'm sending you a check for five thousand dollars to help you start a new life,' he said. 'Then I never want to see you again.'"

So Rebekah saved her father's money and scraped by. The check she contributed to Crewtopia had been her nest egg. My heart gives a painful twist. "Rebekah, I—"

But my friend closes her eyes and gives me a dismissive head shake. "When the check arrived, I wanted to rip it to shreds. But I kept it for the babies." Opening her eyes, she raises her chin at the Subaru. "I loaded that car with all I owned, put it in gear, and headed south . . . for the solitude I heard could be found here. Though I wanted to teach music, I took the first job I found at the hardware store. How else was I going to raise two active three-year-old boys in daycare—who were always hungry, yet outgrew their clothes faster than I could afford to buy more?" She gives me a little smile. "Then I saw the ad you and Griff posted on Craigslist."

The first time we met with Rebekah, we knew she shared our desire to create a close-knit community, one in which we'd all help raise her children. And when we met the darling twins, our connection with them had been swift and profound.

"It still aches sometimes," Rebekah goes on, "like a broken bone badly set. But every morning when I wake up, I pray for my sons and thank God for you guys."

I get up and wrap her in a hug, managing not to poke her with the pin and suppressing the urge to boo-hoo loud and long. But Rebekah rights herself, holds me at arm's length. She inclines a palm for the pin, then shoos me from the porch. "Isn't the watering chore yours this week?"

On trembly legs, I start down the steps. Griffin's SUV grinds up the drive, and I pause. He shoots me a peace sign through the windshield. He's so darned cute. I return the gesture, then get busy poking at the pots of flowers growing along the steps: the showy yellow and pink cliff maids, the orange desert mallow, the riotous red buckwheat, the foxglove. They could all use a stiff drink, as could I after what Rebekah just told me. Griffin, his dark wavy hair still wet with seawater, meets me at the bottom on the small terrace we built with scrap brick.

I grin and kiss his sweet, decent-to-the-bone loyal cheek. "How was the meeting?"

"Good. We settled on some lit formatting for the ads section to attract contributors."

I ruffle his hair. "And the surfing?"

He toes the dirt, then peeks up at me. "Well... the meeting wrapped earlier than we expected."

I tease him. "It did, huh?" I know my guy. A surfer lives spontaneously, preternaturally alert to the capricious combination of wind and water. Griffin can sniff out offshore winds that groom the waves, forming swell sets that make for the longest, most powerful rides. The ones surfers live for. Griff keeps a board in his SUV, a change of clothes. Now he pulls me close. "Well, I'm glad you had some *you* time today," I say.

His espresso-bean eyes capture mine and he gives me his singular smile: the left corner of his lips curling up first, then slowly spreading to the right before revealing a flash of pearly teeth. It's as if he loves me so much he can't help but grin. "What about *your* job," he asks. "Did you finish?"

"I did, but only by a whisker. I don't know why I've been so distracted lately."

"You weren't thinking of last night, were you?" he whispers close to my mouth, his breath smelling of the cherries in the trail mix he snacks on. I kiss his lips, bunching his hair in my hands before letting it fall to his shoulders again.

"Maybe..."

Parker rounds up the boys to put away the baseball equipment. Rebekah comes down from the porch and greets Griff with a high five. They stroll out to the big front yard of the bungalow where our hodge-podge of outdoor chairs sprawl in the shade of mature sycamores. Watching her go, I wish it were possible to unknow something terrible. I give the no-leak spigot a vigorous twist and try power spraying Rebekah's story all the way to L.A. But while wrestling the hose back in its coil, I realize she may have just given me a gift. One money could never buy. A seed of hope sprouts in my midsection: no one makes it through childhood without issues. Even those whose lives seem perfect from the outside. *Is it possible my mother did the best she could?*

Parker and the boys and I join Griff and Rebekah under the trees. Parker lowers himself into the chair next to Rebekah's. I drop a kiss on her head before taking a seat beside Griff. She smiles and puts her bare feet up on the edge of the empty firepit. "Somebody needs to chop more wood before our next fire. I think it's my turn."

Jimi clambers into his mother's lap. "Let me and Miles do it!"

"Miles and me," I say.

Rebekah takes Jimi by the chin and turns his head to look at her. "Don't you go anywhere near that ax, you hear me? That goes for you too, Monsieur Miles. Not until you are twelve."

Parker tugs his baseball cap from his head and gives his sweaty strawberry blond curls a shake. He launches his six-foot-three self from his chair. "Tell you what," he says to the boys, "*I'll* do the chopping, and you can help me haul and stack the pieces." He tosses his cap on his chair, then extends an arm and bends it to make an impressive bicep pop. "Deal?"

"Deal," they answer simultaneously, and then take turns swinging from his big buff arm.

I love Parker, his good-natured teasing. He's as solid as they come. And he has my undying admiration. A baseball-obsessed freckled southern boy, he received a scholarship to play for the University of Alabama, then was drafted by the San Diego Padres and assigned to a minor league team in El Paso. In the first season, he'd been nailed in the left eye by a wild pitch. The Padres organization had paid for surgery to remove the eye and insert an orbital implant to which the muscles of the eye could be attached. Still, the injury had cost him his dream career. Lost to himself, Parker wandered the West Coast for seasons before settling in Los Angeles. Waiting tables at a swanky restaurant and living in a one-room apartment, his feet hanging off the edge of a Murphy bed, he saved his tip money.

One day, Parker met Griff at Huntington Beach. Parker was intrigued by Griff's magazine career, one that could mostly be handled remotely. A year later, Parker built an online baseball career managing the quality assurance of live MLB broadcasts, an ironically solitary occupation when what Parker yearned for was intimacy. When we posted our Craigslist ad, he recognized Griff's name. We met with him at a coffee shop, where he appeared in sunglasses. When our order came, he removed the shades and told us about the eye. We sensed in Parker a deep need for acceptance and that his connection with us was meant to be.

"How 'bout some iced holy basil tea?" Rebekah asks now, and rises.

"These buff beasts deserve it," Parker says, and flashes a grin. "And I'd love some, please."

Jimi falls back in a chair, chuckling, his feet pedaling the air. "Buff beasts!"

Parker grins and pokes him in the side. "You think that's funny, huh?"

Miles, standing behind my chair and smelling of his puppy scent, drapes his arms around my neck. "Hey, Caro, did you hear we rescued a bird yesterday, a belted kingfisher?"

I kiss him on a warm brown arm. "No. But cool. Let's go see it after we've had our iced tea."

Soon the boys and I take off through the grass behind and to the north of the house toward the slabbed outbuilding that shelters the washer and dryer, a rack of Griffin's surfboards, as well as the plethora of tools and yard implements it takes to maintain Crewtopia. Around it, I planted my favorite perennial coneflowers, whose blossoms open like pink cocktail umbrellas. Rebekah made blue gingham curtains for the window. Inside, rows of shelves on the windowed wall belong to the twins, who use them as a small-animal sanctuary. The scent of reusable fabric softener sheets rises above the fugginess of the space. My eyes are adjusting to the dim just as Jimi jumps into the air to yank the string attached to a light bulb.

"Look, Caro, here he is!" Miles says, tugging me by the hand to a shoebox where the bird lies on its side on a bed of straw.

"Oh, he's beautiful," I softly say. "Is it his wing?"

"Yeah," Jimi says solemnly. He points a small finger. "See the black-and-white feathers sticking out under the blue ones? That what's broke."

"Broken."

"Yeah, broken. We might try letting him go in two days."

"Good plan. Birds can usually heal themselves with rest. But if he's not better by then, we'll take him to the nature center and have him checked out." I survey the latest menagerie. The squirrel they found half-starved is swaddled in an old T-shirt and growing round and sleek again. The container of painted lady chrysalides the boys are hatching so they can release them into their school's butterfly garden. Though Jimi and Miles have an affinity for animals and would love nothing more than a puppy, a dog would have a poor chance of survival here with coyotes and snakes in the canyon. "I'm proud of you for being such caring people," I say. For a moment, while they rinse and refill the squirrel's water dish—happy little smiles on their faces—I think about Rebekah. How had she taught her sons compassion when her parents had shown her none at all? Are some people born to nurture, or can it be mastered the way she had learned to piece a quilt together?

Later, when everyone's chores are done, we gather at the round farmhouse table for dinner. As is our custom, we've changed from shorts and T-shirts into something nice, Rebekah and me in cotton midi dresses, the guys in clean shirts and nice pants. Jimi, who for the past year has insisted on wearing a striped clip-on bow tie to dinner, offers our blessing, "Thank you for the world so sweet. Thank you for the food we eat. Thank you for the birds that sing. Thank you, God, for everything." I smile at Jimi. Once I asked him why the tie. He was quiet for a second, in which I saw him peep from beneath his lashes at Parker. Then he gave his shoulders a little bounce. "I just like it."

"Amen, dig in," Griffin says, and passes me a platter of avocado toast. I take a piece for my plate and cut it into pieces with my knife and fork. I take a bite, relishing the hearty sourdough. "Parker, this is *ahh*-mazing."

He nods and wipes his mouth with a blue and orange cloth napkin. "Y'all like the red pepper flakes on top?"

"Love 'em," I say.

Rebekah agrees. "Perfection."

"Gotta keep things spicy," Parker says, and winks at her. *Winks at her!* She rolls an elastic band from her wrist and pulls her long hair up into a knot, then peeks back at him. The two exchange sloppy smiles. *Holy pepper flakes, Batman!* Feeling a little warm myself, I muse about the exchange. *How long has this been going on and why the heck haven't I noticed?* Jimi spins the huge lazy Susan too fast to get more toast and abruptly ends my speculation.

"Why are we the only kids at Crewtopia?" The adults' heads swing as one to look at Jimi. I eat a couple of spoonsful of chicken lentil soup, composing an answer.

"Well, it's because you're special, the coolest kids ever," I say, blotting my lips with a blue striped napkin and looking from him to his brother.

Miles chimes in. "Why don't you and Griffin have kids? You love each other, don't you?" Griffin watches me, and I wonder if he'll answer. I wait a beat, but when he says nothing, I take a breath to keep the disappointment from my voice.

"We sure do, honeybunch. But all of us are a family." I look over at Griffin, whose upturned glass obscures his eyes. This isn't the first time one of the boys has said something about us having children, but it's always me who answers, and every time, it feels like a test. Like Griffin's waiting to see if I'm still fine not having kids. And lately, though I haven't broached the subject with him, I've begun to wonder if I am too.

"There are all kinds of families," Parker says.

Jimi waves a dismissive hand. "Yeah. Mrs. Bing says that at school all the time."

Rebekah blots her mouth and changes the subject. "Mike's bill for the roof repairs came today. Two grand." Parker whistles. The boys try to imitate him, and Miles blows spit on the table. Rebekah raises a disapproving brow at her son.

Griffin steeples his fingers beneath his chin. "We'll all pitch in. And I'll work out a barter with Mike. A discount in exchange for website support hours." I smile at his ingenuity, the gift of his time on our behalf.

"Thanks, bro," Parker says, squeezing his shoulder.

I shrug. "So we'll tighten our belts." I'm the girl Friday of the crew, the one who makes our schedules from chores to activities, the one who keeps us organized. But my mind leaps to the summer. I slap the table with a palm. "Oh man. There goes Coachella. And I heard Stevie Nicks has committed." I glance at Rebekah. Heat rises in my cheeks. I sound like a spoiled princess, the person I could've been if I'd followed Mom's path.

But Parker shakes his head in sympathy. "Yeah. I was thinkin' of going to Burning Man with my Los Angeles buddies. The curve balls just keep on comin'."

"Why did it rain so much and make leaks anyway?" Jimi asks.

Griffin starts to sing the chorus of "It Never Rains in Southern California," and we adults join in.

Miles studies our faces. He's the empath of the twins, and his tummy hurts when we're upset. "Well, the rain barrels are full. We'll have lots of water to help our vegetables grow."

"You're right, Miles," I say, rubbing circles on his back. "Way to find the silver lining." While Rebekah and I clear the table and stack the dishwasher, Griffin goes to get the laundry from the dryer. He comes back and tosses a mountain onto the table. Rebekah puts the boys into the tub. Parker pours a cup of coffee and heads back to his room to monitor a ball game. Rebekah returns, and she and Griffin and I fold. From the front bathroom, the boys sing the Beatles' *Octopus's Garden*.

"How is it I *always* end up with two mismatched socks?" I say.

Griffin looks at me and waggles his brows. "I'll see your green and blue stripe and raise you a pink plaid." We grin and swap out the socks, our fingers grazing each other's just a tad longer than necessary. Often just a touch of his hand turns me inside out.

I see Rebekah glance down the hall. She sighs. "When did you two know you were meant to be together?"

My mind flashes back to the exchange between her and Parker at dinner.

Griffin speaks up, surprising me. "When I couldn't imagine life without her." He shrugs. "She's the girl for me."

I smile tremulously, take his hand, and say to Rebekah, "Same."

She sighs again and gathers a pile of her sons' undies.

When the laundry's put away, the boys tucked into their bunks in Rebekah's room, Parker's still working. The rest of us take glasses of wine outside to sit beneath a sift of powdery starlight. I'm dying to ask Rebekah about her feelings for Parker, but something tells me she should be first to breach the subject. "Hey, 'Bekah," I say, "you have time for yoga before heading to town in the morning? We haven't practiced together for too long."

"I do."

"Griff?"

He grins. "Baby, I'm up for anything."

Chapter Three

Dare

"Dare, you're wanted for police questioning," Carmen says. "Chief Woodside called me a few minutes ago." I close my eyes and swallow around a big lump in my throat. Seraphina has half risen from the other sofa and looks poised to perform the Heimlich maneuver. I raise a palm to restrain her. *This couldn't have to do with the car accident.*

"Why?" I ask Carmen, my mind scrabbling for some other reason. I've always striven to act responsibly and adhere to the *Journal*'s mission. *Had someone complained about the interviews I'd conducted over the Civil War monument protests?*

"Because the party was held at your home," Carmen explains, "and apparently a few of the intoxicated students are still minors. Miss Ahern's a week shy of twenty-one herself." My hands go cold. *The girls were secretly drinking? But they can't hold me responsible for that, can they? I was in the house—on the property the whole time.* My mind races to catch up. "Carmen, Miss Ahern wouldn't have had time to get that drunk while she was here. And the students were all gone by, like, 5:15. They were here a little more than an hour. What time was the accident?"

Carmen pauses. A wet gnashing tells me he's working at the stump of the unlit cigar he wedges in the corner of his lips when he's stressed. "The report says 7:42 p.m. Officers rounded up the girl's friends for questioning. With graduation coming up and their records clean, they were only too willing to tell what they knew. An empty pint of Grey Goose was found inside Miss Ahern's handbag. She spiked the punchbowl at a college-sanctioned event. Her friends said she then belted a boatload of beer at another party. But there's still the matter of the drinking that went on at your property. The alumnae will be questioned. Listen, don't panic about the questioning. You know Doug. He was gracious enough to arrange to meet us here at the paper rather than the station." Thank God for that. I've known Doug Woodside since he was a rookie cop. Droplets of relief ripple through me. I get up, shove my feet into my clogs, and begin pacing the room, half listening to Carmen go on about what I should expect from the questioning. Seraphina would probably give up one of her pinkie toes if I put the conversation on speaker.

"Carmen, I'm so sorry you got caught in the middle of all this. I'll be there in ten." I end the call and scurry to use the powder room, where the floral wallpaper seems to swarm and shift as Seraphina yells for the details on the other side of the door.

"And the vodka! Squirreled away in the fake Kate," she says, still marveling. I brush past her and out the door. A husky "I'll save you the last petit four" follows me as I climb into the car and slam the door.

I huff a sigh and say aloud, "Go ahead and eat the damned petit four. It's my *ass* that may need saving." I fumble my key ring and curse as I grapple for it on the floorboard.

Putting the Toyota in gear, I aim it for the *Journal* and my destiny.

At the paper, Chief Woodside is kind but gives me a grilling. When he has stripped my professional reputation away like a husk of corn, I stump toward Carmen's office. The reek of cigar meets me halfway. He's broken his rule of no smoking in the office, so I know he's as aggrieved about what he has to do as I am. Rounding the corner, I stand before his battle-scarred desk. I hang my head. "Carmen, I'm so sorry the *Journal* got caught up in this mess."

"Hey, kid, don't beat yourself up. This thing will blow over." He lays his cigar down and rubs his eyes with both thumbs. Now get outta here and get some sleep."

"Will you sleep?"

His smile is a bleary line through smoke. "Like an old bear."

I find a sturdy cardboard box in the mailroom and load it with my belongings. Hefting it to carry to my car, I spot the supply company name on the side. *Hopewell.*

The next day, I plod to the end of the driveway to collect the morning edition, then sit on the front steps to open it. I scan the piece, written by the news editor as our protocol dictates: straightforward, economical, and nonjudgmental. But my colleague has zinged a grace note to my heart by including a quote from our boss: *Dare O'Day has never done a reckless thing in her life.* Back in the kitchen, I sit at the island with a cup of coffee, my clogs hooked around the rungs of the stool, wondering how readers will react to the article. I reflect on Carmen's words. The only real truth to his statement is that I am predictable. When I arrived in Foxfield six years ago, the townspeople had sat back and, with the farsighted, unembarrassed eyes of small-town citizens, waited to see what the new journalist in town would do. Would I raze my mother's gem of a Georgian and erect some contemporary horror in its place? Take on the city council? Take a lover? Take to drink? But I'm certain I've dashed all their hopes for entertainment: I've tended my genteelly decaying home the way an A-list actress would tend her face; I didn't vote in the 2016 election; as far as available men go, suffice it to say that Foxfield isn't burgeoning with talent, and my last date was with a visiting professor months ago; and on Monday mornings, when Bo's Recycling hauls my plastic bin to the truck, its contents clink and clank no more than anyone else's on Fourth Street.

Though I had a higher profile position with the *Washington Times* while Caroline was growing up, I'm happy with a small paper. I'm dug in here. I've built a solid reputation. Those of us who work in news are either above reproach or ousted. Thankfully, Carmen had merely suggested I take a brief leave of absence. Still, the idea of going into town now that the article's been published makes me grateful for Seraphina, who's appointed herself emissary of errands. Yesterday, when she went to pick up my dry cleaning, the gum-smacking clerk did a double take at my name on the ticket and tried pumping my housekeeper for information about what happened at the party.

Seraphina let loose a string of Spanish that made me blush when she told me about it, and I only understood half of it. But penned up inside the house, cabin fever's getting real. Now that I've stopped beating myself up for what will probably be judged as careless naivety, although charges could still be filed, I'm damned bored. I open the kitchen windows for fresh air. Maybe I'll take Lucie out to the back garden this afternoon. I'll sit in the sun in my pink Adirondack and read a new book. I slump into my chair at my kitchen desk, noticing the moans and ticks of the refrigerator. My eyes fall on the big cardboard box on the floor. I haven't opened it since I brought it from the office. I give its contents a moment of consideration and concoct a rationalization:

If I unpack it, I lose my job.

If I leave it packed, I keep my job.

Then it will be that much easier to schlep the stuff back. Hope well.

"The *Journal*," I whisper, my heart a tight-balled fist. I can't help but go over the article once more. Fortifying myself with more coffee, I settle again before the paper. For the first time, I study my photo, an old one from the files. Even in black-and-white, I look grim, washed out, my shoulder-length hair lusterless. I might as well be holding a black placard with white letters beneath my chin:

Rockfish County Sheriff's Office

Dare O'Day

DOB 9-1-75

Closing the paper, paranoia plows through me. "Could I *actually* end up in the clink?" I ask Lucie. My pet pokes her head up from the depths of the dog bed under the table. Before the leave of absence, Lucie had served as the paper's mascot. When she wasn't roaming the halls of the office, scouting treats from soft-touch staffers, she'd sleep in my office. Now she peers at me as if to say *Then what are we going to do?*

"That's a good question, cookie dough." Lucie executes a down-dog-stretch-yawn combo. I consider taking up yoga. If I'm not stirring cake batter with a boat paddle in prison, I'll have more time on my hands. It seems everyone's a yogi now, not only hippie types. I picture my uber-curvy thighs and bottom in skintight yoga pants. Maybe not yoga. Caroline practices, and as far as I know, she lives what's pretty much a hippie lifestyle—at least a 2.0 version of one—where she and her roommates, all college grads, integrate hippie values with well-paying jobs they can do from their compound. That she chose to attend college clear across the country and make a life there afterwards spoke volumes about our relationship.

My chest full of ineffable regret, I rise and upend my solitary coffee cup onto the top rack of the dishwasher. I look at the clock and allow myself a two-minute cry. Lucie props her chin on the side of her bed and eyes me warily. My tears end when inside my head my Italian friend Lina says *basta*: enough. I grab a dishtowel and wipe my nose on it, thankful Seraphina's out or she would have given me hell, first for contaminating the towel and then for feeling sorry for myself.

I go to my built-in kitchen desk and open my laptop. While it boots up, I run my hand over the desk's handsome granite surface. When I inherited my mother's home, I updated the outdated surfaces—desk, island, and countertops—with a granite pattern reminiscent of the rich earth tones of Virginia, predominantly its mineral-rich clay. I'm frugal by nature and the replacements were expensive. But thanks to America's obsession with Taft's Chocolate Raft Bars, I have more money than I could spend in two lifetimes.

In fact, since I've lived in Virginia, besides making my usual charity contributions, I've made a single withdrawal from my jumbo money market account. That day, the teller at Foxfield Federal ceased a surreptitious scan of a tabloid rag and fixed me with a megawatt gaze. "This must be for something special, Miz O'Day."

"It is," I assured her with a smile. The paper had reported that, though the PTA had sold wrapping paper to every soul in Foxfield, the county school system was still vastly short of the funds needed to purchase two buses in which to transport special needs children.

Noting the teller's nametag, I wrote a figure on a slip of paper and said, "Monica, will you please wire this amount anonymously to the Foxfield County Schools and stipulate that it's to be used to purchase the buses?" The teller's sharp inhalation made me fear she'd hyperventilate. But she recovered and issued my receipt with aplomb. I offered her a wink and my thanks for her help.

It's strange sitting at a desk with no work on it to demand my attention. The only inhabitants of this surface are my home computer, my collection of charming Rifle Paper Company pads and stationery, and a framed black-and-white high school graduation photo of Caroline, glossy-lipped and staring back at me with my same wide-set eyes, a strand of pearls around her slender neck.

What if I wrote Caroline an email? The possibilities wash past. I'd make it newsy and light. Tell her about it in a casual it-happens manner. But would she make the time to write me back? Or just send me a text? I sit back and indulge myself in a glowing dreamscape fantasy: a concerned Caroline clutching the sheet of stationery in her hand, picking up her phone, saying how sorry she is about what happened, and how we should get together and *really* talk about our lives. I huff a little laugh. *Get real, O'Day.* But maybe, just maybe I'm wrong about Caroline's feelings. Maybe she believes it's I who doesn't care. The only thing that's clear is that she doesn't need me.

A fact whose bony little fingers have been scrabbling at the door of my consciousness suddenly gains entrance: I've never really known my own child. A sob rises in my throat again. *Oh, Caroline, is it too late to make things right?*

Lucie appears on the floor beside my chair and issues her yodel that lets me know she wants in my lap. "Well, c'mon, pup." She springs onto my lap and I cuddle her close. A single tear falls onto the black spot atop her head.

Outside, old Barrett Chipley from next door starts up his hog of a riding lawn mower, though his front yard is, like mine, no bigger than a putting green. The afternoon sun is streaming through the branches of my pinking dogwoods, and for the first time in forever,

I think of walking with my husband Finn around the D.C. tidal basin at cherry blossom time, a breeze ruffling his fire-colored hair. I sigh, wishing I still had someone to whom I could pour out my heart.

When the vacuum roars to life upstairs, I realize Seraphina must have come home through the laundry room door and headed up the back stairs. Of course, I have Seraphina, who was an integral part of Mother's life and my own, but she's not family. And as much as I love her, she is still my employee. I have two close friends with whom I share a book club: Lina, who's my boss Carmen's wife, and Georgie, both professors at the college. I love our monthly meetings for fellowship, wine, appies, and a sprinkling of book talk. I consult my calendar. It's another week before I'll be with them again.

Stroking Lucie's one ear back over and over, the way she likes it, I lift the current April wall calendar page to look at May. Caroline turns twenty-seven this year. I've already written *Caroline's B-Day* with a big heart around it in the twenty-fifth square. Not that I could ever forget her birth date, but somehow seeing it there every time I look at the calendar makes me feel closer to her. Like we're special to each other. Like if she saw her name written there in my prettiest handwriting, she'd feel my love. "Remember the pretty lady that came to visit at Christmastime?" I ask Lucie. "She brought you your stuffed hedgehog."

It's been months since I've gotten the few precious hugs Caroline and I exchange when she's home for Christmas. I close my eyes and imagine stepping into her fragrant embrace, the Moroccan oil she uses in her auburn hair superseding everything else for that one instant. My nose stings with fresh tears of longing. I haven't been to California since I attended her graduation from the University of Southern California in Los Angeles. She's never invited me to visit the house she shares with five others in Topanga Canyon. I'm sure it's because she thinks I wouldn't approve of her unconventional living situation. It sounds so different from the way she was brought up. Maybe she's right. But it still smarts to be so uninvolved in my daughter's life that I haven't even seen where she lives.

On the street, a flash of movement catches my eye and distracts me from my fretting. Light reflecting off the chrome of a passing car. But then cardboard signs being held aloft shuffle and bounce along the sidewalk at the end of the driveway. *What is going on?* My heart lurches. *My house is being picketed?* Clutching Lucie to my chest, I stand and edge toward the window, keeping to one side behind the open blue and white buffalo check curtains. *Protestors?* And then a late-spring blizzard of voices arise. Angry and strident. The women—only one of whom I recognize, old Miss Gaffney from the neighborhood, who's a fierce member of MADD—swarm. "Protect our students," they chant. Thanking God Seraphina must not be hearing the fracas over the whoomph of the vacuum, I crane my neck to read more of the swaying signs: SERVING MINORS IS A CRIME! DRUNK DRIVING DESTROYS! and WERE YOU PUNCH DRUNK? I can't take my eyes off the *you* painted the color of fresh blood.

A shrill bark escapes Lucie and scares the hell out of me. She squirms to be let down. I release her when a different voice rings out: "Aren't you a mother yourself? How could you?" I can't believe this bellicose backlash. The vacuum cleaner gives up rumbling, and Seraphina's size five navy lace-up Keds squeak down the stairs.

"What is *going on*, chica?" she says as she reaches the bottom, her dark brows practically meeting over her nose. She stands smack in the middle of the window for all the world to see, her hands forming fists at her sides.

"Seraphina, ignore them. We're taking the high road."

"I'll tell *them* which road to take, the one that leads the hell away from here." Seraphina strides to the front door, scooping up Lucie, who has begun her most menacing growling, and tucks the dog under a scrawny arm. Flinging the door open, she shouts "*Abrase*: leave here," as well as something I'm glad I don't understand and hope that none of the protestors do. I peek around the curtain for Mr. Chipley, whose lawn mower has ceased its clamor. I wonder if he went in and called the police because, in the oblique view I have of my living room window, the calvary has arrived in the form of a patrol car trolling the street, its blue light revolving.

A decades-old memory snatches the breath from my body: the demonstration. Luke "Anti-Nuke" Henry. The blue lights, the sirens, the swirl of blinding dust coating my throat. The human chain, my hand wrenched from Luke's for the last time. I press my hands against my head, then give it a brisk shake. I will not allow these people to send me spiraling back to a time I have no business revisiting. But abruptly, the cacophony dwindles away, and a weariness overtakes me. I trudge upstairs and lie down. But over and over, one voice, the most injurious one of all, replays itself in my head: *Aren't you a mother yourself? How could you?* What kind of mother wouldn't predict the behavior of girls giddy about having finished their exams and preparing for graduation parties? To realize that, even though the alumnae were fundamentally responsible for any ebbs and flows in the event, something can *always* go wrong.

Only Caroline and I know what kind of mother I have been. And my mother, Taft, while she was alive. Old Taffy knew because the detached and fear-based manner with which I raised my only child had been cut from the wrinkled pattern of her parenting. Would things have turned out differently between Caroline and me if my husband Finn had lived? Would his presence have tempered the way I scrutinized her every choice?

I awake disoriented and grope for my phone. But I must have left my cell in the kitchen. How long did I sleep? Past dinnertime? Momentarily, Seraphina's footsteps fall across the hall, and I hear her usual rap-rap, rap-rap against the door. "Come in."

She enters and gives her head a sorrowful shake. "I'm sorry that happened, Dare," she says, and hands me my phone.

"Oh, thanks."

"*Un policía*: a policeman said he will make passes by the house tonight."

"Oh wow." *Good old Doug.* "That's comforting." I glance at my cell, wondering if Carmen called, but the only message is from the vet's office, reminding me of Lucie's next appointment. I turn the phone upside down on the bedside chest that I chalk painted and waxed to resemble an old French piece and consider the pretty blue and white Asian-inspired lamp. This is my home, my sanctuary, but I feel as if it's been violated. Not only by the protestors but by the unsettling memories of Luke drifting the air currents, recirculating through the vents in the old planked floors.

"I'm making you empanadas for dinner," Seraphina says.

The mention of Colombian comfort food, the half-moon pinch pockets filled with cheeses, makes my mouth water. "That sounds delicious. Thank you."

Later, I've showered and washed my hair. I'm propped in bed, Lucie snoring at my feet. I'm binge watching *Virgin River* on Netflix and spooning Ben & Jerry's Chocolate Therapy ice cream between my lips. My phone chimes: Carmen DiMora.

"Sorry to call so late," he says, "but I just got word that the man hit by the student's car has died." I sit up, overturning the ice cream container.

"It's vehicular homicide now," I manage to say while getting up to pace the room.

"I'm afraid it is, Dare. There's also word from the folks down at the Haven. They've physically identified him as one of the homeless men that turns up there from time to time. He was twenty-two."

A torturous picture flashes through my mind: the poor boy, his body battered and bruised, stiffening on a gurney in the morgue.

Carmen continues. "Since the victim had no official ID on him, Doug's team has no way of contacting his family. If he even has one."

I want to cry at that. A young person dying homeless and alone without family. Without a mother to gently fold whatever clothes and personal effects he had and hold them against her heart.

Carmen goes on. "So it's likely the only charges that may be filed would be by the state. Let's see how this plays out. Even if charges are made, Doug's not going to consider you a flight risk. When you've had some time to deal, let's get you back to work."

I loll in a hot bath with a big glass of Pino Gris. The scandal that has evolved into a tragedy weighs heavy on my mind. As a wealthy woman, I could be the target of some kind of civil suit. I shiver at the thought, despite the heat of the water. Lucie, lying on the aqua bath mat, blinks at me without raising her head from her paws. Now that the community has read the *Journal* article, the far-reaching tendrils of the Foxfield grapevine have put Marvin Gaye's to shame. Without my work or family to support me, I feel hollow inside. But I *have* had time to think about Caroline in ways I haven't before. Maybe there's fruit there. Her birthday comes to mind again. What if I called her instead of sending a card? But millennials aren't phone talkers. The last time I called, we spoke like polite acquaintances. I knew the exact moment when things changed, when her voice frosted, when I said the wrong thing again, when I asked her if she and Griff planned to stay in California. If only we didn't live so far apart.

None of the neighbors has brought *me* a casserole since the protesters showed up. Except for Mr. Chipley, they seem to be keeping their distance. Only Lina and Georgie have called and come by to check on me. With distance in mind, I need to put some between the scandal and me. Get out of town. I have the money to go anywhere. My heart says, *Go to Caroline*. From Seraphina's room down the hall, a snore rips the silence. I know just what that gutsy gal would say: *Grow a pair and go see your daughter*. Caroline could turn me down, say she's too busy with work. Or she could surprise me and say yes. Only one way to find out. I pull the plug from the drain, get to my feet, and reach for my towel on the toilet lid. I say to my dog, "Hey, Lucie Boots, how would you like to take a trip?"

Chapter Four

Caroline

Griffin's father has a brain tumor.

Griff's mother called from Hawaii with the news. Stricken silent, Griffin pulled an all-nighter to get the May/June issue of *Quiver* shaped up for his editor, Collin. Tomorrow he leaves to be with his parents while his father undergoes surgery. This morning, Rebekah made goat cheese and spinach omelets for breakfast. Griffin choked one down with almond milk, then went back to our room and slept a couple of hours. He worked all afternoon and evening, saying little to me and missing dinner entirely, our door firmly closed. When I came to bed, he kissed my forehead distractedly and took his laptop to work in the kitchen. He evaded me both physically and emotionally.

I wake now and raise my head to look over the ridge of his body at the clock on his side of the bed. But Griffin's not there. We both sleep starkers; no wonder I'm cold. It's 2:10. Did he ever come to bed? I rise quickly, put on my robe, and cinch the belt tight. I pad down the hall to peek into the kitchen. He's there at the table again, his shoulders bunched over his laptop, his earbuds in, and I'm sure listening to the Steely Dan he plays while he's working. Deciding to pee before interrupting him, I tiptoe into the hall bathroom and sit on the toilet. The twins' plastic action figures on the side of the tub remind me of the blissful naivety of childhood, before one discovers the world of pain. I flush and survey a couple of Disney princesses in a corner cluster but pick up Rae from Star Wars. She's the strongest of the Jedi warriors. I could use a strength talisman. Rae's a badass. Like Seraphina. My head snaps back. There's a blast from the past. My mother's housekeeper, my grandmother's caretaker before that. The tiny woman who taught me the art of independence my eighteenth summer. I smile at the memory, wash my hands, and tuck Rae/Seraphina into the pocket of my robe.

I walk into the kitchen. Griffin looks up, flinches violently, and rips out his earbuds.

My heart stutters. "Oh, darling. I'm so sorry I startled you."

Griffin's face is naked with exhaustion. And what looks like fear. *He's afraid his dad will die.* Gingerly, I lay my hand on his shoulder and give it a little squeeze, watching as he resumes cropping a slick photo of a surfer hitting the lip of a wave. I take a seat in the chair beside his, hooking my bare feet around the rungs of the chair. I speak in a dulcet tone. "What if you came back to bed for just a couple of hours? I could set an alarm and make sure you're up when you need to be." He scrubs a hand over his eyes, his face, and sighs, then gives me a tiny go-away shake of his head. His eyes return to the computer screen.

I get up quietly, put on a kettle of water for tea, and measure a chamomile and lavender blend into the strainer. I stand miserably at the sink, looking out onto the porch, and think of staying up with him. The kettle takes a light year to come to a boil. I pour myself a cup and turn to Griffin. "How about some tea to help make you feel drowsy?"

He looks up wearily, his face blasted. "I'll take wide-assed awake tea, strong. Don't you know I can't afford to sleep? I have to leave for the airport in"—he peers owlishly at his phone—"six hours. I have to finish before time to shower."

I carry my cup to the table. "Can't Collin finish it up?"

The way he snaps at me is unprecedented. "This is not *Collin's* responsibility. It's *mine*."

I practically drop my cup on the table. Tea sloshes onto the surface and courses perilously close to his paperwork, his computer. I squeeze Rae through my pocket. Griffin swears horribly. An oafish nuisance, I hustle for a dishtowel.

He gets to his feet, swooping the computer aloft. "Just leave it; I'll get it."

In our bedroom, I lean against the closed door for a moment, tears rimming my eyes at his pain. I look at our desolate glacier of a bed. I won't climb back into it without Griffin. I shrug from the robe and put a long-sleeved T-shirt and yoga pants on underneath before cinching it closed again. I take up a quilt, head down the hall, and let myself out the front door. If Griffin notices my passage, he doesn't say a word.

I ease myself into the rope hammock at the end of the porch and tuck my robe around me. The tears come then, streaming my cheeks and sliding into my ears. I've made things worse for him when he's at his most vulnerable. I dry my face, remembering the unsettling supposition that took hold of my own mind in the last week or so. One I need to talk to Griffin about. But with his father's situation, my issue will have to wait.

I wish he'd seek me out for my love and support right now. I push myself up to see if I can get a look at him through the kitchen window, but I can see only the light, a slice of the table. I lie back. I count one hundred heartbeats and peek again. The left sleeve of his soft, old blue shirt. I can smell it and him in my head. I recite the Lord's Prayer and the Pledge of Allegiance and peek again. Only the light.

I lie awake, wishing I was holding him, until the sky brightens and a lemony splotch of sun begins to ooze along the tops of the mountains. My grandmother Taffy said "Everything looms larger at night," and she was right: Griff will be okay. His father will be okay. My gritty lids close with exhaustion.

The next thing I know, he is standing beside the hammock in jeans and a nice shirt, his hair in a man bun. His backpack is slung over one shoulder, and another bag lies at his feet on the boards of the porch. It's my turn to startle, to sit straight. The hammock rocks turbulently, and my empty stomach does a seasick roll. With a lift of his knee, Griffin stops the hammock's tipping. "Caroline, I'm sorry." The left side of his mouth kicks up, but the smile stops before reaching the right.

"Oh, darling," I say trying to extricate myself from the hammock. He reaches out, helps me to my feet. "Did you get your work done?"

"I did."

"I'm glad; now you'll sleep on the plane."

"Hope so." He steps closer and takes my cold hands in his warm ones. He studies our hands, rubs his thumb across the peaks of my knuckles. "I'll be in touch," he says.

"Okay. Be safe. I'll pray for your dad." There are so many more things I'd like to say, but they will have to keep.

"You be safe too. I love you. Thanks for praying." He leans in, kisses my temple. Then he steps back, picks up his bag, and heads down the steps.

I stand gripping Rae in my pocket and watch until the Jeep grows small—just a smear of blue that turns left and out of sight.

"Good morning, crew," I say nonchalantly. My nose has led me from the porch and into the kitchen. Parker's making one of his grand-slam breakfasts.

"Mornin', sunshine," he says from the stove. His sweet Southern accent, long and runny around the edges like his eggs, makes me feel as though I might make it through the day.

"Morning, boo," Rebekah says from the table as she pours glasses of almond milk for the boys. I notice that Parker's coffee cup isn't on his usual placemat across the table from Rebekah but on the mat next to Rebekah's at my customary place. I smile to myself. *Okay, then.*

"Where you been, Caro?" Miles asks.

"Saying goodbye to Griffin." Miles cocks an eyebrow at me, looking like a stamped-on miniature of his mother, but seems to accept my answer.

The boys call Parker's square waffles bases. "I'm on second base," Jimi says.

"Please don't talk with your mouth full, son," Rebekah says, and wipes syrup from his chin with a berry-print napkin.

"I'm on third!" Miles says, always the competitor.

"No homers today, guys," Parker says. "You'll be late for the bus."

When I've eaten scrambled eggs, bacon, and reached first base myself, Rebekah walks the boys to the end of the drive to meet the bus. I sit back in my chair, pull a foot beneath me, and sip a second cup of coffee. What's happening in Hawaii? Why hasn't Griff been in touch? What if his father has died? What if he's so distraught that he stays in Hawaii where the surfing on Oahu's western shore is the stuff of legends? I tell myself I'm being ridiculous, to get up, and spend the day socked away in my room, working on a new translating job.

While helping set the table for dinner that night, Miles requests that we play a Beatles album. "The one with 'Ob-La-Di, Ob-La-Da' on it."

I cross my fingers under the table, hoping she says yes because maybe the music will drown out the scream of Griffin's empty chair. "Okay. But our grace first, please."

Miles puts his hands together and says the God-is-good-God-is-great blessing.

"Play the album with the submarine," says Jimi.

Rebekah rises. "Miles asked first." Parker smiles at her form as she strides across the hall, her footfalls dying as she reaches the deep-shag living room rug.

Jimi sticks out a pink tongue at his brother. I tweak his bow tie, give him the Seraphina side-eye, and send myself a mind note to speak to him later—let him sweat it out a bit. *Seraphina again!*

After a moment, the plonking piano intro to "Ob-La-Di, Ob-La-Da" begins at a low volume. One of us will have to get up and move the needle to skip over "Happiness is a Warm Gun" before it starts. Children. What pains they can be, I think uncharitably. *Whoa, where did that come from?*

But after dinner, when the twins produce construction paper cards they have made for Griffin at school—*We are sorry about your dads brian, but he will be well soon*—I wrap them in hugs and kisses until they squeal and fuss. So Rebekah had chosen to tell them where Griffin had gone. Maybe that's the best way with kids, tell them the truth.

The boys need to rehearse paper-bag book reports for school tomorrow. So we adults drink tea at the table, watching them take items they've chosen to represent story elements out of the sacks, and explain their significance. "I was going to put Rae in *my* bag, but I can't find her," Miles says.

My cheeks warm. "Oh, I'm sure she'll turn up. Strong women always do."

Rebekah puts the twins to bed, then says she'll spend the evening working on lesson plans. She curls up in a living room chair and frowns at her laptop. I hover in the doorway, the chill space comforting me: our soft chairs and ottomans; nubbly throws; one wall covered in colorful local art; bookcases spilling with classics from our combined collections; two big baskets of the twins' picture books; a stereo system and turntable; and like most homes in the Canyon, no television—though we adults often sneak in shows on our laptops, Parker and me, *Outlander*. "Are you going to stand there all night?" Rebekah asks.

As my surprise at her sarcasm hits home, Parker traipses down the hall from his room. After only two innings, the game he was troubleshooting was called because of rain. He says he's going out to look at the stars. One of the best things about nights at Crewtopia is the absolute blackness, the nearest streetlight miles away. Parker raps his fingers against the living room doorframe to gain Rebekah's attention. "Who wants to come?" he softly asks, but I'd bet my back teeth he's hoping that only she will go. She gives him a brief aggrieved shake of her head. With a final rap on the frame, he lifts his chin at me and heads outside.

"I'm sorry I bothered you, babe," I say to Rebekah, then grab a heathery throw from a peg in the hall and head outside. Parker's tipped his chair back, the right side of his face with the sighted eye turned to the sky. Wrapping the throw close, I make my way barefoot across the grass and take the chair to his left, then follow his gaze to the stars. Sirius is so bright I have to peep through my fingers to take it in. "Dude, heaven's putting on a show tonight."

"Yeah, it's gorgeous. Think Rebekah might change her mind and come out?"

"Nope. She was pretty intent on her planning."

Though our chairs aren't touching, I can feel one of Parker's legs bouncing up and down on the earth. One of the things that had attracted Griffin and me to him was his energy. Despite the tragedy that befell him, his face was so full of sun, it was as though he'd frowned twice in his life and been merely passable at it once. Now I start to ask him about his feelings for Rebekah. But a scholar of my expressions, he says to me. "Okay, spill it."

I let go a ragged sigh. "Oh, Parkie, I just feel so, like . . . displaced right now, so detached from Griff. He was super upset last night. I was only two when my father died. But Griffin's dad was . . . *is* . . . a key figure in his life. He's this big tough navy captain. He was pretty hard on Griff in high school when his surfing became way more important to him than his grades. But Corban's a good father. Griff's love for him runs deep."

Parker gives a trio of nods. "Our Griffin's lived a charmed life. He's a great surfer. He built his dream surfing magazine. It's like, what," he says, twirling his hand in the air, "number twelve or something on the Top Hundred Indie Magazines list?"

Eleventh. "Yeah, something like that."

"This crisis with his father is probably the worst thing our golden lad ever faced. But he's strong. He'll be ah-right, you'll see."

I draw my knees up in my chair, pull the throw over them. "What would I do without you? You're the big brother I never had."

He smiles at me in the dark and reaches out to rest a long arm around my shoulders, give them a squeeze. My phone lights as bright as Sirius. "A text from Griff!" I read it aloud. "Everything's okay. I love you. Call you in five?"

"Told ya," Parker says with a grin. He rises, smooths a hand over my head, and strides toward the house. As I wait for the phone to ring, I wish on a star: that my friend lands a love of his own.

I awake the next morning to the familiar *whup-whup-thrum* of Parker's 4Runner turning over. It's Thursday, the day he spends in Los Angeles. I grin, thinking of the scene I encountered in the living room last night after my call with Griffin. Rebekah in her chair, her computer askew in her lap, Parker seated on the ottoman in front of her, holding her bare feet on his long thighs, massaging her insteps. Rebekah's head was thrown back, her eyes closed, whether from embarrassment or bliss. But Parker was studying her face as though it were a treasure map. Was he that much in tune with her that he knew a massage was just what she needed? I tiptoed past the door without either of them noticing, feeling glad for them, but missing Griff all the more.

Now I draw on my robe and head for the shower. As the hot water sluices off my body, I think about how when we drew up our covenants for Crewtopia, we were the core four. Griffin and I were a couple, so we'd share a bedroom, Parker would have his own, and Rebekah and the twins would share the largest bedroom. We agreed that if Rebekah or Parker became involved with someone, we'd negotiate adding a member or members to the crew. I held a hidden hope that the two of them would fall for each other. And now that seems to be coming to fruition.

Back in my room, I dress in work clothes, pull on my boots. What I'd really like to do is burrow beneath the covers and sleep until Griffin comes back. Will this experience with his father and spending time with his traditional family change him? Will he see the life we've built in a different light? I can't wait to see his face when I tell him I love him, when he tells me he loves me back. When I'm sure things are okay between us again. And when I can finally tell him what I've been thinking about. Until then, I'll immerse myself in my assigned chores as well as his. I'll stay busy at night with my translating work.

I find Rebekah at the kitchen sink, drying the dishes. I study my friend. On the graceful and willowy scale, she's a ten, while I might pass as a five. She turns. "Ahh, Caroline," she says, wiping her hands on a yellow dish towel. "I'm sorry about being salty with you yesterday. I think I had a near-fatal case of PMS. I got my period this morning, and my ovaries feel like they're about to implode." Often our cycles are in sync, but not this time. "To top it off, I didn't finish my lesson plans last night."

Ahh, but you had a fine foot rub, n'est-ce pas? "Oh, lovey. It's okay. I haven't been myself either. Why don't you prop up in bed with your laptop and work until the twins get home? I'll check on you later, bring you a cup of tea."

"OMG, yes. That would be lovely. Parker said Griff called. When's he coming home?"

"In two days!"

"Oh, I'm glad."

Between loads of laundry, I sweep out the shed and then decide to tackle the front porch and courtyard too. One of our roosters struts across the front yard. I heave a sigh before chasing him down and tossing him back over the fence. "Why fly the coop when you've got it made in there with the ladies, huh?" I collect four eggs from the henhouse, take them inside to wash them, and make a cup of tea for Rebekah. I tap on her door before peeking inside.

"Come in, Caro." She accepts the warm cup, her eyes soft. "Thank you."

"You are very welcome." I turn to go.

"Caroline, if you ever need me, you know—"

"I know." Smiling a wobbly smile, I leave her quietly, letting the door snick closed behind me.

Grabbing a hat from the hall tree, I head back out for one of my fave chores, gathering the living still lifes of vegetables and herbs from the garden: dusky green broccoli; chard with veins of yellow, pink, and red; fuzzy green snap peas; yummy soap-scented cilantro;

and robust flat-leaved parsley. I take the brimful basket to the house before washing the produce and storing it. I gaze out the window over the sink, watching for the yellow flash of the boys' bus. When the twins get home, I'll feed them a snack and then take them with me to tackle the composting. They were buzzed at breakfast about helping do one of Griffin's chores.

I'm washing apples when the bus stops at the end of the drive. The boys sprint for the house, their packs riding their backs like unwieldy jockeys, and fling open the screen door. Miles gets his words out first. "Jimi forgot to say one of his book report cards, but Mrs. Bing still gave him ten points 'cause he did a good job. And I got all ten points too!"

"I knew it. That's terrific!" I say, bending to wrap them in a group hug. While they dash back to see Rebekah, I slice the apples in half and add a couple of cheese slices to the plate.

Later, the twins and I thread through the garden and out to the special bin in the clearing before the piney grove. Miles snaps skin from his apple with his teeth. "What do we need *compose* for?" The boys carry paper bags of the food scraps we collect and keep in the shed refrigerator, and I, a long shovel.

"Com-*post*. Instead of using fertilizer from a store that has dangerous chemicals in it, we make our own out of the parts of the foods we don't eat for free. First I need you to gather some pine straw and twigs 'cause we're going to layer them with the food scraps." I unlatch the top of the big aqua bin. The boys stand on tiptoe to look inside. The smell of decay wafts upwards. Miles drops what's left of his apple.

"Pee-yew!" Jimi yells, backing up three feet. "Smells like skunk in there!"

Miles cackles and pulls the neck of his T-shirt up to cover his nose. I stagger back from the bin myself and bend at the waist. "Are you okay, Caro?" Miles asks through his shirt. "I think I'm gonna barf!"

"Me too." I take deep, even breaths. "Somebody forgot to add brush to the mixture last week. Please go round up those twigs now, a couple handfuls each." I stand, my forehead against a pine tree and inhale the fresh tang of resin. *It must be true.*

The boys have gathered their twigs. Steeling myself, I approach the bin again. "Sprinkle those over what's in there, and then the eggshells, coffee grounds, and fruit peels. Add your apple." I watch them accomplish that task. The rankness subsides to a tolerable level. "Now let's shred the paper bags and pile them over top. Next week we turn the mixture over with the shovel. In about three months, all of this will turn brown and crumbly and be ready to sprinkle around our plants."

"When's three months?" Miles asks as I firmly latch the bin.

Jimi looks at him as though he's grown a pair of antlers. "It's *May* now, Miles. Remember the banner above the whiteboard at school? May is the fifth month. What's three more past May?"

Jimi looks heavenward and moves his lips as he counts. "August!"

Miles gives his brother a fist bump.

"That's right." My stomach slowly settles. "By August, you should be able help Griff spread the fertilizer."

By that time, my pregnancy will be confirmed and hopefully my morning sickness over.

Chapter Five

Dare

My daughter answers her phone professionally. "This is Caroline O'Day."

I try and pitch my voice not too high, not too eager, but just right. "Caroline. Hello. It's Mom." A clink and some rustling on her end. Abruptly her voice grows louder. "Mom? Is everything okay?"

Of course she would think I was calling about something out of the ordinary because that's the essence of our communication. "Oh yes, everything's *fine*," I say as cheerily brisk as though wishing her happy Friday.

Silence on her end.

"How are you?" I ask.

"I'm pretty good. Busy."

"Still getting a lot of translating business?"

"Yes, thankfully. And there's always a ton to be done out here."

"I'll bet. I try and picture Crewtopia. I'd like to see where you live."

"Well, it's pretty much . . . perfection."

"And Griffin? Is he well?"

"Um, yeah . . . but his father just had surgery. For a brain tumor."

"Oh, my Lord."

"No, it's all good now. The tumor was benign. He's fine. Griffin's been with his parents in Hawaii, but he called Friday night. He'll be home . . . any minute actually."

So Griffin's a caring son. I like that. "I'm so glad to hear it. What a serious procedure. I bet Griffin was frightened."

"He *was*," she says. Then she's quiet for ten seconds that go by like ten years. *What is she thinking? I feel like a dolt, trying to have a conversation with my own daughter. I have to get to the point.*

"Caroline, I'm sorry to lay this on you now, but I'm actually in a bit of a pickle."

I may be the first person on the planet to ever *hear* someone stiffen. "What's wrong, Mom? Are *you* sick?"

I spend the next few minutes spilling my guts about the garden party, the girl and the vehicular homicide, the possible charges against me, and my protocol leave of absence from the paper. Caroline's quiet again. The pits of my blouse dampen. *Has the call dropped? Have I been yammering into a black hole?* "Caroline?"

"Yeah, sorry. I'm here, Mom. I'm really sorry about what you're going through. That's terrible. I can't even."

I let out a silent shaky breath at her compassion. "I know. Thank you. I was thinking . . . your birthday's coming up. I need to get away. I'd like to come and see you."

A resonant male voice floats in Caroline's air. "Baby? I'm back."

A trio of thunks tell me Caroline's fumbled her phone. "Um, Mom, can you hang on a second, please?"

Before I can respond, a cryptlike silence indicates that she's muted the call. Griffin's back. I wait. I breathe. I hope. She's welcoming him home. Maybe I should have asked her to call me back, but she didn't give me a chance. I try so hard not to annoy Caroline, but I feel like a fool sitting here on hold. I take the phone from my ear, check the screen, and note the timer. Six minutes and fifty-four seconds: the typical wait time with an insurance provider call center. *Is she telling him that I want to come? Will he feel put out?* I know nothing about him other than that he grew up a navy brat, mostly in Oahu, that he's a surfer and the publisher of a magazine.

"Mom? I'm sorry about that," Caroline says when she's back on the line. "I have a lot on my mind. We'll make it work. I mean, *of course* you're welcome."

My heart sprouts wings. I ask her when would be the most convenient time for me to arrive and for a hotel recommendation.

"Mom, there are no hotels in Topanga. You'll stay here with us."

I think of the others, the crew, as she calls them, and how I've imagined them. Especially Griffin. *Is he still in the room? I'm not on speakerphone, am I?* "Okay, thank you. Great. Maybe I can even make myself useful."

"Maybe you can."

"Oh! Is it okay if I bring Lucie? Are the little boys—I mean, do you have a pet policy?"

Caroline is quiet. I've made her place sound like an Airbnb. I shrink inside my clothes.

"It's fine as long as we keep her indoors or on her leash. The boys will be stoked. They've always wanted a dog. It's just... there are coyotes in the canyons."

Coyotes? "Oh. Of course. I'll have her leash and keep a close eye on her." *Maybe I can score a point or two with the children.*

"Well. Great. Email me your itinerary and I'll pick you up at LAX."

"Oh, I could take an Uber or something. I mean if you're working." *Take an Uber? Stop being obsequious, for the love of all things holy.*

"Mom, it's cool. I'll pick you up."

I try and picture riding in Caroline's car in the passenger seat, sitting close to her for the hour or more it must take to get to Topanga Canyon, and I'm filled with a mixture of elation and presentiment. "Thank you, Caroline."

"Of course."

"Darling, I am looking forward to seeing you."

"Well, me too. I'm glad you're coming."

I'm dead at her kind words but manage to reply with an even casualness. "Talk to you soon. Bye now."

Hope ignites in me, but it fizzles and sputters when I look out the window. My property has been TP'd. For the *second* time since I became the town pariah. The first time was a half-baked effort, a few rolls casually tossed here and there. But this one is a multi-treed, double-ply extravaganza—the swags and garlands and loop the loops perversely festive. Seraphina and Barrett Chipley—*God bless them*—are already down there, grappling with the dew-damp shreds. As I dress to go out and help them, I feel like my life has switched channels from *The Golden Girls* to *Ozark*. Can I get out of town before things get worse? How can I leave Seraphina behind to deal with all this? But then I realize exactly what that plucky piranha would say: *Get the hell out of Dodge and go see Caroline.*

Lucie the super dog is poised for flight.

She weighs less than twenty pounds. *Check.*

She has a new TSA-approved soft-sided, well-ventilated pet carrier. *Check.*

It will fit under the seat in front of me. *Check.*

I've completed all the paperwork, reserved her space, paid the extra fees. *Check. Check.* And *check.*

I have filled a ziplock baggie with her favorite treats for my handbag. *Check.*

We've visited the pet relief area where, thankfully, Lucie peed a river. *Check.*

I inch aboard the jet, the pet kennel bouncing against my shins. I take my first class window seat and give Lucie a whispered pep talk through the top of the kennel before pushing it gently beneath the seat. "See how cozy this is?" I say before slipping a treat through one of the big openings in the front. As luck would have it, no one comes to claim the aisle seat. Since most flights are overbooked these days, I'll take this as a good omen.

Tucked in my suitcase is a package of Taft's Chocolate Raft Bars for the twins—it'll be just my luck if their mother says they can't have candy and I start off on the wrong foot—and a nice assortment of gourmet teas for the adults. *Crewtopia.* I've tried so many times to imagine it, and in just a few hours I'll be there.

The seat belt light has been turned off. A little curly-haired girl licking a red Tootsie Pop across the aisle, who's traveling with an older, well-heeled woman with upswept gray hair, approaches me shyly. She's wearing a long-sleeved *Frozen* T-shirt, leggings, and sparkly red shoes like Dorothy's in *The Wizard of Oz*. Adorable. The captain's voice comes through the speakers, scrabbly and shrill. Lucie lets out a chuff. The little girl and I cover our ears with our hands. He says we may experience a bit of turbulence when we reach the air above St. Louis. Whether it's the image of a pitching and yawing plane or a slippery memory about sparkly red shoes, my stomach knots. "Is that a dog in there?" the child asks, pointing at the airline-approved travel carrier. Lucie has slept in her sturdier kitchen kennel since she was a puppy and rarely needs to be coaxed inside as she feels safe and comfortable in the niche. We call it her cozy home.

"It is. I'm Dare. And that's Lucie. I'm sorry I'm not allowed to take her out so you can meet her."

"Tell her your name, dear," the woman prompts as though she is QE2.

"Ava," she says, exposing a tongue as pink as Lucie's. "That's Grandmother."

I smile. "It's a pleasure to meet you, Ava." I turn to acknowledge her grandmother, but she's opening *The New York Times*. My heart falters. *The* Journal... *how I miss it.* The grandmother barricades herself behind the *Times*. *Just like Taffy*, I think without warning. Ava's grandmother should be reading a book to her. My mother didn't take the time to read to me once I was nine or ten, and she would have been as likely to give me candy as she would a stick of lit dynamite.

"I bet if I get down here like this," Ava says, crouching in front of the aisle seat and laying the Tootsie Pop on the nubbly fabric, "I can see Lucie in there."

"Sure you can," I say. But I freak out a little at the unwrapped candy on the germ-infested, seat, the thought of all the bottoms that have lingered there. I glance down the aisle, where a flight attendant is moving slowing toward front with his cart, serving drinks and snacks. "Until the flight attendant gets here with the cart, and then you'll have to go back to your seat." Ava presses close to the carrier. "She's white with black polka dots!"

I laugh. "She sure is."

"Aww, hi, girl. Hi, Lucie." Ava pokes a sticky finger through a vent. Lucie snuffles and licks it. Her tail whaps against the side. Ava grins up at me. "She must like cherry."

"She must."

Ava startles and quickly draws her hand back. "What happened to her ear," she asks, her tone quavery and high.

"It's okay, honey. Someone wasn't very kind to her when she was a puppy. But she's perfect now."

"Oh, she's a rescue dog. I know what that means."

"She is. And I love her very much." The service cart is two rows behind us now. The woman on the aisle shouts her order of a gin and tonic with no tonic and two limes. Her companion snorts with laughter and cries, "Girl, *same!*"

"I love her too," Ava says wistfully. She laces her little fingers and holds her hands under her chin. "I wish I could hold her."

"She'd love that. But you have to go back to your seat now." Gingerly, I pick up her candy and hand it to her.

Ava takes it, pops it right back into her mouth, and settles into her seat. Her grandmother doesn't notice. Unbelievable. The flight attendant appears at my side and cocks the cart in place with a foot. He offers me a beverage. I order a Diet Coke and then ask him for a wet napkin to wipe my fingers and the seat. When he moves past, I look at Ava again. Her lap tray is down and she's doing string tricks with a length of yarn. I watch her create a Jacob's ladder. I smile to myself. It's neat that kids still do that. But I bet Ava's string is sticky.

Without warning, a sneak of a memory about red shoes grabs me by the shoulders. I wasn't allowed to trick or treat as a child. But when I was in the first grade, my class had a Halloween party. I begged my mother for a store-bought Smurfette costume with plastic mask like the other children were choosing, but instead, Taffy had her tailor fashion me a stunning Dorothy costume. The tailor had even taken a pair of Mary Janes and overlaid them with red glitter. When my mother's driver, whose responsibility was to transport me to and from school in a long black car, pulled up in front of our house on Massachusetts Avenue the afternoon after the party, I gusted through the door, bursting with news about the fun I'd had but blissfully unaware of a salient piece of information: my hands and Dorothy pinafore were streaked with chocolate. Unhinged by an anguish I couldn't reconcile, Taffy clapped swollen eyes on the chocolate stains and burst into fresh howls.

Mommy! I'm so sorry! It was M&M's. They're 'posed to melt in your mouth, not in your hands. But grabbing my wrists, she pinned me against the kitchen sink and jerked the faucet on. As I wailed, my mother scoured my hands with a plastic scrubby until they were the pink of skinned baby rabbits, all the while telling me my father had been 'bezzling her money and skipped the country. I figured 'bezzling was stealing. But I couldn't wrap my mind around my formal pipe-smoking father skipping along anywhere.

The sticky-fingered bastard she called him before slumping to the floor in exhaustion.

My breath is coming staccato in my throat. I reenter the present scene, fumble the magazine pouch at my knees, and locate an airsickness bag. Ava's grandmother is still blockaded behind her newspaper. Ava is out of her seat again and chatting up a couple sitting in the row in front of her. She points in my direction. "That lady has a polka dot doggie under the seat. But someone wasn't very nice to her when she was little." The couple turn to me with flummoxed faces. I look down at my hands, more veined now, and clench them against a fresh onslaught of nausea. While Lucie's scars will be with her until I bury her beneath the cherry tree in my garden, my scars are visible only to me.

A female flight attendant with a bouncing ponytail approaches from the galley. "What a good passenger you are," she coos to Ava. "The captain has some wings for you."

We're nearly there? My eyes dart to the window. Below gauzy low clouds, mountains rise in olive and sage-hued ridges and crags, rough-edged hickory zigzags. We're in California. Ava's grandmother folds her newspaper into perfect thirds as Ava takes her seat. The attendant slips a pair of gold plastic wings from her apron and pins them onto Ava's shirt.

"You have been a very good girl today," the grandmother says coolly. "Your mother will be pleased." Ava lights like sunrise, sits stickpin straight in her seat.

"Lucie is a good passenger too," she says to me across the aisle.

Lucie lets out a give-me-some-attention yodel, and I absently slip her another treat.

"Yes," I say faintly, and force a smile.

By the time I realized my sticky-fingered father wasn't coming back and that it would be in my best interest to keep Taffy happy, I made sure that I was always a *very good girl*. That I had unimpeachable manners and finishing school elocution. That I won writing competition awards. Top grades in high school. That I was salutatorian of my graduating class and one of a handful of reputed virgins.

Ava's grandmother tucks her newspaper into a Harrod's tote. A month ago, my boss at the *Journal*, Carmen, made a statement in my defense to the citizens of Foxfield: *Dare O'Day never did a reckless thing in her life.*

He didn't know about my eighteenth summer before I left for college.

When I reckoned it was high time I was a bad girl for once.

Chapter Six

Caroline

I got over my diffidence about making love in the daytime *en déshabillé* the time Griffin and I spread a blanket in a thicket at the botanical gardens. We went at it, me giggling breathlessly, my eyes tightly shut against the sun haloing his dark head, until he whispered in my ear, *"Caroline, open your eyes to us. We're a perfect thing."*

This morning, he arrived from the airport at the worst time, in the middle of a phone conversation with my mother. While I kept her on hold—feeling ruder by the second—he and I made a snap decision, agreeing that with her predicament it was the right thing to do. Then I tossed my phone aside and said the world and everyone in it could wait, and I told him to bolt the door. We'd been apart too long. I was desperate to reach that transcendent state where I can't tell where Griffin leaves off and Caroline begins. And by the light of our bedroom window, his eyes and fingers grazed my skin, my generous breasts and bottom with the admiration of an art curator reveling in his most prized acquisition. And despite the tumult of my thoughts, his homecoming was as nourishing and carefree as I had planned.

But while Griff's in the shower, I dress to the tom-tom beat of my fretting heart. I sit on the bed, forcing myself to take cleansing breaths and preparing for the profoundest conversation we may ever have. The bathroom door opens, soap-fragrant steam roiling into the hall. Griffin rounds the corner, wearing a towel around his hips and the sheepish I'm-sorry-but-I-have-to-go look I know so well on his face.

My heart slips a notch as he closes our door. "Say it isn't so."

"Baby, I have to run to the Santa Monica office and meet with Collin and Ed. Collin's leaving for New York tomorrow. But I'll be back before dinner, I promise." He combs out his wet hair and dresses while I stare at his perpetually burnished back, his narrow waist and broad swimmer's shoulders, the marble-pale bottom that would rival any sculptures in the Louvre, my indignation at his leaving so soon coming to a simmer.

When he called from Hawaii to tell me the surgery was a complete success and that both his parents were doing well, we talked for two hours. He apologized for disappearing down a rabbit hole for two days without getting in touch with me. But Griffin Panakis is very likely about to find himself smack dab in the middle of a life he never imagined. I almost feel sorry for him. But it can't be helped.

The twins pound down the hall, giggle at the door. They're all awhoop that Griff's home. I can't tell him we're pregnant here, with four sharp little ears around every corner, with the rest of the crew milling about. I have to take him somewhere that we can be completely alone. In the morning. And maybe it's best that I confirm the pregnancy first anyway. Today. The two of us work best with absolutes. So while he's away, I'll go into town and buy a test. I'll be ready.

Feeling calmer, I walk him outside, then cringe as his Jeep clears—by what looks like inches—the roofer's titanic truck coming down the drive. I call to Rebekah, who's in the chicken coop collecting the eggs, and incline my head to the truck. "Let the wild rumpus begin!"

"Man, this is the day, isn't it? Too bad I'm not teaching in Topanga today." She shoos the hens from her shins and hands me the bowl of eggs so she can latch the gate. "I wish we could get out of here."

Rebekah and I don't spend enough time alone. Sometimes I wish my mother were the type of mom I could confide in. But Rebekah's a mother, and having her with me will be comforting. She'll understand. "I'm actually going into town. How about a girl's trip?"

She flashes a grin. "Give me ten."

She hurries to the house to change. I wave to Mike the roofer and his crew and then stand a moment, surveying the eggs before taking them inside. One of the seven is good-luck green. Lucky seven. Seven, according to Rebekah, the number of completion in the Bible. I still until my free hand finds its way to my tummy. Seven, the number of people who may already be living at Crewtopia.

In her car, Rebekah grins and waves a CD under my nose, Bill Withers's *Menagerie*. I flip down the sun visor on the passenger side and smile up at her two other favorites—Miles Davis's *Mellow Miles* and Jimi Hendrix's *Songs for Groovy Children*—wedged in the slots between classical CDs. She plugs *Menagerie* into the dash. "Lovely Day" begins as we bump along the gravel. "It's a rare occasion when I get to feel free," Rebekah says. "Let's roll down the windows and pretend we're cutting school." Her hair is natural today, and it blows wild, the mimosa honey scent of her conditioner wreathing my head. I unleash my ponytail and let my own hair fly.

It *is* a lovely day, and Rebekah's exuberance makes my mission feel like a divine adventure.

"So where are we headed?" she asks, drumming on the steering wheel along with the music. "The boys are staying late for chess club today. They won't be home until four thirty. How about Santa Monica for lunch!"

"Let's do it!"

My situation reaches up and tugs me back to reality. Griff's probably arriving in Santa Monica as we speak. But he'll be downtown, not near the beach. Rebekah and I reach Topanga and pass the farmer's market, where we buy goat cheese, black bread, and fruit on Fridays. I remove a strand of hair from my mouth. "Actually, I have a stop I need to make first. I had . . . an ulterior motive in asking you to go out today."

Rebekah brakes at the light before Lucy in the Sky Café and Hen-Peck Feed. She gives me a slantwise look, then turns the music down. "What is it? Should I be worried?" The single vertical line on her otherwise smooth forehead deepens.

I sigh. "Remember the other day when you said if I ever needed you—"

"That I'd be there. Right."

"Well, I need you today." She pulls the Subaru to the roadside in front of Sister Suki's dress shop, where tie-dye frocks on outdoor racks float with the breeze and flag the tourists down. She searches my eyes. My words have gone slippery and out they slide. "I'm probably pregnant."

My friend's expressions mirror my emotions: a gape, a bite of her lip, a grin, a fist over her mouth, a look at the ceiling, a grimace, a Mona Lisa smile. Then she nods briskly and gets down to business. "How late are you?"

"I think four weeks or so."

"Does Griffin know?"

"He has no idea. Let's find a pharmacy. I need to take a test."

"You mean you're going to pee on a stick in a pharmacy bathroom?" Her voice rises an octave on the last two words.

"Well, you were so excited to get out, I guess my plan slid from the grid."

"Well, I'm sure it's been done before," she says, and makes a wide U-turn.

"Where are you going?"

"To Wyler's Pharmacy."

"No! WTF? They might recognize me in there!"

She throws back her head and laughs, her graceful reserve flying out the window. "Well, we'll find one in Santa Monica, then." Another U makes my stomach flip, then the Subaru is winding the curves out of town, past the tumbledown and long-closed palm-reading shacks, the beautiful chaparral-covered hills, the fruit trees and roadside stands along CA-27 toward the beach and my destiny.

"Wish me luck." I climb ratty-haired out of the car outside the entrance of a drugstore whose window display resembles that of a head shop's. Only in Santa Monica. Inside, I pay for not one but two tests for good measure. I take them into the bathroom and go about the inelegant commerce of peeing first on one stick and then the other without making a mess.

Outside, Rebekah looks up in astonishment as I open my car door. "That was quick." I buckle my seat belt and read the randy slogan on the brown paper sack: PHARMACY TECHS DO IT OVER THE COUNTER. How had Griffin and I done it last? When had we conceived? Rebekah gives me a look usually reserved for Jimi when he's on her last nerve. "Well?"

I shove the bag at her. "I couldn't look. You look."

"Whaaat? Caroline O'Day, this is the *wildest*, most unconventional thing I've ever done in my life."

"That's saying a lot."

She punch-jabs my shoulder, then pulls the sticks out by the handles I'd carefully dried. She peers at one stick and then the other.

Rebekah looks at me with the pearly gaze I've only ever seen her bestow on her sleeping twins. "You are going to have a baby." It's real. My silent nightly soliloquies to the contrary, the holding back, the stress of not knowing. It's over. A dam bursts from my eyes. Rebekah rifles through her glove box for one of those little travel packs of tissues. She feeds them to me one by one as I wail.

"I've had some time to get used to the idea, but I wasn't sure how I'd feel if it was true. But I feel . . . happier than I've felt in my life," I blubber. "But Griffin! I have to spring this on him. What if he can't handle it? What if he leaves me? *And oh Lord,* my mother's coming!" Panic races my veins. "How will I deal?"

"Caroline—" A couple comes out of the pharmacy, their eyes naturally moving to the yellow car parked in front, its two occupants. Rebekah starts the car and punches at the window roll-up buttons, then slams the car into reverse—narrowly missing a Beamer whizzing behind us into the lot, whose driver flips us off—then looks both ways and peels out. The Subaru careens back onto the highway. "Woo-hoo! That felt great," she says, beating on the wheel, then quickly turning an apologetic look on me. With my emotions slip-sliding all over the place, the floorboard filled with twisted tissues, my boo-hoos turn into guffaws, and Rebekah joins me. "Oh, honey," she says when our laughter wanes and my mind speeds ahead. "*Griffin* can handle it. He won't leave you. As for your mother—"

"Here. Stop here," I say as we come to the first in the strand of beachfront diners, The Palisades. "I either need to eat something or hurl."

Rebekah brakes and whips into the sand-strewn lot. It's early. Only two cars are parked in front. "Let's get some food in you."

Inside the restaurant—decorated with a flotilla of life preservers, fishing nets, retro beach signs, and giant lobsters—the host takes one look at my disheveled hair and ruined face, clears his throat, and addresses Rebekah, who's managed to rebraid her hair between the car and the restaurant door. "Right this way, guys." He leads us to a table in a far corner behind a partition.

A bowl of soup would be good. And some crackers. A baby. And Griff doesn't have a clue. A baby, probably the size of a poppy seed, is growing inside me. Is it already taking nourishment from what I eat? I have to get online and read about fetal development. Territory I'd left uncharted. A waiter wearing purple eyeliner appears with sweating blue tumblers of water, and introduces himself to Rebekah as Venus. We give him our orders. I honk into my napkin. He scuttles away.

I sip my water. "I have to tell Griff but not at the house."

"Drive up to the Top of Topanga Overlook. It won't be touristy this time of year, and nobody much's up there early in the day. Go tomorrow."

"Now that," I say, reaching for my utensils rolled in a paper napkin, "is one brill idea. But what if he's upset that I haven't told him yet?"

Rebekah reaches for her water. "It's not your fault that he's been away. And you wouldn't have wanted to tell him over the phone."

"I know." My belly fumes at me. I open two packages of crackers just as Venus returns with a bowl of vegetable soup for me and a burger for Rebekah. I push a spoonful of soup from the front of the bowl to the back before lifting it to my lips, as Mom insisted. She annoyed me then, but today when I see people eating with both elbows on the table or stirring beverages with a clanking spoon, I'm grateful she taught me proper etiquette.

Rebekah runs a fat fry through a puddle of catsup and pops it into her mouth. She uses her napkin to wipe her fingers. "Caroline, remember the day we talked on the porch, when I said your mother loved you?" *Do I ever.* "And that even if she's not the grandmotherly type she would rise to the occasion if you and Griff had a baby? Well, Griffin *adores* you, and he will too."

"But we made an intentional decision against having kids."

"But why?"

I raise a wait-a-sec finger, eat a couple of crackers, and break the rest into my soup, which is delicious. "He doesn't think it's fair to bring a child into this broken, scary culture. With all the hate. With the political corruption and turmoil. He's concerned about the threats against the U.S., about North Korea and their missiles. He worries about climate change. The oceans and the problems children of the future will inherit. Pandemics."

Rebekah nods slowly, then speaks to me as though I'm someone whose dough hasn't quite risen. "Caroline, *everyone* worries about those things. Besides, that was *five years ago* when you were still in college, still getting to know each other. He's matured since then."

"There are people a lot older than us who don't want kids."

"Well, maybe those people don't have what you and Griff have."

Though I figure I'd cried every drop of water in my body, hot tears spill over my lids. "I know."

"Of course you do. Now. You've told me why Griffin didn't want kids, but you haven't told me why Caroline didn't want them."

Venus approaches to refill our water glasses. I ask him for the check.

"I think," I say to Rebekah, "that back then I would have agreed to drink a cyanide martini if Griffin Panakis was pouring." She dips her chin and gives me a that's-ridiculous half smile. "And as you know, I didn't think I would be a good mother, since I come from a lineage of subpar ones."

"Hold that thought. Let's walk the beach." We lay cash atop the check, then use the restroom before exiting the restaurant through the back doors and heading for the beach. We take off our shoes. The sand is warm and soothing. Rebekah collects her train of thought. "Do you think when I got pregnant I thought I'd be a good mother? I had such a blazing torch of hate in my heart for Denzel and my father, I was afraid it might make me hate my boys."

"Oh, lovie," I say, stopping her and hugging her hard. "But you didn't. And now you're just . . . the perfect earth mother. You had it inside you all the time."

Moving on, she links her arm in mine. "Caroline, I'm far from perfect, and so are my children, but where there's love, there's completion." *Completion again. A crew of seven.*

"But how do I learn nurturing?"

"Caroline, don't you realize how nurturing you are not only to my children but to me?"

My face flies to hers. "That's like the best thing anyone ever said to me in my life," I say, a sob swelling in my breast again. "Thank you," I manage to say around it. I think of the applicants we sifted through when we were completing our crew, including the woman who brought along her collection of voodoo dolls, and am doubly grateful for Rebekah.

"You are quite welcome. I bet you'll even be nurturing to your mother when she comes."

My mother. "The dynamic is going to be so weird with her here, especially while the news about the baby is fresh."

"Well, maybe she could come *next* month, when things are more . . . settled."

"No. She has to come now. She's in trouble."

Rebekah looks at me, her eyebrows shooting up two inches. "Trouble?"

We've strolled all the way to the pier by the time I've finished telling her about what went down in Foxfield.

"You know you can handle this. And we'll all be there to support you." Shading her eyes with a brown hand, she regards the gigantic Pacific Wheel. "Hey, this is our girls' adventure. We must ride the world's only solar-powered Ferris wheel."

Before I know it, my shoes are back on my feet. I'm on a Ferris wheel bench with my friend with the safety bar in place, laughing and loving the feel of the breeze on my tear-tender face.

"So what's Dare like anyway?" she asks when we stop halfway to the top, the bench swinging.

"She's smart—a newspaper editor—and energetic with my light green eyes and curvy figure, though she beats herself up about hers. She's really pretty. Her hair's brown. The auburn," I say, fingering a strand of my hair, "I inherited from my father." I'm quiet for a moment. "Friends have asked me why Mom never remarried, and I tell them the truth: I don't know. I've wondered what she does for sex, not in a literal way because that would be skeevy. She had me when she was eighteen, so she's only forty-five—but if she dates, that's another thing we don't talk about." The wheel is rising again, closing in on the top. "She has Seraphina, who's a total trip and a badass. And she takes the same care of Mom that she took of Taffy, but I still feel like Mom's lonely."

The wheel stops with Rebekah and me at what feels like the top of the stratosphere. "Trust *moi*," she says. "It will all work out."

I smile at her, tickled by the smattering of French she's picked up from me.

I look out over the long pier and the city of Santa Monica where Griffin is working and clutch the safety bar. I will tell him tomorrow. And it will all work out. I look at the ground where six-inch-tall parents hold their children's hands and wait to board the wheel. Our bench rocks. My stomach rolls greasily. And my lunch hits the ground without a sound.

Griffin and Rebekah have prepared a sesame ginger beef stir-fry and mandarin spinach salad for dinner. After losing my lunch earlier, I'm ravenous, eating everything in sight. I snare another piece of bread from the basket. Wide-eyed, Griffin gets up to grab the butter dish from the counter. Rebekah is asking the boys about their school day. Griffin asks the boys, "Guess who has a birthday soon?"

"You!" Jimi says.

Griffin laughs. "No, mine's in January. But you're close. It's Caroline's."

"Yep, it's me all right," I say, slathering butter on a roll. "My twenty-seventh birthday."

"We'll make you the best cake ever, Caro," Miles says. "Chocolate."

I give him a wobbly grin. "Yum-*mo*. I can't wait."

He turns to Miles. "Yeah, and we found our Rae figure! We could put her on the top!"

"That's a great idea," Rebekah says, smiling at me.

"Since we're strapped for cash now with the roof repairs and can't go to Coachella for your birthday," Griff says, "why don't we try the Topanga Days Country Fair? I hear they have a great lineup of local bands. It's a fraction of the cost, and the kids can go too."

The boys raise their voices in tandem and pump their fists. "Yes!"

"Kids in our class are going to that," Jimi says. "There's a parade, bounce houses and sack races—"

"And crafts and 'buying stuff' for the grown-ups," Miles interrupts.

"I happen to like sack races," Parker says to Miles.

Miles grins up at him. "But you're too big for a bounce house."

I put my knife and fork down and smile at the twins. "I have something to tell you first. Something I think you'll like a lot." Rebekah and I talked about my mother's visit that afternoon, and she briefed Parker on the details. He offered to sleep on the living room sofa so that Mom could have his room. The boys stare at me in anticipation. "My mom, Dare, is coming to visit us all the way from Virginia."

"She is?" Jimi asks.

"She is, and guess who she's bringing with her."

Miles says, "Your dad!"

Rebekah puts her arm around his shoulders.

"No, my dad died when I was only two. It's okay, sweetheart," I say as his bottom lip wobbles. "It was a long time ago."

"We—Jimi and me—we don't have a dad either. I mean, if that makes you feel better."

"No, sweetie, I'm fine. But there's better news: Dare is bringing *her dog*. Lucie."

"A dog at Crewtopia?" Jimi falls back against his chair, pretending to faint with delight. We all laugh.

Miles blinks. "What *kind* of dog, big or little?"

"Well, she's pretty little, and white with black polka dots. A terrier mix."

"Aww, I bet she's cute," he says.

"She's very cute. But there's one thing. She has only one ear."

"One ear?" the boys say in tandem.

Miles's mouth quivers. "What happened to her?"

Parker, seated next to Miles, ruffles his hair. "C'mon, big guy."

"Lucie was a rescue dog."

Jimi points his fork at his brother. "Me and Miles know about rescue dogs, right, Miles?"

Miles nods.

I dip my chin at Jimi. "*Miles and I*. So Lucie was mistreated when she was just a pup, and her ear had to be removed."

Jimi's face tightens. "Can she *hear*?"

"She can hear just fine."

Griffin smiles at me and reaches for my hand under the table, gives it a squeeze.

"I will be very good to Lucie," Miles says. "She'll sleep in my bed."

"Not so fast, monsieur," Rebekah says. "No animals under your covers. Parker's giving Dare his room while she's here, and Lucie will be cozy with her."

"Well, then," Jimi asks his mother, "where will Parker sleep? In our room in your big bed?" Rebekah opens her mouth like a gaffed fish.

Parker chuckles. "Hey, dude, I get the living room sofa *all to myself*."

"But there's more," Rebekah says, recovering her equanimity and diverting the boys from sleeping arrangements. "Caroline's mother owns . . . wait for it . . . a candy company!"

Both boys sit bolt upright, their eyes the size of coasters. Miles thrusts out his chin. "Like *Willy Wonka*?"

"I'm speechless," Jimi says, pulling at his shirt collar, his bow tie. We all crack up.

"Knowing her, she already has Taft's Chocolate Raft Bars packed in her suitcase for you." The boys, who are allowed minimal candy, jump down and dance around the kitchen like football players after scoring a touchdown.

"This is gonna be the best time *ever*," Miles says. But I'm absorbed in the look on Parker's face. It's like in missing out on sharing Rebekah's bed, he's lost a second chance at the big leagues.

Later, when the excitement has died down and everyone's in bed, I lie still beside Griffin, though my thoughts are all over the place. He reaches for me, nuzzles my neck. "I loved watching you with the boys at the table. You're so good with them." His fingers trace my side, my hip, slide to the inside of my thigh and tease there. "They love you. And I love you."

But will you still love me tomorrow? "Hey, Griff?"

"Hmm?" he says into my neck.

"There's some stuff I want to talk to you about," I say lightly, though my heart beats like Edgar Allen Poe's telltale one. His hand stills, then moves from my thigh to my tummy, my breastbone, my neck, the curve of my cheek. He rolls over and looks at me. "I know you just got back from Hawaii and have a lot of catching up to do, but any way you could take part of the morning off? Maybe take me to up to the Top of Topanga Overlook?"

He yawns hugely. "Baby, that's the beauty of working from home. I'd love to take you. But let's go early."

I smile tremulously. "Yes, first thing."

The next morning, I awaken to the scent of coffee, of butter and sugar. Rebekah's up baking? Before Griff wakes, I slip out of bed, shower, and dress in the yellow cotton dress he says is his favorite, then tiptoe to the kitchen. Rebekah is sitting at the table in her pink chenille robe, drinking coffee. "Good morning," she says in her soft, quiet-time voice. She smiles and nudges the handled basket on the table toward me. "I thought you might like to take breakfast with you." Inside is a thermos, two mugs, and a cloth-wrapped bundle of muffins.

Tears sting my nose. "You made those for us?"

"I did. They're good-vibe muffins."

I pull Rebekah from her chair and hug her long. "Thank you, my friend." Shower water begins to drum in the tub down the hall. She resumes her seat, tucking her robe around her. "The father's *up*, and this thing's going *down*," I whisper.

"You've got this," she says, and inclines a pinkie to me. I crook my pinkie with hers and squeeze, then move to open the stubborn drawer where we keep things we don't often use: kitchen twine, cookie cutters, parchment paper. The bathroom door opens. I freeze until the bedroom door snicks closed again, then slide from the bottom of the drawer something else I want to take to the overlook. I tuck it beneath the muffins in the basket. Rebekah tilts her head curiously.

I tip her a wink. "I have a plan." I head back to the bedroom but meet Griffin in the hall.

"Howdy there, pretty lady," he says, kissing me. The boys and Parker haven't stirred, so I whisper that I'll meet him in the kitchen, that Rebekah's packed us a breakfast.

Fifteen minutes later, I'm behind the wheel of my Highlander, Griffin riding shotgun. We wind along Topanga Canyon Boulevard. With no other cars about, I park the SUV in the first spot of the parking area. Then I'm out of my seat belt and trotting toward the overlook. Griffin catches up with me. *"Look!"* I say, scanning the masses of early wildflowers amongst the grasses at the top of Topanga.

It's a day for marvels. The sweetly cupped red-orange poppies, the summer blue lupines, fringy lemon-yellow coreopsis, and spiky amethyst fireweed have awakened to the May sun. There couldn't be a more beautiful place to tell my love I am carrying a miracle. Though there are half a dozen benches scattered beyond the parking area, we stand leaning against the warm hood of my car for a space of time, just drinking in the lovely.

"It's incredible," Griff says. The morning air is abuzz with pollinators and sweet with the perfume of the flowers. It's so clear, the chaparral-robed crags of the Woodland Hills stand out in sharp relief. And in the far distance, the City of Angels sprawls and thrums beneath its veil of smog. I rub my hands along my arms, whether from chill or anticipation or both. "Don't we still have that quilt in the car?" Griff asks.

"We do. I'll fetch it, if you'll fetch the basket."

We lean back on our favorite bench—the one with the choicest view—and wrap the quilt around us. Opening the thermos, I pour the coffee. Griff takes a long sniff of his, sighs with pleasure, and takes a first sip. "Thanks, 'Bekah," he says to the sky as I unwrap the muffins. He smiles into my eyes. "This was a great idea, babe."

When we've eaten and Griff's on his second mug, I set my mug back into the basket and withdraw the item I'd brought from the kitchen drawer: a small bound notebook, the title on the cover written all fancy with a Sharpie marker: CREWTOPIA COVENANTS.

Griff's dark silky brows rise. "The covenants?" He huffs a little laugh. "Where have those been?"

"Before we lean into this, remember that day at Pomegranate in Los Angeles when we came up with these?"

"I do," he says, studying my face.

I run my hand over the cover. "Well, this... paradigm was important to us then." I open the notebook to the page with the bullet-pointed list we developed. Balancing the notebook on my palms, I read the list aloud:

- A nurturing environment
- Creativity and personal growth
- Sustainability
- Resource sharing
- Shared chores
- Shared meals
- A work/play balance
- Satellite internet (we *do* have to work)

I look at him. "We laid down the principles for our community."

"Yeah." He gives me his most attentive three nods in a row. "And they became a reality. We've survived longer than most intentional communities. I mean, we became family. We're happy and still committed to what we're about."

My chin begins to quiver. "But we didn't lay down personal covenants."

"*Personal* covenants? You mean between you and me? What's wrong, sweetheart?" He looks alarmed now.

"You said when we got together, senior year of college, that you felt strongly about"—I take a shaky, silent breath—"about not... having children. And I agreed for all the reasons we discussed. But we didn't put it in writing."

Griff turns his body toward me and puts his hands on his knees. He fingers his slender leather bracelet, the one I gave him with our initials etched into it. I swallow a hard knot in my throat. The quilt slips from his shoulders. He looks vulnerable somehow in only his T-shirt and board shorts. I feel awful springing this on him. He raises his gaze to mine. "Are you saying you've changed your mind, Caroline?"

"Griffin, I'm pregnant."

He blinks at me rapid-fire and pushes to stand. He spins around, his hands covering his head as if the sky is falling on it, then staggers to the edge of the clearing.

The sheer distance between Griff standing at the edge of the overlook and me on the bench makes my teeth chatter. I draw my feet up, pull the quilt tight around me. I wait. He pockets his hands. Hangs his head. And his shoulders begin to heave. Tears roll down my own cheeks; I've never seen my guy cry. I suspect he needs the release.

I give it to him.

I empty my mind.

I pray.

After a while, he wipes his face with his T, turns, and comes to me. He surveys my face, his own face blasted. "Caroline, I love you more than life itself ... but I just came through a huge ordeal with my family." I shoot him a look. "You know what I mean—with my *father*, my *parents*—that family. Came back jet-lagged and then had those *senseless-ass* meetings all day yesterday." He stops. "How long have *you* known?"

"Three days."

"Well, you've turned a page on me. I mean, I might be in shock right now," he says wonderingly. He does look pale beneath his perpetual tan. "I need a minute. Can you understand that?"

I look at the man I adore, whose child has set up camp in my womb. "I can." He leans down, pauses, then kisses my forehead. He only ever kisses my mouth. Is he pulling away from me, from us? I rearrange the quilt, drawing it and my strength around both of us.

He shivers, draws in a wet sniff, and stills. "When I was in Hawaii, I thought my father might die without me telling him I loved him one more time. All these memories flashed past. Of the times I let him down, my mother too, but how I knew they loved me no matter what. I realized how good I had it growing up with two caring parents. I prayed with my mother that God would spare Dad's life." He takes both my hands and twists them with his. "I thought about how my parents helped make me the man I am. The man you love. And I thought about you and me making a family of our own."

I feel like I did when I was nine, the time I fell from the branches of a crepe myrtle and knocked the breath out of myself. "You did? But you said you didn't want to bring a child into this terrible world and—"

His face darkens. "I *know* what I said. I was a pinheaded punk then, a fucking pragmatic *idealist*." He's squashing my hands, punctuating his words. He looks in the direction of my tummy like he wants to touch it. "But this, *this* is real. And don't you see that we unwittingly created the perfect place to raise a child?" He turns to face me. "We have this insular world at Crewtopia, but we still have to interact with the big old scary world. Terrorist bombings, synagogue and school shootings, riots. Every day there's a chance Jimi and Miles won't get off the bus. But we have *hope* that this next generation, the boys and *this baby*, will be the ones to make the difference. Look what fine little people Jimi and Miles are because they've been loved. And think how much laughter and joy they bring us."

"So you want the baby?"

Griffin's laughter echoes off the canyons. "*Of course* I do, crazy girl." Cool clean ripples of relief course through my entire being. He offers me his adorably crooked grin, the left side of his mouth rising a beat before the right. "I see how you are with the twins. They love *you* to pieces. And Rebekah's been a good role model for you."

Even after the way her parents treated her. "Definitely."

"Maybe you can break this . . . matriarchal detachment curse on your family. Hell, maybe this child can even heal what's wrong between you and your mom."

I give an internal smirk. "Maybe." *I don't want to wreck the moment by listing for Griffin the things I don't know if I'll ever resolve with my mother. At the top of the list, the scene she made with Lisette that long-ago, awful afternoon.* I drill my eyes into his. "But I don't want to tell her about the baby right away, okay? I haven't been to a doctor yet. And she's been through a rough time lately. We need to get her settled in and, you know, *used* to all of us before springing the news."

"All families go through growing pains. Our crew family will too. I think the others will be happy about it. You *know* the boys will be stoked."

I briefly tell Griffin about my day with Rebekah. "So since she already knows, you want to be the one to tell Parker when we get home? But *not* the boys yet."

Griffin pushes out his chest and nods out over the vista: a landowner surveying his kingdom. "Yeah, sure. I'll brag about what a stud I am." *Oh God. Don't do that.* "JK," he adds. Then he turns to me again and all the feels seem to cross his face. "Ah, Caroline. The first time we met and I looked into your eyes—the color of the ocean that runs through my blood—I knew your essential goodness, the love you had to give. I don't know . . . maybe you were born with it, or maybe your mother did better than you thought she did." *Maybe.* "The first thought I had when you told me was Wow! A baby inside Caroline? That's before I fell apart for a minute," he adds, glancing back at the overlook. "It's a miracle."

After a moment, his brow furrows. "By the way, how did your birth control ring fail?"

I give him a sheepish look. "I forgot to put a new one in soon enough."

"Well, you know, everything happens for a reason. This baby's meant to be. I feel like hopping on my best board and executing a rodeo flip like the freaking god of the sea."

I shyly peep through my lashes at the freaking god of the sea. "I think you'll be a wonderful dad."

"Hope is the answer. Who can live without it? So we're going to do this thing, O'Day. We'll raise this child because we have hope. You'll see. It will all work out."

I smile my sunniest smile until the sun abruptly sets behind my bottom lip. I close my mouth as though to make it last a little longer, but a breath escapes me when I remember that my mother's coming to stay in our home. "I hope."

Chapter Seven

Dare

A guy on the jet bridge was joking about a sentiment on Twitter: *In SoCal, we don't say I love you. We say yes, I can pick you up at LAX.* My heart soars because Caroline not only came to pick me up but has come inside the terminal. She stands near the baggage carousel in a pair of white jeans and an indigo top. Behind her, the sun streams through the expanse of windows and ignites the shine of her auburn hair. She catches sight of me, smiles, and lifts her pretty chin.

I approach her and she meets me halfway. We awkwardly move to hug each other at the same time. "My darling, it's so good to see you," I breathe into her hair.

She lets go first, as is her habit. "It's good to see you too, Mom. And look at Lucie there. Hi, Lucie. The boys are *dying* to see you. *Both* of you."

Ava and her grandmother have queued up at the carousel, Ava doing some little jazz steps in the red shoes. "Do Jimi and Miles know about her ear?" I ask Caroline. "It can be shocking at first." I'm congratulating myself for remembering the boys' names when I spot my behemoth of a suitcase dropping down the chute. "Hang on. Here's my bag."

I haul the bag over the lip of the carousel and double-check the tag before raising the handle and wheeling it toward my daughter. We make for the sliding exit doors. "Oh yeah. No, it's fine. They know. Miles—he's our tenderhearted little dude—wants her to sleep with him. Car's this way."

"That's so sweet." We emerge into the bright California day and navigate past a taxi line as long as the Vincent Thomas Bridge. Before we get to the parking garage, I manage to get Lucie to potty in a patch of scrubby grass. I screech as she sniffs at what looks like a used condom. "Don't eat that!" *Welcome to Los Angeles.* I've never seen Caroline's car because of course she flies to Virginia, so when we've reached her handsome silver 2019 Highlander, I compliment her on the good deal she made on it. Though she rarely taps her trust fund, I'm glad it's there for her if she needs it.

Caroline inches the car along a line at the pay station while I secure Lucie's kennel in the back seat. Caroline is digging through her bag. She comes up with the shabby wallet she's had for years and slides out cash for the attendant.

"How about letting me buy you a handsome new wallet while I'm here?"

Her chest rises high and falls. "Mom," she says, tight-lipped, "I think you offered to buy me a wallet last year, and I believe I said I liked this one."

"Oh, of course." *Well played, Dare. Pissing her off before we've even left LAX.* I have to make this work, build an adult relationship with Caroline, or I could lose her forever. Breaking free of the airport congestion, we pass gas stations and rows of fast food joints where the first palm trees snag my attention. "It's neat seeing all the palms out here."

"Are you hungry, Mom?"

"No, I took a sandwich on board. I'm good."

"It's Griffin and Parker's turn to cook dinner tonight. We'll make it an early night because you have to be tired from your travel day."

"How thoughtful. Are they good cooks?"

Caroline grins. "Better than Rebekah or me."

"Well, I can't wait to meet everyone."

"Yeah, they're excited too."

I release a quiet breath. *Okay, we're doing well.* "Oooh, I might like a Starbuck's, though. May I treat you to something yummy, like a caramel latte?"

"Sure, that sounds good. There's a Starbuck's ahead before the turnoff."

Minutes later, our coffees in hand, Caroline calmly glides through traffic that makes me wish I'd ordered mine decaf. She asks after Seraphina and how it's been going at home. I surprise myself by telling her—in vivid detail—about the protestors and TP'ers. She shakes her head and murmurs words of disgust. I sip from my cup, feeling warmed not just by the coffee but how Caroline and I seem to have fast-forwarded to the place where we're easy with each other. An hour later, we pass the Santa Monica sign. Lucie stirs and stands up in her kennel as if asking *Are we there yet?* I slip her a treat from my purse. "Is this where Griffin surfs?"

"No, he goes up to Malibu or Huntington Beach. The best waves are there."

"Oh, there's the pier and the giant Ferris wheel! I remember all this—from when I attended that journalism conference when you were in high school. I bet the twins like to ride the wheel." When Caroline doesn't answer, I look at her. Below her sunglasses, her face has paled.

"You okay, darling?"

She swallows hard. "Oh yeah, yeah. Sometimes the combination of the milk and high sugar in these coffees upsets my stomach. Go figure."

"Oh yuck. Sorry. I have some Tums in my bag." I reach for my bag on the floorboard.

"Mom, thank you. But I'm really fine."

"Are you sure?"

Lucie whines.

Caroline looks at me flatly. "Mom. I don't. Want. A Tums."

Silence descends.

I've done it again.

What would Seraphina say? *Shut the hell up, Dare. Just let it be. She's a grown woman. Don't smother her.*

I want Caroline's friends to like me. How much has she told them about me? If I'm ever *really* going to get to know my daughter, I will have to accept her lifestyle and the people she loves. I also need to be myself. But if I keep sticking a size eight leopard-print J. Crew driving moc in my mouth, it's going to be permanently stained with red lipstick.

At CA 27N to Topanga, we leave the palms behind and pass through an evergreen forest of manzanita, rosemary, and coast live oaks. I roll down my window in hopes any lingering tension will escape the car like a hornet that's been trapped inside. I take a sharp inhale. As the pungent pine and lemon tones of the fresh rosemary rush my lungs, I swear my blood pressure drops five points.

And then I've got it! I'm a journalist, for Pete's sake. I'll pretend I've been given an assignment to explore a way of living that mainstream America may not understand. While I dwell amongst the people of Crewtopia, I'll study the connections between them and discover the gifts each of them brings to make intentional-community living satisfying. That solved, drowsiness overcomes me.

Ten minutes later, a lilting sigh from Caroline awakens me. She's flipped on a blinker just before a gravel road.

"Is this Crewtopia?" I ask, fluffing my hair. The stale air from the plane seems to have permeated my skin. I scramble to freshen my lipstick.

"It is," she says, a beatific smile transforming her face.

I smile back at my daughter, hope washing over me.

I've totally got this.

As Caroline's car crunches along the drive, a man comes down the front steps of the house. He stands, hands in the pockets of tan pants, blue shirt sleeves rolled up tanned, muscular forearms. "Here's my Griff," Caroline says so adoringly I'm convinced I've arrived in paradise.

"Ah." Caroline has told me a bit about him over the years, but I was unprepared for how gorgeous he is. My stomach does a little rhumba step as the Highlander draws alongside him. I'm no cougar, but the guy is a cross between Giacomo Giannotti on *Grey's Anatomy* and a handsomer, younger, and decidedly cleaner Johnny Depp.

I give him a little wave as Caroline parks, and then the bungalow that is the heart of Crewtopia commands my eyes. It is utterly charming. I step out onto the gravel—peripherally aware that my daughter and her boyfriend are greeting one another with hugs and kisses—and lift Lucie's kennel from the back seat.

As Lucie sniffs like mad at the new place, I survey the house. The French blue paint is offset by crisp white trim. Pots of rowdy flowers and searching tendrils almost obscure the front steps leading to a long front porch slung at one end with a rope hammock and brightly colored pillows and a black woman sitting behind what appears to be a quilting frame at the other. She waves at me and stands, stretching her back.

"Mom," Caroline says, leading Griffin by the hand, "I'd like you to meet Griffin Panakis. Griffin, this is my mother, Dare O'Day."

Griffin inclines his hand. "It's a pleasure to meet you, Dare."

Though I'm still shook by his film-star appearance, I muster my firmest, most professional shake. "I'm happy to know you, Griffin. It's good to finally be here."

Griffin smiles. "I'll grab your bags."

"Thank you."

"Mom, come meet Rebekah." I take my purse and Lucie's kennel and follow Caroline up the steps.

"The flowers out here are magnificent."

Rebekah meets us at the top in a cool column of batik cotton, her brown arms bare and supple. She laughs and inclines a cool hand. "Your daughter's the one with the green thumb. I'm Rebekah."

Caroline's a gardener? How many other things don't I know about my girl? "How nice to meet you. Your laugh is musical. It's like ... the tinkle of ice in a Jefferson cup." Griffin bumps my honking bag onto to the porch, and he and Caroline exchange amused glances as she holds the screen door open for him. I give my shoes the once-over.

But Rebekah saves me and instantly becomes a BFF. "Well, you've paid me the perfect compliment. I'm a musician. I play the flute and teach music."

"Oh, I hope you'll play for me while I'm here. And you're a quilter too."

She smiles. "I will. And I am. But foremost, I'm the mother of active twin boys."

"Miles and Jimi. I can't wait to meet them."

Rebekah gazes down the drive. "It's their late day at school, but the bus should be here soon. This must be Lucie," she says, squatting down to poke a finger inside the carrier. Lucie's tail beats a rhythm on the nylon side.

"Mom, come inside," Caroline calls. "Why don't you set Lucie in the living room so she can get used to being here before the boys bombard her."

"Great idea." Rebekah shows me into a cozy-looking living area, and I set the kennel on the deep-shag rug. The abundance of books—leather-bound classics *Pride and Prejudice*, *The Great Gatsby*, *Slaughterhouse Five*, *A Tale of Two Cities*—crammed into a bookcase commanding an entire wall surprises me. Colorful modern posters are displayed on the others. These kids are not only well-educated but well-read. And they've done a wonderful job with the old place.

I compliment Rebekah on the room and then follow her across the hall into a large well-ordered kitchen. Caroline holds a red tea kettle under the sink faucet. "Would you like a cup of tea? Or would you rather freshen up first?"

"I'd love to freshen up."

Caroline flips on the stove and sets the kettle on a burner. "Watch that for me," she tells Griffin. "Come on back, Mom. You'll be in Parker's room in the rear addition. We just replaced the roof over that section and put a fresh coat of paint on the ceiling." She leads me along wide-planked old floors and stops at the first room on the left. "This is Rebekah's room. The boys bunk with her. And they mostly use the front bath here across the hall." We continue down the hall, the floor sighing and groaning. Caroline grins. "You can't sneak around here on these old boards." She continues the tour. "Down here on the right is mine and Griffin's room."

"Nice," I murmur, trying not to stare into the room but dying to see what's inside. Rambling left, we enter the addition, where on the right is a bathroom with an old scratched soaking tub.

"Parker and Griff and I share this bathroom, and you're welcome to it too." *Sharing a bathroom with guys I don't know will be a first. But hey, I can do this.*

"So this is where you'll be," she says, walking into Parker's room.

"Oh, it's great," I say taking in the king-sized bed where Griffin has set my suitcase, the plain functional furniture, and a massive desk with three computer monitors on top. "Are you sure he's okay with me taking his room? I feel badly about that." *Damn, did that sound like a put-down on the house, that I think it's too small and there's not enough room for a guest?*

But Caroline gives me a don't-sweat-it wave. "Parker's chill. But he *will* need to be back here when he's working. Hopefully you'll be comfy hanging out in the living room or outside." Caroline claps a hand over her mouth and squeezes her eyes tight.

"You okay, darling?"

She stumbles past me into the bathroom and shuts the door. *For the love of God, don't offer her a Tums.* I hear the clunk of the toilet lid—*there you have it, share a bath with guys, and the seat gets left up*—and hurry down the hall before her retching can reach my ears. The others are in the kitchen, talking above Fleetwood Mac's "Songbird." I follow the music to the living room, where *Rumours* spins on a turntable, and look in on Lucie, who's sacked out and snoring. Across the hall in the kitchen, Griffin, Rebekah, and a cute freckle-faced guy in a baseball cap are drinking tea at the table. "Dare, meet Parker," Griffin says.

Parker rises and sweeps his cap from curly hair, but I wave him down and extend my hand. "Hi, Parker. I'm Dare. Thank you for sharing your bed with me." I scream inside my head, but he laughs along with the others as though I've made a saucy joke and shakes my hand. So I smile, shrug a shoulder, and pull out a chair.

Parker says, "We usually have our tea before the boys get home ravenous for their snacks. You a tea drinker?"

"I'd love some. Oh!" I say, still holding onto the back of the chair. "I have something for you in my bag."

"Where's Caroline?" Griffin asks.

"She—oh, we drank a Starbuck's on the way up and it didn't agree with her. She's in the back bathroom."

Rebekah and Griffin exchange a look I can't read, and he gets to his feet. "I'll check on her."

Instead of following him back there to open my suitcase, I sit and accept a warm mug from Rebekah. *Let Griffin take care of Caroline.* I'm chatting with Parker about his work in baseball when in storms a blur of boys and backpacks. "Is Dare here yet?" they say in tandem.

"She sure is," Rebekah says, and plants a kiss on both their tousled heads.

I wave at them from across the table. "Hi, guys. I'm happy to meet you." They rush the table, but Rebekah stops them in their tracks.

"Go wash your grimy paws and faces first, please, and then you can hug Dare. They are little lovers," she says with a doting smile as she watches them go.

"Aww." *Hugging a child. How long has it been?* I breathe in the steam from my tea—jasmine—and marvel as the flower opens inside the cup. *If only I'd snuggled with Caroline in her middle years. If I hadn't been consumed with my career and maintaining a perfect façade. If I hadn't hired Lisette in the first place. So many regrets. So many wrongs to be made right. Stop this!* I breathe and remind myself of the assignment I gave myself: to get to know the crew, to explore and discover how they make an intentional community work.

Parker is searching for cookies in a high cabinet. I do a double take as he locates a white tin with red and yellow flowers that looks like one Taffy had. I bet they found it in a consignment shop. I glance at Rebekah, who's toying with fringe on a napkin and giving Parker's athletic body the once-over. As he arranges cookies on a red plate, a wistful smile plays about her lips. *How many years has it been since I looked at a guy like that?* I cradle my mug with both hands. *Luke Henry. The turbulent summer of 1992.* Rebekah giggles at something Parker says, and he replaces the tin in the cabinet. *Caroline hadn't said anything about them being a couple, but I'd have to turn in my girl card if I didn't notice that she is into him.*

The boys return, smelling of wind and citrusy soap. Jimi speeds around the table and falls against me, hugging me tightly and kissing my cheek with a loud smack that makes the adults laugh. Miles hangs back a second, not shyly but as though assessing my comfort level. *Has he sussed out my inability to nurture?* My arms tremble as I extend them to him. He comes to me, wrapping his arms around me and laying his petal soft cheek against my shoulder for a moment. Warmth thrums along my arms. Around the tears that clog my throat, I manage to say, "Thanks, guys. That was a sweet, sweet welcome."

The boys attack the plate of cookies. "Who made these?" Jimi asks. In the midst of chewing, Parker raises a hand. Jimi raises his brows at me. "Parker makes the *bestest* cookies."

Miles freezes, a cookie halfway to his mouth, and his brow knits. "You didn't bring your dog."

"*I did too.* She's in the living room."

The boys look at each other, as rapt as if Santa had popped in and emptied his sack while they were at school. Jimi says, "You're kidding." And everyone laughs.

I rise. "Come with me."

But Rebekah says, "Now, don't rush the dog; give her time to get used to you."

The boys follow me into the living room and fall to their knees in front of the kennel. Lucie lets out her aren't-I-the-best-dog-ever yodel.

I sit on the floor and unzip the door. "Lucie, come out and meet some new friends."

Lucie trots out, shakes herself, and makes immediately for the boys' outstretched hands. "She's sooo cute!" Jimi says. "And her ear. It's not bad. I was afraid it would be gross."

The adults have drifted in to watch. "Jimi!" Rebekah says.

"That's okay, Jimi," I say. "I know what you mean."

Lucie goes to Miles, and he wraps her in his arms. "I love her."

"You know what?" I say. "She probably needs to go out for a tinkle."

"What's *that*?" the boys ask, perplexed.

Parker chuckles. "It means she needs to go take a whiz."

"Ohh," Jimi says. "Can we take her?"

"Well, let's get her leash out, and I'll go with you."

"Looks like you've hit a home run with the boys," Parker says.

I return his smile. "And they with me."

The twins and I take Lucie out into the sunshine. She is in her element, out for a total sniff-o-rama. "Have you seen our chickens, Dare?" Miles asks.

Chickens? I was crushing hard on the cute bungalow when I first arrived. I failed to notice the ramshackle, scat-spackled henhouse enclosed by wire fencing on a scratched-out patch of earth not twenty yards away. A great squawking and flapping of wings bring chickens out to slipping and bobbing their way down a plank. "We got six eggs yesterday," Miles says. *My daughter, USC magna cum laude graduate, raising chickens?* Lucie squats to tinkle. "And you *have* to see our vegetable garden. It's *ginormo*," he says, throwing his arms out as wide as the moon.

"We pretended it was a jungle when we were *little* kids," Jimi says with a sniff. Lucie in the lead, we wind through a hedge with pretty yellow blooms. Beyond it, running almost the length of the fenced property, is a massive sprawl of burgeoning green, some stems as big as my arm. "Caroline keeps the vines tied up on stakes. See up there? Or they'll go *everywhere*." He spins in a circle. "She calls it our Garden of Eatin'. That's a joke."

"I got it." *Caroline, an accomplished gardener. She certainly hadn't picked that up from me. It was Taffy who had established the garden at my home in Foxfield long before she passed away.*

"Look at the tomatoes over here. They're air loom," Miles says. The fruit *is* beautiful, scarlet red, plum, the yellow of Dijon mustard, apricot. "They're ready too," he says, twisting four off the vine and rolling them up in the front of his T-shirt to reveal a cute little outie of a belly button.

"Yeah, and look how many purple peppers. We have to come back with a basket. But let's show Dare our compost box first," Jimi says, emphasizing the final consonant on compost.

Wordlessly, I move with them beyond the garden through yards of tangly roots and scrub brush, clutching Lucie's leash, my eyes zigzagging the ground at our feet. "Are there snakes out here?"

"Mostly California kingsnakes," Jimi says. "They're good snakes. They eat the rats and gophers and squirrels that munch on our vegetables. But they're more ascared of you than you are them."

I sincerely doubt that.

"Sometimes we have Pastific rattlers here. And they're major-league poisonous but pretty shy. They don't like being around people," Miles adds.

Usually? My heart inches toward my throat. "Pa-cific," I murmur.

We reach a small clearing. In its center squats a huge hexagonal aqua box. The ventilation holes and horizontal air pockets, the squiggled door hinges on the top make it look as alien as if a spaceship had hovered the clearing once and jettisoned the thing.

"We put our scraps and pine straw and stuff in the compost box and it turns into fertilizer for the veggies. But it's *real* stinky. Want me to open it?"

"No. Thanks, though. I'll take your word for it."

Lucie gives a shrill bark, and I shriek like a banshee.

"Oh, that's just a skunk. Mostly, though, they come out at nighttime," Miles says as the business end of a small black-and-white creature waddles into the brush.

Oh, my God. Snakes and skunks and coyotes, and who knows what else? "It's time to get back to the house, fellas. I want to see about Caroline."

Miles asks, "May I please hold Lucie's leash on the way back?"

"No fair," Jimi says, glowering at his brother.

"Miles can hold it halfway. And you can hold it the rest. And give the tomatoes to me."

"That's fair," Miles says. He takes the leash, and off we go, the boys Lilliputian bodyguards at my sides.

Lucie brakes and hunkers down for a poop. "Okay, how about Jimi takes over now? Oh, I forgot a poop bag."

Both boys giggle. *"A poop bag?"*

"You know, to collect animal waste."

"You collect animal waste," Jimi deadpans, peering up at me. "We don't. It . . . just stays on the ground wherever the animals drop it. But we've never had a dog here."

"I see."

Jimi takes control of Lucie's leash. I hold the tomatoes and watch the ground all the way back as though at any second it could collapse beneath my feet.

"How did it go?" Rebekah asks as we finally reenter the house. "Shoes off, please." Along with the boys, I gladly slip off my mocs and expel a big breath.

"We did great! Lucie *tinkled* and pooped too. And I picked four tomatoes."

Tickled that Miles has picked up my word, I set the tomatoes on the counter and relax.

"Thanks for bringing those," Caroline says. She's drinking tea with Rebekah, the color back in her cheeks. Food is cooking, but the men are nowhere in sight.

"Are you feeling better?"

"*Much* better. I took a little toes-up."

"I'm glad." The boys have nestled in the hammock on the porch with Lucie. I step out to make sure they have her leash tightly in hand.

"We clipped it to the chain," Miles says.

From the porch, I scan the north side of the property, which appears fairly ordinary, the grass neatly mowed where a double clothesline sways with the breeze. And in the far corner, a homely yet well-proportioned baseball diamond. I smile. *Parker's doing, no doubt.*

In the center of the yard where a parliament of outdoor chairs is pulled around a brick firepit, Griffin and Parker capture my attention. They stand beneath mature shade trees. Parker reaches out to clap Griffin on a shoulder, give it a shake. But Griffin pulls Parker in and goes for a bro hug. I'm liking the man my daughter loves.

Back in the kitchen, I compliment Caroline on a splashy patch of yellow and purple Johnny-jump-ups near the porch. "Your grandmother grew those in her garden. Said they couldn't wait to pop up in the spring and say . . . oh, wow, I've forgotten the rest."

"'How do you do.' It was 'how do you do.'" I turn to gape at her. A wistful smile on her face fades as the color in her cheeks rises. She begins fidgeting with the wooden tea box.

"Did I tell you that? Or is it a thing people say? Because I thought Mom made it up."

"Not sure," she murmurs, arranging the tea bags by color. "It's catchy, though."

"It is," I say to the top of her head. "Well. Okay if I take a shower now?"

"Of course," she says, looking at me again. "The clean towels are in the cabinet over the commode. Make yourself at home, Mom."

Clean of that airplane-body feel and dressed in a denim skirt and white blouse, I head to the kitchen, carrying the wrapped gifts I forgot to take from my suitcase earlier. But I pause at the door of Caroline's room. The floorboards squeal. I still. Everyone seems to be in the kitchen, so I risk a peek inside. The room is lovely, one side chic and romantic. My daughter has good taste. A folding screen covered in a French chinoiserie fabric obscure hers and Griffin's work spaces: two stand-up style desks strewn with papers and trailing tangled nests of cables and cords.

"Mom?" Caroline calls from the hall but beyond my sight. Heart in mouth, I reverse my steps. My daughter gives me a squinty-eyed crooked smile. "Dinner's almost ready."

"Oh good. I was just . . . admiring your room. The covered work screen was a great idea."

"Well, thank you. I inherited my good taste in decorating." Buoyed by her generous comment, I skim along the hall, where music from a Crosby, Stills, Nash and Young album floats from the living room, and follow her into the kitchen. Everyone is jostling about, bringing food to the table, and dressed in fresh, neat clothes, darling Jimi in a collared shirt with a jaunty little clip-on bow tie. Dressing for dinner is something my mother always insisted on, and when my rebellious days ended, I found I appreciated the practice.

The food smells wonderful. Even if it's some kind of strange hippie dish, I'll be polite and choke it down. A place is set for me beside Miles and across from Caroline. I pull out my chair and set the gifts on the table. Miles face swoops to mine.

"Presents?" he asks, his features a mash-up of curiosity and delight.

Jimi leaves off wiggling a loose front tooth with his tongue and gapes at me. "For us?"

"Yes, for you and for everyone else. Little happies."

"Should the boys open theirs after dinner?" Rebekah asks, guessing correctly that I brought candy.

"How 'bout we open all of them after dinner because dinner's hot and ready," Parker suggests. At the phrase "hot and ready," Rebekah stares at Parker, raises her hand to her lips, and bites the side of her thumb.

"Good plan," I say, setting the packages aside and wondering about Rebekah and Parker again. Just then, Griffin leans over and kisses Caroline's temple. There's no paucity of pheromones around here.

Dinner is a marvelous-looking platter of spaghetti and meatballs, a big salad of fresh vegetables, and a hearty grain bread. I guess not all version 2.0 hippies are vegetarians, like most of their predecessors. Miles surprises me by tenting his hands and announcing that it's his turn to say the blessing. I bow my head. *Who cultivated spirituality in the children?* My thoughts distract me from Miles's words. While Caroline was growing up, we said the blessing on special occasions like Thanksgiving, Easter, and Christmas, and attended church about as often. When Miles is done, Rebekah gives him a big wink and smile.

Plates are filled and the song "Our House" beats from the living room. I smile around at everyone and compliment them on their taste in music.

"We like old music," Griffin says.

"Our youthful appearances are an illusion. We're old souls," Parker adds.

I laugh. "Do you all take turns cooking?"

"We do," Rebekah says. If you want Italian, the guys are your best bet. And South American? Wow. It's Caroline."

I look at my daughter, my head tilting like Lucie's when she's heard the word "treat." I'm wondering how and why Caroline chose to master South American cuisine when Miles asks, "May I have some juice, please?"

Griffin smiles and compliments him on his manners. "I'll pour it for you." Griffin and Rebekah discuss the merits of the tomato varieties they're growing. Caroline picks up her utensils. I suddenly recall that she began using both a fork and knife—even for burgers and sandwiches—before she left for college. *I just don't like getting my fingers messy*, she explained. But I worried for a couple of days about whether or not there was a genetic component to my mother's phobia now manifesting in my daughter.

Jimi spears a meatball and holds it aloft. "So are you like our grandma now, Dare?" I cough into my sleeve, my eyes darting to Caroline, but her face clicks shut. Jimi continues, "I mean, Miles and me—"

"Miles and I," Caroline dully mutters. *Me, a grandmother? With my track record as a mother? And with my recent and epic fail at protecting underage kids?* Caroline sips her water, then looks at her lap and resituates her napkin, pulling it almost up to her waist.

Jimi starts over. "*Miles and I* don't have any grandparents." I look at Rebekah for help. She smiles and offers me the same wink she gave Miles before.

I'm only here for a short time. How badly can I mess this up? The boys are looking at each other with you-know-she'll-say-yes grins. *Isn't that what a grandmother would do, indulge her grandchildren any request?* I take a deep breath, let it go, and smile. "I suppose I could be your *honorary* grandmother."

"Even when you go back to Virginia?" Miles asks. Caroline turns her face to Griffin's, raises her eyebrows. And he gives her what I hope is an encouraging nod.

"Even then. We could be pen pals."

Jimi pops the meatball in his mouth, lifts a victorious chin.

"Awesomesauce," Miles says. "What's a pen pal?"

I turn in early, prop up in Parker's comfortable bed with Lucie, and text Seraphina:

Hey, S! Day one at Crewtopia. Despite a few blunders on the part of you-know-who, Caroline and I are getting along. I'm channeling your wisdom. Her friends are nice, but they could just be using their party manners. The reporter in me has sniffed out some intriguing dynamics. The twins are DOLLS! They asked if I was their grandmother! I didn't get a full read on how Caroline feels about that. Everyone was thrilled with the chocolate and specialty teas you suggested I bring. Lucie is a total hit with the twins. Griffin and Caroline are very much in love.

The bungalow is darling, the CA flowers gorgeous. Caroline is full-out gardening! OMG, parts of the property are wild and untamed. And my girl is raising chickens! My plan is to stick close to the house. Hope all's well. If you see my photo on the wall at the post office, let me know.

Love, D.

P.S. The Andy Garcia would wear a paper bag over his head if he caught sight of Griffin Panakis.

Chapter Eight

Caroline
Washington, D.C.
2012

My mother. Is. Making me. Freaking. Cray.

Since the first college acceptance letter sailed through the slot in our townhouse door, she's been campaigning for the University of Virginia. I've been accepted by three more schools, including the University of Southern California. *If you choose UVA,* Mom said, *you could be home in two hours for a home-cooked dinner and a cozy sleep in your own bed.* That we eat mostly neighborhood takeout or Lean Cuisines because she works late must have slipped her mind. Tonight I went out for Chinese with friends without calling her to let her know. I got home at seven. She met me at the door. "I *bought* you a cell phone so you could keep in touch. The food is getting cold."

I pull my pink Motorola RAZR from my jeans pocket. Flip it open. Two missed calls from her. "I didn't realize you were preparing a meal." I look past her shoulder into the kitchen, where a big grease-spotted bag from Buca di Beppo slumps on the counter, the receipt still stapled to the top. Her cheeks are pink, but an instant later, her indignation rallies.

"As long as you live under my roof, you will obey my rules."

I stand there thinking, with the way we've been fighting, why would I be jacked about coming home from college to sleep under said roof? I lift my chin. "C'mon, Mom. You're a writer. You're not going to use that trite expression, are you?"

Her lips practically solidify, but she hisses through them. "You will not leave this house the rest of the weekend." I stand there a moment, honestly wanting to ask her, *Weren't you ever eighteen, aching for an identity apart from your mother? Or for an identity, period, like me?* Instead, I turn to sashay up the stairs.

Later, I'm sitting on my rug, listening to Taylor Swift and painting my toenails. Mom taps on my door. She holds a mail order catalogue. She smiles, helps herself to a seat on my desk chair, then holds out the cover of *LOFT*. Makes it shimmy and dance. "How about we pick you out a nice new wardrobe for college? The works?" I'm sure she's afraid I'll embarrass her at move-in weekend (wherever I end up moving in) wearing the retro grunge my friends and I wear. I almost say, *Mom, have you ever seen me wear anything remotely like the clothes in that catalogue for, like, middle-aged ladies?* But I don't want to start another argument. So I downshift. "Thanks, Mom. But I'm actually good with what I have."

She smooths the catalogue across her lap, eyes the cotton balls blooming between my toes, the blue polish, and sighs. "Okay, darling, but if you change your mind . . ." She leaves, closing the door. I pinch the catalogue between my fingers and drop it into my trash can.

If my father had lived, maybe he could have been a buffer between Mom and me. Maybe she wouldn't have scrutinized everything from boyfriends to blemishes to bumper stickers. Why can't our relationship be like the one Peach has with her mom? She takes her shopping at Urban Outfitters. When Peach put a purple rinse on her hair, her mom took pictures for her Facebook page, adding *LOL*. They even go to the movies once a week. Sometimes they invite me along, but I don't want to screw up their mother-daughter time. Peach will actually miss her mom when she leaves for school.

I turn up the next song on the playlist and lie on my bed, crossing my arms beneath my head. Unlike Peach, who's headed for Duke in North Carolina to study special education and play basketball, I should make a sign to wear: I HAVEN'T DECIDED WHERE I'M GOING TO COLLEGE YET, SO DON'T ASK. With a childhood French au pair and five years of private school French under my beret, the only thing I'm sure of is my major. I ease open the drawer of my bedside table. I withdraw a black-and-white strip of photos from between pages of the book of Job in my first communion Bible. Lisette and ten-year-old me, imping, pouting, and grinning behind a photo booth curtain. It's been so long since the day my mother banished her that, without the pictures, I have a hard time conjuring her face. But wherever she is, I bet she'd be happy to know she inspired me.

My phone chimes with a text.

Peach: *How's it going at The Rock?*

I laugh and type: *Cell's pretty comfy. No scuttling rats. Come over?*

Peach: *B there in 10.*

I replace the photo strip, pass my mother's closed door, and head downstairs to wait on Peach. When she gets here, we snare a bag of pretzels and two Diet Cokes and tiptoe upstairs. In my room, we sprawl across my bed. Peach toes off her canoe-sized Vans sneakers and they fall to the floor. I flare my nostrils. "Pew-wee. Ever thought about washing those?"

"Well, I'm going to camp; they'll be stinkier when I get back." Peach leaves in two days to spend June and July as a camp counselor for special kids in Maryland. On my bedside table, an envelope embossed with my grandmother's return address catches her eye. She picks it up and raps the edge against her palm. "How original. The Taffster sent you a check for graduation."

"Well, seeing how she knows *le zéro* about me, she couldn't give me something meaningful."

"True dat." Peach opens the bag of twisty pretzels and pops one into her mouth; she'll suck the salt off before chewing it.

"Oh, Peachie," I whine. "I have to figure out school!"

She chews thoughtfully. "Get away and go to camp with me. I know for a fact they're still minus two counselors. We'll figure it out together."

"You know that's not my thing. I'm a city girl."

"Well, duh, so am I."

"Yeah, but you like sports and outdoor stuff."

Peach sighs at the envelope and replaces it. "I'm sorry, Caroline, but it's weird as shit that you and your grandmother don't know each other." Peach knows that Taft only visits when she returns to D.C. for quarterly board meetings and never stays overnight. "And she never asks you guys to go to Foxfield. That's just wrong."

"Well, she's just strange."

Peach's eyes gleam. "Maybe she's an eccentric! Eccentrics can be fascinating. You know, like Andy Warhol. Or Tilda Swinton. Maybe if you got to know her, you'd find out she's cool. Look at all she's accomplished." She sits bolt upright. If she was in a comic, there would be a light bulb over her head. She looks toward the door. "*Look*, tell Dare you're going to camp with me. But drive to Foxfield instead, on the sly," she says, punctuating the last three words with jabs to my knee. "Show up on Taft's doorstep. Tell her you're there to polish her andirons, hang out with her and what's-her-name."

"Seraphina." I get up and pace the room, my thoughts pinging around my head like pinballs. I stop and stare at Peach. "That's *tres brill*. I mean, getting some space between Mom and me is a no-brainer. And I think I might be psyched about doing something outside my comfort zone—"

"'Like, for the first time in my life,'" Peach finishes for me.

An hour later, she's left for home and I've turned out my light. But filling in the Sudoku squares of my plans leaves me staring at the ceiling. I know Mom will be okay with me going to camp with Peach because that would be doing something good in the world. And she's been promoted to features editor with The *Times*, so she'll be working more than ever.

I'm eighteen. It's time I grew up. How can any living thing grow and thrive if it's deprived of its root system? I'll get to know my grandmother, get in touch with my roots. I might even figure out why my mother's the way she is.

I'll learn where I come from. And maybe where I'm going.

I sit in my car in front of my grandmother's house. The things I planned to say first fly from my head to roost in the branches of the trees rising from the manicured grass. Since I was here seven years ago, ivy has scampered up the white brick, giving the grand two-story house even more appeal. I wish we had flowers in the narrow swath of yard at our D.C. townhouse or even a pretty window box. But though Mom loves flowers, she's never been the outdoorsy type, and I wouldn't have a clue as to how to make a garden grow. "The place is *dope*," I murmur aloud while pulling my Accord into the driveway behind my grandmother's car, the sleek navy Bentley she's had as long as I can remember, and what must be Seraphina's ride, a gold Trans Am. I take off my sunglasses and lay them on the dash. The clock there reads 3:15. Do old ladies nap in the afternoons? Mom, who would shit a brick if she knew where I was, is still at the newspaper, probably thinking of what she'll pick up for dinner.

I'd imagined all the ways the encounter between my grandmother and I might play out. The odds are fifty-fifty: She will be reservedly pleased to see her only granddaughter and place a dry old-lady kiss on my cheek. Or she'll push me off the porch for arriving unannounced. Either way, it's time to cross the Rubicon.

I climb out of the car and stretch myself long. Leaving my Vera Bradley duffle in the back seat, I shoulder my purse. The summer air seems fresh washed, heady with the perfume of flowers. Do I go around to the back door like family? Or to the front? Front, I decide, and start across the brick walk where a troop of summer flowers—in uniforms of orange, pink, purple, and yellow—nod their caps as if saying *You, go girl*. At last I'm standing at my grandmother's glossy gray door. Do I use the federalist eagle knocker or ring the doorbell? Remembering the Westminster chime tone of the bell I thought was fancy when I was a little girl, I grin and stick out a finger. But a slight middle-aged woman yanks the door open before my finger makes contact.

"We don't want any," she says. The smirk on her face makes a smile tug at my lips.

"Well, good," I quip back, "'cause, I don't have any."

A grin splits her face. She shakes a loose finger at me. "You're Caroline."

I feel like I've stuck a knife in a live toaster. "You . . . know who I am?"

"Course I do. You're the spitting image of your mother. The same eyes, the hair, though yours is more auburn than her brown."

I take in her outfit: plastic fuchsia earrings, pink blouse and white crops, curly permed hair. "And you're Seraphina. I remember you."

"Come in, *cariño*," she says, holding the door wide. I picked up enough Spanish from Peach, who studied Spanish, to know that Seraphina's called me sweetie. *But will Taft be glad to see me?* "Your grandmother's upstairs." The forgotten familiar smells of lavender furniture polish, wool, and something cooking with saffron greet my nose.

"Oh, please don't wake her."

Seraphina waves down a palm. "She's not sleeping. She's planning her next move to one-up me." Another grin has its way with her mouth. She sidles over to the broad staircase, pumping her arms like she's doing the funky chicken, and tilts her head toward the top in a watch-this gesture. "Oh, Taa-afft! You have a visitor."

"Who the devil is it?" my grandmother replies from beyond my sight.

"Come and see for yourself."

"You know I don't like surprises."

Seraphina flips up a light switch. "You'll like this one."

I stand in the foyer, an ornate chandelier illuminating my nervousness, awaiting the formal and couture-wearing woman I remember to appear.

When a stout figure wearing a pair of overalls clumps down the stairs in yellow garden clogs, I'm blown away. "Grandmother?" My voice ricochets off the walls.

Taft Marston now has a bit of a dowager's hump that forces her neck and head forward. Her topknot, similar to the one I'm wearing—though hers is gray—bobs with her nod. She puts her whole body into examining me. "Caroline Marston O'Day."

Her subtle Virginia lilt reminds me of the proper south-of-the-Mason-Dixon-Line response. "Yes, ma'am."

"What took you so long?" she asks with a broad smile.

I'm sure this rip-roaring laugh of Taffy's was never heard in a boardroom. The faded overalls are slaying me. If Mom could see her! After a tour of her beautiful home, which stirs fewer memories than I expect, I follow her to her backyard and garden, clutching a napkin-wrapped glass of the best iced tea with fresh mint I ever tasted. My grandmother fixes a hazel gaze on me. "How long can you stay with us before leaving for college?"

I drop my gaze to a brilliant blue butterfly on a bush with fuzzy white flowers. I should have been prepared for the question. But she asked how long I *can* stay, not *how long I'm staying*. I'm clearly welcome here. Slowly releasing a pent-up breath, I extend a palm to the butterfly, whose gossamer legs step onto my thumb. I smile at Taft, whose nod and benign expression give me the nerve to say "I'd love to stay long enough to get to know you."

She studies my face. "And I you, kiddo." She takes a swallow of tea, her glass obscuring her features a beat longer than normal. "Well, then, I'm going to teach you the art of gardening. First, because of this iron-hard Virginia clay, I had to dig down a few feet, then layer on topsoil and compost."

Seraphina, who has trailed us out and is perched on the gracefully curved brick wall surrounding the terrace, chimes in. "Now, don't have Caroline believing you did all that yourself. The nursery outfit up to Mountainsburg came out and did the digging and spreading."

Taft straightens and pockets her hands. "That information is superfluous to this conversation."

"Just making sure you're not playing fast and loose with the truth," says Seraphina. I poke my tongue into my cheek to keep from grinning.

Taft consults her watch. "Shouldn't you be in the kitchen figuring out what we're going to feed my beautiful granddaughter for dinner?"

Seraphina taps her temple. "It's under control: arroz con pollo; salad with *queso fresco*, peas, and cilantro; and for dessert, my tres leches cake. I had all the ingredients on hand."

Taft grimaces. "That damned sticky cake again?"

I hadn't stopped for lunch and only nibbled a protein bar. Now my mouth waters at the suggestion of a homemade meal. Especially the cake. "That sounds amazing. May I help you?"

Taft smiles. "Not on your first night. Tomorrow you start pulling your weight."

I give her a thumbs-up. "Deal." Seraphina smiles as she heads into the house.

"Now. The backbone of a garden is perennials." She points out the tallest rows of flowering shrubs in shades of pink. "The peonies, hollyhocks and joe-pye weed. But old joe's anything but a weed. I won a prize for a bouquet last year at the flower show. But don't mention it to Seraphina or she'll give me shit about tooting my own horn."

I laugh then. "Are the perennials the ones that come back every year?"

"That is correct." She shields her eyes with a weathered hand and regards the swiftly slanting sun. "Would you like to work out here with me tomorrow?"

"I'd love it," I sputter.

She eyes my sundress. "Did you bring anything besides dresses?"

I laugh. "I did. I was hoping you wouldn't mind me wearing shorts."

"Heavens, child, why would I mind?"

"I, uh well, I thought you were more . . . formal."

Taft gazes past the garden and north as if she can see clear to D.C. "I dressed in a very conservative manner when I led the corporation."

Seraphina's voice startles us. "She's mellowed in her old age. Just wait and see."

"Hush your pie hole," Taft says, leading me from the garden. "I lend dignity to any garment I wear. *Especially* my overalls," she says, hooking her thumbs through the shoulder straps, her big belly poking out. Don't you agree, Caroline?"

"Oh, absolutely."

"But now we *do* dress for dinner. It's a holdover from my previous life. That pretty frock will be fine."

"Dinner will be ready in an hour," Seraphina says. "How about cocktails out here tonight, Taffy?"

"That would be delightful. But I must shower first. Where are your bags, dear?"

"In the car. Just a humongo duffle actually."

"Well, bring it in and get yourself settled in your room."

My room. "Okay. Then BRB. Oh, that means—"

"Be right back. I may be old, but I'm quite hip. I am a member of Faceboard."

"Face*BOOK*." The word fires like a torch from Seraphina's mouth.

Taft grimaces. "Do I smell candy on your breath?"

Seraphina pushes her lips out and cuts her eyes to one side. "Just a Jolly Rancher to tide me over."

"I do hope you washed your hands after discarding the wrapper into a proper receptacle." With a roll of her eyes, Taffy ambles across the terrace and indoors.

I laugh all the way to my car.

I use the back door and weave through the kitchen, my bag bumping against the island, and say to Seraphina, "So the candy heiress is still freaked out by anything sticky?"

She eyes me sharply. "You know about that?"

"Well, yeah. My mother told me."

"*Es algo real*: It's a real thing. I looked it up on the internet." She casts a furtive eye toward the stairs. "Viscophobia: the fear of anything sticky or messy. I've been trying to desensitize her for years. And she's better." She grins. "That's how I get away with messing with her."

I return her grin. "She seems to like it."

"*Ella adora el suelo sobre el que camino*: she—"

"Wait! I think I know what that means," I say with fanfare. "She . . . worships the ground you walk on?"

Seraphina sets the oven temperature. "*Tu hablas español, cariño!*" she says, her eyes lighting.

"Un poco," I say, holding my forefinger and thumb an inch apart. "My friend Peach took Spanish in high school."

"Peach, huh?" My grandmother asks, entering the kitchen wearing a linen tunic and pants, clinking bracelets on one wrist. She's pulled her hair back with a beautiful barrette. Seraphina takes a salad from a massive stainless fridge.

A pang of missing Peach squeezes my heart. I need to FaceTime her at camp. "Yes. Peach. Her real name's Priscilla."

"I like it," my grandmother says to me. "I support nonconformity."

Seraphina hoots. "Taft's a hippie now."

Taft ignores the hippie remark but addresses her caretaker. "A glass of Pinot Grigio for me, my fiery angel. That's Seraphina translated," she says to me. "And for you?"

A blush climbs my cheeks. "I'm only eighteen."

She peers at me. "Well, I guess you are, aren't you?"

"I'd love a sparkling water with lime, though, if you have it, please."

Seraphina gives me a side-mouth click of approval. "You got it, *cariño*."

Taft and I have our drinks at a table on the terrace. My antennae are raised for personal information. "You look nice tonight, grandmother. I like your outfit and cool bracelets."

"You must call me Taffy."

I grin. "Taffy. A pretty slick nickname for someone with a candy empire."

"That is the assumption most people make. But in fact, I was born with a head full of taffy-colored hair." She smiles. "The press was delighted with the moniker. Ironic that my name is associated with the stickiest stuff on the planet."

I'm sipping my drink, engaged in an internal debate about whether or not I should ask her why messy things bother her so much when she spends so much time digging in the dirt, when Seraphina calls us in to dinner.

Taffy pours glasses of wine.

"Just tap water for me, please," I say. "Oh, I meant to tell you, Seraphina, your Trans Am is sick."

Taffy returns with my water and chuffs a laugh. "What a thing to say, Caroline." She nudges the breadbasket in front of me and motions for me to take a slice.

Seraphina rolls her eyes. "That means the car is cool. *Sick* is a compliment. Thank you, Caroline."

Taffy arches a brow. "I'll be certain and add it to my vocabulary."

The dinner is delicious and mildly spicy. I shovel the first bites in as though I haven't eaten in a week, then wipe my lips with my napkin. I use my fork to give my plate an emphatic point. "I am seriously in *love* with this food. What region of South America is it from again?"

"North. I grew up in Colombia."

I shake my head again. "I've never cooked a single dish in my life."

Both women regard me as though I'm some undiscovered variety of plant that sprang up in the garden. "Dare never taught you to cook," Taffy says flatly.

"Nope. She doesn't cook that often. We eat a lot of takeout." Taffy and Seraphina exchange looks. I feel like I've thrown my mother under a bus. "But you know how hard she works." I shrug as though I'm totally cool with it.

Seraphina's eyes are soft. "Would you like to learn Colombian cooking, *cariño*?"

I grin. "How do you say 'hell yes' *en espanol*?"

Seraphina hoots again. "*A huevo*. Tomorrow we'll tackle empanadas, then." She rises to clear our plates. "Now, how about a piece of the best cake in the world?"

"Yes, please!" I say, though my belly nudges at the waistband of my underwear.

My grandmother hauls herself to her feet. "I'll take my coffee into the living room while you consume that gooey mess. Thank you for a delicious dinner, Seraphina. And I know you'll wipe that counter down well."

"You are most welcome, Taft."

Seraphina and I tuck into the three-milk cake. "This was my mother's favorite dessert. I was making it myself by the time I was five."

"*Five?* Cool."

The living room TV comes alive, loud, with the bouncy theme from *Jeopardy*. Seraphina snickers. "That's Taffy's show, but I usually wax her ass at it."

"This I gotta see."

Taffy calls out. "Seraphina! There are candy wrappers on my Italian table! I almost spilled my coffee."

Seraphina tips me a broad wink. "I'll get 'em, I'll get 'em."

I chuckle and inhale cake crumbs, cough, and pound my chest.

"The category is universities," Alex Trebek booms. I scrape my plate for the last of the icing as he gives the answer: "In 1979, this West Coast university marching band was invited by Fleetwood Mac to perform the song 'Tusk' for their twelfth album."

As triumphant as an Easter trumpet, Taffy answers, "What is the Stanford University marching band?"

Seraphina cocks a thumb toward the living room. *"No,"* she calls out along with the host. "What is the University of Southern California marching band?" My pulse skitters as the host confirms the response. *Why of all the universities the show could have featured did they choose USC? Is this a sign?*

Taffy asks, "How the hell did you know that, *bruja*: witch?"

"Told ya," Seraphina says, her eyes agleam.

I'd grown used to sleeping late that summer. So when my grandmother raps on my door the next morning, I almost topple from the bed. I tussle for my phone and squint at it through sleep-ratted hair. *Six frickin' thirty?*

"Good morning, Caroline. Breakfast in fifteen minutes," she calls as chipper as though Liam Hemsworth is whisking eggs in the kitchen wearing nothing but an apron. "We need to get in the garden before the sun's too high."

"I'll be down in a sec." I throw off the covers, use the bathroom, then dress in cutoff shorts, a brown David Bowie T-shirt I poached from Peach, and ankle socks. Carrying my Nikes downstairs, a dazzling aroma greets my nose.

"Is that *béarnaise sauce*?"

"Eggs Benny this morning in honor of my favorite granddaughter's first day as a gardener," Taffy says from the stove. She's wearing a big denim apron over a zip-up caftan. Seraphina slumps on a stool at the Formica-topped island, her hands cradling a cup of coffee.

"Morning," she mutters.

"Morning. May I help you, Gra—I mean Taffy."

She points out a damp paper-towel-wrapped bundle on the counter. "Snip some parsley for garnish, please? I brought it from the garden. The little shears are in that drawer."

"Sure thing!"

"My *caretaker* is not a morning person, so if I am to have a nice healthy breakfast instead of that preposterous Lucky Charms she sneaks into the pantry, I make it myself."

Seraphina raises her head. "Breakfast with a leprechaun just might sweeten you up, old woman."

"I *sweetly* suggest that you replace your surly expression with a pleasant one before sitting down to breakfast with my granddaughter." I pull out the crew neck of my T-shirt and aim a spate of giggles inside Bowie's spiky head. Seraphina gets to her feet and drops Taffy a half-baked curtsy.

Taffy asks me to add parsley to the plates, pointing out where the leaves should go. "This is like the *Great British Baking Show*," I say. "The plates look so fancy."

Taffy unties her apron and hangs it on a hook inside the walk-in pantry before joining us at the table. A long-sunk memory bobs to the surface of my mind. "Do you still have a white metal tin with little raised red and yellow flowers in the pantry?"

Seraphina grins. "It's still there."

I'm on my feet. "I have to see it." I find the tin on a middle shelf and run my fingers along the flowers. Everything inside me turns over and sighs. I *do* have memories here. Why didn't Mom and I visit more often? I have to ask Taffy when the right moment comes. Was it because of her or because of Mom?

I return to the table and put on a smile. "It's just like I remember."

Taffy returns my smile. "Before I leave this earth, I shall I bequeath it to you. Seraphina, remind me to amend my will."

Her words make my breath hitch. I spread my napkin across my lap. "Just don't be leaving it anytime soon."

And that's the moment I discover that, despite her aloof façade, I love my grandmother.

Five moany bites into the eggs Benny, I raise my face and produce a chef's kiss. "The two meals I've eaten here have been better than any I've had in, like, a year. And this béarnaise is per-*fec*-tion."

"Careful or you'll give her the big head," Seraphina says around a bite of egg.

Ignoring her, Taffy lays her fork across her plate and pats both corners of her mouth with her napkin. She rests her elbows on the table, her chin on clasped hands. "Are you going far from home to college, Caroline?"

I pick pretend lint from my T-shirt. "I . . . might go to California."

"After studying humanities at Bryn Mawr, I packed my cases and headed to Paris for culinary school."

"You went to all the way to Paris by yourself?"

"I did. I wanted to be Audrey Hepburn in *Sabrina*, though I wasn't running off to forget a man but my parents' expectations. They had orchestrated my whole life. And I loved Paris, though at first I found myself in a bit of a fix. One night my landlord, an unscrupulous sort, used his key to sneak into my flat. My scream ran him off. But I worried he might return. The next day, I bought a large rodent trap. That night I not only captured three of his toes but the attention of the other tenants when I drowned out his howl with screams about resident rats. But you know what I discovered?" Tethered to her every word, I shake my head. "Self-reliance; self-respect. When I returned to Washington, I took the helm at Marston. I married your grandfather. I was ready to handle a career and a relationship on my own terms. And I was one helluva French cook."

I lick the last bit of béarnaise sauce from my fork. "Okay. You are like my hero now. I mean it." *Why hadn't I heard that story?*

Taffy laughs softly. "Well, now, Caroline, whether I'm worthy of such adulation remains to be seen. Don't forget I'm putting you to work today." She and Seraphina rise from the table, gathering dishes.

"I'm ready! Just let me run brush my teeth. Excuse me." I skim the stairs, my head full of unanswered questions. I want to hear every one of Taffy's stories.

When I am back downstairs, Taffy is already outside. Seraphina is cleaning the stove. I sneak up behind her and put my hands on her shoulders. "Hey. I just wanted you to know I'm a fan of Lucky Charms. Straight out the box. OMG, the crunchy marshmallows."

She throws back her curly head and directs a boom of a laugh to the ceiling. "I'm sure glad you're here, *cariño*. You're a breath of sweet air."

"Speaking of air, I better get outside."

Seraphina stares out the window at Taffy. "Hope you learn a lot today, kiddo. And have fun while you're at it."

"Oh gosh, Taffy," I say as I mix fertilizer into a five-gallon bucket of water. "I forgot to thank you for your graduation gift!"

She redirects a bumblebee intent on orbiting her head. "Oh hell. Writing checks is what I do."

"Well, it was a super nice check. And my mother would kill me for forgetting to write you a thank-you note." I reach for the special sprinkler attachment Taffy asked me to use for gentle watering and work it onto the threads at the end of the hose.

She smiles at me. "It's much nicer to receive your thanks in person. Maybe you can spend the money tricking out your dorm room." I give my head a mental shake. *That check could redecorate the palace of Versailles.* Taffy interrupts my thoughts. "Okay, start on the coneflowers, then work your way toward the foxgloves."

I mince my way through the flowers to turn on the spigot under the kitchen window. Retracing my path, I stop short, curiosity and presentiment twinning in my head. Taffy's examining the face of a sunflower, her fingers gently skimming the seeds as though reading a message there. As the water saturates the petals of the tallest perennials, the intensity of the pinks and purples are almost too much to take in. A butterfly floats by, nothing on its mind but nectar.

I suppose I'm feeling a bit of what Taffy must. At that moment, I know I'll spend her check on something in her honor. The spray casts rainbows. The bees thrum. The birds chatter. The wind soughs amongst the Virginia pines. I'm filled with an emptied-out peace, one where my relationship with my mother and where I'm going to college seem as far away as Pluto.

Taffy, who's cutting twine with a pair of shears, calls to me when I've used up my third bucketful of water. I rub at my upper arms, knowing they will be the good kind of sore tomorrow. I close the distance between us. "What's the string for?"

"Vine vegetables—peas and beans—and the heavier ones like tomatoes and cucumbers require a trellis support structure to train the plant as it grows."

"Oh, makes sense. How'd you learn all this?"

She winces at a pain in her back and takes a seat on the wall. "I had a dalliance with my neighbor."

A lover! My mouth falls open. "You did not!" I jump up and down. "Which neighbor?"

She cocks her head to the property on the far side of her driveway. "Barrett Chipley. Summer of '97," she says smugly. "A widower with a marvelous garden. Taught me everything he knew. I taught him a few things as well. In his gazebo," she says bouncing her brows. "Naked as jaybirds."

"Grandmother!" My thoughts swoop and scamper. *Well, I wanted to get to know her.* "Taft Marston, you've just done a number on my head."

"Shhh, now. I don't want Seraphina getting wind of this."

I can't help myself. "So what happened?"

"By the time a hard freeze took the last of the perennials, the bloom was off the rose, so to speak. I had fallen in love, not with Barrett but with gardening. But we've remained friends."

I pitch my voice low. "I could never get naked outside with a guy."

Taffy snorts. "Growing older frees a woman."

I stand there like Lot's wife, a mind movie starting in my head, starring me and a yet-to-be and faceless man lolling on a blanket in the great outdoors.

"Your cheeks are red as radishes, Caroline. Do you need one of my hats?"

The mind movie fades to black. "Oh no, I'm fine."

"Then here," she says, draping lengths of twine across my hand. "Help me string these between the stakes and tie them off. Nice and taut, mind you. It's time to get ready for the vegetables." My admiration for my grandmother flourishes. She treats me as an equal. Not an eighteen-year-old kid but a woman. I give her a grateful smile. After a moment, she quietly says, "Caroline, I'm glad you've come to me. You and I share a special affinity or connection." I stare at her, her words sinking in, wonder spreading through my chest. "But it seemed that connection skipped a generation."

Every hair on my arms raises. *Tell me why. Please tell me why my mother is so aloof while you are so . . . not.* I dig my nails into my palms to keep from crying like a six-year-old but still come out sounding like one. "Don't you love my mother? Why didn't *you two* have the connection?"

She searches my eyes as though reassessing my maturity. The air between us ripples with charge. "The day my husband left me, the phobia that had ignited inside me consumed me like . . . a flashover. I was . . . severe with Dare, though she didn't deserve it. And instead of grieving our loss together, we grieved alone. Dare slowly withdrew from me. I loved the child, but I couldn't or didn't reach beyond my own pain to draw her back." Taffy's confession squeezes the air from my lungs. I gasp at the grim reality of my heritage. She pats my arm absently. "Shortly thereafter, I took on the role of CEO at Marston. I never sensed that Dare lacked for anything. She had friends, but she was independent and driven to excel. Perhaps she was simply emulating me. I don't know." I am crying in earnest now, snot running from my nose and over my lips. Taffy pulls a bandana from her pocket and hands it to me. "I wondered why your mother didn't come with you, and I don't believe you've even mentioned her. Do you two not share a special bond?"

One tiny word made enormous by disappointment, by regret, and by anger squeezes from between my lips. "No."

Tears fill her eyes and course her creased cheeks. She reaches blindly for my hands. I am not sure where to place the anger that simmers low in my gut. But I've just come to know Taffy and I don't ever want to be without her again. I drop the twine and hold tightly to her hands. The sun beats down. We stand like two sorrowful scarecrows staked in the middle of Eden. "Please, Caroline, you're at a crossroads in your life. It *can't* be too late. Talk with Dare when you go home." I nod dumbly and release her hands to wipe my face on my T-shirt.

Taffy pours three glasses of wine at dinner that night. I am so emotionally exhausted that, by the time I've drunk mine with one of

Seraphina's empanadas, my eyes are at half-mast. The wind rises outside, sending dogwood branches to scrape against the window. "Can we sleep with the windows open tonight? The air's so fresh here."

"You bet," Seraphina says.

As soon as I've nestled my face against the pillow, I conk. But an hour later, I'm tiptoeing across the hall to the bathroom. I wince as I lower my sore gardening thighs onto the toilet. Wind billows the sheers, and the scent of weed meets my nose. *Weed? Who the hell is down there?* I dart to the hall window, hoping for a better view.

From behind me, Seraphina lays her hands on my shoulders. I jump so hard I expect to see my skin unzipped and lying at my feet. "Sorry, *cariño*," she says, her head against mine.

I spin around, impaling her with my eyes. "That's Taffy down there?"

"Sí . . . the bud helps to ease her pain."

Dread races along my sore limbs. "But . . . what's wrong with her?"

"Ah . . . old lady *enfermedades*: maladies." I stare into Seraphina's loving eyes. And after a moment, they tell me a different truth. The façade of my grandmother's immortality dashes like pottery to a floor. With it lie the shards of my anger.

Two weeks of watering the garden gives way to a luscious rainy morning. Taft's reading in her living room chair when I come downstairs. She refuses breakfast for *just coffee, please.* Seraphina and I eat Lucky Charms at the kitchen island, and for the first time, instead of eating the marshmallows with my fingers, I let them plink into the bowl along with the cereal, cover them with milk, use a spoon.

Seraphina heads upstairs to collect dirty linens. I pull the dusting supplies from the pantry and take them into the living room to start my chore. Taffy lays her book aside as Seraphina returns. "How the hell someone who weighs eighty pounds makes such a racket galumphing down the stairs is a mystery to me."

Seraphina drops a pile of sheets and towels and plants her hands on her slight hips. "I'll have you know, Dr. Avery weighed me last week, and that slidey thing on the scale stopped at three marks over one-hundred. *Además*: furthermore, for someone who's a hundred and six, you have the ears of *el burro*." She puts a thumb on either side of her head, making flopping donkey ears. I'm holding in so much laughter, my entire body shakes.

"You make anyone believe I'm one hundred and six, and I'll fire you faster than you can say one-way-ticket-to-Cartagena."

Seraphina grins. "Hee-haw!"

I compose my expression. "Now, Seraphina, Taft has a beautiful youthful complexion. It runs in the family. No one would ever believe she's a day over a hundred."

My grandmother raises her brows at me before dissolving into helpless giggles.

Seraphina says, "Only because she spends a fortune on skin cream made from the placenta of lambs." I've grown used to their banter, but this one makes me want to ROFLMAO.

Daily, I learn something new from these women. Seraphina is teaching me to cook and, by example, how one manages a household. And that, like my fave pink coneflowers that signify strength, I have the power to decide the best course for my life. Taffy and I tell each other our stories. With her eccentric views, we riff on crazy ideas. And her reservoir of wisdom is endless. She says that when you lose your looks to old age, the good Lord grants you wisdom in exchange.

One day she lets me know that I'm in charge of the vegetable part of the garden for the remainder of my visit and drops an armload of gardening books on my bed. After dinner that night, she tells me she has a special book to give me for keeps. "It lives on my bedside table. Go up and get it, please? *The Language of Flowers*, illustrated by Kate Greenaway."

I hop up, excited that Taffy's giving me something that's meant a lot to her. But when I locate the floral-covered book cover amongst the things on her table, it's just an ordinary little thing, something one's eyes would skip over in a consignment shop. I sit on the edge of her bed, open it, and one whiff tells me it's an old copy. Gingerly, I thumb to the copyright page. The book is a first edition. And Taft has inscribed it to me. *To my granddaughter gardener Caroline O'Day, for the best summer ever. Taft Marston.* Closing the book, I hold it against my emotion-crammed chest.

Downstairs, Taffy and Seraphina are gearing up for *Jeopardy*. Cradling the little book, I drop to a seat on the floor in front of Taffy's chair and lay my head on her broad lap. "How can I say thank you? For this... incredible... treasure. For the inscription. For loving me." I peek up at her face.

She smiles. "You just did, my darling."

Weeks pass like dandelion seeds blown from the stalk by a child. The sun drops a little lower in the sky each day, and my heart follows suit. Now that I know where I come from, I can hardly bear the thought of leaving Taffy and the garden for an uncertain new life.

July is galloping into August, bringing the message that it's time to return to Washington and pack for college. One Monday morning, after many hugs from Taffy and Seraphina, I climb into my car and drive away. Beside me on the passenger seat is the metal tin with red and yellow flowers filled with Seraphina's still-warm dulce de leche cookies. I tell myself I won't cry. Instead I'll spend the drive home making up my mind about school. At the light at Fourth Street, I idle behind a woman driving an SUV. On the back window is an implausible-for-this-area collegiate decal that lights when the woman foots the brake: the University of Southern California. I let out a whoop of a laugh that sounds a lot like one of Taffy's.

And just like that, I know where I'm going.

Chapter Nine

Dare

1993

My best friend Tricia and I lie sunning ourselves on her freshly mown backyard. Tricia ogles Jeff McBride—who's moved on with his gas-powered mower to the Rosenbergs' lot next door—through her huge Kurt Cobain-inspired red sunglasses. "Damn, he's fine," she murmurs. It's only been a week since our high school graduation, but Jeff's arms and legs are tanned, and his lean muscles ripple in the sunlight. "Maybe I should offer him a cold soda when he's done."

"Go for it," I say as though I hadn't heard her big-talk-movie-of-the-week-aspiration *The Seduction of Jeff McBride* about a hundred and twelve times. I run my fingers through the tender new grass beside my towel. But I can't imagine running my hands over Jeff McBride's muscles. I'm not sure what my type is, but it isn't him. Finn O'Day and I date on and off. We've been close friends since seventh grade, but when it comes to chemistry, we aren't blowing up the science lab. Most of the boys we know I find as lackluster as melba toast. Not a snack I'd choose if someone told me it was the only one I could have for the rest of my life.

The Rosenbergs are more particular about their lawn, insisting on a geometric pattern. Each time Jeff reaches the end of a strip, he pauses to raise his face to the sun, slick his blond locks back with a lazy hand, and toss a bored glance our way.

Tricia's eyes light. "What if I accidentally let my top drop and give him an eyeful?"

"He'd probably run the mower over his foot. That would end his glorious football-punting days."

"Dare! Gross!"

I give her an evil grin and take a long sip of my Diet Coke. She turns on her boom box. Mariah Carey warbles "Dreamlover." Tricia's eyes trail Jeff again. Of the handful of reputed virgins in our senior class, she and I are the last two holdouts as word has it that Sarah H. and Linda B. defected from our dubious "club" on prom night. "Is this all we're going to do this summer?"

"Well, *my* brain needs a break from finals. You know I have to work harder than you do. And this way, we'll have great tans when we get to UVA for rush."

I sit up abruptly. *"Rush?* I'm not going through rush!"

"Well, your mother thinks you are."

"I'm sick and tired of doing what my mother expects. And I'll be damned if I'm going to lie around watching jock frat boy wannabes mow grass all summer."

"That hurt."

I gentle my tone. "I'm sorry, but do you really think you have a chance with Jeff?"

She swallows around a hard lump. "No."

"Look. We've never had an adventure. Let's sneak off and do something wild before college."

Tricia sits up and faces me, gives me her old smile. "So, wild thing, what do you have in mind?"

The Greyhound bus engine hisses to a crescendo as it pulls from the station house. Tricia clutches her hobo bag to her chest, her eyes wide. "We're really doing this."

While I was thinking of ideas for our adventure, a big chunk of luck fell in our laps. A Tri-Delt from UVA sent Tricia an invitation to a house party on the Outer Banks at her family's monster of a beach home and urged her to bring a friend. Both our mothers had been thrilled, and just like that, we had a week away from home.

Now from our third-row bus seat, I turn and take a casual survey of the passengers behind us. I smile at a toddler with a fistful of

Goldfish crackers. "You can relax the death grip on your purse," I whisper to Tricia. "These are mostly old people and mothers with babies. Except for Joel Rifkin sitting across from the bathroom."

Tricia flinches horribly and grabs my arm. *"The serial killer?"*

"I'm kidding! You know he's in prison. We heard it on the news. Relax, this trip will be smooth as a cat's belly."

Tricia pulls her notebook from her purse to double-check the itinerary. She sighs. "I'm just a little freaked out that we're actually doing this." I give her a look. "I know. I know. You did your homework."

And I had, after spying a flyer for an anti-nuclear demonstration on the bulletin board at Ben and Jerry's. The protest would be held at a power plant in Massachusetts. My chocolate ice cream had run from the cone to my elbow as I devoured the information. Members of MUSE—Musicians United for Safe Energy—would attend.

"Jackson Browne, Neil Young, Tom Petty, Bruce Springsteen, and *Dan Fogelberg* will be there," I told Tricia from a phone booth outside. Gorgeous Dan Fogelberg had earned our allegiance as the thinking girl's heartthrob. "This is exactly what we're looking for! We'll be revolutionaries!"

Once I convinced Tricia, I studied the Greyhound bus schedule and located the teeny town of Millimack on a Massachusetts map. We paid cash for round-trip tickets. We packed sparingly—only hip T-shirts and shorts—but crammed handfuls of Magic Markers and tape in our duffle bags, reasoning we could buy poster board in the little town and make anti-nuke signs. What was a protest without cool signs?

Now on the outskirts of Philadelphia, the bus driver announces a stop. Tricia and I get out to stretch our legs and line up inside the service center for the bathroom. "Look," she says, doing Macarena moves down the aisle when I come out of the ladies. "Sugar Babies! I haven't had these in forever."

Back on the bus, I dig through my duffle and produce my portable CD player with Dan Fogelberg's *Captured Angel* ready to spin inside. We share the ear plugs, resting the tops of our heads together. Tricia hums and munches her candy, her heels up on the seat. My mind drifts with the music. What if I met Dan in person, got his autograph? I check my watch. In fewer than two hours, we'll be in New York City, where we'll change buses. *New York City!* What had ever been this exciting?

Tricia eases the plug from her ear. "Wait. After New York, your itinerary says we stop in Boston, Massachusetts... but the route ends there." She waves the notebook in front of my face. "Just how do we get to Millimack?"

I shrug. "I don't know; it must be walkable, though." I'm embarrassed to tell her I'd forgotten to bring the map. Tricia leaps to her feet, swaying with the movement of the bus, her face pinched with fear. "I'm going to ask the driver."

"Wait. Shhh," I say, my eyes darting to the drowsing slack-mouthed passengers around us. "I don't think you're supposed to bother the bus driver." I'm pulling her back down by an arm when a skeevy-looking couple, probably in their twenties, in the seat in front of us turns around and stares.

The girl, a blonde with glazed moonstone eyes, grips the bar on back of the seat with both hands and rests her chin on them like a child. Her breath reeks of onions. "You headed to the anti-nuke protest too?"

"We are," I say, trying to regain my cool and breathing shallowly through my mouth.

The guy gives us a wobbly smile. His pupils are like flecks of cracked pepper. The girl speaks for the two of them again, further polluting the air. "Man, Boston is the end of the line." She giggles. "From there, it's thumbs out on the highway."

Hitchhiking? "How far is Millimack from there?" I ask the girl, my voice quavering with dread. Tricia is shaking so hard her feet tap a beat on the floorboard. The guy bobs his head to their rhythm and bites into an onion, apple-style.

The girl pushes at his shoulder, nearly toppling him from his seat. "How *far*, hon?"

The guy drops his onion, and it rolls across the aisle under a sleeping man's seat. He gazes at his empty hand and then blinks at her. "Huh?" A runner of drool escapes the corner of his lips. My stomach lurches.

"How far do we hitch?" the girl practically yells into his ear. People are waking and shifting and turning their faces to the ruckus on rows two and three. My eyes fly to the giant rearview mirror. The driver is looking at us, a homicidal glint in his eyes. What if he throws us off the bus? What if we're stranded in the middle of nowhere? My revolutionary persona pales.

The stoned guy chuckles. "Like a hundred miles, I guess. No, no, maybe 'bout ten."

Oh, dear God.

Tears trickle Tricia's cheeks. "Why'd you have to mention the serial killer. Why?"

We board a newer, fresher Greyhound in New York City, though without so much as a peek at the Empire State Building. The youngish driver's nod and smile are so bolstering, we take the front seat to his right, and I'm encouraged to lean over and ask him the distance from the Boston stop to Millimack. "Forty miles," he says, pulling the big lever to close the folding door.

The bus takes off, and I hope the loud blast of slipstream wind drowns out Tricia's wails. "Listen, sweetie, it's going to be okay. We'll find somebody nice to ride with. Trust me."

"T-trust you," she says, sniveling into a bandana from her bag. "I thought you had it all figured out!"

I feel like a bush-league bungler. I put my arm around my friend's heaving shoulders, hoping she can't feel my own case of the shakes. "I'm so sorry."

The hippie couple who were in front of us on the other bus are slumped across the aisle, the girl already passed out on the guy's shoulder.

A tap falls on my shoulder.

Loathing the thought of interacting with another unsavory character but afraid to come off as a snooty princess, I slowly turn my neck. Two guys are seated behind us, one skinny with straight brown hair and a bandana tied around his head. All I can see of the other guy is a corona of longish, curling ginger hair and freckled hands holding a chunky paperback before his face. The skinny one offers me a friendly smile with a top row of white teeth. He was the tapper. "I'm Blake," he says, then gestures to the other guy with a cocked thumb. "The big guy here is Anti-Nuke Luke."

Luke takes two beats too long to lower the book, *The Fountainhead*, from his face, as though nibbling his way through a savory passage before finding a place to swallow. But when he does, I'm paralyzed by his singularly fabulous face. My heart races as he dog-ears a page and extends a big square hand. "Luke Henry," he says, his lips rosy, his voice smooth and low.

Tricia warily takes his hand. "Tricia."

"Nice to meet you, Tricia."

His eyes slide to me, but I'm boneless, incapable of lifting my arm. "I'm . . . Dare. Dare Marston."

His ginger brows lift. "Dare? Cool name. And are you?"

I blink. "Am I what?"

He holds up the cover of his book about a rogue young architect. "Daring."

I sit taller. "I suppose I am."

"It's nice meeting you." He gives my shoulder a friendly squeeze. These guys are several years older than us and no elitist frat boys. Luke's ruddy complexion, the tiny wrinkles at the corners of his eyes speak of outdoor adventures and good times.

Blake says, "I couldn't help but overhear your conversation earlier. A lot of people probably *will* thumb it," he says, gesturing vaguely toward the back. "But a couple of our old high school buddies are—bada bing, bada boom—picking *us* up outside Boston. We could squeeze you both into the van." I give him a smirk. *Yeah right. Crawl into a van with a bunch of strange boys?*

Luke offers up, "Zen the Archer's bringing his girlfriend. You won't be the only women." *Women.*

Tricia presses my hand, her eyes asking, *Could we be saved?*

I slide down in my seat and hiss into her ear, "Weren't you the one just freaking out about serial killers, and now you want to throw in with guys we've known for five minutes?"

"Hey, check it out—sunflowers ahead on the right," Luke says. I pop up in my seat.

Tricia and I get up on our knees as the bus passes vast fields of dazzling yellow. "It must be like a sunflower *farm*," I say, dizzied by the brilliance. It can't have lasted more than fifteen seconds, but when the show's over, all of us are quiet. Still on my knees, I lower my face to Luke's. His face is turned up to mine. A beam of sunlight captures his expression and lingers there for a moment. It's not unlike one of the flowers that's just aligned itself with its source of sustenance.

And just like that, I'm pulled into Luke Henry's orbit.

Behind us on the zooming Greyhound, Blake gets to his feet. "Shouldn't we cop some sleep?"

"We probably should too," Tricia says.

Take a nap? With the most intriguing guy I've met in my life sitting right behind me, his cinnamon breath stirring my hair? "I think I'm too keyed up. But you go ahead. Get some rest."

Blake shrugs thin shoulders and brings a bed pillow down from the overhead rack. He surveys the rows of seats behind him. "I'm going to grab an empty row and stretch out."

Still behind me, Luke asks close to my ear, "Want to talk awhile, Dare Marston?"

I turn. *For the rest of my days.* "I guess so."

Tricia pulls her blue jean jacket from the duffle at her feet and balls it up to use as a pillow. Luke is on his feet. "Here," he says to her. "Take my seat so you can spread out."

She gives me a hope-you-know-what-you're-doing look, and she and Luke squeeze past each other. I slide toward the window seat, and Luke sits on the aisle.

The temperature of the bus rises ten degrees.

As he situates himself, making room for his big hiking boots, I study him as though I'll be sculpting him later. Down: campy looking shorts, knees square, legs heavily muscled and ginger-furred down to his hiking socks and boots. Up: a green Save the Whales T-shirt he fills out perfectly. I look into his face, liking the mischievous up-tip of his nose, and long to touch it with a finger. Instead, I tilt my head and toy with one of my silver earrings. "Anti-Nuke Luke, huh?"

He laughs for the first time. "That's what they call me."

"Where else have you protested?"

"Jersey, Arizona, Virginia." He looks at the roof a second. "Pennsylvania, Ohio." He gazes at me through sherry-colored eyes and purses his lips. "You're a virgin protest-wise, right?" My heart feels like it will fall out of my body.

"Is it that obvious?"

"You're just out of high school." How does he know that? My eyes fall on my hand and the shiny class ring. I ball my fist and smile an I'm-a-dumbass smile. "You eighteen?"

"I am." I pull my auburn hair over one shoulder and stroke it like a pet. "How old are *you* . . . Anti-Nuke Luke?"

"Twenty-one."

"You just graduated college?" I don't bother looking at his hand because this guy wouldn't buy something as conventional and short-lived as a class ring.

"Nope. Didn't go." *He didn't go to college. What would my mother think?* Suddenly I don't give a rat's ass about what Taft Marston thinks. *But what do I think?* I look at the book beside his leg, and he notices. "I'm a reader, though."

"I loved that book."

He dips his chin at me and arches a brow, indicating his approval. "Did you identify with Howard Roark?"

I look out the window as we pass a blur of black and white and green—pastured cows. "I *understood* him, but I'm not sure I could be as"—I grin and form air quotes—"*daring* as he was."

"Not to change the world?"

"Is that what you're going to do?"

"I am." There seem to be vast, uncharted canyons within this guy.

"Tell me about nuclear energy and why it's so bad." He begins then, turning sideways in his seat to face me and sending a rush of happiness along my limbs. I hang on his every syllable until the sky dulls to dusk and Tricia rouses, her face flushed and, after a moment, resolute.

A trickle of miles outside Boston, the driver announces, "End of the line folks. Boston, M-A."

We reach above and below, collecting our things. Tricia and I troop down the deep steps with our unwieldy duffles. Blake and Luke wait with some of the others as the driver unlatches the cargo holds in the belly of the bus. Both of them lift out enormous bound tarps and bags, and Luke palms the driver a five-dollar bill. "Hey, thanks," the driver replies, pocketing it. That was a classy thing to do; a nice thing to do. No one else had tipped the man. I'm liking Luke more and more.

Blake looks at Tricia and me. "Where's your camp gear?"

Tricia laughs. "Camp gear? Oh, we're not camping. We're going to find a cheap motel room when we get to Millimack."

Blake looks at Luke and shakes his head—but not unkindly—at our folly. "Sorry, ladies, no motels there. But most protestors are laid back, friendly folk, especially when the reefer's flowing. Everybody shares tent space."

Pinpoints of light appear on Tricia's lashes. *Don't you cry again,* I tell her with my eyes. I throw my shoulders back. "Hey, it's cool. We came here for adventure," I say to everyone, and then glance at Luke. "And to save future generations from the effects of toxic waste, of course."

Luke grins hugely. "Well, let's get to it." He shoulders his load, struggling for a moment to maintain its balance, then waggles the fingers of one hand at me.

And just like that, I take it.

But I don't feel claimed, only shepherded. Luke's different from any guy I've ever known. He's brawny and sexy and brainy, yet affectionate. A string of people stays at the main road, their thumbs out. Some tramp on along the shoulder, laboring under large packs. Tricia and I with Luke and Blake—and about a dozen lucky others awaiting rides—bivouac under what may be the only streetlight in town on a littered lot in front of a derelict ice cream stand.

It's full-on dark and getting chilly by the time Blake spots their friend's Chevy van and waves both arms to flag it down. The van bumps to the side of the road, the round headlights momentarily blinding us. The side door slides open, and the crew inside exchanges *Hey, mans* and *Hey, dudes* with Blake and Luke. Blake introduces us to the group. Scuzzy-looking Zen the Archer's girlfriend's name is Cricket.

Tricia whispers. "I gotta pee."

"Me too." I shiver. Why hadn't we thought to go on the bus?

As though he's read our minds, Blake inclines his arm. "Last bushes before Millimack, if anyone needs to go."

Cricket, wearing a tank top and tight jeans, pipes up. "Me! C'mon, chickies!" She slithers from the van and produces a flashlight. Balancing in squatting positions, we laugh at her banter and manage not to pee all over our shorts. Cricket seems self-assured. By the glow of the flashlight, I notice that blonde nests at her armpits match the color of her waist-length hair. She must be a hippie, but not like the girl on the bus. She produces a travel pack of tissue for wiping and shares it with us. I remind myself to suggest to Tricia that if we get separated from Luke and Blake, we should keep our eyes on Cricket.

Fisher-Price-like barn and silo outlines punctuate what the others say is a checkerboard of dairy farmland. It's hard to believe that ahead is a plant that dumps poison into the river embracing its land. Blake is at the wheel, silhouetted against the dashboard lights. Next to him, Luke hasn't spoken since we climbed into the van. Once in a while, he bobs his head to the Lynyrd Skynyrd tape. Maybe he's meditating or praying or psyching himself up. After forty miles of nausea-inducing close quarters, the comingling odors of breath, bodies, and humid paper sacks of produce, we reach the city limits of Millimack. *"We're here!"* I whisper to Tricia, who has also not uttered a single word. Blake steers the van from the pocked main road and winds it up an immaculately maintained drive.

"The river's there, just below the road," Cricket says. "You'll see it tomorrow; it's too beautiful," she says in the voice of a dove.

So she's been here before. I smile, my confidence in her surging further up my shore. And then, floodlit and rising from what looks like a tree-dotted mall parking lot, appears the Millimack Nuclear Power Plant. At one end, a squat but massive silo dominates a colony of oddly shaped buildings strung together. I imagine for a moment that it's a candy factory—like the one in *Charlie and the Chocolate Factory* that my candy-company CEO mother read me when I was little—but then I shudder, remembering the insidiousness that Luke said is going on behind the façade. No singing oompa-loompa would be stirring a vat of marshmallow fluff inside the Millimack. And then I catch sight of a mini version of the tent cities I studied about in school.

Blake parks the van along a row of other ragtag vehicles, and we pile out. There are a few nice pop-up campers amongst sturdy new tents, but most tents are poorly-staked and sagging. "Wonder where the musicians park their big buses," Tricia says, then asks, "Where will they put up the stage?"

"Maybe we'll get the lay of the land tomorrow," I say but with a sinking feeling. I glance at Luke gathering his gear and realize how woefully unprepared Tricia and I are. And a minute later: *How the hell are we supposed to shower? I'm already shivering, and there's not so much as a pillow or blanket between us, much less food. We're going to have to mooch off people! And we thought we'd be eating meals at a kitschy little diner in Millimack.* Zen the Archer and a few other guys string up what Cricket says will be our mess tent. *Dear God, we've joined the army!* Cricket, who has produced a black stocking cap with kitten ears to cover her blonde head, begins unpacking supplies—a cooler, pots and pans, a Sterno stove kit—and supervising the doling out of quick sustenance. I try and talk to Tricia, but she has shut down. I ask Cricket if I can help her, but she waves me down. "You can help with breakfast." A new stream of protestors, who've either hoofed or hitched, arrives. They plod past, leaving a new breed of stench in their wake. A rush of dread lodges in my bones. I've made a mistake of colossal proportions. Then Cricket hands me a warm(!) foil-wrapped burrito. I wolf it down.

Sometimes a warm burrito is all it takes to turn the world right-side up again.

I open my eyes the next morning to shards of hazy sun piercing through a canvas tarp. Tricia and I had unzipped and spread out the sleeping bag Zen the Archer lent us—*Cricket and I don't mind sharing hers*—and slept on that. Now there's no sign of Tricia. Stiff and wincing, I sit up, put on a clean shirt and my sneakers, exit the tent, and follow the voice of Cricket. "Each person is allotted one jug of water for tooth brushing and stuff, so use yours sparingly. Write your name on a sticker there and slap it on your jug." Tricia nods like a dashboard bobblehead.

What I hadn't seen last night are the lush tree-covered mountains that ring the area. My heart lifts. Along the river, which is truly stunning in the morning light, perch a posse of porta potties. My mother would die. "I'll be right back to help," I call to the girls, and gamely stride to one with an open door. But locked inside the evil smelling one holer, it's easier to believe the plant is poisoning the water, the fish, and life within it. Where is Luke? Tricia and I had been so exhausted last night, we took the first spots available in a tent with some of the people who have become our group. Luke and Blake had not been amongst them.

After we help serve breakfast—which is bowls of cereal, since the milk will be the first thing to spoil—the call to come and make protest signs ripples our way. Tricia grins for the first time since on the bus to New York, and I give her an impulsive hug. We dive into our duffles, coming up with our markers and tape, and head to contribute to the cause. By the time the sun is at its zenith, we've joined a hundred others in forming a line around the plant's chain-link fence. Though cars enter the plant's main gate and workers come and go between the buildings, no one seems to pay us any attention.

Abruptly, Anti-Nuke Luke squeezes in next to me. We grin at each other like a couple of possums. "Having fun yet, daring one?"

"I am," I say, giving my sign that reads SAVE MOTHER EARTH FOR FUTURE GENERATIONS! a little waggle.

He looks up at the sun. "You're going to roast." He pulls a little tube from one of his pockets and squirts some white paste on a finger. "Do you mind?" I feel as safe as a bullseye at a rigged carnival shooting gallery. Holding my sign between my knees, I take off my sunglasses. The cream is cool as he gently rubs it across my nose and cheeks. "Now you are war painted."

"Well, I do happen to be at war," I say, then shout, *"against nuclear energy!"*

Some guys around us whistle and cheer. Luke takes me around the waist, leans down, and hoists me to sit astride his big shoulders. His hands are warm around the skin of my calves. I whoop and laugh and wave my sign like the wild thing I've become.

We sit on the grassy bank, roasting hot dogs on long sticks our group had scavenged from a nearby wood. We built a bonfire downwind of what everyone now calls Porta Potty Place. Despite our rocky start, after a full day of incomparable and exhilarating sight, sound, and sensation, I know I have to remember every minute of my time at the protest rally. I liked writing in high school and found I had a knack for it. "I'm going to write about all of this," I say to Tricia at supper.

"Go for it," she says, licking mustard off the side of her hand.

"I'll be like a reporter. Maybe interview some of the protestors? Like, find out why they came. May I borrow your notebook?"

Tricia smiles. "It's in my duffle. Help yourself."

When Luke sits next to me, smelling of wood smoke and sweat, I realize how I must smell, despite tooth brushing and sponge bathing. My hair is oily for the first time since I had flu in ninth grade. People begin pairing off and drifting away from the cooling fire. Luke and I sit talking about the books we've both read. It has to be part of the curious connection between us. After a space of time, he asks, "Where did you sleep last night? I looked for you to see if you were okay."

"In Zen the Archer and Cricket's tent. I was exhausted when I lay down and didn't realize I was cold until I woke as a human popsicle."

"Sweet Dare," he says. "I'll lend you my sleeping bag tonight." He reaches to stroke my dirty hair along its length. "How much water do you have left?" Instead of feeling mortified as I would've only a week ago, I close my eyes and scrunch my face, thinking about the level of the jug. "About half."

He grins again. "'Bout three-quarters. And I left it in the sun all day so it would be warm. Let's wash our hair. I'll do yours; you do mine."

"Oh. Let's."

Hand in hand, electricity leaping between our palms, we make our way through the tents. Luke stops before a small battered canvas triangle. "Home sweet home."

"You have a tent all to yourself?"

He laughs. "My old Boy Scout tent."

Inside, Luke kneels to light a lantern and rummages through a bag while I wait at the entrance. He withdraws a tube of shampoo, grabs a wooden folding chair, and joins me outside. He looks toward the river, his eyes stony. "Too bad we can't bathe in there. Fucking toxins!" He shoots me an apologetic look. "Sorry, but it gets to me."

"You shouldn't apologize for feeling passionate about what matters to you." After a moment, he smiles a little and seats me in the old chair. I lean my head back as he pours a trickle of the still warmish water from his jug over my head and begins rubbing in the shampoo he says is biodegradable. I open my eyes to him, a smile trembling across my mouth. He rinses away the shampoo. Holding the clean hank of my hair in his hand, he gives it a squeeze and leans down to kiss me once, twice. He nips at my ear.

I am claimed.

And a glutton for the taste of his lips again. It's my turn to wash his curls. He sits, the chair groaning with his weight. Brazen, I work a leg over to straddle his lap. He moans and clutches my shoulders. I apply a tiny bit of water and shampoo and massage his scalp in swirly suds. He raises up to kiss me, but I—who have *never ever* teased a guy—murmur, "I'm not finished with you yet." When I've rinsed him, he shakes his head like a wet dog, showering us both, and pulls me to him for another kiss. With a great splintering crack, the chair gives way. We lie on the ground, laughing fit to burst. "Sorry," I say as we struggle to our feet. "Tell me the chair's not a Scout heirloom."

"It *was*. My father made it for me." *Oh, my Lord.* "But that's the *best possible way* it could've broken. I'll never forget it."

"You're very gracious, sir. Might we go inside?"

He swallows, and his fervor darkens his eyes to whiskey. "Thought you'd never ask." The top of the tent is so low, Luke has to hunch over inside. The lantern wick sputters gold. I pull my T-shirt and shorts away from my shivering body. "These clothes are kaput."

Luke sheds his T-shirt, revealing sleek wet ginger fur that saunters from his pectorals to his tummy and beneath the waistband of his shorts. I am breathing like a pair of bellows. He takes a flap tie and wraps it around a metal loop, securing the entrance. Thirty seconds later, we are out of our wet things and together on a big wooly sleeping bag. He rubs his hands briskly over the skin of my arms, my back, warming me. He wraps a fuzzy leg over mine and squeezes. I'd had only a glance at the exuberant rise of his manhood as we undressed, but its heat against my leg now launches an inferno in my core. The wind off the river whips at the tent as though it wants inside, but no wind could cool our desire. Luke kisses my lips, face, and neck, and holds me close. I realize I've been starved for his arms, his *affection*, my whole life. My eyes slowly adjust to the darkness. Stroking the soft fur of his chest, I work my way down to his tummy. His sighs are spaced like notes on sheet music.

He nips at my ear again and speaks into my damp hair. "Darling Dare, are you a virgin?"

Does he feel the uptick of my pulse? "Does it matter?"

"No," he says, kindness in his eyes. He raises up on an elbow and scrapes his fingers through his drying hair. "I just need to be sure you want this."

My body is a cupped hand for him. "Oh yes," I whisper into his ear. "But do you have . . . protection?"

A condom materializes in his hand. "I'm a Boy Scout, remember?" And then softly, "I don't want to hurt you, Dare."

"The only way you could hurt me is if you stopped now."

Day 5: Millimack Power Plant, Millimack, MA
From the Journal of Dare Marston

The buzz: Zen the Archer says, "The musicians are coming!" Will Dan Fogelberg and Tom Petty—

Behind me, the grasses rustle. Tricia has found me on the river bank, sitting on a rock and writing in the notebook. I interviewed four people the day before, three women and one man, and am fascinated by the reasons they each had for attending the protest. "Hi, you," she says, sitting.

"Hi! How are you? Ready for a big day?"

"I'm ready, I guess." She takes off the red Curt Cobain sunglasses that had made her feel cool. "Lonesome too." I search my best friend's face. "I mean, you've spent the nights in Luke's tent, leaving me with Cricket and her babbling. Have you noticed every shirt she has is, like, warning-light yellow?" She sighs. "Then we're protesting all day. I guess I thought it would be different."

"I guess I did too. But I fell in love, Tricia."

"I know. You're shellacked in it."

Day 7: Millimack Power Plant, Millimack, MA
From the Journal of Dare Marston

The buzz: an enormous influx of protestors. We're amongst a thousand people. If any musicians are here, nobody has seen them. Our water jugs are bottoming out, Cricket's never-ending food supply almost depleted. I smell. Tricia wants to go home. I'm feeling cluster-phobic. But most everyone's optimistic the numbers may finally gain the attention of the plant administrators. The plant will bus in its workers today for fear of the mob.

I find Luke in Zen the Archer's tent. The group is strategizing joining the human chain to block the plant entrance. "Look at everyone now and memorize the color of their shirts," Zen says. "Cricket's always easy to spot."

"This isn't my first insurrection," she says to us. "Just stick with me and hold on strong."

At 7:45, Luke hugs me long.

Hand in hand with both Luke and Tricia, I make my way through the mob and toward the plant entrance. The first Greyhound rounds the bend. *How my life has changed since I first stepped on one of those.* I tighten my grip on my friends' hands. The driver sees the people ahead and slams on his brakes. The bus swerves back and forth across the road, tires steaming, big body swaying, and so does the next one and the next and the next. The workers, their faces pale through the windows, stay aboard as they've been instructed. Protestors who've somehow produced gas masks run past us, screaming for us to form a chain, locking arms around the perimeter of the plant. This is not a day for carrying signs.

Helicopters appear high overhead, the sound of them like feet of snow slumphing from roof tops. We step into the line, Luke with a death grip on my right hand. Tricia's on my left. Zen the Archer and Blake stand stalwart on her other side, linked with others from our group. *But where's Just-stick-with-me-Cricket, our leader?* A stroke of omniscience peals in my head.

Some along the chain murmur into each other's shoulders, a few of them weeping. A screaming strobe of color weaves through the mob and the buses, hurtling past the entrance and gaining the main road. Cricket, yellow outside and in, has bolted. Sirens ring out. Police park and run toward us. They begin roughing people up. My legs buckle. "You're all under arrest," one of them bellows through a megaphone. Tear gas blooms in the air. Luke's hand is wrenched from mine. Darkness crawls over me in waves, and I fall.

I wake dazed, dust and gas in my nose and mouth. I scratch and claw at the turf for Luke. For Tricia. Crying their names. Tears flood my eyes, temporarily clearing them. Tricia finds me and clutches at me like a baby animal desperate for its mother. I hold her tightly, pride in her filling my chest. She was so brave. We gain our feet. Finally forced to run for our lives, we leave behind our possessions. And our ideals. We flee with about one hundred others, not faltering until we've gained the main road again. Tricia retches and throws up but wipes her mouth on her filthy T-shirt. Taking her arm, we stagger on. Ten minutes later, we're slumped in the back of a dairy farmer's truck. Though I stink of BO and vomit, the blue shirt I borrowed from Luke and wore that day still retains his scent.

I pray he made it out alive.

We spent six nights in his sleeping bag, exchanging *everything* but our addresses.

I howl with the rush of the wind until I'm emotionally debrided. In Boston, the blue-eyed farmer, who says he has daughters of his own. escorts us into the bus station and purchases two chocolate milks, two sandwiches, and one-way tickets to D.C. for us. He shoves his stained cap back on his head and hands us each a quarter. "Call home."

In the D.C. Greyhound station once more, I say to Tricia, "We can't go home like this. We have to clean up." I drop my quarter into a pay phone.

"Who are you calling?"

"Finnegan O'Day."

All Taffy had to say when I got home after showering at Finn's and borrowing an outfit from his sister was, "You're awfully pale to have been at the beach for a week."

My heart breaks afresh each morning. I get ready for college and try to make peace with losing Luke. Until the day I realize the red tide of my period isn't going to show.

I never listen to Dan Fogelberg again.

Chapter Ten

Caroline
2020

"Yoga in ten, clothing optional!" I call into the house from the porch as the boys' bus trundles out onto the main road. Everyone's working from home today, so we should be able to get in a practice before addressing our computers and the individual demands that keep our pantry filled.

My mom giggles from in front of the kitchen sink, where she volunteered to wash the breakfast dishes. "Caroline, you are so funny. Where did you get your sense of humor?"

My mind slips into the country of the past. *Probably from Taffy and Seraphina. A good dose of it wouldn't have hurt you either.* "Just lucky, I guess." Mom's rubbing at an egg-stuck plate with an old dish rag. "Hey, Mom, please use the Tough-Love scrubby under the sink for that. And would you mind not letting the water run while you're washing?"

Her back stiffens. "A scrubby?" she says, so softly I can barely make out the word.

"Yes, please. They're down there by your right foot."

She turns and looks at me, her expression miles away from any I've seen on her face. Her eyes are wild, like a first-time skier who's just swooshed past a black slope marker. I reach around her, turn off the faucet. She relinquishes the dishrag with a trembling hand. "Mom, what is *wrong*?"

If she notices the crew when they come down the hall carrying their mats, she is unfazed. "That . . . buckwheat in the pancakes must not have agreed with me. I'm . . . going back to bed." She literally trots down the hall and shuts Parker's door. As I stand gaping down the empty hall, the latch on the door slides home. *What the hell?*

"Hey, guys," I manage to call back through the screen, "start without me?" I reach beneath the sink for the scrubby and turn it over in my hands. I know terror when I see it. This is no upset stomach. I finish the dishes myself and head outside, where the others are gathered in the shade.

A half hour of lovely stretching, strength poses, and a restorative Shavasana later, we're seated in a circle. Allowing myself to become aware of the world and its issues again, I pick at a clump of dandelions in the grass and tell my friends what happened with Mom. "I have no idea what got into her. But she was scared to death without even seeing the scrubby. It's like . . . the *idea* of using it scared her to death."

Griffin shakes his head. "Maybe a childhood thing? Everyone has things that happened when they were kids that haunt them in one way or another."

"Damn straight," Rebekah says, closing her eyes. Only *I* know what will haunt my friend to her grave. I lean to give her a hug.

"We'll just have to be gentler with Dare, give her some space. I'll shower in the front bath today," Parker says.

Rebekah smiles at him. "How about getting a ball game going when the boys get home? Maybe that'll draw Dare out. Maybe the neighbors can come."

Parker peers up through the gently fluttering leaves. "It's a fine day for baseball." He smiles at her. Her chest rises high and falls.

When the boys are home, they're pumped at the prospect of a game. Jimi talks around the bite of Marston bar that Rebekah's allowed them for a snack. "Where's Dare and Lucie? Taking a nap?"

"Hopefully they'll be out in a bit," their mother responds, and crosses her fingers for luck behind her back for me.

Chewing, Jimi makes a wrinkly-nosed face and spits something onto his palm. "My tooth came out!"

"Luc-ky," Miles says.

Rebekah smiles. "Well, good! That's your fourth."

Jimi feels the new empty hole in his smile with his tongue.

Rebekah takes the tooth and rinses it off under the tap for the tiny tooth box she keeps.

"When will I lose another stupid baby tooth?" Miles grouses. "I've lost only two."

Jimi taunts him. "It's because I'm the oldest and you're the runt."

"Yeah, three minutes older. Big deal, big shot."

"Hey, guys," I say, "let's take our competitive spirit to the field."

It's the bottom of the fourth, and my team—Griff, Miles, and me—are at bat. Our neighbors, the Moores, couldn't make it today. In the field, Parker's playing first, Jimi's covering both second and short stop, and Rebekah's playing third. "You're up, Caroline," says Griff, who's pitching for both sides and looking fabulous with his dark curly hair bouncing about his shoulders. I grab the bat, tap the plate with it, give him a big grin, and get in position. Griff tosses me an unprecedented underhand pitch. I swing, making contact. But Miles easily catches my fly ball.

"Yerrr out!" he yells, a four-foot-tall umpire. "That's two away!"

Jimi frowns, rising from his crouched position. "Hey, Griff, why'd you pitch underhanded?"

Griffin glances at me as I take a seat again and adjusts his ball cap. "Just being easy with my lady."

Jimi persists. "So we're going to have ladies' rules now?"

Griff turns back to him, his hands on his hips. "Hey, pipsqueak, who's the pitcher here, huh?" This is a running joke between him and the boys. Jimi is Pipsqueak One and Miles, Pipsqueak Two.

"Okay, let's go!" Jimi says. "We need a pitcher, not a can of corn."

From the mound, Griffin calls to me. "Look who's making an appearance." My mother is coming down the steps of the house, a darting and sniffing Lucie in the lead.

Miles catches sight of them. "Hey, Granddare's here!" *Granddare? When had they come up with that?* Mom smiles at Miles and joins me on the wooden player's bench that Parker scored from the high school when they installed new ones. The boys think it's cool because the few players who went on to the big leagues had once warmed it.

Still tethered by her leash, Lucie gives up sniffing and hops up. Quick as a keyboard tap, she's curled in my lap. Stroking the pup's back, I look at my mother. "You feeling better, Mom?"

"Fine." She surveys the field. Lucie yips and chuffs along with the chatter and cheer from the field. Mom smiles a little. "Guess Lucie's a baseball fan. Who knew?"

"Any of us can figure out that we're fans of new things we try when we embrace nonjudgment and aren't afraid to take risks. I know I have."

Mom gives me a captivated please-tell-me-more look. But Jimi shows up, dusty and with chocolate on his chin. He stops to give Lucie a pet and then takes a seat right next to Mom. He loops an arm around her shoulder. Diverted from our unfinished conversation, she gives me an *aww* grin over his head. "Hi, guy," she says.

"The game's almost over. You want to bat, Granddare?"

She looks into my eyes. "I'll give it a try, if you'll hold Lucie."

Jimi jumps up and does a not-bad cartwheel. "Miles! Granddare's going to hit! Here, girl," he says, taking Lucie and putting her over his shoulder. Lucie bathes the chocolate from his chin, making him squirm and giggle.

Mom takes the bat and winds up. Griffin pitches the ball underhand again and even slower than he threw for me. Then open-mouthed, his head swings to look past third base, where the most unathletic woman I know (besides myself) has walloped the hell out of the ball. Everyone goes nuts and runs to congratulate her. Griffin gives her a high five. "Well *played*, Dare!"

Parker retrieves the ball. "That was *awesome*. Guys, look at this." He holds the ball aloft. The laces on one side have split down the seam. We marvel at it as if it's a meteorite fallen from the sky. Parker howls and slaps a big knee. "Dare O'Day just knocked the cover off the ball."

Mom and I look at each other and say as one, "Oh. My. Gosh."

Jimi jumps up and down. "Hey, the men should carry Granddare around the field on their shoulders like real baseball players do!"

Mom chuckles and waves her hands in front of her as if warding off a bee. "Oh no, no. We'll skip that custom. The last time I sat on someone's shoulders I weighed about a hundred and fifteen pounds."

Rebekah turns to Parker. "You were lovely to make Dare a hero," I hear her say. Parker swoops off his cap, holds it over his heart, and gives her a little bow. "Thank you, milady." Signaling the game's end, Griff calls to Parker to come and help collect the equipment. Watching him go, Rebekah sighs long. "He's adorable." We sit back on the bench. I cross my legs, gladness and pride sliding with the sweat down my spine. Granddare, the conquering hero of baseball, joins us.

"Mom, that was unbelievable! When's the last time you hit a baseball?"

"Like seventh grade? It must have been some kind of savant thing." Rebekah and I hoot with laughter.

"Mom," Miles yells. His face is all scrunched up and he's pulling at the back of his shorts. "I need some help inside, please."

"Oh, bless him," she says, rising. "He sometimes waits too long when he needs to poop."

"Caroline did that too," my mom says, her mouth twisting against a grin.

"I did not."

"Yes, you did. Several times." *Well, I'll be damned. What a thing to say, and in front of Rebekah.* Undaunted, Mom watches as Rebekah stops where Parker's stacking the bases and says something to him that makes him grin and nod. "That girl has it bad for Parker."

"She does? How do you know?" We watch Rebekah climb the front steps with Miles.

"Maybe too many sexy novels."

"Well, ding-dang, Mom!" She laughs a little as I sit stunned and slightly queasy at the thought of my prim and proper mother reading erotica.

"Is Parker aware of her feelings?"

I'm pleased that Mom's getting to know the crew. "I—I'm not sure how they feel."

She looks at me and grins. "Mark my words, she wants him bad."

I guess I'm not too old to be excited that
Today's my birthday!
I tick off on my fingers the things I'm grateful for today:

- Griff and I are going to my first OB appointment to hear the baby's heartbeat.
- We're going to Topanga Days this afternoon to celebrate.
- My mother's here.
- Rebekah and the boys have made a chocolate cake for me.
- The loveliest man in the world is sleeping *toute nu*: in the buff next to me.

I thrash my arms and legs around under the covers with excitement.

Griffin wakes. He licks his lips. "Happy Birthday, baby," he says, rolling to me and hooking a leg over my hip. His grin is lazy, his eyes at half-mast, performing for me what he knows is his sexy look. I bite my lip and look over his body at the clock.

"We have, like, fifteen minutes."

He grins. "A quickie?"

After we're showered and dressed, we stop in the kitchen to grab one of Rebekah's muffins. "Happy birthday, Caroline," everyone sings out, Dare's voice falling a beat behind the others.

"Wow, birthday girl," Rebekah says, "you look so beautiful."

Mom sets down her coffee cup, my cup, the lovely one she gave me for my last birthday. She cocks her head, considering me. "I'd love to see you in lipstick, darling. I couldn't do without my signature red.

Color brings out your inner beauty." Everyone stops in midaction and looks at me.

"You know I'm not into lipstick, Mom. I prefer my natural cruelty-free lip balm."

"Caroline's gorgeous just the way she is," Griffin says evenly. I give him a sheepish smile.

"Where're you going?" Miles asks.

Rebekah says, "I told you they have something to take care of in Los Angeles, remember?"

He smites himself on his forehead. "Oh yeah." We all laugh at his antic.

"Would this be a good time to tell them our news?" I search Griffin's eyes. He nods in confirmation.

I look first at my mother, with whom I'm still annoyed about the lipstick remark but who is the woman who gave birth to me, gave me all the advantages of life. "I'm going to have a baby."

Mom bites her bottom lip and bursts into tears. "My baby is going to have a baby," she says, her tone a sloppy mixture of incredulity and delight. I go to her, and she rises. We reach to embrace at the same time. My heart slips a notch when Mom lets go first, but she turns to Griff, reaches for his hand, then leans in to kiss his cheek. And just like that, he gets up and gives her a hug. "Congratulations, Griffin," she says.

"Thanks, Dare. You too."

Jimi and Miles, who are on their feet and engaged in some kind of elaborate slide-clap thing, come to an abrupt halt and consider their mother. "Does that mean we're going to have a baby brother or sister?"

Rebekah reads the answer on my face and smiles. "Well, yeah," she says to them.

I lie on a comfy heated table in Dr. Bhakta's office, my feet in hand-knitted booties in the stirrups, a starchy paper blanket over my bare lower half. Griff, who's an OB/GYN office first-timer, stands beside me, marveling at the examination setup, checking out the screens and equipment, a fool for cool technology.

Dr. Bhakta comes in and greets us with her lovely lilt. I introduce her to Griffin. "Mr. Panakis, if you wouldn't mind taking a seat, we'll see what we have here." She conducts her internal exam, finding everything in order, then squeezes a warm gel across my abdomen. She glides the ultrasound wand over my lower belly and then, from her machine, brings to life a large wall monitor. "You'll see the baby up there, Papa." Tears of joy leak from my eyes as the grainy black-and-white image of our child appears on the screen. "Look, Griff, he's real."

He tilts his head. "Is that *the head*?" he asks cautiously.

Dr. Bhakta presses down, giving us a better view and reminding me how badly I need to pee. "That it is."

"Do I see eye sockets? How big is he?" Griff asks.

"Yes. The fetus is about the size of strawberry."

Griff shakes his head while forming the size with a thumb and forefinger. "That's so little."

"The fingers and toes are formed but are still partially webbed."

"Like a little duckling," Griff says tenderly. Tears stand in his eyes.

The doctor smiles. "Soon the extra tissue will be reabsorbed to reveal individual fingers and toes."

"Can you tell the gender?" I ask.

"It's a wee bit early yet." She completes a series of rapid taps on the enormous gestalt of her keyboard, then nods to herself. "With your irregular periods it's tricky to pinpoint conception, but I believe you are farther along than you thought," she says, looking back at my chart and flipping a page. "Which means I believe you'll deliver sometime around December 20. We'll know more later."

"A Christmastime baby," I say, an excited tickle zipping throughout my abdomen.

As the doctor ends the exam, my mind flicks to Rebekah's vastly different ultrasound experience, her agony when Denzel left her so abruptly and permanently. But Griff bends down to me and kisses my lips, one of his tears plopping on my cheek. "I can't wait," he says.

I step back inside the door at Crewtopia, and my stomach turns at a potent chemical odor. Griffin grimaces. "What the hell?" Rebekah comes down the hall, fanning her face with a hand.

"Dare sprayed Febreze to freshen the air."

"Where did she get that?"

"She made the grocery store run for us this morning. Believe me, that was not on my list."

Mom comes through the screen door with Lucie and the boys. Jimi pinches his nose. "What stinks?"

"Mom," I say, careful about hurting her feelings or embarrassing her, "we don't use chemical sprays in our home. But I'd love to show you how we purify the air with a bundle of sage."

"Oh, I'm sorry." Her cheeks pink. "But the sage sounds fascinating. I'd love you to show me."

My heart rises. "Great, then. And thanks for getting the groceries. That was a big help."

Parker comes in for lunch, his nose twitching. *Don't say anything,* I tell him with a brisk shake of my head. We put sandwiches together. Rebekah reaches atop the refrigerator for some pears in a bowl but comes up short. Parker comes up behind her, easily snaring the fruit. I swear I see him smell her hair. Her honey-mimosa shampoo that takes me back to the day we drove to Santa Monica with the wind whipping through our hair. A giggle bubbles in my throat at the memory of taking the pregnancy tests in the pharmacy bathroom. It strikes me that, until today, Rebekah was the only one who knew about the baby, but she kept my secret. I give her a fond smile as she washes the pears. Mom, in jeans and a plain T-shirt, is setting the table. Guilt takes a small bite of me: I hadn't told my own mother first; that's how indifferent our relationship had become.

We've all finished our work by the time the boys sprint up the drive from the bus. Miles manages to ask between pants, "Can we go to Topanga Days now?"

"May we," my mother and I say in tandem. She gives me a little wink.

"*May* we, puh-leeze?"

A band is already on stage, the music pumping as a parking guide motions to a spot for Parker to drive his SUV—with the extra third row seat—on the grass. We pile out and get our bearings. Not a cloud mars an azure sky for this yearly celebration of local music, arts and crafts, healing arts, and Mother Earth. "Why couldn't Lucie come?" Miles asks. "She'd love it here, all these smells. People will drop food scraps too."

Rebekah smooths back his hair. "The rules say no pets allowed. You just didn't think of it last year because we didn't have a dog."

Jimi beams at my mother. "We do now, though!"

Griff looks at me, and I know what he's thinking because, after the Febreze fiasco, he asked me again how long Dare was staying. "We'll see," I only said. I'm not sure how I feel about living under the same roof with her yet. Sometimes I'd like to strangle her, while others, I'd like give her a big hug. And despite her few gaffes, she seems happy with us. I haven't asked her when she might go back to Foxfield and the *Journal*.

Mom says, "Maybe we can find some sage here with the healing art items?"

"Bet we can," I say, and give her a grin.

"Who wants popcorn or a brewsky?" Parker asks, directing the last word at Griffin.

"Popcorn," Jimi says, rubbing his tummy and licking his lips. "But can we go do the kids' arts and crafts first? Mrs. Bing is the boss of the arts and crafts."

Mom grins and addresses the adults. "How about you guys go do your thing, and I'll take the boys to see their teacher."

"*Go, Granddare!*" The boys chant.

"Well, okay," Rebekah says, scanning the amassing crowd. "But stay right with her."

"We will!" Jimi says. And they're off, both of them holding her hands and jabbering like chipmunks. The four of us watch them locate the tent, then stop at the first food vendor and pay for a couple of bags of hot popcorn.

A Rolling Stones cover band is warming up, and the guys want to join the gyrating swarm in front of the stage. Rebekah and the guys purchase cups of local craft beer, ginger for me. We nod and speak to neighbors and townsfolk, many of them in shorts and T-shirts like us, others in garb born of years of tradition. I wonder if anyone can tell I'm pregnant.

The color of it all is my favorite part: the women in crowns of wild flowers, tie-dye shirts, muumuu dresses, and bare feet; floppy hats, peace buttons and vintage hippie jewelry; men with Willie Nelson-style braids; girls in teeny bikini tops with long swishy skirts; a small troupe of Elvis impersonators; the homemade signs protesting this or that concern of the moment.

Two beers in, Rebekah says she's going to check on the boys and crisscrosses her way through the crowd. The band launches into "Wild Horses," and Griff asks me to dance. As I step into his embrace, Parker goes in search of another beer. But only minutes later, he's back, out of breath, his face a mask of tension. Griff and I drop hands and stare. "Miles is missing," he says.

"How do you know?" I ask stupidly, looking wild-eyed about the gaudy crowd. "Where's Rebekah?"

"I met her lookin' for him near the food. She's about half hysterical."

"Where's Dare?" Griff asks. The three of us exchange glances and hurry for the arts and crafts tent but meet Rebekah halfway, her face blasted.

"I can't find Miles!"

"We know, babe," I say, putting an around her trembling frame. "What about Jimi?"

"He's still painting something ... back there."

"And Mom's there?"

"Yes."

"What color shirt was Miles wearing?" Parker asks.

Rebekah presses her fingers against her forehead and closes her eyes. "His green school T-shirt with the dragon on it."

Still at the arts and crafts site, Jimi absorbedly paints a wooden glider with a small brush, a triangle of pink tongue protruding from the corner of his mouth. My mother is sitting on a bench, her head down, her lips moving as though in prayer.

"Wait, babe, let me. You stay here with one of the guys," I say to Rebekah.

"Mom," I say, crouching in the dust at her feet, "what happened?"

She looks at me, mascara puddles beneath her eyes, makeup streaked by tears, her lipstick chewed off. "He was right there ... between Jimi and"—she points to a kid, wearing a dress, daisies woven into his long, curly hair—"that ... child there."

"Have you been sitting here all this time?"

"No!" She practically shouts into my face, a bead of spit landing on my cheek. The other parents gathered around not so nonchalantly look over their shoulders at us. "I ran out onto the path and found a security guy and asked for help. He thought I should stay here in case Miles came back. He got on his walkie-talkie and asked someone to announce his name over the PA system."

I rise and pat her shoulder. "That was a good thing to do, Mom."

Jimi turns to us from the table, blowing on his freshly painted glider. "Miles isn't back yet?"

"MILES JACKSON, YOUR MOM'S LOOKING FOR YOU AT THE SCHOOL ARTS AND CRAFTS TENT. MILES JACKSON," the lead singer from the band roars through his mic on stage, his voice as cragged as Keith Richards' face.

A copse of porta potties two tents away catches my eye. They've been placed in a different spot from last year.

The door on the right end one opens a sliver. I keep my eyes on it.

"Mom," I murmur in her direction, "come see."

A small brown hand reaches around the door.

The door opens another six inches, revealing Mile's face and green shirt.

My mom rasps, "Miles!" If Parker hadn't shown up just then and grabbed her arm, her legs would have folded like a TV tray.

The door opens all the way.

"I'll go tell 'em the kid's been found," a kind man behind us says.

Miles stands in the doorway, his eyes as big as lily pads, his chest heaving. He holds his hands over his face in the posture of a much younger child's if-I-can't-see-you-you-can't-see-me way.

Rebekah beats Wilma Rudolph's best time reaching the shed. She swoops her boy and his humiliation into her arms and whisks them away toward the parking area. The rest of us thank the security guards and the other parents as Parker rushes after Rebekah. We trail them through the grass, Mom with a grip on Jimi's wrist. The band's playing a new song, "Mother's Little Helper." Miles couldn't have been missing more than ten minutes, though the time had seemed to pass like the space between two birthdays. Cradling the child within me with both hands, I go cold at the realization of the tremendous responsibility of parenthood.

My mother, who I'm coming to understand was a better mother than I thought, had lost Miles. How can Griff and I keep a child safe when he or she could vanish in the time it takes for one to delete a spam folder? A greasy, humid blast from the vent of a Mexican food truck hits me in the face. I stagger toward a rusted 55-gallon trash drum, clutch its sides, and unleash a slew of ginger beer and popcorn. *Happy Birthday to me.* Griffin has turned around to locate me. He strides to the drum and shepherds me away, lifting the tail of his shirt and wiping the vomit from my chin.

This man, the father of our baby, will always be there for me.

We reach the car. Astride Rebekah's hip, Jimi is sandwiched between her and Parker, his dirty hands wrapped around both their necks. Parker and Rebekah, partners.

Miles falls asleep in the car. The others of us talk about what happened. Miles had gone to where the potties had been located last year and had to double back in search of their new locale. Mom apologizes profusely to Rebekah. "It could've happened to any of us," gracious Rebekah says, and reaches to squeeze her hand. "Think no more about it."

Then she says to me, "Oh, Caro, we'd planned to have your cake and ice cream tonight." She regards Miles. "Maybe we still can if we let him finish his nap—"

"We don't have school tomorrow, so we can stay up late," Jimi says.

"Okay, then. But let's get ourselves cleaned up first," Rebekah says as we climb out of the SUV. Griffin carries Miles into the house. My mom washes her hands at the sink. "Hey, Dare," Rebekah says gently, "will you turn the water off while you're soaping your hands?"

"Oh sure. Of course. I forgot."

Miles awakens and wiggles to be let down. Rebekah gets into the front bath shower with both boys. Before his shower, Parker sets the oven temperature and pulls the pizzas we reserve for emergency dinners from the freezer while Griff and I head for the shower in the back.

Miles won't look at Dare.

After we've wolfed the pizzas, Rebekah serves my favorite chocolate cake with salted caramel ice cream. "Will you play "Happy Birthday" on your flute for Caro, Mom?" Jimi asks.

"Good idea. I'll go get it." Parker lights the three candles for past, present, and future. Rebekah returns with her instrument, begins to play, and everyone sings. The boys help me blow out the candles.

"That was lovely, Rebekah," Mom says.

"Thank you."

Jimi says, "Remember when I said we could put Rae on your cake? See her in the middle?"

"I do."

Miles speaks for the first time. "I put the other princesses on there too because, well, you're pretty, like them."

Jimi squints at his twin and shakes his head. "That was a jackwagon thing to say."

Rebekah puts down her fork. "Do *not* call your brother names, young man."

Griffin swallows a spoonful of ice cream and gives the boys a weighty look. "Guy rule number one: never pass up the opportunity to tell a girl she's pretty." He taps a temple. "Keep that in mind for later." He leans over and plants a lingering kiss on me. The boys whoop.

Rebekah rises and gives Jimi an ear twist for his earlier comment before collecting a small pile of packages from the counter. "Oww, Mom!"

"Remember that the next time you're tempted to talk ugly to your brother."

I open my presents. Mom has given me a handsome leather journal. "I thought you could use it to write about your feelings as you grow your baby."

I smile and run my hand over the cover. "That's a great idea. I love it, Mom." Miles still assiduously avoids my mother's face.

The boys painted me a sturdy wooden box for jewelry. "Or whatever you want to put in there," says Miles.

"Thank you both. I love it." Parker hands me his gift, wrapped in a pretty vintage dishtowel that would have been gift enough, but inside is a tiny plastic bag filled with special wildflower seeds.

"While you're growing the baby, I thought, well, that you could grow some new flowers."

"That's the perfect gift, Parkie. Thanks so much." I unwrap Rebekah's gift, a dog-eared paperback copy of *What To Expect When You're Expecting*. She gives me a diffident little look.

"I know you can get that in e-reader form now... but I wanted you to have the copy I read when I was expecting my boys."

I gulp and touch my chest, then reach to give her a hug. "I couldn't love anything more. And I hope I'm half the mother you are, mousekin."

"You will be terrific."

My mother echoes her. "Yes, you will." My eyes fill.

"Okay," Griff says, "before everyone ends up boo-hooing, I have a gift for you too." He pulls from his pocket a little box. *Tiffany's?* He shrugs, his cheeks darkening. "I figured this year would be a good one for a splurge.

"What have you done?" I ask, my heart hurrying as I slowly open the unrivaled blue box. I hold up a silver bracelet for everyone to admire. It's elegantly simple: a flat band bisected by a bar clasp. "Oh, Griff, how gorgeous."

"Read the little card inside."

I read it aloud. "'This Tiffany collection represents courage, strength and optimism—just like the women who wear it.' I love it."

"Are you going to make out again?" Jimi asks, hands up and poised to cover his eyes.

"Dude," Parker says to him, "look at me. Guy rule number two: never miss an opportunity to kiss a beautiful woman." Rebekah gives Parker a sidelong glance, and he catches her. They exchange knowing smiles.

"What are the other rules?" Miles asks, oblivious.

"You rookie guys are on a need-to-know basis."

"No fair," they say, and then laugh through their pouts.

I watch from the doorway as Rebekah tucks the rookie guys into their beds. My mother enters the room quietly. "'Night, Granddare," Jimi says sleepily. On the bottom bunk, Miles stares at the underside of Jimi's mattress and says nothing. "Miles," Mom says to him, "may I sit down for a second?"

"It's a free country," he says in a very small voice. Rebekah and I move into the hall but carefully park ourselves on either side of the doorway.

"Miles, I'm so sorry about what happened today, the way I lost you. Do you think you'll be able to forgive me? I love you and want so much to be a good . . . granddare to you."

"But it wasn't *your* fault."

"It *was*, Miles. I'm the grown-up, and I should have kept a closer eye on you."

"But I was the one who ran off . . . to find a bathroom. I shoulda told you I was going, but I had to go real bad. I've been scared all day that you were mad at me and didn't want to be my grandma anymore. I want to be a good grandson."

"You . . . and Jimi are the best grandsons ever. Miles, I had a little girl once, and I didn't always care for her the way I should have."

"Did you lose her?"

My mother lets out a big breath. In the hall, I place my forehead and hands on the wall in anguish. "In a way I did."

"Was it Caro?"

"Yes. It was Caro."

"Well, she's not lost; she's standing out there in the hall listening to us right now." Busted, Rebekah and I slide down the walls to the creaky floor, holding in our laughter, tears coasting our cheeks. Miles is quiet for a space of time.

"But you are gonna have a *real* grandbaby soon."

"Yes, I am. But I have enough love for all three of you. No matter what happens, even when I go back to Virginia, I'll always be your Granddare."

I say goodnight to Rebecca and go to bed with Griffin but get up an hour later, my heart a riot of emotions over all my mother said. I take a breath to rein them in and pad to the kitchen to make a cup of tea. The boys' bedroom door is open, and soft lamplight still burns there. Rebekah's bed is still made, and she's nowhere to be seen. The blanket over Mile's chest rises and falls. And at the foot of his bunk, my mother still sits.

Watching over him.

Chapter Eleven

Dare
2020

I am the first one up this morning, though I sat up watching the twins sleep until almost one a.m. The boys, who are typically up no later than 6:30, sliding up and down the hall in sock feet, pretending to surf and "accidentally" bumping into doors, must be exhausted from yesterday's drama. I sip a cup of coffee, feeling quiet and pensive. Light footfalls approach from down the hall that by now I've come to know are my daughter's. "How're you doing today, Mom?" she asks kindly, and drops a kiss atop my head.

Hope sparks in my chest, glowing and foolish.

When Caroline's busy with the coffee maker, her back turned, I say gently, "I'm okay, sweetheart."

She notices my hazelnut Coffeemate on the table. "I need to get *my* creamer out." She opens the fridge to retrieve the raw almond milk she gets from a farmer down the road and comes to sit next to me with her cup.

I look at the discrete products sitting together on the table. "I appreciate that our preferences can coexist here," I say with a smile.

She returns my smile over the rim of her cup. *"Moi, aussi."*

I notice Parker's packet of wildflower seeds Caroline left on the table overnight and take a sip of courage. At once the words come to me the way they do when I'm expressing myself through writing. "I'm embarrassed that you heard my conversation with Miles last night. I realize I have to deal with my doubts about being a good grandmother when I wasn't the best mother." I press my hands tightly between my thighs to keep from fidgeting.

Caroline sets her cup down and levels her green-eyed gaze at me. "I've seen the way you are with the twins. They adore you. And no one faults you for what happened to Miles. He left without telling you. It could have happened to any of us."

Her generous reply fortifies me until I realize she hasn't refuted my claim about not being the best mother. So much for my fishing expedition.

At the clamor of boy noise in the hall and bathroom, Lucie gives a yip from underneath the table. The twins rush around the corner and skid into the room. "Where's Mom?" Jimi asks without concern, only curiosity. Miles crawls under the table.

It hits Caroline and me at the same time, and we lock eyes. While I stayed up late with Miles, Rebekah had not gotten into her bed but had doubtless slipped down the hall and into Parker's. Now she flies around the corner, still poking her arms in the sleeves of her billowing robe. "Here I am, you rascally rabbits." Miles comes out from under the table with Lucie, bumping his head and wincing. He rubs at the spot. "Where have you been, Mom?"

"Oh, Parker shared his room with me," she says, gathering them both as well as Lucie into her lap.

"Oh. Okay," says Miles. "What's for breakfast?'"

Wise Rebekah. She had told Miles nothing more than he wanted to know, and he was satisfied. A brilliant mom's way of keeping a can of worms firmly sealed.

Saturday morning, everyone's "up and doing," as Parker likes to say. The boys have installed themselves in the hammock with Rebekah's old iPod and an excited Lucie, where they are permitted to watch the old Warner Brothers cartoons on YouTube. Lucie paws at the pad. "Hey, Granddare," Jimi calls, "Lucie likes Pepe LePew!" My pulse thuds as I remember the skunk we saw in the garden and how I vowed to stay away from there.

"Well, so she does." Caroline heads down the steps and for the chicken coop, Griffin to the shed to get the lawn mower, and Parker to take care of the composting. How he can tackle that job with a full stomach is beyond me. Rebekah's about to pull out her quilting frame but I quickly ask her, "My doctor in Foxfield sent an eScript to Wyler's Pharmacy in town. Do you have a few minutes to take me there?"

A beam of light turns her eyes to the satin of chocolate ganache. "For sure. There's actually a prescription I need to renew myself..." She knows I know, and she's unabashed. When I first realized she still trusted me after what happened at Topanga Days, I felt like we'd become real friends, like we'll keep the starch in each other's spines. Soon we're off in her little yellow Subaru.

"You know, I've noticed your strong faith," I say quietly.

"How so?"

"The way the boys ask the blessing at dinner and just some of the things I've heard you say. Do you come from a family of faith?"

She navigates a hairpin turn and then glances at me, a trace of cynicism crossing her features. "Why do I feel like I'm being interviewed here?"

"Oh, sorry. I must have slipped into journalist mode." I watch her profile until the corner of her mouth turns up again.

"You miss writing." A Yoda action figure has rolled from under my seat and I pick it up.

"I do! I've been thinking about doing some writing from here. But I need to get in touch with my editor." *Wonder how Carmen feels about me being away for a month already?*

"About faith?"

"Pardon me?"

She consults her rearview mirror and changes lanes. "Well, that's what you were asking me about. I thought you were going to write a piece on faith."

I wonder what she'd think if she knew I was contemplating writing about intentional communities. "No, I'm just curious about how you have done so well as a single mother—of twin boys, no less—when I didn't do so well with one daughter."

Rebekah downshifts as we enter the town of Topanga, and the downturn of her mouth in profile makes the ceiling feel like it's pressing closer. "My parents, who proclaimed to be people of faith and were about this far away"—she takes a hand off the wheel and creates an inch of space between her forefinger and thumb—"from being snake handlers, disowned me when I got pregnant."

Her words lay heavy across my shoulders. *"No!"*

"Yeah."

A stifling silence fills the little car, and simultaneously, we reach for our window handles. Rebekah gives me a little well-you-asked look. "I'm so sorry."

"After that, the real God stepped in. Whenever I was scared I couldn't do right by my boys, a voice would whisper: *Do it by faith.* Not my parents' version but the one God packaged for me along with my children."

Her words bolt down my spine.

I compose myself and finally turn to her. "I wish I'd had that faith, Rebekah. I mean, I know my situation was a stroll down the Champs Élysées compared to yours." Beyond her, out on the sidewalk, a laughing woman in a tie-dyed sundress holds the hand of a little girl who's jumping to avoid the cracks in the cement. "I think because I was raised by a . . . wintry woman, I wasn't prepared to be the attentive and affectionate mother Caroline needed. It's taken me way too long to figure that out."

Rebekah wheels the Subaru into the small shopping strip where the pharmacy's located. "So, Dare O'Day," she says, easing into a spot, shifting into park, and sliding her aviator sunglasses up into her hair, "how long do you intend to beat yourself up over it?" Tears climb the ladder of my throat. "Dare. Look at me. Screw the past. You've been given another chance with Caroline," she says, at once making the tears descend again.

I set Yoda on the console. "How will I make it up to her?" I wait for Rebekah to channel and quote some Jedi wisdom.

But she puts her warm hand over mine and comes out with the wisdom of Solomon instead. "By faith."

Though Caroline's baby no longer has webbed fingers and toes and is two fruits farther along the size chart (a kumquat now), Griffin still refers to him or her as duckling. I decide to celebrate the progress each of us have made by preparing a special dinner for everyone. I scoot all them all from the kitchen, tie on Caroline's apron, which is more than a tad too small, and chop vegetables for ratatouille, one of the few dishes my friends Lina and Georgie raved over in Foxfield. I'm flipping wall switches to activate the garbage disposal when I realize they don't have one. I stare into the sink full of vegetable peelings and woody stems. "Why the hell don't they have a disposal?" I mutter.

Griffin obviously hears me from the living room. "Dare," he says, amusement in his tone, "you just now noticing we don't have one? You know we compost."

I've instantly plunged from town pariah of Foxfield to the village idiot of Topanga. "Sorry!" I call out. "I forgot."

Griff says, "Just wrap your scraps in one of the newspapers from the pile, and I'll take it to the fridge in the shed." I throw back my head, my mouth falling open, and roll my eyes at the ceiling. *Thank God.* "Thanks, Griff!"

I spy the white paper bag of bread. At least I know I'll hit a home run—I grin at how I'm subconsciously tossing off baseball metaphors—with the special loaf. After years of shopping at Marie Bette Bakery in Foxfield, I know bread. Caroline and I drove out to the Topanga outdoor market that morning. The sexy Frenchman selling bread, in a baker's coat with HENRI ST. MARTIN embroidered on the front pocket, the sleeves rolled up tanned and well-muscled forearms, waxed forth, "I use local flour, giving the loaves a Topanga terroir and this beautiful dark caramelized crust," he said, waving a slim palm over a round loaf.

"*J'en prends deux, s'il vous plait*: I'll take two, please," my daughter said like a shot. The man smiled and loosely bagged the bread, his blue eyes sweeping not over Caroline but me. "Bread buying should be a daily routine, Madame. And you must come every day."

"Many thanks," I said prissily, and handed him cash.

Caroline clutched my arm on the way to the car. "Mom, Henri was into you."

"He was not!"

"He was."

"I know! He *was*. And that double-entendre!"

"OMG," she says. We laugh together, and she locks her arm companionably with mine.

"He's an expat. And about your age."

"I came out here to spend time with you, not to find a man."

"Face it, Mom, you are ripe for romance."

"He did get my attention," I said. "Maybe I'll go back next week and see if he remembers me."

Now in the kitchen, I set a green salad next to a dish of room-temperature butter and the gorgeous bread on the table. Henri. Gelled back gray-streaked dark hair, and a broad insouciant smile. I *could* go back tomorrow . . . ask him to recommend something tasty to spread on the bread. Henri. The way the French pronounce it, Ahn-ree, is so sexy. *Oh, my Lord. Luke Henry. How had the name connection not occurred to me before?*

Miles calls, "Is it ready yet, Granddare?" I press a hand to my chest, take a deep breath.

"Yes. Dinner is served."

When everyone's seated, I bring the casserole of ratatouille and set it on the lazy Susan with a flourish.

"Dare, you've outdone yourself," Rebekah says. "This looks fabulous." The others murmur their agreement. "Now, whose turn is it to ask the blessing?"

"Mine, I think," says Miles, and launches into a lengthy six-year-old discourse on the merits of good food and being thankful for it.

"Jimi," I say when Miles is done, "I love your bow tie. But I'm curious about why you wear it every night, about your tradition."

"Oh, he always wears it," Miles says. His forehead wrinkles. "Why *do* you anyway?" he asks his brother.

Jimi tears off a small piece of bread and butters it without comment.

Rebekah pipes up, "Dare is a journalist, Jimi. And I salute you both for being curious. People who asks questions learn more about the world."

Miles furrows his brow. "What's a jurnolisk?"

"Jour-na-list. It's someone who writes stories for newspapers or magazines."

"Oh."

Jimi swallows his bread and looks up at last. At Parker. His small face wide-eyed and darkening up to his pointy little ears. "Well, last year in first grade, Mrs. Sadler told us about a boy she saw on the news who made bow ties for boy shelter dogs. Male dogs, I mean," he says, flushing again and making a fist on his knee. "Mrs. Sadler said the boy thought that if the dogs looked dapper—she gave us that word for a bonus spelling word."

Mile's interrupts. "D-A-P-P-E-R."

Jimi continues, his voice wobbly, "They had a better chance of getting adopted."

Seated next to him, Parker says, "Hey, big guy, what's all this?" Jimi steps down from his chair and leans into Parker's side. He peeks round at the rest of us and then turns and speaks into Parker's shoulder. "If the dogs looked dapper, they might get picked for adoption." Parker holds the child. The room is silent as glass. Parker looks at Rebekah, who's clutching her napkin between her hands, her eyes enormous.

Jimi speaks. "I always wanted you to be my daddy. Because you're the funniest person ever, and you love baseball. And you have a cool fake eye. Carter at school has two daddies, and Miles and me don't even have one. I thought if I wore my bow tie, you might, you know, want to adopt me."

Parker blindly reaches for Rebekah's hand. Then, "C'mere, Miles," he says. Miles moves to stand on Parker's other side. "I need to ask your mother a question," Parker says with a sniff. He gazes into Rebekah's dark eyes, takes her hand. "I don't have a ring yet, but Rebekah Jackson, I love you. Will you marry me?" The rest of us dissolve into a puddle. Someone wielding a giant mop may have to squelch in and wipe us up before we dissolve through the cracks in the old wood floor. Rebekah softly says, "Yes, I will marry you, Parker Randall. I love you."

Parker kisses her fingers, then looks solemnly at the boys. "Then I will be your daddy forever." Both boys press against his long torso, their narrow backs heaving. "Hey, look at me, fellas." They do. "How 'bout we take a guy trip into Los Angeles and get a matching set of bow ties for the wedding?"

The boys pass fists over their wet eyes and look at each other. "Huzzah!" they say in tandem. Miles bends to look beneath the table, where Lucie stalwartly awaits crumbs. "Can we get a bow tie for Lucie to wear, even though she's a girl dog?"

"Sure we can. Some females wear bow ties anyway."

Rebekah stands. "A wedding. A real wedding," she says, her voice like flannel. Parker scoots the boys from his lap, and she takes their place, sidesaddle.

"*Yes, a real wedding*, for a real bride. A real *beautiful* bride."

Jimi, holding onto the back of the chair, jumps up and down. "We could have it on the baseball diamond!"

Absorbed in Parker's eyes, Rebekah says almost shyly, "Not on the baseball field, but I want to have it here at Crewtopia, under the trees." The sycamores, the sun-dappled yard. I picture her raven-gloss hair in an updo entwined with flowers and in bare feet like Jenny in *Forrest Gump*.

"Whatever you want, my love, you shall have."

"Course, old Griff will have to go with us on the guy trip to get a bow tie 'cause he'll be my best man." Parker looks at Griffin with question marks for eyes.

A sniff from Griff. "You bet."

Rebekah looks at my daughter. "Caroline, will you be my maid of honor?"

"I'd be, well... honored." With a little laugh, she takes a last dab at her eyes with her napkin. Everyone lets out giggles of relief and all together dig into my ratatouille, which is tepid at best. Still, the praise flows. But it's the bread that brings moans of contentment. *Henri.*

Miles suddenly looks at me. "What will Granddare be in the wedding?" I start and stuff another bite of bread in my mouth. *Oh, Lord, don't let me impose in any way.*

Rebekah tilts her head and squints her eyes at me. "I see Granddare as a young, honorary MOB." Though I thought I was done with crying, my nose stings with fresh tears of love.

Jimi pipes up in the nick of time. "Mob? Like for gangsters?" He studies me as though I'm wearing the striped pajamas of the bad guys in cartoons, iron balls chained to my ankles. I feel Caroline's eyes and wish I could turn the clock back two minutes and somehow prevent this moment. Her gaze is maddeningly neutral.

Rebekah swallows a bite of salad. "That's what is called an *acronym*, where letters stand for words. MOB stands for mother of the bride."

"Cool," the boys say again in tandem, and go back to eating as though I'm not visibly trembling.

"Dare's not my mother, though sometimes I wish she could have been. But she's Caro's mother, so she's special." Caroline looks up from her plate and gives me a small closed-lipped smile. Instead of choking on tears, I decide I'll nourish myself on Rebekah's generosity and Caroline's smile of acquiescence, and wash them down with gratitude.

Later that night, Rebekah and the excited boys help me move my things from Parker's room and into theirs. "Are you sure about this, Dare?" she asks.

"Are *you*?"

"Oh, surer than I've ever been about anything."

"Then hurry up and get down that hall. Your man awaits you."

Chapter Twelve

Caroline
2020

Another sun-washed Saturday morning. "Hey, Park, walk with me a minute?" Since the evening of Jimi's revelatory admission and Parker's out-of-left-field proposal to Rebekah, the man has been like a plucked bowstring that never settles.

"Sure," he says, and drops one of the two-by-fours he's using to shore up the bottom of the henhouse. He rubs his hands down the hips of his jeans. We walk beyond the coop and down the brick path toward the garden. A black and yellow fellow, a striped racer, at the edge of the path raises his head, showing us his pink underside and bisects our path with long lunges and quick heaves to the other side. I'm glad I've grown accustomed to our good snakes, but if Mom had seen that one, she'd be running down the LAX tarmac to catch the next plane out.

"Thanks," I say when we reach a verdigris bronze bench we found buried under a pile of rubbish when we claimed the old property. I point at it. "You're benched, Randall."

Parker takes a seat, removes his cap. He looks up at me with a half grin. "Yes, ma'am!"

I sit beside him. "I suppose it will seem like I'm poking my nose into your business, but I need to talk with you about your intentions regarding Rebekah."

"O-kay," he says, drawing out the two syllables.

I shift on the bench to face him. "Let me explain. The boys are out of their minds about finally having a dad. I know you love them, but do you truly love Rebekah? Enough to spend the rest of your life with her? Your proposal was pretty fast. Rebekah's my best friend, and I would never want her hurt."

"I've been nervous about how the rest of you must feel." He leans forward, his elbows on his knees, swings his cap. He gives a mighty sigh, stirring the flowers on the other side of the path. "I don't want this to sound the wrong way, but remember, I met *you* first, before Rebekah came. In the movies, you'd be the director's dream to play the girl-next-door: rosy-cheeked, whip-smart, and kind. And I had a little crush on you."

I cross my arms over my chest. "Oh. Well. That's sweet."

When his cheeks redden, I motion for him to get up. We walk to the chicken coop and enter it together, he with his boards and me to collect the eggs, a task I haven't done since the day Rebekah and I went to Santa Monica. He shoves a board up against the bottom of the henhouse and digs in a front pocket for some nails. "And then Rebekah shows up, and no offense, but she's this goddess. And . . . *exotic* to this white boy from Alabama. He sets the nails down and pulls his shirt away from his back as though the sun's just dialed it up five degrees. "When she told me what happened with the twin's biological father, I realized that her out-of-my-league façade was her way of protecting herself and her children. But damn, when she let me in . . . let me close, I've never felt closer to another human being. And that boho earth mother part of her is so damned sexy. I'm plumb nuts about her."

"I think she feels the same. Rebekah will take as good care of you as she does her sons."

"I promise to tend them well." We smile at each other in the dappled sunlight.

"Here, let me hold the board while you nail it in place."

He wipes his brow on a sleeve. "Thank you, Caroline. For everything."

It seems like Parker's always shoring something up. Today it's my confidence in his intentions toward my best friend. "Thank *you*."

I carry the eggs in the house and set them in the sink. Griff's cutting up fresh fruit, filling the air with citrus and his Griffin smell. I kiss him, and his lips are sticky with pineapple. These days my arousal can get from Mercury to Venus in nothing flat. Rebekah's book says pregnancy sends an extra rush of blood to a woman's vulva. Griff's reorganizing the topsy-turvy cabinet full of mismatched Tupperware. I locate the colander to wash the eggs, but I'm preoccupied with the T of his back and shoulders, his perfect buns. He is as hot as an oven latched for its self-cleaning setting. I breathe a sigh and count the eggs. Seven. My hands still. *But we're going to be a crew of eight as long as Mom's here. C'mon, Caroline, you're acting like Seraphina, superstitious and foolish.* Nevertheless, after washing my hands, I take a quick pinch of salt from our salt box, turn my back to the sink, and toss the salt over my shoulder.

Griffin burps the container of fruit and stows it in the fridge. He tilts his head meaningfully toward the living room where Mom is reading Kate Camillo's *The Miraculous Journey of Edward Tulane* to the boys. "I caught her letting the water run while she was brushing her teeth last week. For like five minutes. I thought you'd talked to her about that. *And* she put the coffee grounds down the sink."

"Griff, she's not going to do everything perfectly overnight."

The boys and Mom walk from the living room. Mile's tone is accusatory. "If you're a jour-no-lisk, how come we never see you writing?"

"Pipsqueak Two, that's a great question. I've really missed my writing . . . but I *have* been making some notes about a story I'm interested in."

Jimi leaps up to smack the kitchen doorjamb with an outstretched palm.

"Stop doing that, please, or you'll leave dirt marks," my mother says. Looking at her, Griff's back and shoulders stiffen as though he's annoyed with her for correcting the boys.

"*All* the kids at school do it."

Miles folds his arms over his chest, taking a rare-for-him smart-ass stance. "Yeah, and they get in trouble for it too. The principal said we couldn't do it anymore."

"Miles can't do it. He's too short," says his beaming, benevolent brother.

"Whether you are capable of accomplishing such an act of dazzling daring," my mother says, "has little to do with the disobedience accompanying it." She bends down to eyeball them. And expels a high-pitched fart.

Jimi howls with glee, "Good one, Granddare!"

My mother sends out a fusillade of sputtering—*Oh, my Lords* and *Oh, I'm so sorrys*—her face violet.

Parker had managed to saunter in just in time to witness the ruckus. "Don't sweat it, Dare," he drawls. "You have fart blanche at Crewtopia."

She stands and straightens her skirt. "I'll have no such thing. That's common and disgusting."

Parker does a prizewinning job of holding back a guffaw. "Well, if you let one slip again, just remember it happens to everyone. In fact—"

"Pipsqueaks to the yard, please," Mom asserts, "but please go get the dog shampoo and a towel from our room first. You're bathing Lucie." She heads out the screen door. The boys exchange a twin-grin and zoom to get the supplies.

The three of us, Parker, Griffin, and I, stand on the porch, watching them unroll the hose and spray the dog down. Parker says of Mom, "She's pretty cute, all prim and proper."

Griff looks at me. "That's one of the things that attracted me to you when we first met. I appreciated that you were ladylike. The way you eat and sit and walk. The way you speak in cursive. It made me feel like swooping you up on a white horse."

"Well, Griff, that is very sweet," I coolly say.

Failing to note my tone, he runs on. "Then there's the badass part of you that turns me—"

In the yard, Miles shouts at Jimi. "My turn now. Move it!" My mother raises a stop-that finger that would rival Seraphina's best.

Oblivious, Parker gives a trio of nods. "You know, *Dare* just may make a decent badass one of these days." Griffin laughs.

When Lucie's clean and shaking rainbows in the sun, the boys are talking a mile a minute. Mom drops the hose and reaches for the towel. Water from the hose streams down the gravel drive. "Dare," Griffin calls, "the water?"

"Oh, sorry! I wanted to wrap Lucie up first." Jimi looks at Griffin and rushes to turn off the spigot.

I've had enough. I speak to Griffin through clenched teeth. "May I see you in our room, please?"

Catching on, he glances back at my mom, then follows me inside to sit on the bed. "Look, Caroline," he says, spreading his hands. "I know what you're going to say. And I'm sorry; I overreacted."

"The hose was left running for fewer than two minutes. Are you *insane*? You embarrassed my mother. She's become the pied piper of Topanga with those boys after living alone for almost ten years. And I believe I can speak for Rebekah when I say she's allowed to correct the boys when they need it, just as the rest of us do. The twins are loving spending time with her, and she's great with them. Remember how all of *us* had to get the community MO down while still being ourselves? We have to give her more time, that's all."

"But *we* were learning to get along as part of a *permanent* arrangement. You still haven't said how long Dare's staying."

Do I want her to stay? "She hasn't said, and I haven't asked. But for the first time, I feel like I'm getting to know my mother. I love having her here."

"Well, that's a good thing, sweetheart." He strokes my hair. "Speaking of mothers. I told mine about the baby."

I jerk my head away, my annoyance flaring again. *"You did?* Why would you do that without *me*?"

"Well, Caroline, my mother called to chat and report on how dad's doing—very well, by the way, since you asked."

"Well, Griffin, I'm sorry, but I've had a little bit on my mind."

"I know you have."

Slightly mollified, I say I'm glad his father's doing well.

"And then she hit me with a barrage of questions about a wedding."

"A wedding? What did you say?"

"I told her the truth. The conversation took a header at that point. I told her we'd talk soon." *At least my mother's not giving us the business about getting married.*

"Hey, remember when I told you about the baby that day at the overlook and you said maybe he or she would help heal the matriarchal detachment curse on my family?"

He purses his lips to one side and slowly nods. "Yeah. I think so."

"Well, maybe that's already happening."

"Baby," he says, tentatively inclining his head to kiss me and rub my tummy, "I'm sorry I upset you. I promise I'll be more tolerant with Dare. Why don't you take a nap before dinner?"

"A toes-up *would* do me good."

"I love you."

"I know," I say. He goes out, shutting the door behind him. I close my eyes, wrap my hands around my now peapod-sized baby, and whisper, "No matter what, I'll never deprive you of a grandmother."

I cajole Mom into the chicken coop and ask her to latch the gate. She stands holding the egg bowl like an altar boy with a vessel and flinching at the chickens as I duck in and out of the henhouse collecting eggs. "Mom, I know it's hard being out of your element. But you're doing great." I place three eggs into the bowl. Mom looks at them and purses her lips. "You're really contributing: shopping and cooking and being so great with the boys. But we want you to be free to be yourself." A hen takes a peck at her driving moc. She glances down at it as though assessing whether or not a scratch will have to be buffed out. "I mean, none of us want you to feel like you have to walk on eggshells." I grin as her eyes dart to the ground beneath her feet and then back up at me. She laughs.

"You know, part of who I am is a writer, and though it took me a minute to realize how much I've missed it, I've started writing again." I hand her the last egg: only four today.

"That's great, Mom! What are you writing?"

"I'm just making notes, brainstorming ideas." I wave her out the gate and latch it behind me. We mount the front steps. "Darling, are you sure you should be handling those... dirty eggs while you're pregnant?'

"After washing the eggs, I'll thoroughly wash my hands, just as I always do. You might want to wash yours too, BTW."

"Caroline, you are. You're funny."

That night, after Mom has read the boys to sleep, she comes outside to find us in our chairs under a sky where only a smattering of the brightest, most determined stars hangs. Parker raises a bottle. "Hey, Dare. Like a glass of wine?"

Mom looks at me. "I love wine, but I'll abstain with Caroline."

In the dim, Griffin peers at the wine in his glass. He tosses the wine over his shoulder into the grass, sets the glass down, and smiles at my mother. "You're exactly right, Dare. I shouldn't drink either while Caroline's on the wagon. Thank you for that. I mean it." He lays his head back and interlocks his hands across his belly like a man at peace.

"Well, you're welcome," she says, smiling and taking the seat on his other side, then asking Rebekah something about a recipe. I grin and poke Griff's knee with a bare toe. He rolls his head along the chairback and gives me for the first time in a long time the smile I fell in love with: the left side of his mouth curling up and then the right before turning into a grin.

Chapter Thirteen

Dare

My phone hasn't rung in a sea turtle's age. I typically text back and forth with Lina, Seraphina, and Georgie. But one morning at ten o'clock, while the crew is working from home, I'm sweeping the front porch and longing for a toad strangler of a day like we had in Virginia to lay the dust when I hear my phone trill from where I left it in the kitchen. It's my *Journal* editor, Carmen DiMora, calling, and I'm glad he's remembered the three-hour time difference between Virginia and California. When he called with the highly anticipated word that I had been absolved of all wrongdoing in the Allie Ahern case—though I was thrilled—he had woken me before the first chicken cheep.

"Dare O'Day, how's the Wild West treating you?" he asks now.

I laugh. "So far the wildest things around here are six-year-old twin boys, but I never know what I might encounter." My eyes fall on the baby-fruit poster. "But big news! My daughter's expecting a baby!"

"That's wonderful. Congratulations. But does that mean I can't inveigle you back to the tame world of Foxfield?" Like the great editor he is, Carmen never wastes time getting to the point. Before I can find my voice, he keeps plunging ahead. "It's time you were back in the office, Dare."

"Actually, I've been thinking of writing remotely, if that's something you would consider. I mean, you could send me assignments. But actually, I'm onto a pretty great human-interest story as it is."

"I'm all ears." Grinning at the thought of Carmen's oversized auricles, I head out to a chair in the front yard. There I spend a half hour describing intentional communities to him and how they've evolved from the hippie communes of the sixties to groups of educated young professionals living together to achieve higher ideals in a family setting.

"I mean, I've been living in one for six weeks. I have a lot of material."

What I *don't* tell him: I've not asked the crew's permission to write the piece.

What I *do* tell him: I'm not sure yet how long I'm staying in the "Wild West."

The scritch-scratch of a ball point—Carmen's a habitual note taker and prolific doodler—ceases. "Sounds like a compelling piece, especially for people back East who aren't likely familiar with the concept. Why don't you get it to me by month's end?"

"Thanks, Carm. Love to Lina."

There's so much sex going on at Crewtopia, I can barely concentrate on my writing. I take my laptop outside a lot. But on one such occasion, Lucie and I walked to the baseball field and stumbled on the sight of Rebekah and Parker getting it on at home plate in a position I didn't stick around long enough to comprehend. Lucie, who, thank God, didn't woof, even tilted her head in a perfect parody of puzzlement. And though I hoped my daughter had grown up without sexual inhibitions, there are enough coos, moans, and guttural cries morning and night behind hers and Griffin's door, it sounds like a live feed from a documentary on the mating habits of land fowl.

When I think about men, my mind pushes Finn (and the men I dated after him) aside and makes straight for Luke, which is weird because, while I spent 168 hours with Luke (we'd done the math while twined around each other in the sleeping bag that last morning in Millimack), I was married to Finn for two whole years. I wonder for about the seven thousandth time what Luke Henry looks like after all these years. If he still has ginger-red hair. On his head.

His chest. Elsewhere. Would Caroline look like him if they stood side by side? When she was born with dark auburn hair and brows to match, those who thought that Finn and I got married *awfully fast* were silenced. I'm not a Facebook person, and if Luke has stayed true to his Anti-Nuke Luke-ness, he's a guy who'd be more into Mideast Peace Accords than GIFS of *The Simpsons* or someone's post of "Happy Birthday to Grandma in Heaven." I wonder if he finished school and has a professional career, as I do.

I've begun dreaming of him more often. He makes cameo scenes where the actor with that part steals not only a scene but an entire film. A couple of years after Finn died and Luke's daughter was learning to walk and talk, I—with all the savvy of a twenty-year-old—hired a shark of a private investigator, the first one listed in the D.C. phone book. "Mr. Henry has spent time in several artsy cities in the Northwest," the gumshoe wrote me after taking my money and a year of my time. I *didn't* take my time firing the dick.

Guilt over not telling Caroline her father could still be alive clutches at the hem of my skirts. Should I try to find him again before telling her? If Luke has died, what would be the point? Caroline and I are finally building a relationship. She has a loving mother who is there for her at last. But shouldn't a relationship be founded on trust? There is so much about me that she doesn't know. So many secrets. Every day I'm with her, I commit the sin of omission.

At forty-five, I'm a rookie Granddare and a soon-to-be biological grandmother. And I'm damned lonely for romance.

Maybe I should hire an Oregon-based detective, one renowned in that area.

Maybe I should pay another visit to the market for some specialty bread.

Two days later, Rebekah, the boys, and I wander the Topanga market stalls in the shade of the big-leaf maples. When my black-mascaraed eyes have located Henri's white coat, my breath catches.

He's offering samples to a bevy of simpering women gathered before his white-tableclothed altar. Rebekah and I purchase jam and honey from other vendors and casually make our way toward Henri's after the women have moved on, laughing, their color high. "

Dare!" Henri says, revealing a white grin. Greeting him, I introduce him to Rebekah and the boys, who stand in front of us, their fingers clutching the edge of the tablecloth at wide-eyed level with Henri's confections. "I'm offering samples of my madeleines and canelés today," he says.

Each of us takes a small piece of the pastries speared with picks. At one taste of the canelé, Rebekah gives me an eyes-to-the-skies-good glance, and I moan. "Hen-ri," I say, drawing his name out, "that's the best thing I've ever tasted. We'd love a dozen, please." I can't help licking my fingers, and I twitch as he notices.

Jimi's face lifts. "But you said we were only coming here to buy that good bread again and not to ask for anything else, Granddare."

Now the only attractive man I've met in Topanga knows I'm a grandmother. I grimace at Jimi, longing to pinch his head off. Blinking, I answer him in the voice of Glenda the Good Witch, "Which of the breads would you like?"

Miles points at an item listed on the menu board. "Isn't this the one we had last time, the five-grain bastard?"

Rebekah looks as if she's swallowed a bone. "That says *bâtard*! And where did you hear that other word?"

"I don't know . . . at school?"

Henri bites one side of his lip. "*Bâtard* is French for a short oval loaf," he says, tracing a finger above the bread to indicate its shape. Just as I was contemplating crawling under the tablecloth, crazed laughter erupts from my mouth. *I can't help it; this is suddenly the funniest thing I've heard in months.*

"Excuse me," I manage, my shoulders still bouncing.

"Miles must take home a *bâtard* today." Henri studies his creations. "And I think Dare must take something sweet to savor." My cheeks aflame, I pull at the neck of my blouse. "I have a little café, Le

Normandie. Would you join me for dinner there on Saturday evening?" *He has a restaurant?*

I'd forgotten Rebekah and the boys are still here until she speaks. "I know it. Le Normandie is one of our hidden gems. But I haven't been there yet."

His eyes troll her long black hair. "You must come another time, Rebekah."

"I will," she says.

"Will you meet me on Saturday, Dare? Allow me to cook for you?"

"Yes, thank you. I'd enjoy that." His face incandesces.

"Bien. Meet me at eight, when my work is finished in the kitchen?"

"You can take my car," Rebekah rushes in before I think of a reason I can't go.

Back at Crewtopia, we're unloading the produce and the goodies from Henri's stand from reusable shopping bags. Jimi is filling Caroline in on the whole shebang. I turn to the sink, rinsing vegetables and hiding my smile. "Go out and play now," Rebekah urges the children, then watches them go.

"Some-body has a da-ate," Caroline says, all singsongy. "And with the hot French baker and restauranteur no less."

"So he has a café. He'll cook for me, and I'll get a fine meal out of it. I mean, not that I don't have fine meals here every day."

"People come from Los Angeles to eat at Le Normandie and the larger, fancier spot down the road from it, Inn of the Seventh Ray. You'll probably see a few celebrities."

I turn to them, drying my hands on a towel. I've reached for a paper towel at least fifty times since I've been there, but paper products are taboo with the crew. I've meant to ask them why bathroom tissue is okay but have kept my mouth shut since the Febreze fiasco. "Oh, my word. How dressed up should I get?"

Both women survey my figure. "An LBD," they say in tandem.

"You think I have a little black dress rolled up in my suitcase ... I mean I had no idea we'd be going anywhere fancy."

Caroline grins. "We'll hop over to Malibu! Make it a girls' trip and find something great to showcase your curves."

She takes my hands and makes me jump up and down with her until the thrill of it trickles from my head all the way to my toes.

Saturday evening, I hand the keys to Rebekah's Subaru over to a hipster valet in front of Le Normandie. Henri seemed eager enough for both of us, so I'm showing up fashionably late in the great dress Caroline and I found. When my daughter came into the dressing room with me, her arms laden with choices, and as casually as if we giggled in dressing rooms all her teenage years, it seemed like the fathomless friction between us was only a bad dream. She turned to the side and gaped at her stomach in the mirror. "Look at this, Mom. I'm showing!"

I smiled, misty-eyed. "You sure are. Finally. And it's lovely. What's the fruit this week?"

"A nectarine. But Griffin hasn't given up on duckling." In the close dressing room, I breathed in the Moroccan oil product in her hair, the decaffeinated coffee from her breath, and remembered the tension-filled day she had picked me up at LAX and driven me to Topanga when I'd been so bossy and uptight. And as I was supposed to be looking in the three-way mirror at the fit of the dress, I couldn't help comparing Caroline's wide-set celadon eyes with my own; her auburn hair, brows, and pert nose with . . . Luke's.

Now I clip along a slate walk to the door of Le Normandie in a pair of heels borrowed from Rebekah. A doorman peers at me through one of those tiny speakeasy doors and opens the big door wide. "Bonsoir, Madame." The aroma of rising dough, tarragon, and chervil rush past my face and into the cooling night. My stomach mumbles.

"Dare!" Henri calls, removing a flapping apron and handing it off to a server. Stepping magisterially through a maze of small tables, he gestures toward a corner one where a single coral rose tilts prettily in an old glass bottle. Reaching me, he takes my shoulders and kisses first one of my cheeks and then the other. Henri's sleek in a dark gray dress shirt, exquisite silk tie, and black slacks. He smells grassy, of vetiver and thyme. My mind turns over, empties like a bucket. I cannot speak until we are seated and a waiter sets a bottle of water and two glasses before us. I drain all of mine. Henri squints at me as though he has mistaken me for his real date while I take a seven-second inhale/exhale.

"Henri, thank you. I felt a little light-headed there for a moment. But I'm happy to be here. Le Normandie is quite lovely."

"Ahh, bien," he says, relaxing in his cane chair. "And you look lovely this evening, just as I imagined." *He's been thinking of me.* I whisk off my shoulder wrap and drape it over the back of my chair. An annoying hanger strap I should have cut off along with the price tag is sticking out of my right armhole. Another server appears, and Henri introduces him as Corban, who so resembles Samantha's boyfriend Smith from *Sex and the City*, he must be an aspiring actor. While the two discuss wine selections, I gingerly tuck the strap inside my bra. I smile at Corban, then watch him saunter away. *Shazam.* I study the low-lit space, feeling as though we're in the north of France. Corban returns with a bottle of wine for Henri's inspection and a basket of warm bread so fragrant it ought to be a felony.

I'm poised to pillage the napkin-covered basket when Henri uncovers it for me. "You must try my new loaf with toasted pumpkin and sesame seeds." He nudges a ramekin of white butter my way. "And my homemade goat butter." I anoint a slice with the butter, take a bite, and close my eyes. *Nom.* "So you are a *grandmere*, Dare. But you cannot be more than forty?"

"Forty-five." I refocus my gaze on his handsome face. "And you are?"

"Ahh, I am just right for you. Thirty-nine." *Thirty*-nine? I take a huge sip of wine, clinking the base of the glass against my bread plate on its way to the tablecloth. I give him a quizzical look. "I'm into older women," he goes on. "They are more independent. Much better in bed. Prudent. And above all, discreet," he says, leaning to lay a slim finger across my lips.

Deciding to ignore his touch and last remarks at least for the present, I tell him about Rebekah's boys but admit that my twenty-seven-year-old daughter is expecting a baby. He seems about as intrigued as if I were extolling the virtues of talc-free face powder, even turning to watch for Corban's approach with our first course: duckling *a la Rouennaise. Is he that insensitive?* I feel slightly queasy as I slide the tines of my fork under the smallest slab of saucy pink meat, Griffin's pet name for the baby in mind. But I'm impressed with the taste—and as I look around at the other patrons heartily digging in—I do as when in Topanga Canyon.

The tables clear the way they do in time lapse photography. I press my tongue against my top teeth to keep from gaping when Ryan Gosling materializes from one dark corner with his gorgeous wife and they take their leave, his hand at the (very) small of her back. I sip my wine, trying to recall her name from the tabloids at the grocery store when Henri takes my hand. "You have such lovely skin, Dare," he says, his eyes moving from my hand up one bare arm and to my neck. "Just as my breads are best with fresh butter, I know your skin would taste delicious with a little of this." He looks pointedly at a new ramekin that Corban has delivered with the salad course. Corban refills my water glass and glides across the small room to wait on two beautiful older women wearing swirly Stevie Nicks layers.

Henri turns my hand over. This is not going to go well. But no one in their right mind would reach for the TV remote or change the channel while his slender fingertip is dipping below the surface of the ramekin and coming up with a dab of butter. He smiles again and spirals the finger around my palm, creating a creamy labyrinth.

The muscles by my mouth jump. *This has to be a joke. It is the most ridiculous and embarrassing thing I've ever experienced.* I look to the table to our right, where a woman is scowling at her husband, and a memory flashes. The scowly faced protestors surrounding my home in Foxfield. I'm feeling now as I had then.

Incredulous. Humiliated.

I didn't stand up to the crazed protestors, only ignored them and gone upstairs, and then let them get away with TP'ing my home. Twice. But since then, I've traveled cross-country with my dog, revived the most important relationship in my life, taken up residence in an intentional community with no paper towels or garbage disposal, knocked the cover loose on a baseball, and become an honorary grandmother. I glance around the now mostly empty cafe, my stomach twisting. Henri's kneading away at my hand like a sourdough. The staff has migrated to the tiny bar area at the back. *Is anyone noticing what's going on? Is this practice a thing with him?* The last patron is one of the women from what had been the table of two across the way. She is either researching a documentary on the craft of seduction by dairy or else waiting. For Henri. She crosses her bronzed legs, leans an elbow on her table, and drinks her wine.

Meanwhile, my date murmurs, "The emotions that crossed your face that day at the market when you tasted my canelé. Oof. I wanted to watch your face as *I* tasted *you*." *My God, the man is a cannibal.* Taking a break, he peeps up at me with those gorgeous eyes. The woman across the room hoots and applauds.

I'm suddenly seething with anger. "Henri? What is the word for *enough* in French?"

He looks up, his lips buttery, his eyes dazed. "Enough? *Suffisant*."

I slip from his grasp and get to my feet. I slide a finger around the edge of the inside of a ramekin, dislodge the entire contents, and smear it down his beautiful tie. Slick hands on the hips of my nice new dress, I puff out my sizeable bosom, cock a hip. and bellow as loud as a Le Havre fish wife. "*Suff-i-sant! This* older woman *is* prudent. She knows better than to stay for one second more of these kinky shenanigans. Your aesthetic is *cheesier* than your camembert." I swoosh my wrap from the back of my chair, collect my clutch, and raise my chin at the woman across the way. "You're up, buttercup!"

Henri regards me mildly and shrugs a shoulder.

I make a grand exit and slam the door of the cafe. In the small lot, Rebekah's little yellow Subaru looks for all the world like Cinderella's expired pumpkin, and I can't wait to crawl inside.

But I turn back.

I slide the little speakeasy window open and call through it. "BTW, this older woman? She's *spectacular* in bed. An independent journalist. Oh, and the heir to the Marston Candy empire."

The next morning, a Saturday, after the others have breakfasted and are at their chores or computers, I pour a monster tumbler of coffee and stroll out to the ballfield. I take a seat on the bench and a long sip of caffeine, remembering what had gone down last night, how Caroline and Rebekah had hooted when I told them about the disaster date. Then I gave myself exactly two minutes to remember how Henri had made me feel. The way he shrugged when I left, as if I were some slut. As though his actions had no consequence. I won't be buying fancy bread at the market again.

Digging my cell from my pocket, I dial the number I found days ago: a private detective of unimpeachable reputation in Salem, Oregon. His name, honest to God, is Samuel Spade. I can't help but picture him as Humphrey Bogart. Listening to the rings on his end, I wonder how often the man is teased with the abbreviated Sam. Detective Spade, as he says he prefers to be addressed, tells me he will be happy to meet with me in Salem on July 3 at nine. A week from tomorrow. His rate is a jolting $450 an hour. But the amount is a drop in the bucket compared to what I'd pay to see Luke Henry again. All I have to offer the detective is a decades earlier physical description: Luke's full name Luke Hollins Henry, and he *may* have been arrested at the Millimack Nuclear Energy Plant at age twenty-one.

Just as I've ended my conversation with Detective Spade, Miles comes trudging out to the field, his legs coltish in a pair of shorts, a partially eaten banana in his hand, the blackening peel draping around his little fist. He reaches the bench, sits, and kicks sulkily at the dirt with the toe of a sneaker. "What's up, Pipsqueak One?"

"I'm Pipsqueak Two," he says sorrowfully. He kicks the dirt again, and a cloud of it roils into the air.

"Oh, my bad. And please don't kick that dirt up again so that it gets on me. It's inconsiderate."

"Well, my brother is inconsiderant."

"Inconsid-er-ate."

He waves away my interruption, my correction. "Jimi broke the Mike Trout bobblehead that Parker bought me when we went to an Angels game." After he tells me about the squabble, I get to the root of his upset: he's worried that Parker likes Jimi better than him. It's as if it's the most important thing in his life, because to him at that moment, it is. I remind him that Rebekah and his father-to-be have a special love in their hearts for both boys. And that feelings of jealousy are natural. He folds his banana peel in a neat package and gives me a small smile. I tip my forehead to his and remind him that I love him and why he is special. Then straightening, the two of us sit side by side, my arm around his thin shoulders.

Neither of us hears Caroline approaching. "Miles," she crisply says, making both Miles and me jump, "will you please go and help Parker with the composting?"

"Oooh, I'll take my banana peel!" And Miles is off like a bowshot.

Caroline takes a seat on the bench, and the look she gives me is like a knuckle to my breastbone.

"I can't believe what I just saw." My hands go numb in my lap. Now it's time to listen to my daughter as if whatever's on her mind is the most important thing ever. Because to her it seems to be.

"What is it Caroline?" I ask, keeping my voice mild.

"Lisette." *Lisette?* Caroline is back on her feet. She spins slowly around, face to the sky, clutching her sweater around her hillock of belly. "Lisette!" she cries. "Why, Mom, why did you send her away?" Though her anguish is a dart to my heart, I sit quietly, waiting. She clenches her fists at her sides. "I saw you place your forehead against

Miles's. Like Lisette used to do with me. She loved me, made me feel important, like I mattered, played games with me, read to me, and took me on adventures in the city."

"Well, that *is* why I hired an au pair," I say gently. "It *was* her job."

"Because you were so devoted to your precious paper, even working late when you didn't have to. I loved Lisette, but you had to make that big scene and send her packing!"

I could never forget going home late from work, dead-dog tired after a grueling meeting with the publisher. I walked into Caroline's room and saw her forehead resting against Lisette's. Nestled like two tulips in a vase. And for the first time, I understood that I'd become like one of those women, a princess or politician, whose nannies raise their children. I stepped into a firing kiln of anger. *Lisette*, I hissed through tick-tight lips, *Get out of this house this instant. Take your things and hail a taxi. I will arrange to have a ticket to Besancon waiting for you at the airport.* Stricken silent, her head low, Lisette rose and crept to her room to pack. I watched through the front window as she flagged a cab and climbed into it with her neat little bags while ten-year-old Caroline howled in her bed. After the harrowing episode, I took a vacation from the paper and apologized to my daughter a million times. And though I spent time with her, that day marked the beginning of the emotional distance between us.

"Caroline, darling. Sit with me?" She does so, sniveling and wiping her nose on the inside of her T-shirt like a child. "I had no idea that hurt still lingered."

"Well, I guess it has. Seeing you with Miles brought it back."

"Caroline, I was jealous of how close you were to Lisette. She had taken my place." The arched brow she gives me puts me in my place. "I know, I know. It was my idea to hire her. My reaction that day was awful, but you know, it was a one-time event. What is it you are so afraid of now, Caroline?"

"I'm afraid of losing it the way you did and that my baby will end up hating me!" *Oh Lord, she hated me?* "What if our relationship ends up the way yours and mine did?"

"Darling, you won't. You live a very different life than I did. And you have Griffin, who will be there to emotionally support both you and your child. I was widowed and lonely. I buried myself in my work. It was what made me feel alive after your fath—after Finn was killed. My mother was a powerful career woman, and I guess I wanted to be one too. But you and the crew have created a life out here of peace and love and understanding. You work, and I'm so proud of your success, but you also make it a priority to spend quality time with this family."

Caroline looks at me, her eyes wary. "What was Taf—your mother like? I mean, when you were little." I pull one leg up and over the bench, straddling it to face my daughter.

"Is this a day for telling family secrets?"

She looks up at the sky, then regards the path back to the house. She blows out a big breath. "I suppose it is."

I release a breath of my own. "Remember the day in your kitchen when you asked me to use your special . . . scrubby?"

"Yeah," she softly says. I remind her of the phobia Taffy had as a young woman and then spill it: my father's sudden defection, the Dorothy costume I stained with chocolate, the way Taft had scrubbed my hands. Caroline, who has been crying soundlessly, reaches for my hand, but then swiftly pulls it back. "So what if it's some genetic defect in the women in our family and history repeats itself?"

"Taft never did anything like that to me again. But it did damage our relationship. I wanted so much to please her. I did everything I could do be the perfect daughter until . . ."

"Until?"

What my daughter doesn't know about the summer of *my* rebellion and the truth of her paternity goes through me, twisting and hurting. Caroline averts her gaze to stare beyond second base, past the manzanillos and the slice of the Santa Monica Mountains the property affords.

"There are secrets even in Griff's pretty-near-perfect family. He told me his mother once backhanded him across the face for mouthing off to her in the car. And his grandfather, a prominent judge, committed suicide. And gosh, look what happened to Rebekah with her parents." She looks me in the eyes and nods. "She told me she told you about it."

I puff up my cheeks with air and slowly let it out. "She did. God bless her. All families have secrets, some uglier and more scandalous than others. I think somewhere along the way, you and I fell into the trap of thinking that we knew each other. Just because we had a long history together didn't mean we knew how each other thought or felt . . . or made sense of the world."

"Acknowledged."

I give her a little smile.

Near the house, Griffin calls out to Rebekah. Caroline says, "You know, Griffin's parents have been disapproving and vocal about us not getting married. I really appreciate how you've respected my choices, even just Griff and me living together. That means a lot."

My heart fills with affirmation. "I try. Get over worrying about being like Taffy or me. You're your own woman. An independent woman. And I'm super proud of you. No parent has or ever will be perfect. But I fully expect you to be a lovely mother."

"Thanks, Mom."

"Caroline, always remember. You have my *hand* and my *ear* whenever you need them."

Chapter Fourteen

Caroline

Mom and I move quietly about Crewtopia. She's extra gentle and considerate with me. She says she wants me to remember my pregnancy as a beautiful time of anticipation and joy. And maybe it's some kind of mommy intuition, but I get the feeling her own pregnancy wasn't a magical time. Maybe she's hoping my experience will make up for that. I wish I could ask her about when she carried me, but with things as chill as they are between us right now, it could be like stepping onto an ice-fringed pond that cracks and submerges the progress we've made. Though she never talks about her husband either, I'm sure she loved Finnegan O'Day. But I get the feeling not passionately. Not the way I love Griffin.

The summer I spent with Taffy, I asked her what my father was like. She told me he was a lovely boy, that his father owned an investment company, and a Finnegan was considered a modest but respectable match for a Marston. She had been pleased with the marriage. Finnegan was a glass-half-full kind of guy, a skilled tennis player who enjoyed poker and whiskey at his club and had a penchant for fancy cars. When I asked Taffy why my parents had married so young, before Mom even started college, she simply answered, *it was time* and changed the subject. I figured Mom must have gotten pregnant. The way Taffy was back then, she probably made them get married to save her own reputation. Mom kept a picture of Finnegan in our house in D.C., not on her bedside table like you see widows do in the movies, but above the fireplace in our formal living room. I'd passed the framed photo a thousand times, but other than recognizing the red hair and fair skin he passed on to me, I felt no affinity with the man on the mantle.

My mind moves away from a past that's irrelevant now and

turns to Griffin. Though he's been annoyed with Mom several times, that happens with most men and their mothers-in-law. And lately, he's been more patient with her. My lover has made me feel even more beautiful and desired since I've been pregnant. And to think there was a time we didn't want children! Our love is deepening, and I get teary every time we make love. This week Griff's duckling is the size of an apple. "A big ol' Crimson King," he said proudly, noting the more pronounced lift of my top and reaching underneath to rub the growing mound of my belly. I can't wait to see the baby's face, what he or she will look like. And to watch Griff as the cutest dad ever.

This morning, Mom has been watering my container garden at the front terrace and stumbling around working out the kinks in the hose. I stand behind the screen door listening to her and Rebekah talk about flowers. Lucie waddles to stand next to me, her over-long nails clicking on the floor. I pick her up for a snuggle. But I pause, my hand on the frame of the screen door, before going out to join them when I hear Mom say my name. "I want to make a significant bouquet for Caroline, one comprised of flowers with distinct meanings." *She's trying so hard.* "Do you know what any of—"

"Ca-ro?" Jimi calls to me from his room. I turn from the door and release Lucie to go play with Miles in the living room. "Yep? What's up, squeak?

"Will you please help me zip up my backpack? I'm taking my baseball card collection to school for show-and-tell, and I can't get the zipper to go all the way up." The singular hiss of the school bus's exhaust brake meets my ears, so I hurry back to his room to help.

"Caro, you're the best," he says, hugging me around the waist. Then he stops and pats my tummy the way he would Lucie's head. "Sorry, little apple baby."

I smile. "You can't hurt the baby with a gentle squeeze." I follow him back to the front hall. Miles and Lucie are tussling on the living room rug, but when we walk past, Miles pops up to scare his brother. Jimi messes up Miles's hair in retaliation. But Miles just slicks it back in a move worthy of a young Elvis Presley. "Au revoir, Monsieur. Cool." I say with a grin.

When I pad back down the hall toward the shower, I do a double take at an unexpected shape inside my room. It can't be Griffin back so soon from a morning surf at Huntington Beach. I step inside. It's not Griff. It's my mother, sitting on the edge of the bed holding something in her hands. She must have come in while I was helping Miles. "Mom?" She jumps, but then slowly lifts her face. On her palms lies *The Language of Flowers*, open to the page where Taffy had penned her note to me.

Oh no. Oh no, no, no. Her hands tremble, and she grips the book. She reads the words aloud. "To my granddaughter gardener Caroline O'Day, for the best summer ever." Chagrin races my veins. "Twenty twelve? The year you were supposed to be at camp with Peach?" Mom's voice is brittle. "You went to Foxfield. And spent the summer with my mother."

"And Seraphina."

"*That,* my dear, is one whale of a secret," she says hotly.

Embarrassed to be confronted, I lift my chin. "Why were you snooping in my room?"

"Rebekah said you had a book about flower meanings on your bedside table. I wanted to look something up."

This isn't about the book; it's about what I did that summer. I sink to the bed, leaving enough room between us for an orca. She stares at the wall. I watch the trembling of her downturned mouth in profile, then note the deepening of her crow's feet, the slight sag of her chin. Suddenly, I feel like shit.

She breaches the silence between us. "I wish you hadn't felt you had to lie to me."

"Well, so do I, *now*. But you and I were always fighting. And I was angry with you for not . . . facilitating a relationship for me with my grandmother when I had so little family. No father. No siblings. Only a short-term au pair. I wanted to see what Taffy was like. And hopefully what made *you* tick."

A tear slips down the cheek I can see, but she flicks it away. "I'm afraid that door swung both ways, Caroline. Taft was a strange bird. She made very little effort to see us either."

"You told me so little about growing up with her. But while I was in Foxfield, she mentioned once being severe with you and how much she regretted it." I sigh. "But regardless of what went down between you, I know I would still have come to love her. Is that selfish? Or didn't I deserve that for myself? She'd become super mellow by that time in her life. She was really cool, chill, and funny. I had the best time with them."

Mom finally turns to look at me. Tears drench her face. I stretch across the bed to reach a box of Kleenex on Griffin's bedside table and hand it to her. "I wish I'd spent time with her then," she says, plucking out a tissue. "I have so many questions. I've lived with Seraphina myself for ten years now. I can't believe she never told me about your visit."

I purse my lips and offer her a gentle shrug. "Blind loyalty?"

"I didn't even know about Mom's cancer until Seraphina called me the next year to tell me she was dying." Mom begins boo-hooing in earnest. I scoot over and slip my arms around her. *I think of the night I found out Taffy smoked bud for her pain. Seraphina didn't come right out and tell me Taffy was dying. But I knew. I could have told my mother. Why didn't I? Was it an immature eighteen-year-old's miscalculation?*

When Mom's crying abates, she blows her nose. I ask her why we didn't have a funeral. "I was mad at you for not having one," I say drearily.

"Remember, you were in the middle of finals. There was no need to call you home. Her wish was cremation and no memorial service. Only to let her ashes blow across her garden."

"I'd have loved to do that. Well, I guess not *with you*. Not at that time, anyway." I give her a rueful smile.

She pats my knee. "Well, guess what? The ashes are still on my mantle in Foxfield. In an old wooden box."

"They are?"

"I tried to spread them three times, but something always stopped me."

Low and deep, I feel a feathery fluttering. *The baby.* "Mom, I just felt the baby move. There it is again! Here, feel." She places a hand over the spot and gives me a happy smile.

It's as if all the clouds blow away.

She tells me I need to rest. I tell her she needs to do the same. Though she's wrecked, I allow her to tuck me in the way she missed doing so many times. She makes for the door, then turns and gives me a look I'm too tired to parse before letting go a big breath, slipping out, and closing the door softly behind her. As I'm drifting off, a pink Post-it catches my eye. It's stuck by one corner to the side of my bedside table, as though it had slipped there and barely managed to hang on. Written in Mom's fine hand are three values, each followed by a dash. Honesty. Forgiveness. Renewal.

Is the honesty about how I lied to her? Does she wonder what happened to the Post-it or been back in here looking for it? If I gave it to her, we'd probably end up rehashing the conversation. I don't think either of us wants that. *The Language of Flowers* is in the exact spot it's been, beneath *What to Expect When You're Expecting*. I pick up Rebecca's book and stick the pink note inside it for a book mark. Maybe Mom looked up the flower meanings online.

The baby flutters again and fills me with hope. No matter our past, I know Mom loves me. I hope she and I can strew Taffy's ashes in the garden. Now that all our family secrets have been outed, we can start over.

I feel like she wants us to be friends, the way she and Taffy never got to be.

I want that too.

So I'm shook to the marrow when I get up the next morning, and she is gone.

Chapter Fifteen

Dare

The next morning, I find Parker up early, drinking coffee on the porch. He is at once so typically receptive and generous with his time, driving Lucie and me to the Amtrak station in Los Angeles before the rest of the crew even stirs. Parker tells me how he had to learn driving all over again after he lost sight in the one eye. He points out the extra-large side-view mirrors he installed on his SUV. And he still doesn't drive at night. But sanguine as ever, this morning he flips on Sirius XM and drums his fingers to the beat of America's "Sister Golden Hair" on the steering wheel. Parker always soothes my jangled nerves. I tell him I'm headed to do some Northwest sightseeing. He flicks me—what is for Parker—a skeptical look, then launches into what he knows about the area from his time of wandering about when his dream career in baseball splintered like an old wooden bat. "It's rustically beautiful, like Cali," he says with a smile, "but different. Course, it's a hiker's paradise. All these incredible geologic formations and the lakes and forests. I mean, Oregon's gorgeous. Whitewater rafting. And on the coast, caves full of sea lions." He shakes his shaggy head. "Portland's a crazy blend of hoity-toity wealthy people and folks who ride bikes nekkid." I crack up. He sips his coffee and tells me about the capital city and commerce of Salem as we pass through Santa Monica.

"What about the art scene?" I ask after we've made the turn onto Interstate 10 toward Union Station. I pluck my iPad from my purse and start typing.

"God. You're such a reporter," Parker says with a grin.

"I just want to remember what you've said." *I am. Such. A reporter.*

"Artsy areas . . . Silverton? Clingman Falls might be your best bet. I spent a couple weeks there. Besides the falls themselves, there's a lit food and wine scene, sculptures, and a shit-ton of galleries." He looks at me. "Knowing you, you'd be stoked about the boutique hotels and shopping." I hoot and poke an elbow into his side. "And the best? No sales tax."

"Nice."

He pauses and finishes his last sips of coffee. I appreciate everything he's told me, but the best thing he said is that he knows me. I feel a flicker of guilt about slipping away but considered it the least complicated way to go. It seems my conversations with Caroline of late have ended in tear fests. If high-wire emotions jeopardize her pregnancy, all the progress we have made could unravel like a seam in one of Rebekah's prize quilts.

When we arrive at Union Station, I give Parker a big hug of thanks and cash for the gas, which he stuffs back at me. I tell him I'll text Caroline from the train and let her know where I'll be.

"Take care, Dare. And enjoy yourself."

"I will." As Parker drives away, I stand with my suitcase in one hand, Lucie's carrier in the other, and the strap of my computer bag hanging from a shoulder, wishing for a moment that this was going to be the kind of trip I've led him to believe. My stomach lurches. *Merde!* Another lie. But one told to protect my daughter. If I find Luke Henry, Caroline and the crew will soon know everything.

I queue up at the tracks with other passengers and wait for the first leg of my mission to find Luke to begin.

Maybe my private eye has already located him.

I hoist myself, Lucie's kennel, and my suitcase up the steel steps of the Coast Starlight on which I've splurged. The trip from LA to Salem is twenty-three hours. And I'll take every measure of comfort I can get. Wine and food await in the car behind mine. My strategy is to explore the Salem area for a few days before my date with destiny, aka, my head-to-head with Sam Spade.

I text Caroline, telling her I'm going to Oregon to do some sightseeing and to give her some space for a week or two. She seems nonplussed, but I tell her not to worry and that I love her. Then I pull my computer out, boot it up, and review my notes on the article I'm writing. But too soon, I'm captivated by the stunning scenery. Missing Caroline already, I feel a tug at my heart as the train crosses the border from California into Oregon. The conductor announces that Clingman Falls is the next stop and that there are thirteen hours to go until we reach Salem. I knew it would be a long ride, but the thought of thirteen more hours suddenly seems interminable. My conversation with Parker that morning raises a supposition in my mind. The Luke Henry I knew wouldn't settle in the capital city. If he had settled in Oregon, it would be in an artsy town. *Clingman Falls.*

An irresistible notion or force majeure propels me to my feet.

I grab up all my items, including Lucie's kennel. She lets out a what-is-happening yip. I bump my way down the aisle, swerving to and fro with the motion of the train. Lucie lets out a yodel of distress. "Shhh, Tootsie Roll, we'll get our bearings in a minute." At the end of the car, I disembark with my entourage of terrier, suitcase, computer bag, and handbag. I stop at an empty bench before springing Lucie from her kennel and settling my baggage around me. I leash and potty my pup, then hold her as I study Yelp for a dog-friendly hotel. "Hundo-P!" I say, like the kids at Crewtopia when I score a small boutique hotel two blocks away.

Instantly, I'm snatched up by more guilt over not telling the twins goodbye. What kind of grandmother, even an honorary one, leaves without saying goodbye? A perfectly imperfect one, I decide, and let myself slip off the hook. Lucie and I make our way to a small station house, where I sweetly tell a surly ticket agent that I'd like to spend a few days in her beautiful town before heading north. She neither smiles nor issues me credit for the aborted leg of the trip to Salem. I'm stuck with forfeiting the price of the ticket, but if it means finding Luke, it will be worth the money. I wrangle a disgruntled Lucie back into her carrier, tossing an appeasing treat from my pocket in after her, and set off down the bustling street. The name of the hotel—to which I'd paid distracted attention on Yelp—is Folly, painted on a navy sign in three-foot-tall white letters: FOLLY.

Folly. Is this a fool's errand?

I begin muttering to myself as I shove my unwieldy load through the revolving door. I mean, there's probably an artsy town behind every rock in Oregon. But why had Parker chosen Clingman Falls to tell me about this morning when he could have described anyplace? And why had I felt the need to get off the train here so strongly? I'm trusting my gut. If the cosmos has aligned and Luke is here, I'll find him.

I'm starving, and Lucie probably is too. I check in, and when I reach a clean and cool room, I dump everything on the bed. I feed my dog, then shower, and change into a linen A-line dress and sandals. I put Lucie to bed in her cozy home, stroll out into the cooling night and down the still-hopping brick street in search of food and drink.

The sun is the top half of a neon orange sphere, dropping behind a fetching brasserie, *Le Petit Chien*: The Little Dog. Another good vibe. From the open yellow door and windows curls a rich aroma that roots me in my tracks, blindsided by the memory of Henri's cafe. And his butter. I run my palm down my dress as though it's still greasy, approach a bored-looking hostess who's picking at her nail polish, and ask for an outdoor table. Strands of twinkle lights celebrate my arrival, coming on one by one as she leads me to a table in the courtyard. Most tables are occupied, people finishing dinner or wine, the laughter and conversation lively. My excitement about the possibility of Luke being near heightens. I rub my hands over the wrought iron tabletop. What if he has sat right here, in this same chair? I'm indulging in a fantasy where a smiling and mature Luke is seated across from me when a young server with tatt sleeves introduces himself as Dalton. Poof! Mature Luke is gone.

I order a vodka martini with a twist. Dalton hands me a menu, from which I instantly choose the mussels in wine and garlic. I'm two martinis in and happily empty plated when he checks on me a final time to chat and work on his tip. The vodka has loosened my tongue. "Have you lived in Clingman Falls long?"

"Just a couple of months."

"Do you know a man named Luke Henry?"

"Luke Henry," he says, peering down and pulling at his goatee. He looks at me again. "No . . . I don't think I've heard that name." *It couldn't have been that easy.*

"Hey, Ruby," Dalton calls to an older server with a silver braid to her waist who's laying out fresh cutlery, "do you know a guy named Luke Henry?"

"Nope." She eyes me. "You a tourist?"

"No. I'm here looking for an old friend."

"Wait," Ruby says. "The Henry part threw me. The only Luke in these parts is known as The Hermit."

Dalton chuckles. "Oh, the old *hermit*. I've heard of him."

The patio wobbles and spins. *Please don't let this be true. Luke, a hermit?*

"Ah, he's not old," Ruby says, surveying me. "He's about her age, I'd guess."

"No offense," Dalton says quickly.

Ruby gives me a level look. "You'd be about as likely to find The Hermit in town as you would Sasquatch. Tourists love juicy legends like that. Hermits are mysterious and intriguing, you know." She rests her hands on the back of the chair opposite me and narrows her eyes. "You sure you're not a tourist?"

I raise my palms. "Truly, I'm not."

Ruby consults her watch and asks Dalton to bring her a beer.

"Add that to my tab, please," I tell him. "And bring me another?" I invite Ruby to join me. She pulls out the chair and sits, letting out a grateful moan at getting off her feet. Dalton returns and puts a new glass directly into my hand. I dunk the lemon peel under with a fingertip and take a sip, sloshing half of it down the front of my dress.

Ruby grabs me a wad of napkins from the dispenser on the table. She sips her beer while I blot at my dress, my mind a tizzy of turbulence. *Calm down and get to the bottom of this thing, Dare.* I take a deep breath. "How long has Luke... The Hermit lived here," I ask, quailing at my use of the appalling title.

She peers at me over the foamy rim of her glass. "Are you some kind of reporter or something?"

I manage a smile. "Not lately."

"What's your name, anyway?"

"I'm sorry. It's Dare." Watching the last couple leave the restaurant, I take a big breath and slowly let it out. "So if Luke's a hermit, he's not married or partnered, right?"

"Now, *that's* a right fair question." Ruby surveys my ringless left hand, and her voice softens. I feel like someone who's sustained a bad ding in her windshield and fears it will send out spiraling cracks at any moment. "I'm not one to gossip, but I don't think The Hermit ever made it to the altar. There's Margaux Chiles, his agent. And if the rumor mill grinds it right, there *might* be something between them."

His agent! Why would a hermit need an agent? "What is Luke's, uh, business?"

She sits back in her chair. "He's an artist," she says as though she's personally responsible for his success. "But only we locals know that."

An artist! My chest fills with a measure of hope.

"So, Dare, you got your mind set on seeing... Luke?"

"Absolutely."

Ruby looks furtively around as if watching for interloping tourists. She puffs out her sizeable chest. "Only we locals know where to find him," she says with a broad wink. "Up near Clingman Falls, down a *posted* private road that takes you up to an old foundry. He claims the foundry as his address. But somewhere beyond that he has a little house." She peers around again, then slows and lowers her voice, like a storyteller who's getting to the best part of her tale. "But *nobody I know* has ever seen it."

Finding myself caught up in Ruby's spell, I match my voice to hers. "How would one go about getting that address?"

Dalton treads over to say he's heading home. Ruby tells him to have a good night and pauses maddeningly until he's strolled halfway down the street. "The Hermit allows our local taxi drivers to bring people he does business with up there on occasion, but *never* tourists." She drains her glass and grins, revealing two gold teeth. "Now, there are two ways you can get yourself up to the foundry: call a taxi—that's Western Taxi, mind you—not an Uber. Those kids come and go with the ski season and don't know squat. *Or,* since you treated me to a beer, *I* could give you directions and you could hike up there." She bends to look under the table at my rose gold Jack Rogers whipstitched sandals. "If I was you, I'd take a taxi."

That night, my sleep is splintered by dreams, images of scary storybook hermits with long beards. Roaring forge fires. Smoke and heat. The tear gas at the Millimack protest. Crewtopia in flames. By five, I'm done with the hard bed and damp and toss-wrinkled sheets. I check the charge on my phone before stepping into a scalding shower. There's a spike in my skull from the martinis and lack of sleep. Before I set off helter-skelter, I decide on breakfast downstairs at the inn. I'll regroup, get a better lay of the land and maybe more information about Luke.

I can't believe that I could be *this close* to seeing Luke after twenty-eight years. The restaurant doesn't open until seven, so I feed Lucie and take her for a walk down Main, a pedestrian-only brick street. The morning is deliciously cool, and I'm glad I brought a sweater. While Lucie indulges in a sniff-o-rama, I stop to admire the arresting array of bronze statues along the sidewalk: a dolphin, a winged gargoyle, a pedestaled pair of kissing lovers, a dancer, graceful with upraised arms, and a grizzly bear at which Lucie gives a menacing growl.

6:30. I take Lucie back up to the room and call Seraphina.

She answers instantly. "WTF, Dare. You woke me up."

"Sorry. So Luke's here! In the Clingman Falls area!"

"No way!"

"Yes way. Can you believe it? But I asked some locals about him last night, and they say he's a *hermit*!"

She softens, rewarding me with a milder response. "A *hermit*?"

"Well, he's apparently an artist who lives up in the mountains near some old foundry, but he doesn't come into town. I just can't wrap my head around him living that way. I had bad dreams all night about dirty old hermits. I'm taking a taxi as far as Clingman Falls today, then walking the rest of the way."

"Maybe Luke just likes his peace and quiet. Now, get yourself to a shop and find something comfortable to wear, nothing prissy. And some sturdy shoes." While it's nice to be known the way Parker knows me, Seraphina knows me a bit *too* well.

"Okay. Am I doing the right thing?"

"I just saw something about this on *Dr. Phil*, I think it was Thursday or maybe Friday. Anyhoo, he said we women owe it to ourselves to be fulfilled, not just as a mother or grandmother or friend but as a woman. Look, it's a miracle you've found where Luke is at all. Dr. Phil would say you have to find out if he was really *the one*. Or else put it to rest. Move on."

"You're right, you're right. And I owe it to Caroline to see if Luke is worthy of a relationship with *her*."

"Besides," Seraphina says with a froggy cackle, "I can't have you living with me the rest of your life."

I laugh. "Right, living with you in *my* house."

"Take care, chica. And keep me posted. Later, gator."

"Thanks, honey. After 'while, crocodile."

People are entering the restaurant now, the older ones with newspapers tucked under their arms and maps in their back pockets, the young ones with their phones. All of them wear the American tourist uniform of shorts, skorts, or jeans and T-shirts, ball caps emblazoned with sports teams from across the country. A red

Alabama cap reminds me of Parker, and I smile to myself. I make a mental note to ask my server about a good shop to find comfort clothes.

Coffee with Advil, grapefruit juice, oatmeal, and an omelet put me right again. My server tells me there's a consignment shop, Re-Threads, just around the corner. I take Lucie out again while waiting for the shop to open and hurry back upstairs to brush my teeth and hair and apply light makeup. I expected Luke to become a teacher or writer, the way he loved books. An artist is somewhere in that realm. *But the town hermit?* I think of the *Outlander* episode where, after the loss of his Claire, gorgeous Jamie Fraser hides out in a cave, growing long greasy hair and beard to match and not speaking to anyone for years. Luke can't have become a hermit because he lost a girl he knew for a scant week. I say a quick prayer that Luke's not become like Jamie.

At Re-Threads, I buy a pair of faded blue jean shorts, a short-sleeved buttoned-down blouse with little blue flowers, and a belt pack for my phone, lipstick, and accessories. The clerk sends me down another block to a shoe store to find thick socks and sturdy sneakers. I'm lacing them up when my phone pulses with a text. *Caroline.*

C: *Good morning, Mom.*

Me: *Good morning from Oregon, darling!*

C: *R U okay? I mean, I've never known you to do something . . . reckless.*

Reckless. One day I'll tell her about the anti-nuclear protest. Hopefully while I'm telling her about her real father, who *cannot* be a dirty hermit.

Me: *I'm great. Just shopped at a consignment store—I know you'll give me points for that—and am headed out sightseeing.*

C: (after a pause) *Hope you'll B back soon.*

I pause, rereading her sentence, my chest warming. She's hoping I'll be back soon. It's the first time in so many years I've heard a trace of need in her voice. With texts, it's hard to get a read on emotion. Is she down on herself because I freaked out about the summer she spent with Taft? Does she believe that's why I left? I take a leap of faith and allow myself to believe she's just missing me.

Me: *Of course I'm coming back. I miss you already. I just thought you could use some space. Got a bee in my bonnet about sightseeing while on the West Coast. How are you feeling?*

C: *Good. And good. I've been sleeping a lot.*

Me: *I remember that overwhelming fatigue when I was carrying you. I'll be in touch soon. Love you.*

C: *Love U too.*

I peer at my phone with tear-clouded eyes and push the red End button. I wipe beneath my eyes, hoping to keep some of my mascara, and finish lacing my sneakers. I think of all the ground I'm about to cover—literally and figuratively—and go back and form double bows. I'm ready to face Anti-Nuke Luke, The Hermit of Clingman Falls.

I call Western Taxi, who sends Ichiro, a man who could talk the ears off a jackrabbit. I decide I'll bail at Clingman Falls after he gives me directions to the old foundry and walk the rest of the way. "Approximately fifty meters past the falls is an unmarked lane on the right," the man says. "You will see a Private: No Trespassing sign nailed to a tree. It is a short walk from there to the foundry. If your friend is not there, his apprentice can help you." I reward Ichiro for that last bit of info with a big tip and climb out of the back seat.

But as he speeds away, the sharp fangs of fear and doubt sink into my brain. I look back. The taxi is still bumping its way down. It would be easy to flag him down, to go back to town and try to get in touch with Luke another way. But no, just no. I had the courage to come all this way by myself from California. I survived the violence of the anti-nuclear power protest and raised his child by myself. This is *my Luke*, hermit or no.

Putting one foot in front of the other, I stride until I hear the rush and roar of Clingman Falls. I stop at a spot along a guardrail where a quartet of tourists have gathered to admire the whitewater cascading like bridal lace veiling columns of black rock. The contrast of the whitewater, black rock, and green, green moss is stunning. I take a picture with my phone and try to text it to Caroline but have no service. I wait until the others have moved on before treading the fifty yards along a rugged road to higher ground and easily spot the private road sign Ichiro described. A puckish wind teases my hair as I tramp along pine straw. Glad I slipped an elastic hairband around one wrist, I put my hair back in a ponytail.

I slow to catch my breath in a wide clearing at the sight of an ordinary-looking industrial building with big barn doors on either end. A newish blue Subaru with balding tires and an older Jeep with immaculate tires are parked in the clearing. Grass tickles the Jeep's hubcaps. Cautiously, I approach the closest door and peek my head around it, my heart booming. Heat rushes out to meet me as though from an oven set at five hundred degrees.

I backpedal. This is no abandoned building where an artist could set up a studio but an active foundry. Does Luke work here to make ends meet? Clutching a splintery wooden crossbeam on the door, I peer around it again. Two men dressed in leather aprons and helmets with face shields hold either end of a pole with a babbling vat of orange hot molten metal inside. Their movements are synchronized as they pour the substance into irregularly shaped containers. Once they've emptied the vat, they step back and lower the apparatus. "Great job, Derrick," says Luke Henry in a voice deeper and more resonant than I remember but with the same inflection, the same tone. *It's him!* "Now grab the tongs and keep them handy, 'cause in these smaller molds, this is going to cool quickly." At once he lifts the helmet and shield from his face. My heart boomerangs in my chest as he shakes out dark ginger curls cut just below his ears and scrubs an arm across his face, dirty not from a hermit's neglect but from work in a hot foundry.

He catches sight of me in the doorway. The space is already cooling along with the metal, so I step just inside, planting my sneakers on concrete. Luke takes a step in my direction, his eyes popping, the corners of his lips rising. He stands looking at me while the other man begins working at the cooling mixture with huge metal tongs.

"Luke?" I say as though talking a jumper off a ledge. "It's Dare. Dare ... Marston."

He removes his gloves one finger at a time without looking at me. I count all ten, my lids stinging with unshed tears. I watch. And wait.

Luke lifts his eyes to mine and slowly ambles toward me at the entrance of the foundry. With arms like a stevedore and bigger shoulders to carry, there's a swagger to his walk. His face is broader, but the freckle patterns are the same, and more of them have shown up to enliven the lines on his mature face. His once-mischievous pert nose has surrendered to gravity, not unlike parts of me. He stops when he is fewer than three feet away. I'm about to ask him if he remembers me when his bottom lip begins to tremble. A single word escapes them. "Dare." He drops his gloves to the floor, moans, and opens his arms wide. I run to him, wanting to leap and wrap my legs around his torso the way I did at Millimack.

Crying now, I try and relax into his arms as, incredibly, tears of his own fall to my neck. He smells of smoke and pine and effort. I never want to let him go. But Derrick calls out. "Luke, these are ready to shape."

I let go first, feeling as though some vital part of me as been surgically removed. Luke bends to pick up his gloves and slaps them against a work pant leg. "Derrick, this is Dare," he says haltingly, as though still brain rattled by my appearance. As though, like mine, his brain is logjammed as it populates with hundreds of unanswered and unexpressed notions.

Derrick removes his face shield, revealing that he is a young black man. "Hello, Dare. Sorry to interrupt, but this process moves *fast*."

Luke looks pointedly at Derrick. "You've been my apprentice over three months now. You've totally got this." He tosses his gloves to him.

Luke guides me out the door and into the clearing. For a moment his hand steals to the small of my back (no longer so small) but then lets it fall, as though it's too soon for such an intimate gesture. After being inside the oppressive heat of the foundry, the fresh air is a bouquet of evergreen with a sprig of snow-fed falls. I breathe deeply and count thirty heartbeats before asking him if he has the time to see me.

He gives me a you've-got-to-be-kidding grin. "Of course I do." Then he gets to it, piercing me with his still bright sherry eyes. "It's still Marston? You aren't married?"

"Actually, it's O'Day. But I was widowed a long time ago."

"Oh, I'm sorry, Dare." He pauses, a mixture of pain and wonder in the eyes that sweep my face. "You're real. But how in the world are you here? What brought you to Clingman Falls?"

I take captive his gaze. Only one answer feels right. "I came for you."

Chapter Sixteen

Dare

Luke and I stand facing each other in the clearing outside the foundry. He surveys his sooty work clothes, the steel toes of his boots. "You should know: I did time in Massachusetts for the protest." My headache starts up again between my eyes. I pinch the bridge of my nose. "When I got out, I tried to find you." He searches my eyes, slowly shakes his head. "Why... *how* could we share all that we did and fail to at least exchange phone numbers?"

"We didn't know it was our last day. I'm so very sorry you were arrested. I wasn't sure if you got out or not. I tried to find you too. But we didn't have cell phones or Facebook, all these things we have now. I'm sure we would have swapped phone numbers if things hadn't ended when they did."

"Oh, Dare, even though we were so young, I had all I dreamed of in a woman with you. And was left with just *nothing*."

Nothing but a daughter.

A white van trundles up the road and pulls behind the other vehicles, kicking dust into the air. Behind the wheel is a blonde. *Margaux? Oh God, why now?* She steps out in painted-on jeans and strides to meet us. Luke shuffles his feet and gives me a sidelong look. "Hello," she says with a magazine smile, and raises her sunglasses into her chic, short haircut.

Luke raises his chin to her, stammers out an introduction, then adds, "Margaux markets and sells my work. And she's a friend, of course." *Of course.*

Margaux puts out a long tapered hand and I give it a shake. "Nice to meet you," we say in tandem. I give her a grimace.

She hands Luke a large sheaf of envelopes. "It's such a beautiful day, I decided to drive up and bring you your contracts." She scans me. "You new in town, Adair?"

"Dare," Luke says firmly. "D-A-R-E."

I grin inside before answering Margaux. I was about to say I'm only here sightseeing when my brain ratchets up the remark. "No, I came to see Luke. I'm living in Cali right now. And Virginia. It's complicated."

She laughs throatily. "Yes, a lot of things are... complicated. Well, nice to meet you again," she says, turning back to her van. "Let me know when you have a chance to look those over, Luke."

"Oh sure. Thanks. See you later."

She drives away, kicking up more poofs of dust. Luke referred to Margaux as a friend in front of me—purposefully, I thought—but I'll get the quickest read in history on that relationship.

Luke tilts his head and smiles at me, his brow furrowing. "California? Virginia? We have to catch up. Will you have dinner with me tonight?"

My spirits soar. Dinner with *Luke*. I open my mouth. Then close it. Open it again. "Where? To be honest, my server at a restaurant last night called you... well, the local hermit. I didn't think you went to town."

Luke throws back his head and laughs with the same cadence and pattern as Caroline's. It's the first stitch in repairing the seam on my time-ripped memories. "I've grown used to being known as The Hermit. I like it. It affords me an extra layer of privacy."

I cross my arms over my chest and look around the clearing. "Are you going to clue me in on why you need such privacy?"

He puts a fingertip beneath my chin, opening the gate for a new slew of memories, and raises my face to his. "I will. Tonight. Let me cook for you in my home."

"Where *is* your home?"

He points to the other side of the clearing and stands close to me, making my pulse pound. "See that green pump house?"

"Ye-es."

"There's a path on the other side of it that takes you up to my home. I use the foundry's address for my snail mail address. For deliveries." Derrick treads out of the foundry, having shed his work clothes and wearing a T-shirt and jeans.

"I'm heading to lunch, Luke."

"Hold up a sec, Derrick? Dare, we'll be done here by five." He frowns and looks back down the road. "Wait, did you *hike* up here?"

"Well, sort of. I cheated and took a taxi as far as Clingman Falls. The driver gave me directions so I could walk the rest of the way."

"Where are you staying?"

"Folly, on Main. I brought my dog with me, Lucie, a little terrier. And I should get back to the hotel and check on her. What time do you want me this evening?"

"If you're ready to head back, Derrick can drive you." Derrick nods his consent. "I'll send a taxi for you this evening. About seven? And bring your pup."

Lucie's been confined so much lately, I leave the kennel in my room, hopeful Luke won't mind her nosing around his home. I stand in front of Folly, holding her leash and waiting for the taxi. A driver pulls to the curb and rolls down the window. He introduces himself as Muhammed. "Ms. O'Day?"

"Yes. You okay with a small dog aboard?"

"Sure. Hop in, small dog." Lucie chuffs and springs from my arms and onto the back seat.

Bob Marley and the Wailers thumps through the speakers as Muhammed takes the road up to the foundry. The ride seems shorter this time because I know where I'm going. *But where will Luke and I go from here?* I fidget, winding Lucie's leash around my hand. *Was I insane making this trip, presenting myself to him like an old box of VCR tapes?*

But I owe it to Caroline. And maybe to myself. Luke had not found me, so I have no alternative: Muhammed must take me to the mountain. I rub

Lucie's head. Too bad I have to call Sam Spade tomorrow and tell him I've cracked his case.

At the thundering falls, my knees tremble. But when I see the water, I sit up and clutch the back of the passenger seat, which reeks of hair oil. "What the—?"

Muhammed chuckles and stops the car. "It's a phenomenon, man. Sometimes when the sun's setting, its rays strike the falls at a perfect angle and turn it into a firefall."

"It's like neon orange!"

"Pretty cool, aye? But it's one of those don't-blink-or-you'll-miss-it things. See there! It's back to white. Firefalls are not even supposed to happen this time of year, come to think of it." He holds tent-fingered hands above his turbaned head and poofs them up, pantomiming his mind blowing.

I sit back as if to better digest what I've seen, "It was like *lava* streaming down." I remember the bucket of molten bronze Luke and Derrick carried today and think of how dangerous things can be beautiful." *Like grizzlies. Or snakes lurking the outskirts of Crewtopia.*

"You timed it just right." At last we make the turn onto the private road that leads to the foundry. "Are you going to see who I think you're going to see?"

"I'm meeting a friend I haven't seen in more than twenty-five years."

He grins again, his eyes widening. "The Hermit. We locals use the term affectionately. He helped put Clingman on the map. He's a good man. And we look out for him."

My stomach executes a somersault. Just who *is* Luke Henry?

Muhammed parks in front of the foundry and blinks the headlights three times. When I get out, he doesn't move until Luke's shadowy figure steps into the clearing. Luke and Muhammed exchange waves before he drives away. Luke smiles as Lucie goes nuts, yodeling and pawing at his shins. I tug her back by her harness. "Sorry about that. Seems she's already taken with you."

"You're a cutie," he says, bending down to pet her. Unlike most people, he doesn't draw his hand back at the appearance of her ear.

Instead he says, "What happened there, little one?" I give him the short version of Lucie's story. "How old is she?"

"Ten, but she still has a lot of puppy in her." Luke smiles and waggles his fingers, inviting me to take his hand, and I'm transported right back to Millimack. To the first time he held my hand when we got off the bus in Boston to meet up with his friends. Zen the Archer. Cricket and the others.

Luke was adorable at twenty-one, but now he's as hot as his foundry. Tonight he smells of soap and clean, warm skin. He's tucked a handsome plaid shirt into a pair of chinos. His rolled-up shirt sleeves reveal not only magnificent forearms but the silky ginger fur I loved to stroke. *Down, girl.*

"There are no lights between here and the house, and the path is zigzagged." He peers down at me in the dim. My breath takes a hike. I'd wondered if I wore the right thing: a black linen dress with a silver statement necklace and black espadrilles. But he rewards me with "You look really beautiful tonight."

"Thank you." After all the zigs and zags and Lucie pulling me off path three times to mark her territory, we reach the house.

I had expected something quaint and cozy, like a hermit crab shell, but I'm unprepared for the rustic grandeur that is Luke's multi-gabled wood home surrounded by a low-slung, natural stone wall. Anticipation rushes along my limbs as he opens an iron gate and we move along a torchlit brick path to the door.

"Luke," I stop and whisper as though entering a cathedral, "this is gorgeous."

"Well, I don't know about gorgeous, but it's built solid and comfortable."

Something in the way he speaks of its solidity with a hint of pride makes me blurt, "Don't tell me you built it."

He grins. "Not by myself. But I helped design it and worked with the construction crew."

"You are a man of limitless talents."

"Most of it's just good old sweat equity. But thank you. That means a lot."

"What's the material?"

"Local red cedar. It's really only a modern cabin." *A cabin.* After The Hermit bit, I'm relieved that Luke lives well. When we step inside, my eyes leapfrog over everything else to an expanse of floor-to-ceiling windows at the opposite end of the wood-ceilinged open space. "What a fab view of the valley you must have in the daytime!"

"Yeah, it's great. The deck gets the morning sun."

He moves through one end of a state-of-the-art kitchen and bar that gobbles up the center of the room. "Feel free to take a look around while I fix us a drink."

"Okay if I let Lucie off her leash? Is there anything she can hurt or get hurt on?"

"Sure. And not a thing." I unclip the leash, and Lucie's off to the races. I turn and survey the front of the space first: bookshelves beneath high arched windows for light; comfy-looking leather chairs and reading lamps tucked into corners. I'm wondering if Margaux had a hand in the decorating when Luke calls, "Hey, I'm making a pitcher of vodka vanilla greyhounds."

Greyhounds? "Did you choose that mindfully in honor of our meet-cute on the bus?"

He laughs. "I'm not that clever. We could have wine or beer or anything else you'd like. I'm a fair mixologist."

"No, the greyhounds sound refreshing. I love grapefruit juice." I turn back to the bookshelves. "Your library! You must have a thousand books."

"I've lost count. But that's a fair guess. And about as many pairs of reading glasses," he says with a rueful chuckle. A thousand books. Like the thousand nights we could have spent together instead of living in parallel universes. At well-placed intervals between books, intriguing pieces of sculpture capture the eye: clay, metal, wire. I watch him pour our drinks.

"Remember what you were reading on the bus?" I ask him.

"Of course. *The Fountainhead.*"

He comes out from the kitchen and places a glass in my hand, the liquid the color of sunrise with a sprig of fresh rosemary. *Wow.*

I grin. "Thanks. Cheers, Anti-Nuke Luke."

"Cheers, Dare the Conqueror." As we tip glasses, he looks into my eyes.

"Did you call me that at the protest?"

"Nope. Just made it up."

"I didn't think I'd forgotten a minute of that week we had together."

"I haven't," he says into my eyes.

I take a sip from my glass. "This is delicious." A silence stretches between us. I wonder if he's thinking of the lovemaking or the exhilarating adventure before everything went wrong. I hope both.

He surveys my long hair and seduces my mouth with eyes that are still clear and bright. My chest fills with fizz. "I've thought of kissing you again all afternoon. May I?" I close my eyes and raise my chin. He takes my upper arms, his touch light. His lips are cool and soft as they press twice firmly before drawing away. At once, I move like a comet right back into Luke Henry's orbit.

He smiles. "I forgot to put some music on." He moves to a stereo system while I sip my drink and continue browsing through the books. *I would love to freelance a features piece for a magazine showcasing Luke's home—the pieces never tell exactly where the homes are—but with his propensity for privacy...* Crosby, Stills, Nash and Young's *Déjà Vu* spills from the speakers. I grin. "I'll drink to that," I say, raising my already empty glass to his.

"Oops." Luke moves back to the bar and brings the pitcher, pours each of us another, and sets the empty pitcher aside.

"Thank you. These are way too good." I scan the bookshelves. "I don't see *The Fountainhead*. I must confess I bought and read it like three or four times. I wanted to read it through your eyes. I thought I could find something of you there." I close my eyes, remembering reading in bed, the paperback propped against my tummy full of Caroline.

"I know what you mean," he says softly, the sun leaving his face. "Unfortunately, it was left in the tent along with all my gear. I do have a hardcover copy," he says, pointing to one of the top shelves. "But you know what? I never read it again." *Like me and Dan Fogelberg.*

The aroma of roasting meat and wine wafts from the kitchen, and my empty stomach grumbles. "Dinner smells divine. What is it?"

He grins and wiggles his brows. "Coq au vin. You like?"

"I love. Can't wait to taste yours." My cheeks heat.

"You haven't seen the rest. But hold on a second. Lu-cie!" He pulls a small bowl from a cabinet and fills it with water from the tap, sets it on the floor. Lucie canters in, her tongue hanging out, and laps greedily from the bowl.

"That's so thoughtful. Thank you."

"No problem." He ushers me to the living/dining area, where two more comfy chairs squat and a sofa faces a massive stone fireplace in which a fire's been laid. Centering the space is an ornate dining table and chairs that would have made Henry VIII burst into song. "Come see the deck. But you won't see much of the view tonight." We set our glasses on the table and then step out French doors onto a terraced deck of blue slate. The town of Clingman is like a smattering of constellations below. But under a sliver of moon, I can make out forest and mountain only in silhouette.

"It's wonderful. I would have my coffee out here every day." The wind rises, bringing fresh pine and fir to my nose and chill to my limbs. I rub at the skin along my arms.

"Nights drop fast up here. Let's go back in and light a fire."

Back inside, I take a seat on the sofa. "How about some wine?" he asks, moving to a rack and selecting a bottle, a Pinot Gris with a colorful label.

"Nice. I *love* Oregon wines. That's what I buy in Virginia." As he opens the bottle and pours two glasses, I breathe deeply, preparing to ask him the questions that have pinged about in my head all day. He sits on the hearth and lights the kindling. Lucie bounds in from her explorations and springs up to sit next to me.

"Luke, what keeps you from going to town?"

He drops the match. His face darts to mine. "Honestly, I don't go to town much because—and this is fucking embarrassing—I'm sort of famous. For my sculpture."

I shake a finger of recognition. "The bronze sculpture along Main Street?"

"Yep. Mine."

"They're incredible! And they're yours?"

"The chamber commissions a new one each year. Tourists come to Clingman to see them. I do small-scale pieces too. Honestly? If I'm spotted, people want to take selfies with me. Margaux runs a studio for my work, sells and ships it all over the world. She's a savvy businessperson, really good at what she does."

"And why don't the locals know you as Luke? Because the server at the restaurant said she didn't know a Luke Henry."

"My *friends* call me Luke." He shrugs a big shoulder. "But to the townspeople, I'm The Hermit or LHH Designs."

LHH Designs. Where have I heard that before? "Well, we have to do what feels right, what makes us feel safe." I survey the room. "And why such a big place for one?"

"When I built it, I thought I might not always live alone. I have friends who come over. We have dinner parties, the occasional game night."

"What are their names?" I ask with intention.

His brows work toward each other. "Well . . . Beck and Julie, Sallie and Max, and Memory and Sean."

"The way you just grouped them . . . does that mean they're all partnered?"

Luke turns to the fire, prods at the logs and brightening embers with an iron poker. "What, are you a psychiatrist now?"

I have to laugh. "No, I'm a journalist."

He freezes, his face a frown. "You're not here to do a story on me?"

"Oh no! Sorry I made you think that. This is personal."

He heaves a sigh. "Well, then, yeah. All my friends are married."

"All but you."

He takes a slug of wine. "Yep. I have all this," he says gesturing at the luxurious cabin. "I'm a forty-five-year-old man without a mate to share my home or feelings. No children to leave what I've built when I'm gone."

I get up, taking my wineglass with me, and move to sit facing him on the hearth. I find a place on the uneven brick to set my glass and take his hands in mine. "You've been lonely a long time."

He stares at me, his lips parting. He nods his head, tears glassing his eyes. I squeeze his hands. He swallows. "I had my books. I had buddies in high school, like Blake. I took girls out to dances and stuff, had sex with some of them. And yes—because I know you're wondering—Margaux and I have had a fling or two. But we're strictly business now. She . . . isn't a kind person at heart." He takes a gulp of wine. "When I started attending those protests, I felt empowered for the first time, part of a group and a cause that was important. I thought I impressed you as a cool hippie dude who would help save the world. But I couldn't even save you. When our hands were wrenched apart and all that . . . toxicity engulfed me, I couldn't even save myself. In one fell swoop, my identity imploded."

A brief shower of anger passes over his face. "All I had to show for that protest was a police record and a persistent case of PTSD. When I got out of jail, I made for my folks' home in Maryland. They were understanding, really good to me. They paid for me to attend counseling. The therapist gave me perspective. She said some people are *born* wired for introversion, and that unless it crippled me from having healthy and nurturing relationships or from supporting myself, it was okay. I had relationships here and there." He looks down at our hands, bounces them on his knees and punctuates his next words. "But the bond I shared with you was the one I ached for, the one that nurtured me." He peers from one of my eyes to the other and back as though making certain he's speaking to my soul. "I'm a man who believes in love at first sight." *Oh, so do I.* "For that week, you were not only my lover but my friend. You sustained me." A flutter moves throughout my body.

But he releases my hands, pushes to stand, and moves to the great windows, his back to me. "I never made it to college. I wandered. Worked construction jobs across the country—always on the lookout for you. I became an apprentice, learned my trade. I became successful. When I landed in Clingman, I felt an inexplicable peace." After a moment, he slowly turns, his eyes as wide as the coasters on the table. "Would it be batshit crazy to think it was because we were *meant* to meet again. Here?"

I stare at him, my heart swelling. I look down, expecting it to part the buttons on my blouse. "It wouldn't be crazy to me." I think of Rebekah. "God moves in mysterious ways." I get to my feet and go to him. Hold him tight. "Luke, I have something else... super important to tell you. I suffered PTSD too after the rally, but my circumstances were a little different," I say, my voice twisting on the last three words. Still holding him, I pull back just enough to capture his gaze. "I had *no choice* but to pull myself together, and fast." His eyes are locked with mine. "Because I was carrying your child."

Disbelief and hope slowly transform his features. "You... were?"

I smile through inchoate tears. "I was."

"We made a baby... on that old sleeping bag? But how—"

"I figure it was the last morning, when you'd run out of condoms." Abruptly, the last of my pent-up emotion breaks free. I begin to sob. I step blindly back and hold my hands over my face. I wanted us to get to know each other before I told him about Caroline.

But Luke pulls my hands free and draws me back to the sofa, plants me there. "Let me get you some water." He dashes to the kitchen. Lucie creeps onto my lap. From the kitchen, glass clinks. Water runs. Luke returns with a pitcher of cold water, two glasses, and a box of Kleenex on a tray. He sits beside me.

I hold a glass in both hands like a child, drink it down. Lucie relocates to the back of the sofa, making a nest there, ears pricked, her eyes on me. I take a tissue, honk through my nose.

Luke pulls me into his big arms, putting his chin over my head until my breathing quiets. He pushes me away from him to look at me, kisses my cheeks, smooths back my hair. He starts to speak, stops, then starts again. "Did you ... keep the baby?" I detect no judgment in his eyes. But his face is painfully naked with hope.

I offer him a tender smile, then shake my head three times in rapid succession. "Her name is Caroline."

He is very still. "I have a daughter."

"You do."

If he's hurt or angry or any of the dozens of things I feared, he doesn't show it. Anti-Nuke Luke is still the poster boy for mellow. "She's ... twenty-seven?"

"And smart and talented and beautiful. And right now she's expecting a surprise baby of her own."

Tears coast his cheeks. He smiles an incredulous smile. "Caroline," he says, tasting her name. He seems to find it sweet. "This is the best secret I've heard in my life. You're a mother." He shakes his head slowly. "So she's married, Caroline?"

"No, but she and her partner Griffin are very much in love." The oven timer shrills. Lucie falls off the back of the sofa and lands on her agile feet, making us laugh a cathartic kind of laugh. "Well, dinner's ready." Luke says.

"You know what? All of a sudden, I'm starved."

"Me too. Do you want to eat in here at the big table?"

"Let's just sit cozy at the bar."

"Come and talk to me while I put a salad together?"

After a delicious dinner of coq au vin, rocket salad, and an apple tart, we are stuffed, but though I'm practically in a stupor, I know he needs to hear more. We take bathroom breaks. When I come out, Luke's back, seated on the hearth. He awakens the fire, the flames highlighting the shades of crimson, coral, and violet in his red hair. He looks up at me, grins and shakes his head again. We move to the sofa and, without words, lie in each other's arms. I bob with the rise and fall of his chest as though on a calm sea.

"Tell me what happened to you after the rally," he says. "I mean, you were still a kid yourself. It must have been so hard."

I speak of my return to D.C. and how, two weeks later, I figured out I was pregnant. Of Taft's reaction and how she lied to her friends, telling them that my good friend Finnegan O'Day and I had been secretly seeing each other for a year. How he stepped up and married me. How he cared for Caroline and me until his deadly crash. The mantle clock reads 12:50. Overcome with fatigue, I ask Luke if we can make coffee. "Of course," he says, getting to his feet. I take another bathroom break, splash my face with water before going back to him.

"Thank you," I say when he hands me a mug. We sip our coffee. Feeling revived, I talk of Caroline's childhood up until she left for college in L.A., where she met Griffin, and how they had formed Crewtopia. A little about the crew. The clock has ticked its way to 1:50.

"When Margaux was here, you said you were living in California and Virginia, that it was complicated."

"It *is* complicated." I humble myself by telling him that my relationship with Caroline has been a rocky one and why. About my relationship with Taft.

He kisses the crown of my head and says into my hair, "I think you're an amazing person."

"Aww, Luke, you're too good, too fine." He asks me to stay in Clingman for a while. "We can get to know each other and figure out how I can meet Caroline."

Shame and regret rush over me like the firefall. I close my eyes. "There's a last secret I have to tell you. And I'd do anything to make it untrue."

"What is it?"

"I haven't found the right time to let her know you exist." His face displays resounding shock. Then it slowly smooths into grace, followed by understanding, though his shoulders have slumped.

"Will you let me help you figure it out?"

I blink and the firefall disappears.

"Yes. How are you so understanding?"

"Because I have faith in you," he says. "Look, we're her parents. We're going to make this right."

When light from the massive expanse of windows finds my face, I open my eyes. Luke's head is still at the opposite end of the sofa as it was when we both floated off, Lucie a black-and-white-spiraled Nautilus on his chest. The clock reads 7:08. I sit up, brushing futilely at the wrinkles in my linen. I gaze at the evergreens and mountains I couldn't make out last night and fill with a bevy of emotions, peace, joy, and hope.

After coffee and croissants, Luke drives me back to my hotel in his Jeep. But when I step out in front of Folly, he turns right and speeds back toward the foundry. I shake my head. It's a paradox that he says he feels at peace in this place.

Could I persuade him to leave it?

How would Luke react to the hive that is Crewtopia? Everyone would be strangers to him at first and would know he can't live in a packed environment. If I stayed on the West Coast, could he leave Oregon and build a house in Topanga? I force myself to toss my premature thoughts aside.

I shower and change clothes for the picnic we've planned to take up beyond Clingman Falls to Wallowa Plateau. Until then, while Luke's working with Derrick, I'll make another trip to Re-Threads, find a toy store to get something for the boys, and pick up a gourmet picnic from Clementine on Second Street that I found on Yelp. I eat a late lunch at a cute sandwich shop with flower-drooling window boxes.

When I step onto the sidewalk again, I look up for the name of the shop next door. LHH DESIGNS: simple gold lettering on a black sign. My breath leaves me. I yank the straw hat I bought at Re-Threads to ride low on my brow and find the gumption to look through the plateglass window. Margaux, in emerald green silk, is talking with a couple. The door is open, and her husky voice floats out. "If you'll excuse me, I'll go in the back and make that call." One of the men says, "That'd be great; take your time."

This is my chance to see Luke's gallery. I hotfoot it inside. The verdigris wall color is the perfect backdrop for Luke's bronzes, pedestaled and labeled with small brass plaques: "The Fir Maiden"; "Oscar's Wild"; "The Hermit," which is a parody of Luke himself looking like Jamie Fraser in the cave. I laugh aloud. The back door opens. I turn and speed it for the sidewalk.

"Who was that?" Margaux asks.

"Probably a tourist."

Back at the hotel, I strip off the clothes I fell asleep in, shower, lie down, and close my eyes. But they pop wide open when something comes to me. In my Foxfield garden is a beautiful piece of bronze statuary I found in Richmond. I was in the city on assignment, and even though it was pouring and I was due at a meeting in twenty minutes, I couldn't resist slipping into a sculpture gallery near the Jefferson Hotel. I wanted something special for the garden. Something lasting that would take on the patina of age.

I shook out my yellow umbrella and leaned it against a geranium-filled urn beside the door. Though I had copper in mind, I was immediately drawn to a couple of unique bronzes. The first was a life-sized figure of a kneeling man, his head thrown back in angst, his arms outstretched as though in supplication. Its emotional quality riveted me. I did a double take at the second piece, my eyes following the stem of a sunflower to its full height of six feet. Its Hula-Hoop-sized face was slightly up-tipped, as though it were early in the day. And my mind was blown. Though the sculpture was way beyond what I wanted to spend, I purchased it on the spot, asking the gallery to ship it to Foxfield. Seraphina and I installed it in the garden. I told her about seeing the sunflower farm on the Greyhound bus when I claimed the flower as my favorite.

Now I frown and fumble for my phone. I place a quick call to her, hoping to catch her at home. I'm in luck. She's sitting on the terrace, drinking a can of her disgusting orange soda. "Hi, Seraphina. Do me a quick favor?"

"I might, chica."

"Please run out to the sunflower sculpture in the garden and tell me what the artist's mark along the stem says."

"Well, now, hold your horses. I have to go in and get my readers."

After ten maddening minutes, she's back and slightly out of breath. I hear her chug at her soda. "It was muddy and I had to brush it off. Got mud on my Keds too." *C'mon, Seraphina!* "But here's all it says: LHH Designs."

As if I'd wandered the Sahara for a month and spotted an oasis: that's how dazzled I am when Luke picks me up for the picnic at 4:30 in front of Folly. From his white grin and glossy red curls to a worn blue T-shirt that reads Protect Our Ocean, to tan shorts with a plethora of pockets, to his ginger-furred legs and running shoes: he's all I ever wanted. I climb into the Jeep, wanting to slip into one of his pockets where I'd be safe forever. Before putting the Jeep in drive, he leans over for a deep kiss. I realize I've forgotten the picnic basket and have to run back up for it on trembly kneed legs.

We drive up to the falls—talking about our lives all the way—and then higher to Wallowa Plateau. The parking lot at the trailhead is empty. "Hopefully, we'll be the only ones up here." His words resound as we set off for a two-mile round-trip walk, Luke carrying the basket and me an extra quilt I borrowed from the hotel closet.

At the meadow, I have to squint at the panorama of wildflowers, the colors almost too much to take in. "I wish I knew more about flowers. Actually, *Caroline* is a gardener. She learned from my mother."

Luke points out the varieties: balsamroot, bachelor buttons, and white yarrow. "Farther ahead are the ones the tourists clamor for." I put my hands over my heart in a can-I-stand-it gesture. I wonder if he brought Margaux here, then decided it didn't matter. We reach the spot he wants to picnic, and I'm truly blown away by the purple lupine and scarlet Indian paintbrush. Luke spreads the quilt in a patch of pink prairie star. We're both starving and dig into the basket, sipping wine and ending the meal with homemade butter mints topped with candied violets.

Luke leans back to rest on one elbow. I look into his eyes and lean down for a kiss. He pulls me down, his lips opening and closing around mine in a way they didn't at his house or in the Jeep. "I want so much to love you again, but I'm intrigued with this older us. I don't want to rush it."

"Me either. But at the same time, I want you *bad*." His mouth forms a grin against mine.

"Oh man." He sits up and offers me a last questioning look. I return it with a wanton smile that sends his fingers for the top button of my blouse. Deftly, he reaches the last one, his eyes never leaving mine. I tug at his shirt, wanting it off. To see and feel his silky chest against mine again. In a minute with wings, we are naked in a meadow—full of bright green wind—that stretches as far as the eye can see. And soon a tangle of limbs and searching fingers, mouths. "I've learned a new trick or two since we were kids," he says, breathing heavily after round one.

I nibble another mint and pass the sweetness from my tongue to his. Slowly, he begins trolling his lips down my body. He looks up at me. "You're still so beautiful, Dare. So authentic . . . and natural. The essence of sexiness." Luke takes his time showing me his tricks. Finally, I'm lying next to him, my breath slowing, his big arms around me, my head resting in the sweet hollow between his chin and chest. A bee with nothing on its mind but nectar buzzes the air.

Abruptly, I raise my head. Fewer than six yards away, a family of white-tail deer: a magnificent buck fronting a blinking doe and spotted fawn nipping at the sea of grasses have paused to study our species. We lie paralyzed with awe until they saunter away with grunts and flicks of their white flags. Rising to a seated position, I watch them go. Luke lifts languid hands to caress my breasts.

"That was amazing. I wish we'd had time to take a picture."

"Sometimes," he says, "your heart clicks the shutter for you." He pulls me to him again. "Dare, I love you."

My heart blossoms, filling my chest. "I love you too."

He looks out where the deer have dwindled to three indistinguishable shapes and speaks with passion. "I have a family now, like that buck. Even though both you and Caroline are strong, independent women, I'd do anything to keep you safe." He gazes across the meadow for a space of time. "Since you told me about her, I confess I've been thinking only about how this affects me. But now that the two of you are finally bonding, what will her finding out about me do to your relationship?"

Though I'd already crossed it a dozen times in my mind, I say, "That's a bridge I'll cross when I come to it." He nods, his face sober.

I look into his eyes, pause, then ask very slowly, "Luke, could you ever leave here?"

"If I did, it would be for you."

I spend another week in Clingman, Lucie and I most days up at Luke's. When we're not making love, he teaches me about metallurgy at the foundry and helps me make a beautiful vase for Caroline. We take long walks, talking and getting to know each other as never before. We play "Tell me something I don't know about you." It's my turn to ask Luke. "Okay. I have an insatiable sweet tooth," he says in answer. "My cleaning lady, Mrs. Fitz, enables me. She tops up my candy jar every other week."

"Where's that jar! I need to inspect it." I fly to his pantry and locate a tin tucked on the top shelf. I hoot when I pull out what's on top: a Taft's Raft Bar.

"Oh no, you can't have that. That's my favorite." He comes for me, grasping and tickling me until I breathlessly hand it over.

There's a smart-ass edge to the brow I lift. "Have you checked the label on those bars?"

He squints at the wrapper. "Marston Candies? You're shitting me! You told me your grandmother's name was Taft... but this means you're a candy heiress." He grins. "Hey, wanna be my sugar mama?"

On July 4, Luke hosts a potluck at his home, introducing me to his small circle of friends, who are nice and fun to be with. Later from the deck, we all watch the pyrotechnic show put on by the Town of Clingman. And much later upstairs in his bedroom, Luke and I make our own fireworks. One night he comes down and spends the night in my bed at Folly, and we enjoy brunch in the restaurant the next morning. A few people smile at him, and fewer whisper a word or two to their companions, but no one interrupts our meal.

My phone nudges me from my pocket. "Oh, a text from Rebekah." My first reaction is that of alarm.

R: *Dare, Caroline's fine, but is spotting. Dr. B put her on bedrest. She & Park were in a car crash and he has broken arm. Can U come back?*

Though a rind of pain has formed around my heart, I answer the only way a mother could: *Will B on next Delta flight. Give C & P my love.*

Chapter Seventeen

Dare

After the flight back to Los Angeles, I blaze with conviction through the automatic doors at LAX. The miasma of heat and pollution is like a carcinogenic cloak after the fresh air of Oregon. I've strapped Lucie's kennel to the top of my rolling suitcase, bulkier now with the things I purchased in Clingman Falls. She watches the hive of activity through the open mesh of the door as if thinking, *This alpha perspective; I'm diggin' it.*

As for *my* current perspective, it has ricocheted from Luke to his daughter. I'm all in for her welfare now and for focusing on what I can do to help at Crewtopia. Lipstickless and unfazed by a coffee spill the size and shape of Florida down the front of my rumpled dress, I consider my transportation options. The taxi line is as long as the drop of Clingman Falls. Where are the freaking Ubers?

A black Jeep slows near a crosswalk and beeps at me. I scowl until the driver rolls down the window. "Dare O'Day! Hey, Dare!" *OMG, it's Griffin!*

"How in the world did you know my arrival time?" I ask after giving him a big hug and we've installed Lucie and my baggage in the back.

His grin starts on the left side and winds up at the right. He replies in the tone of a proper millennial, "Uh, the Delta app?"

"Oh right." I hide my sheepishness by opening the tall bottle of water he's thoughtfully placed in a cupholder for me.

I get to it. "How is Caroline?"

"She's hanging in there," he says, slowly nodding twice. "Miraculously, she came out of the rollover with only a bruised arm and shoulder. But Dr. Bhakta says the placenta is too near the cervix and wants her to stay in bed for a few weeks. Her spotting is lighter and she hasn't had any contractions." He looks at me and smiles. "And our duckling, who is the size of a papaya—is staying put."

"How is . . . are the two of you feeling about the bed rest?" This is Griffin's baby too. I'm grateful for how invested he is in Caroline's care and condition.

He smiles again. "For a couple of liberals, we're glad her doctor is conservative. If it means *months* in bed, we'll deal. Her days are tedious, but Caroline's a trooper." *Had Taffy and Seraphina taught her to be a trooper? Or had I inadvertently made her that way by not always being there for her?*

I shake off my worries and fill my lungs with gratitude. "And Parker. How is he?"

He shakes his head about six times. "The airbag didn't pull any punches. He came away with two shiners and a couple of burns on his face, but it's the arm that has Rebekah popping the top off the pain pills. Luckily, the ER doc said they thought it would heal on its own and shouldn't require surgery, but it's heavily casted."

"Well, I'm ready to help any way I can."

He gives me a side-eyed glance. "There's one thing. Caroline won't let me help her with the bedpan. She says she's afraid it will gross me out and . . . well, you know." A blush scales his neck, his handsome face. "Rebekah's been doing it. But I bet Caroline will let you help."

"Of course. I mean, I changed her diapers, cleaned up after tummy bugs. That's what moms do."

Griff is quiet for a moment. "Caroline's been talking about you."

My circulatory system reverses. "She has?"

"Yeah. Old memories are surfacing." He glances at me. "Maybe because she's pregnant? Like how you read her the *Little Bear* series. Took bubble baths together. How you bought her those animal crackers in the little circus box with the string on it whenever you went to the market. How you loved her."

No sonnet, no symphony, no field of sunflowers could touch me the way Griffin Panakis just did. And he didn't *have* to say it. But he did. I swallow around the lump that's formed in my throat and wrack my brain for a worthy reply.

But at a red light, he turns his full face to me and smiles.

Tell me. Tell me more.

"I feel like she's discovering she needs you. Thank you, Dare."

Chapter Eighteen

Caroline

When you're on bed rest, nothing changes but the hour, the day of the week. I read. Rebekah's *What to Expect When You're Expecting*—with Mom's Post-it as a bookmark—and a few classics that I haven't read in years. I start *Lady Chatterley's Lover*, but even with its archaic language put it down because it got me all aroused. Miles loses a tooth. I phone Seraphina to make me laugh and to hear her call me *cariño*. The baby taps. I nap, though I'm not sleepy and there's *nothing* to make me feel tired. Not even sex. Dr. Bhakta said we can't do it again until I'm thirty-five weeks. The clock ticks. The house ticks. The earth rotates slower.

Mom has been back at Crewtopia long enough that the baby's eggplant sized. Rebekah reports that, though she still hasn't ventured far from the house, she hit the ground running: cooking for everyone, cleaning and organizing, doing the laundry, herding boys and chickens, which she says is about the same thing. She swoops in and out of my room like a barn swallow tending to its young. Every few days, she comes in with blooms cut from my container garden to refresh the ones in the gorgeous bronze vase she bought me in Oregon. I wouldn't be shocked if she poached from her money market fund to buy the vase; it screams artisan crafted. When I took it into my hands, marveling at the fluted top, the verdigris glazing, I dipped my hand into the bottom for a card with the artist's name but came up empty. I asked her the name. Averting her gaze, she tucked in a stray corner of bedsheet. *Oh, an artist in Clingman Falls. There are some great galleries up there.* Now, with as much time as I've had to speculate, I wonder just exactly what she was up to in Oregon. Had she met someone? The sculptor?

Parker is up and around, though, chafing to be shed of his cast and of real help again. To play ball with the boys. He and Rebekah have postponed their wedding until November, when it will be cooler anyway. But they've already met with a lawyer about Parker giving the boys his name, though Jimi and Miles don't know it yet. Griffin set up a workspace in a corner of the living room so as not to disturb me. I dream vivid dreams: of making love with him; of sweet auburn and black-haired babies; of Taffy's garden, the bees carrying buckets of pollen on their legs. When I wake from the garden dreams, I'm swamped with grief, remembering that the baby will never know her great-grandmother.

But the clang of pots and pans in the kitchen makes my heart happy because, like any model prisoner, I know my guards Griff or Mom or Rebekah will soon be bringing me one of my three squares a day. The late August heat wave has the garden bonkers with ripe veggies, and my meals are delicious and nourishing. I ask my loving captors to stay with me while I eat, but they usually have some excuse or another about something that needs to be done. Once a week, the boys pop their heads in my door to report on the size of the baby and likely to make sure I'm still alive. It's as if all of them are conspirators in keeping me sealed in a cube of white peace.

One day when I've had enough—*Suffisant!* as Mom said when she'd stood up to Henri—I call the adults into my room. "I *need* you guys to spend time with me. I'm going *loca*—as Seraphina says—lying here all day by myself. It isn't going to hurt me or the baby, who's obviously healthy because she's kicking like crazy," I say, wincing and nudging at one side of my soccer-ball-sized belly.

Griffin opens his mouth. "But—"

Rebekah cuts him off at the knees. "Caroline knows what's best for her. Pregnancy should be emotionally fulfilling. A fun time." Only I seem to notice the slight shadow that passes over her face. Rebekah's pregnancy had been no Ferris wheel ride. I pull her by the hand to sit on my bed and give her cheek a peck.

My room is colonized.

Rebekah sets up her quilting frame at the foot of the bed and talks to me of babies, her graceful hands in a perpetual and hypnotic motion that lulls me snug and drowsy. Parker calls my bed the mother ship: a place where French documents are translated with Griff propped beside me, working on *his* computer; where the boys lay with their heads on my tummy, singing or telling six-year-old boy jokes to the baby and wriggling with laughter whenever they get a knock of response; where Parker and I sneak in past episodes of *Outlander* on Starz, Parker digging away at the skin beneath his cast with a backscratcher; where Lucie makes herself comfy; where small stains on the bedspread are happy reminders of shared snacks; and where Mom lingers in the doorway.

Now that my spotting has completely stopped, Dr. Bhakta said I can get up to go to the bathroom and take a once-daily shower. Mom found some ceremonial white sage at the market and, with Rebekah's guidance, purified the house, then sprayed the rooms with refreshing rose water. She line dries my pajamas and robe so they feel and smell like sunshine and flowers. She finally understands our aesthetic and seeks to live as one of the crew. But why doesn't she come and sit and talk with me? I wonder if she has forgotten about the Post-it I found and her plan to use it. Is she still smarting about me getting to know Taffy while she never did? Or because she had to cut her sightseeing trip short? *No way* it could be either. Mom is not a shallow or petty person. So I smile at her in the doorway and pretend all is well.

One morning, Rebekah knocks at my half-open door. She steps in, turning back to glance at the hall, then smiles and shakes her head. "Have you noticed Dare's renewed interest in her phone?"

I raise my arms in a stretch. "Of what do you speak, mousekin?"

"She keeps it in a pocket instead of leaving it lying around the way she used to. She giggles like a fourteen-year-old at the screen. Something's sus about that sightseeing trip. She may have found herself a *snack* up there in Oregon."

I raise myself higher on my pillow. "First, gross term to use when we're talking about my mother. Second, how can we find out?" Rebekah cackles and I join in.

A week later, as I lie in bed with my computer, Griff is changing clothes before the chest of drawers. "Your mom's taking a walk on the wild side," he says with a sketchy grin.

"What the *hell*," I say, thinking first of Rebekah's and my conversation and next of the Lou Reed song.

"The wild side of the *garden*. It's nuts, the veggies so heavy with all this heat, they're yanking down the strings you rigged." A memory from Taffy's garden whisks into my head. It was the day she taught me how to construct a string trellis to keep the produce from touching and rotting on the ground. Pulling off his work pants, Griff goes on. "Dare told me to go surfing and said, 'There is a time to reap and a time to sow. I've been reaping long enough.' And the boys can help her since they're on their school break."

I knew Mom had been working in the chicken coop, which in itself is worthy of a lead story, but she's going all the way out to the garden? "Wow . . . I'm so proud of her."

Griffin pulls his surf wear out of the closet and shucks out of his T-shirt and Tommy John underwear. Abruptly, I'm bordering on foaming at the mouth desire. "Oh Lord, Griff, can I just touch you?"

"Not if you don't want to get nailed, you can't. And that, my love, is out of the question." Swiftly, he steps commando into his wet suit, zips it up. "I was heading out to redo the string myself when Dare stopped me."

"I know you thanked her."

"Course I did. Dare's *on it*. She's a lot tougher than I gave her credit for. Do you know she made organic feed for the chickens?"

"What the heck?"

"Yep, the heiress found a recipe online for inexpensive but nutrient-rich feed. If it weren't for the diatomaceous earth ingredient, I'd eat it as trail mix. He perches on the edge of the bed for a moment, hands me a hair band, and softly groans as I take my time drawing his glossy hair into a man bun. "You know, your mom's doing all this for you. She got the big basket from the shed so they can pick the ripe veggies before shoring up the trellis. The boys carried the ladder, one of them on each end. Here," he says, taking his phone and navigating to his photos. "I took a picture for you and Rebekah."

"Oh, how cute! Take more pictures for me, please, so I'm not missing everything."

"I will." He takes my face in his hands and tenderly kisses me and then my belly goodbye.

Later, Rebekah makes Mom and the boys some lunch and then brings me a tray, buzzing about what good work Mom did. The boys finish their lunches first and bound into my room. Rebecca yells from the kitchen, "Do *not* sit on Caro's bed. You're still grimy." They stop as if playing a game of freeze tag and stand next to the bed, recounting for me how slowly Granddare had put her gloved hands into the vines while quizzing them about snakes. "We told her they were more ascared of her than she was of them and that our noise would make them go away anyway," Jimi says. "She was shaking like crazy, climbing the ladder, but we held it tight."

"Yeah," Miles says, "and I told her to think about something fun, something that makes her happy.

"Oh yeah," Jimi chimes in with a grin, "and she said *we* make her happy. Then she put on a brave face—like we do when we get our shots at the doctor's—and got busy. We handed her the string and clippers. We're going back to clean up the tools and put the ladder back in the shed when she finishes lunch."

"Thank you for taking such good care of Granddare."

"Heck," Miles says with a shrug, "we love her." Jimi nods firmly.

"When you've had your baths, get back in here so I can hug on you squeaks."

An hour later, I've finished a translating job and am powering down my computer to do some reading when I hear what sounds like all of hell is exploding up through the ground out back. My uncommonly poised mother is screaming like a girl in a horror movie. The boys are yelling and crying as I've never heard them.

I find myself on my feet at the window, pushing it open, dread lifting the hair from my scalp.

Chapter Nineteen

Dare

Miles asks if we can take Lucie with us to return the tools to the shed. "And *I* get to hold the leash this time," he says to his brother with a six-year-old air of superiority.

Jimi won't be bested. "Big deal."

"Be kind, or go inside and take your baths," I say, hot and bordering on irritability myself. Lucie lets out a low growl.

Jimi studies her. "What is it, girl?" Lucie cocks her head and raises a paw.

Miles follows the dog's curious gaze to Parker's pile of extra boards well beyond the shed. "Rattler," he shrills. The long snake slowly advances, delivering its signature warning like a strand of rosary beads bounced in a hand. My mouth falls open. Miles, with a two-handed grip on the leash, staggers, his feet slipping out from under him. He lands on his bottom with an uumph and squalls. Jimi's eyeballs look ready to tumble from their sockets.

Parker.

He just went into the house. Where is he? I scream his name loud enough to be heard in Sacramento.

The rattler slips from the boards and enters the grass. Both boys are bawling. Lucie turns to snap and bite at her leash, pulling Miles in the snake's direction as though it's her duty to investigate the source of his terror.

Miles digs his bottom and heels into the ground for purchase.

Jimi is at the door of the shed, flinging it open. A scant minute later, he flies out the door, the ax he is forbidden to touch raised above his head, his eyes murderous, snot streaming from his nose.

With my heart knocking furiously against the cage of my chest, I look back at the snake. No more than eight feet away now, the triangular-headed, slit-eyed demon raises its head as though assessing us. Its body slowly rises from the grass, recoiling into the striking position I've seen only TV. *Are you supposed to back away from snakes, or turn and run?* But it's too late now. I sway, my peripheral vision darkening as in vignette. I cannot faint and leave the children to their own devices.

Miles loses his grip on Lucie's leash. He throws back his head and keens at the sky. "Please, God!"

Nearing the snake and sniffing like mad, Lucie does a little jump—four paws off the ground—and abruptly crisscrosses to its right.

Jimi hurls the ax.

Crewtopia seems to hold its breath, the only sound the low scrape of cicadas.

Parker trots from around the house, slip-sliding and clumsily fastening his pants with his good hand. "What the *fuck*? I was in the bathroom."

Jimi falls to his hands and knees, a shiver racking his small body. "Rattlesnake."

Miles roars, "Jimi, get up. Look! You got him!"

Jimi lifts his head. "I did? I hit him?"

Parker grabs a shovel leaning against the shed and stomps through the grass. He gently bunts Lucie back with the side of his shoe. He turns his good eye toward the reptile. "Damn near split its head in two, son."

The twins practically body slam each other in a tight hug, crying their eyes out. As Parker chops at the snake with the shovel, I stumble away, the water of nausea filling my mouth. I swallow it back and inhale sharply, quaking in new places throughout my body. "Did . . . it strike Lucie?"

Parker drops the shovel. He whisks off his shirt, scoops Lucie into his arms, then swaddles her in the shirt. "No, sweetheart. Come here." The boys and I sink to our knees on the ground and gently examine the limp pup. "There's not a mark on her, but she may be in shock."

"Lucie, my little love, you're okay," I softly moan, my tears falling on Parker's shirt.

Parker's throat sounds clogged with tears of his own. "It was a close call... but it's over. Let's keep Lucie swaddled, get her inside where it's cool, and get her some water."

"Caro. We have to go see about Caro," Jimi says.

Caroline. Oh, my fragile child. She has to have heard the chaos. We all turn to look at the house, at her bedroom window, just as her auburn head sinks below the sill. We hurry en masse into the house to see about Caroline. She is the only thing keeping my feet moving. Returning the ax and shovel to the shed, Parker tells the boys he will give them a refresher later about what to do if confronted by a snake. For all their big talk, they are still little boys who were only trying to protect my dog, their dog.

Parker tells the boys to go to the kitchen and get fresh water for Lucie, keeping them busy, I know, until we can get to Caroline. My daughter is a heap on the floor. But she raises herself on her hands, her hair in her face, and asks, "Is everybody okay?" I let out a huge breath. Parker hands Lucie, still wrapped in his shirt, to me. He swiftly picks up Caroline and carries her to the bed. Her pajama bottoms are soaked, and a sad little puddle lies on the floor beneath the window. My heart rate takes off.

"Baby, has your water broken?"

"No, no. I'm okay." Caroline begins to cry but from relief, I think. "I peed my pants. I was hanging onto the windowsill, but I couldn't hang on anymore." She lets out a mirthless laugh. "So much for being a badass."

Each of us murmur our own versions of *it's okay* as the boys enter, Jimi bearing a water bowl. We kick off our shoes and crawl up on the bed to surround Caroline and Lucie—who resembles a burrito supreme—in the middle. Parker takes the water and holds it before the only part of her sticking out, her little black snout. Lucie raises her head, sniffs at it, and lays her head down. She picks it up again and goes for the water with a vengeance. "Not too much all at once," Parker says, handing the bowl back to Jimi. Caroline pulls Lucie close to the side of her belly and strokes her. The five of us, reeking of fear, sweat, and urine, arrange ourselves like cordwood on the king-sized bed. I'm facing my daughter, smoothing her hair, a toasty Jimi at my back. We are like a family on a lifeboat, minus Rebekah and Griffin.

I'll always be a member of this crew. Whether I stay here or not, these are my people.

But before sleep takes me under, I realize my family could never be complete without Luke. I close my eyes, yearning for the surety of his strong and loving arms.

Sometime later, I awake to the sight of Rebekah and Griffin standing just inside the room. "What in God's holy name," Griff whispers. The others rouse and sit up. They begin telling the story to the astonished pair. But Miles is not amongst us. I speak to the burrito, whose tail frees itself from the swaddling and wags twice.

"BRB," I say, untangling myself from the pile of crew. I pad across the hall to the room I share with the boys. Miles lies on his bunk facing the wall, and the memory of the last time I sat here with him flows through my mind. "Milesy love, are you sleeping? Are you okay?" I sit on the edge of his bunk. Slowly, he rolls to face me, his face filthy and stony, his brown eyes dry.

"Is Lucie going to be okay?"

"She drank water, slept, and she just wagged her tail for me. Twice." I stroke his back up and down. "How does that sound to you?"

He closes his eyes, and a single tear leaks from each eye. "Good." Roughly, he brushes them away. "When I met Lucie, I told you I loved her already. I said I would take good care of her." He crooks his elbow across his eyes. "But I let go of her leash."

I pull his arm away from his face, hold his hand. "You held on longer than I could have, bud. The situation was bigger than us, that's all." I decide to let that sink in for a minute, hoping Miles understood the big word *situation* I used. The child remains silent. "Remember the day I thought I lost you at Topanga Days? How bad I felt because I thought I'd let you down? You remember the conversation we had that night, don't you?"

"Yeah." He looks at me and smiles a tiny smile. "It's kind of the same situation, only different, isn't it?"

I grin. "It sure is, smart boy." I get to my feet. "I'll be back in just a sec." I head back into Caroline and Griffin's room, where Rebekah's gathering up the soiled bed linens and Griffin's sitting in a chair, holding Lucie as naturally as I believe he will his newborn.

"Everyone's getting cleaned up," Rebekah says in answer to the question that must show on my face.

"I need to go next," I say with a wry smile. "But may I borrow Lucie first?"

Griffin smiles and hands her over. "I took her out for a pee a few minutes ago. She's a tough little mutt."

I swallow, grateful for this loving man. "Thank you, Griff."

I take Lucie, who does seem fine, and carry her across the hall to Miles. I let her down on his tummy. Her tail is a steady metronome as she licks his dirty face until he giggles and wipes his mouth on his sleeve. "You know what, Granddare? Lucie was protecting me from that snake."

"Yes, she was. Both of you need to rest quietly now." I blow him a kiss and go out, closing the door behind me.

I stand under a stream of tepid water, my thoughts swirling like the dirty water around the drain. Soon Caroline will be off bedrest, and I'll tell her the truth of her paternity. I'm so close to having everything I've ever wanted. My daughter and I are bonding more every day. I've found an extended family. Soon I'll have a grandbaby. And through all the texts and FaceTimings we've exchanged, the new memories from Clingman Falls mixing with the old, I'm falling deeper and deeper in love with Luke. What could breach the sweetness and power of that devouring relationship?

Caroline could.

She could refuse to meet Luke or reject him out of hand. She could be angry enough to send me packing. There are a million flights leaving LAX for the East Coast every day. I could be in tame old Foxfield, skirmishing with Seraphina instead of snakes, before the sun sets on another day. I shampoo my hair, thinking of the *Golden Girls* life I lived there with her. I'd be right back where I started.

I turn off the water and reach for someone's wet towel hanging on the rack. I huff a little laugh at myself, how I freaked out when I first came here about even sharing a *bathroom* with guys I didn't know. I dry myself as best I can, then step from the tub. I pray that it doesn't come down to having to choose between my precious daughter or the love of my life.

Days later at breakfast, Griffin serves us banana pancakes and says he's taking Caroline for her appointment with Dr. Bhakta. Hope zings to my heart. The twins still have a week left of their summer vacation, and Rebekah wants them involved in something creative, perhaps an art project. But the two have another idea. They are co-authoring a book, *The Adventures of Lucie the Wonder Dog*. Chapter two, which they took turns reading to us at dinner last night, is titled "Lucie Takes On the Snake." Rebecca squirmed through the presentation, fearful about Miles and Jimi reliving the event. But after they show us the illustration for chapter two, featuring Lucie wearing a superdog cape, she discusses it with Parker and me after dinner. The consensus is that the writing would be cathartic. After all, the book is about facing fear.

Griffin calls me late morning, so excited I expect him to burst forth in song. He reports they decided against learning the baby's gender. And not only had Dr. B freed Caroline from bed rest, but he was taking her for a fancy lunch date in Los Angeles.

I end the call, grateful that she is physically sound. My mind begins filling in the blanks of the plans I've made for outing my final lie. I hope the truth will prove as cathartic for Caroline as *The Adventures of Lucie the Wonder Dog* has been for the boys.

In the following days, Caroline, round and rosy and happier than I've ever seen her, begins nesting in earnest. She and Griff carve out a niche in a corner of their room big enough for a crib and changing table. I long to buy a French antique cradle for my grandchild, but when Caroline and Griff come home one day with a sweet and simple Moses basket for the child's first months, I'm charmed. Rebekah has been secretly working on a tiny, intricate quilt from the leftover scraps of French chinoiserie fabric that Caroline used to cover the folding screen in her bedroom. She's using that for the top and a soft, soft cotton for the underside. Maybe later Caroline and Griff will allow me to purchase a crib or first bed.

The twins, for whom the baby has been a mere concept all these months, watch Caroline waddle around Crewtopia with eye-popping awe. And by nature of their competitive spirits, they begin a contest on whether the child will be a boy or a girl. They tack a piece of poster board with two columns, one for boy and one for girl, beneath the fruit chart in the kitchen—which reveals the baby's now the size of a cauliflower—and call us all together. They peel off Post-its on which we are to write our names and insist that we stick our notes in the column we think will be the right one.

Caroline, coming in from watering her plants and spreading fresh mulch, grins and says to Miles and Jimi, "What if someone guesses twins like you, but a girl *and* a boy?"

Jimi purses his lips and takes his chin between his first knuckle and thumb. "Well, it's simple . . . then they put their sticky note in the middle!" Caroline laughs, wraps both boys in a squeeze, and pretends to knock their heads together. Jimi hands me a Post-it for the contest. I still, thinking of the other note on which I wrote three values. Though I lost the note, I committed the values to memory. This is the sign I've been waiting for.

It's time the mother came clean with the mother-to-be.

Chapter Twenty

Caroline

Which has been worse during my confinement, not making love with Griffin or not practicing yoga? I swiftly conclude that no sex trumps no yoga, because sex with Griff is not only about the best thing in the world but what made our baby in the first place.

I'm raring to resume yoga. While in bed, I faithfully kept up the deep breathing and meditation part of the practice. But unlike my limbs, the weeks had stretched into months, and my arms and legs pined for the mind-body workout, the strengthening, stretching, and balance poses. I studied prenatal yoga until I could have written an award-winning blog on the subject. This morning, I'm surprising the crew by joining them under the trees.

I stand on the front porch in stretchy spandex, looking down at them in their yoga wear: a goddess bathed in sunrise, a woman making a human, a proud warrior.

Rebekah (clapping): "Woot, woot! You're back! You look so shiny . . . and energized."

Parker: A silent doubtful stare

Griffin (shaking his head): "Oh, Caroline. What about the baby? Are you sure you about this?"

Smiling at each of them in turn as if bestowing blessings, I descend the steps. "Not only am I sure I should be practicing prenatal yoga, but I know how to take care of myself and our baby." Trusting in my man—who supports empowering women—to trust in *me*, I unfurl my mat on Mother Earth and lie back. I roll my head to look at him, and his left-to-right grin sends me his approval. With a happy sigh, I look up into the softly fluttering leaves and begin gentle stretching. After a lovely and successful practice and sweet kisses from Griff, I feel newly minted, ready to enjoy the remaining weeks of my pregnancy.

Mom knocks at the open door of my room that afternoon. I'm finishing up a job at my stand-up desk. "Mind if borrow your vase to refresh your flowers?"

"Aww, you're sweet to keep doing that for me."

She lifts the vase. "I'll be back in a flash."

She returns minutes later, carrying it full of white chrysanthemums. "*How nice.* Those are fun flowers. They remind me of fall back East ... corsages and football games. But where did they come from?"

There is an inscrutable quality to her smile. "I had an errand to run in Santa Monica and bought them specially for you."

"Oh yeah?"

"May I speak with you privately?" she asks, shutting the door.

"Sure. I just need to power down. Have a seat." *What's on her mind?*

Mom sits heavily on my bed. Her hands twist in her lap. I sit sideways at the foot of the bed and face her. "The chrysanthemum symbolizes honesty." *The curious sticky note. The values.*

I grin. "I knew that."

Mom glances at *The Language of Flowers* on my bedside table and smiles thinly. "Touché." She examines her uneven nails, the unprecedented crescents of dirt wedged beneath a thumb and forefinger. Dare O'Day gardening and surviving encounters with snakes. What a long way she's come. *But for the love of God, say what you need to say.*

"The truth, when it comes to our family, is a machine whose gears have a hard time meshing. There's still one last untruth I have to make right."

This has to be about meeting a guy in Oregon. "Why don't you start by telling me about the vase," I say, admiring it anew on my bedside table. "And your trip to Oregon," I add. "Rebekah and I are dead from speculation."

Mom releases a ponderous sigh and crosses her legs. "I'm afraid I need to start a little earlier than that. To 1993, actually." *The year before I was born?* The baby cartwheels.

"When I was eighteen, after high school graduation, I sneaked off. Like you did at that age. But my motives were far less noble. I was hell-bent on rebellion."

I fail to stifle a grin. "Mom! What did you do?"

"My friend Tricia and I were bored stiff that summer. She was jonesing on this pretty boy from our class. All those guys were the same, aspiring frat boys. I didn't know what my type was, but none of them were what I longed for. Taft was set on me being a sorority girl at UVA. Tricia and I received an invitation for a week-long beach party on Nag's Head with the Tri Delts. But before we committed, I found this poster advertising a nuclear energy protest."

My mother a protestor? I look at her as though I've never known her. "You're kidding. What happened?"

"We told our parents we were going to that beach party but took a Greyhound bus from D.C. to Millimack, Massachusetts." She gives her head a shake. "Man, did we have our eyes opened for the first time." Then she smiles softly. "But on the last leg of the trip up, I met the guy of my dreams."

I clap. "Finnegan O'Day! My father. You got pregnant! *That's* why you had me so young. This explains so much. Why did you never tell me?" Mom closes her eyes and pinches the bridge of her nose like she has a brain freeze.

Watching her, I begin sensing that this tête-à-tête isn't a guilty confession about her time as an anarchist, and my heart slips a notch. "Mom?"

She opens her eyes, and her bottom lip begins to tremble. "No, Caroline. It was Luke Henry. Nicknamed Anti-Nuke Luke because of his involvement in other protests. He was twenty-one and didn't go to college but was really well-read." She stares somewhere into middle distance. "He was *gorgeous* with this copper thatch of hair and all swole or whatever the latest word for buff is now, big and strong and sexy. To make a long story short, we spent six nights in a tent together, exchanging everything except our contact information."

"Wow," I only say, too smacked about having this type of conversation with my mother for her last words to sink in. But then they do. "Wait. Wait! You got pregnant then?" I'm on my feet. I push up the sleeves of a hoodie that no longer meets around me and twist my loose hair into a topknot—nothing gets in the way of what's going down here. I shake my head. "Are you freaking telling me that this swole anti-nuke person was *my father*?" Knuckles rap on the door, Griffin's three sets of three knock pattern.

"Hey, baby," he says, and opens the door. He regards my face. "I'm interrupting. It can totally wait." He steps back, pursing his lips at me, his eyes asking whether or not he should stay. A mischievous brown face slides between Griffin's knees to see inside the room. Miles. "Hey, Caro, guess what? We got five votes for a—"

Griffin plops a hand over the top of Mile's head and propels him back into the hall. "Not now, buddy."

I look at Griff. "See you in a bit," I say evenly. My glance darts the room before settling on my desk chair. I move to sit there, putting the desk between Mom and me. I cross my arms. "Yes? You were telling me that my life has been one big lie?"

"Only in the sense of your paternity. Luke is your biological father."

"Wait." I slap my palms on the desk and get up again. "He's alive? You skulked away and found this guy in Oregon," I say, putting a nasty, sarcastic spin on my words. She doubles over as if the breath has been knocked out of her and gasps for air for a moment. "How—"

She sits tall, though it seems a great effort. "Rebekah noticed your constant texting. We figured you'd met *someone* up there." I nod my head about five times. "And I kept wondering why you randomly chose southern Oregon for sightseeing. And the vase." I turn and glare at it. "*He* was the sculptor. Wasn't he?" I want to hurl the vase of honesty flowers out the window, so far that they roll down the driveway and into the road and get flattened by a log truck.

"Yes. I found him and I told him all about you."

I'm momentarily diverted. "You did?" *He didn't know about me before? Do I look like him? Was he interested in me? Oh, my God. How could she do this to me?* "What did he say?"

"Well, lots of things. I told him everything about your life and what a wonderful woman you've become. He wants . . . we want you to meet him."

The fingers of my right hand find a hole in the pocket. I stretch it wider, popping threads, tearing the seam open. "Oh-ho-no. No. No way." The scent of the chrysanthemums has surpassed cloying, expanding like a noxious gas to fill the corners of the room. I stump to the window and open it wide. I turn to her, my breathing ragged. "Are you really that crazy about this guy?"

Tight-lipped, she nods. "Yes." At the crack of a bat, we both glance out the window. *This is so hard. The crew has been my family for years. They were here for me when Mom wasn't. This is the happiest home I've known. Why can't things go back to the way they were before Mom came and this father farce fell on me like a house? Though I don't remember Finnegan O'Day, he was a presence in my childhood fantasies, looking lovingly down at me from heaven.* Friction builds between my past hurts and my reckless pride. Abruptly, I'm like the kid Drew Barrymore played in the movie *Firestarter*, as though through sheer will, I could implode anything in my path.

Chapter Twenty-One

Dare

When Caroline storms out, I lie curled on her bed, praying that the little one curled in her tummy is sweetly unaware of her mother's turmoil. When I hear familiar crew noises approaching the house, I jump up and dart across the hall to the room I share with the twins. I close the door, slip beneath my covers, and pull the covers over my head. The boys' sweaty puppy smell wafts into the room before they do. Jimi speaks first, "Hey, Granddare! You missed—"

"Shush, numb nuts," Miles whispers. "Can't you tell she's taking a nap?"

Jimi murmurs, "I'm telling Mom you called me that. Let Lucie down so she can nap with her." Lucie sniffs around my head. The boys go out, closing the door. I draw back the covers and allow the pup to burrow in. I stare at the coarse ceiling and the tears flow. How could I have been so selfish? Caroline should be enjoying her third trimester, in love with her man and in love with their baby. Why hadn't I waited until after the baby was born to tell her about Luke?

When my eyes feel as though fifty-cent pieces lay on my lids, I force myself to sit up. I'm so embarrassed about upsetting Caroline, I have to look busy if someone comes in. I gather my laptop and charging cord from my bedside drawer and plug in. I spend an hour on the piece I'm writing on intentional communities. Though right now, I feel as much zeal for the subject as I do for reciprocity theorems. I screw up the courage to email Luke. There's too much to text, and there's no way I'd call him. There are six pairs of ears in this house, two of them as sharp as aged cheddar.

I open my Gmail and take a deep breath.

Darling Luke,

I miss you so very much. Remember I decided to tell Caroline the truth about you when she was off bed rest and strong? Well, the time came. She's up, even practicing prenatal yoga. So this afternoon—

Just when I thought I'd experienced enough shock today for the rest of my life, Caroline sticks her head in the door. With shaking hands, I close the computer lid. Jimi crowds in behind Caroline. "Hey Granddare, may I please take Lucie outside?"

"Yes, please."

Lucie springs to the floor and trots out without a backward glance.

Is *Caroline* as eager to be shed of me?

But she stands at the foot of my bed, shifting feet and avoiding my eyes.

"Won't you sit down and get off your feet?" I ask. I draw my knees up, sit taller, and Caroline sits on the end of the bed.

"We're having a cookout tonight. Everyone's out front getting ready."

"Do all of them want to send me out on an ice floe for upsetting you?"

Caroline looks at me so intently, no doubt taking in my swollen eyes, that I flinch. "Nobody knows about our conversation, Mom. I only told Griff that I needed some me time. I took *all* of the laundry out to the shed and sat on the floor while it washed and dried."

"On the floor! That's no comfortable posture for a pregnant woman."

"I'm perfectly fine. I sat on a towel. It was actually very cathartic. Watching the suds lap away at the glass door and meditating to the rhythmic drift and fall of sheets in the dryer. It helped cleanse my anger. There may still be a little behind my ears or between my toes. But laundry therapy. It could be a thing."

What did she think about? "Your meditation," I say delicately. "Did you—"

"I'm sorry I acted like such a brat."

I release a pent-up breath. "Well, the fault is mine for . . . shaking your very foundation. But all pregnant women experience roller-coaster emotions. Having this baby is a huge transition in your life. Transitions are stressful." I flap a casual hand. "Of course, you read that in Rebecca's book."

She nods brusquely. "I want you to tell me about my father." *Luke?* "About Finnegan O'Day." *Okay, it's a start, a healthy sign, I think.*

"Finn O'Day was a dear friend. He and another boy hung out with Tricia and me in high school. He was Irish through and through, and so handsome. Though second generation, he still had that cool lilt from his parents, know what I mean?" She nods and sticks out her chin like *go on*. "He loved to drive fast. His family had plenty of money and he was an only child, so his first car was a Saab 9000 Turbo. Late one night senior year, he drove the beltway at a hundred miles an hour. I don't know why it surprised me when a car wreck is what ended his life."

"But it wasn't suicide," Caroline states, her light green eyes beseeching mine.

"Most definitely not." She closes her eyes, gives a firm nod. "One night we did donuts around Dupont Circle, Trish and me screaming with laughter." I am lost in reverie for a moment, reflecting. "Those crazy times with Finn must have left me predisposed to grasp for the gold ring of that protest pamphlet, rebel against Taft. But if I hadn't gone to the rally, I'd never have met Luke . . . never have had you."

Caroline seems not so much to be looking at me as through me.

I need to see her smile again. "Finn was a happy boy and a happy-go-lucky man. He was super smart. Top marks came naturally for him. He didn't care about accolades." Caroline smiles a little, encouraging me to keep going in this vein. "Let's see, his favorite band was the Rolling Stones. He always had them cranked up. He dated rich girls, who fawned all over him. Slept with most of them but didn't fall in love. Sorry, if that's TMI, but you *are* over twenty-one. Some nights after his dates, he would climb a woodpile rack behind Taffy's house and sneak up to my window. I'd lie on my side in bed, listening to him talk about anything and everything while he sat astride the windowsill, smoking cigarettes and blowing these perfect smoke rings out into the darkness."

Those words have just passed my lips when the odor of charcoal drifts under the door, reminding me how long we've been talking and wondering which of the crew will come looking for us first.

Though Caroline's nostrils flare, she seems locked into her thoughts. "Was *he* in love with *you*?"

I look at her, and my lips tremble into a smile. "He must have been." Caroline shifts and nudges at her lower back. I grab my second pillow, and she pushes it behind her back. "Ahh. Thanks. Go on."

"When Tricia and I got back from the rally, I was sick at heart about the trauma of it all. I could have used a dose of Taffy's love, though she was as stoic as ever. When we learned I was pregnant, her main concern was the family reputation."

"I'm sorry I never knew about those hurts. I feel for you. I know you would have been loving if that had happened to me."

I go on, my nose stinging with hopeful tears. "When I told Finn I was pregnant and Taffy's desperation grew, he asked me to marry him." I shrug and take some deep breaths. "Naturally, we had a lavish church wedding. Finn looked incredible in a dove grey tuxedo." I smile at the memory. "When you were born, he was the proudest father you ever saw. He paraded you around in your stroller, singing 'Dance Little Sister' and 'She's A Rainbow,' Stones songs in his Irish tenor." Caroline grins a little. "He taught you to play peekaboo and patty-cake. You laughed aloud at three months. When you started walking the next spring, we held your hands on either side and ambled around the Cherry Blossom Tidal Basin."

"So he really loved me."

"He *really* loved you." Now we're both crying. I snatch tissues from the box on my bedside table. Pile them on the bed. "If the first two years of a person's life counts, and I believe it does, maybe it was Finn who made you the loving person you are."

Caroline blows her nose. "I think it was both of you together," she says, zinging a valentine to my heart. "It's weird how the three of us—I mean Taffy, you, and me—grew up without fathers. At least mine wasn't a sticky-fingered bastard." We both laugh at that and exchange a little fist bump. "Wonder . . . if in my later years, things would have been better between you and me, if Finn had lived."

"That we'll never know."

"I was pretty much a little bitch to you."

My face pings to hers. "None of how things were between us was your fault. The . . . tenor of a mother-daughter relationship depends on the mother's ability to grow and change with the relationship. It's the mother's burden to make sure it happens."

"Taffy didn't teach you that."

"No, she didn't." I twist a tissue around a finger, pulling it tight. "I learned it the hard way. I think every mother hopes her children will do her one better. And you have, Caroline. You've one-upped both Taffy and me. We didn't know we had it in us to nurture until we were middle-aged." I give her time for that to sink in.

"You are a good mom. And you'll be the best grandmother. The twins think you flung the stars."

I gulp, trying to hold in a freshet of tears but lose it at her next words.

"I bet that's part of what . . . Luke . . . finds attractive about you." As I boo-hoo, she curls around her baby and lies down, her head resting on my thigh. "The photo of Finn on the mantle in D.C.," she says, her voice muffled by blanket. "Do you still have it?"

"It's in a dresser in Foxfield. Would you like to have it?"

"I would."

"I'll mail it to you when I go home."

Caroline slowly rolls back onto one elbow, her eyes wet lashed and wide. "Are you going home to Foxfield, Mom? I mean for good?"

If she only knew the complexity, the despair of my situation.

The front door slams, ushering in a battalion of words, the aroma of grilled beef. Footsteps squeak along the old hall floor.

I sit up and swing my legs over the side of the bed. I capture Caroline's eyes. "I need you to meet Luke before I can answer that question."

A week later, Caroline still hasn't responded to me about meeting Luke. I added nothing more to what had essentially been an ultimatum and left it to her to draw her own conclusions. She has been pleasant with me, though very quiet, spending much of her time on a painting project with Griffin. The two are giving their bedroom a fresh coat, using a gender-neutral-colored water-based paint, Caroline wearing a mask and gloves just to be sure. Parker rigged his big box fan in the windowsill to push the air out. Rebekah and I love the "Intimate White that is the perfect combination of sweet and chic," as the source read. The shade works beautifully with the chinoiseries on both the cradle quilt and their work screen. At first, Griffin had smirked at the color description with the kitchen poster in mind: now Team Boy: 5, Team Girl: 2. But as the paint dried, he agrees it's a great color.

At Caroline's next doctor visit, Dr. B suggests that she interview midwives in case of emergency. She hands her the card of a woman who lives in the Topanga area. One afternoon, Rebekah—who, it turns out, is already acquainted with Kristie Johnson—invites her to come for tea. Kristie's recommendations are glowing. "It's *fantastic* that you're practicing prenatal yoga," she says to Caroline, "because of the minute-to-minute changes that happen during delivery. Labor's unpredictable, and this physical opening of the body is unlike anything else you'll ever do."

I shake my head and look at Caroline. "I wish I'd known all this when I had you because I was scared stiff."

"Well, you were eighteen and didn't have my support system," my daughter says, indicating those gathered at the table.

I smile. "True that."

Kristie goes on. "The deep breathing exercises and strengthening poses are teaching you to stay focused and calm in the moment. Most women can do it almost automatically, and I suspect you will too." Caroline is all smiles. Griffin is quiet, nodding at Kristie as though she's a sage. Our bases are covered.

On Halloween night, the community of Topanga meets at the outdoor market for a party, games, and tailgate trick-or-treating. Miles and Jimi were set on wearing superhero costumes, but when I order in a case of Taft's Raft Bars, they come up with a more creative idea. They've just read *Charlie and the Chocolate Factory* and decide to go as a pair of Oompa Loompas. Despite my childhood Halloween nightmare, I go along to the party. When Miles and Jimi pass out everyone's favorite chocolate bars, they feel like superheroes after all. And when they introduce me as their grandmother, I cloak my fears with a superhero cape of my own.

I continue to await word from Caroline and finally send the email—the one I began writing the day I told her about Finn—flying through cyberspace to Luke. Most mornings, an urge quick and sharp as a trowel sends me to the garden to prune and pick. I harvest some of the last vegetables, the leeks and carrots, their roots trailing dark rich earth, and reflect on my own mucky situation. Though Luke and I continue our lovey-dovey texts and FaceTimes, he doesn't reply to the email. I let it be. I figure he has a lot of reflecting of his own to do. Afternoons, I work on my piece for the *Journal* or help clean the house.

And then one day, when Caroline is thirty weeks along, the baby the size of a cantaloupe, I receive an answer from Luke.

> *Dear Dare,*
>
> *I die a small death every day I don't see you, kiss your pretty mouth, hold you in my arms. And I long to meet Caroline. I see her face (in the picture you texted me) in every mold, in every vat of molten metal, when I open the microwave, on the pages of the books I read. But if she decides she doesn't want to get to know me, I won't come. I want no part in reopening the wound in your relationship that is finally healing.*
>
> *I love you forever,*
> *Luke*

Though I adore him all the more for his sensitivity, for his sacrificial support of my relationship with my daughter, something inside me begins to ratchet tight. I remember a conversation we had on ocean preferences while I was in Oregon. Though Luke had grown up near the Atlantic, it was the Pacific he grew to love. "But the Atlantic's only a half day's drive from Foxfield," I said, "the water *warm* in the summer with golden or white sand that squeezes just right between your toes."

"The Pacific is my home ocean; I knew it first... I know its moods, its color, its nature," he mildly replied, quoting Steinbeck while gazing out at the rocky shore. Silently, I punctuated the quote with a colon instead of a period, for Caroline still hasn't asked me to stay in Topanga, and I'm hoping that if Luke and I are meant to be together, one possibility would be for him to live in Foxfield. But even now—with my fondness for our quaintly sophisticated, academic hamlet—no matter how hard I try, I can't see Luke Henry in Foxfield. The ratcheting grows tighter and tighter.

Still wound tight late that night, I manage to finish my piece on intentional communities. Then I pull up the flight schedule from LAX to Foxfield and purchase a ticket. I'll give the work to Carmen—who must be the last editor in America who prefers to read a hard copy—in person and spend a week seeking comfort and wisdom from Seraphina. So that Caroline won't worry, I'll tell her I'll be back in a week or two, tops.

Someone once said that life is full of comings and goings. I wish they had been a little more specific.

The friend who dropped me off at LAX couldn't be more different than the one who picks me up at Mountainsburg Airport in Virginia. While that morning elegant Rebekah listened quietly to my Luke angst, this evening Seraphina smacks gum and sips from her can of orange soda while running her mouth about a man. "He's the *owner* of the new gym in town, came here from Richmond. Jimbo Aronoff," she says, "a former jockey! A little bitty guy. But everyone calls him Jumbo. Get it?" She's off into one of her galloping whoops of laughter.

"I get," I say, turning to her, a grin working its way across my face despite my ever-present consternation over Luke. "Seraphina Perez, have you become *a gym rat*?"

"*Hell* no, chica! I *volunteer* there to fold towels. And to watch Jumbo in action. He's all *músculos y hombros*. A narrow waist and a six-pack." She punches the fan button on the Trans Am's dash to its highest speed, sending a chill over me but pushing the odor of the Caribbean Colada Little Tree deodorizer hanging from her rearview mirror—that had me inhaling inch-deep breaths—to the back seat.

"Seraphina, you are good medicine for me."

She turns the fan down on the AC. "Now tell me, chica, about my *cariño*."

"Oh, honey. I never really told her that much about Finnegan because she had no memories of him. I figured he was a moot point. But I was so wrong."

"Si. You were."

I glare at her. "Well, why the hell didn't you tell me that?"

"Some things you have to learn for yourself."

"Acknowledged." I sit back as we enter the city limits of Foxfield, and something loosens in me. Foxfield is ablaze with summer flowers, the sidewalks pristine. "Learning about Luke made Caroline feel insecure. She needed to know that Finn had loved her. We talked a long time. God, it was emotionally draining. But it brought us closer. Still, as far as I know, she hasn't come closer to wanting to meet Luke."

"She needs time." Nodding once, she points out a sign with a long pink fingernail where workers are installing an irrigation system in someone's yard: PROCEED WITH CAUTION. At last, we reach home, and she corners the Trans Am into my driveway.

I walk through my house, tears welling in my eyes. Though I've missed its familiar beauty, the grand Georgian feels so small, the view afforded by the curtained windows narrow. I imagine Luke gazing out his great windowed wall at the mountains and evergreens, the valley below. Suddenly needing air, I hurry to the garden.

Seraphina's done a great job watering and keeping things pruned, but I miss the roughness of the garden at Crewtopia, its wildness. The bronze sunflower winks in the sun. I reach for my phone and take a photograph. I haven't told Luke about this evidence of our enduring connection but can't wait to do so. Stepping out amongst the perennials Taffy nurtured, I reach the piece, skirting it until I spot the LHH artist's mark on the back.

The next morning, I'm on the doorstep of the *Journal* at eight a.m. Everyone is happy to see me, and I them. Carmen is seated at his desk, the unlit stump of cigar wedged in the corner of his lips. He looks up. "Dare O'Day! Come in and save me from this," he says, hovering a hand over the chaos that is his desk. "You look like fresh print. I take it I've lost you to the West?"

"That remains to be seen." I fetch us both a cup of coffee and recount the highlights of my weeks away—not the headlines, only the fluff news. He weighs my article in his meaty hand and nods as though impressed with its depth. Then I resign from the *Journal* in my official capacity. Carmen will get back with me soon. Now I'm free to write wherever my future takes me.

I spend the next few days visiting with my friends, Lina and Georgie, and talking late into the nights with Seraphina, who has had a first very satisfying date with Jumbo. I'm caught off guard by a call from Griffin. He says that Caroline, heavier and unwieldier, seems to have lost some of the joy she discovered before I left Topanga. He asks if I can come back earlier than I planned.

The last available seat on tomorrow's flight to California is assigned to Dare Marston O'Day.

Chapter Twenty-Two

Caroline

Griff grins and pulls from under his pillow an action figure he's poached from a set he gave the twins: a surfer, much like the little green army men he played with as a child, though these toys promote not war but fun and fitness. He peels the sheet back from my mountain of bare belly and waits for the baby to roll again. I roll my eyes. But secretly, I love the boyish things he does where the baby's concerned because I know what a fun father he will be. He will lavish the baby with love the way Finnegan did me. And later he'll teach him to love himself and others, to enjoy reading, to surf, and to care for the earth. I've begun to wonder what Luke Henry would have been like as a father. The way my mother talks about him, he would have taught me to work hard, take nothing for granted, to be grateful, open-minded, honest, and allowed me to be a citizen of my day and age. In other words, Jesus the carpenter, Abe Lincoln, and a rugged Mr. Rogers all rolled into one.

"Little surfer, little one," Griff sings to my belly—"whoa, here comes a big one," he says, interrupting the song as the baby obediently creates a swell. He makes the action figure ride the crest of the baby's turning, complete with sound effects, trying to make me laugh.

He looks up at me with his aw-c'mon-sweetheart face, his lips poked out, then plants slow kisses over my skin. He lays his head on my pillowy breasts and resumes his song, gazing into my eyes. When he gets to the part where he asks if the surfer girl loves him, I smile tenderly. "I love you more every single day."

"Me too you." Blotting my happy tears with the sheet, he says he has to get up and get to work because the baby will need clothes and her own surfboard when she is eight—the age he's told Miles and Jimi he will teach *them* to surf. "Bring you a cup of coffee in bed?"

"Yes, please," I say with a mighty stretch of my arms.

Once Griff has left for a meeting in Santa Monica, I prop myself high on our pillows, admiring the new wall color, the way the young sun has added shades of yellow and pink where the walls meet the ceiling. My thoughts return to Luke and the fabulous house that Mom described. She showed me his photograph. He's broad-chested and freckled, ruggedly handsome, with hair the color of mine and my same slightly upturned nose. His eyes are not my green but sort of amber. I know Luke's a big reader, but what are his favorite books? Does he speak in a cultured voice? Is he a man of faith? Does he use good manners? I look at the vase on the bedside table, the chrysanthemums now on their last legs. How did he become interested in sculpting, in working with metals? What kind of music does he listen to? I know Luke appreciates the natural world. Would he like gardening, playing baseball? Is he athletic? What kind of food does he like? Does he know about wines? Is Luke slow to anger like Griff? Is he quick to smile?

Though I haven't told anyone but Griffin, a week ago I received an email of introduction from the man. He simply said he would like to meet me someday and sent his best wishes for the birth of a healthy baby. It was short and sweet. I suspect he Googled my name and got my address from my translation business website. I don't believe Mom would have given out my address without asking me first. My mind whirs on.

When Griffin sails through the door that evening, he says he has a surprise for me, actually two, and that I have to wait until dinner to find out what they are. Parker has made breakfast for dinner, one of his grand slams with a precipice of pancakes. Jimi, secure in Parker's love, no longer wears his bow tie. I smile at Parker as he turns from the stove. Miles asks the blessing and God if the baby will be a girl or a boy. "Wish it was that easy," Rebekah says, "but God reveals things to us in His time." I glance at the Post-its on the chart.

"Somebody's been doing some rearranging," I say, mock stern and accusatory.

Team Boy: 2

Team Girl: 4

Everyone is suddenly fascinated by their eggs, slathering butter on pancakes, passing condiments, and munching bacon. In turn, they look up at me with insistent it-wasn't-me faces. I laugh. "We'll soon see."

Griff takes a long drink of juice and wipes his lips with a pink napkin. He grins at me. "Speaking of soon, I talked with Dr. Bhakta today."

I fumble my knife with a great clank against my plate, making everyone jump. "You what? You did? Why?"

"Who's heard of a babymoon?"

Jimi raises his hand the way they do in school. "I have! Iddinit when the moon is a tiny sliver, a crescent?"

Griffin chuckles. "Super guess, but no. It's a special trip that mothers- and fathers-to-be take before the baby comes and turns the house upside down." The boys knuckle their eyes and make wa-wa baby cries. "You've got it." The baby gives a two-footed push off against my belly as if turning a handspring. Griffin goes on, looking now at me. "I called Dr. B to ask her if I could take you away for a few days. She said, 'By all means, take a babymoon, but do it now. I don't want Caroline traveling past thirty-four weeks.'"

Miles points at the calendar. "Our wedding is right after that. See? On November 27." The "our" melts my heart. "Mrs. Bing even wrote it on our class calendar."

Rebekah touches her chest. "That is sooo sweet. You tell her I appreciate that."

"Okay," he says around a bite of bacon.

Griffin pushes his plate away and rests his elbows on the table. "So we could leave tomorrow and be back well before the wedding." He reaches to squeeze my hand.

"*Tomorrow?* But I have to pack and stuff!"

"Don't sweat it. I'll help you pack. It's a casual destination." He winks at me and turns his attention to Rebekah and Parker. "But I wanted to talk with you. With Dare away, would us also being away create a hardship for you?"

"Not at all!" Rebekah says at the same time Parker says, "No problem-o. We'll make it work."

Rebekah shrugs. "Thanks to Dare, the garden's in great shape. And the wedding is pretty much a fait accompli. The cake's ordered. And we have time to iron out the small details."

"We still have to get Lucie's bow tie," Jimi insists.

"We'll get it," Parker says, putting an arm around the boy and giving him a squeeze.

Griff kisses me. "Okay, then. We're on!"

"But where are we going?"

He points to his chest. "*I* can't tell you that. It's a surprise."

My heart leaps with gladness for the first time since before Mom left for Foxfield. I rub Griffin's foot with mine underneath the table.

"Okay, *Big Daddy*, you're on."

Chapter Twenty-Three

Dare

I return to California to find that Caroline and Griffin have left for a babymoon. But a surprise from her awaits me in my room. The bronze vase is triumphant with twisty purple tulips. An envelope with the word *Mom* written in Caroline's hand leans against it. I breathe in the fresh scent of the tulips before sitting on the bed and taking the envelope in my hands. Never has opening a card been more intriguing or exciting.

Dear Mom,

As we both know—ha ha—the purple tulip symbolizes forgiveness. I'm so sorry that it became too late for you and Taffy to have an adult relationship, but I've enjoyed telling you what she was like. Funny old life! If I hadn't sneaked away that summer, neither of us would have come to know or understand her. Or each other. And maybe ourselves.

But it's not too late for you and me. I understand why it was next to impossible for you and Luke to find each other in the early nineties, and why you married Finnegan. I'm grateful you told me about him, adding color to pages of my story I never realized were neutral. So I'm reconciling my past hurts with my pride and asking you to forgive me my childish reactions. I suppose that's adulting, huh?

Each day I'm more curious about Luke. Maybe sometime soon we can meet.

Now that our secrets are out and you and I are developing a happy and healthy relationship, I would love nothing more than for you to stay on in Topanga. I can't imagine not having you here to love the baby and watch him/her grow.

When Griff invited me on a babymoon, I jumped at the chance to get away. Sorry we left before you got back, but we had a brief window of time. You can thank Rebekah for having the flowers delivered. I love you.

Caroline

P.S. When I asked if you could stay in T.C., I didn't literally mean in the house. As you know, we are bursting at the seams. But definitely nearby. Close by. XO

I hold the note card to my chest, where something bright kindles.

I receive a rave email from Carmen about my piece on intentional communities. The *Journal* will run the article by editor-at-large Dare Marston O'Day, now a freelance journalist. And he'll submit it to other publications. I've done it! A freeing light boomerangs inside my chest. Then abruptly, I realize I've failed to share what I wrote with the crew before turning it in to Carmen. Though the article is not specifically about *this* community and no names or actual locations are used, will they be affronted?

In the spirit of full disclosure, I ping Carmen and ask him to put the brakes on the article until I've emailed each crew member a copy. I sit down and do so, anxiety worming its way into my head. I have to have a unanimous vote of confidence. When we're back together, I'll discuss it with them.

I stay busy helping Rebekah and Parker with last-minute wedding tasks. She and I make paper flowers with patterns from Etsy for the backs of the rental chairs. Rebekah will carry fresh flowers in her favorite palette of red, purple, orange, and burgundy. The fall color at the Top of Topanga has faded, and still there's been not much-needed rain to lay the summer's dust. And then, when the wedding is four days away, we wake to a splendid all-day soaking, the sky platinum. Rebecca dances in the rain in her nightgown. "It's a spa day for the earth, all of it renewed and revitalized!"

Lucie lolls in the fresh grass. Parker, the human ladder, strings white lights in the bows of the trees, beneath which he will marry Rebekah. He takes the boys for a gourmet burger lunch in Los

Angeles, where they find the perfect bow tie for Lucie. I receive compliments on the intentional community piece from Rebekah and Parker. They agree that the piece could inspire others to consider their supportive way of life. Two down, two to go.

Two days before the wedding, Rebekah and I are in the kitchen when Griffin's Jeep swooshes down the drive. I step onto the porch, the chambers of my heart opening in welcome. *Had Caroline's babymoon been all she hoped?*

While my eyes are glued to her smiling face in the front seat, Rebekah drops a dish towel onto the counter. "Who's that with them?" The car doors open. The sun, glinting off the chrome of Caroline's door, obscures my view until Luke Henry steps out onto the fresh earth.

He lifts a bag in each hand, shrugs, and raises expectant eyebrows at me. I run to him. Dropping the bags, he meets me halfway and wraps me in his arms. "You're here!"

"I'm here for you."

I kiss him, my thoughts awhisk in cream.

Caroline and Griffin, who've unloaded their bags onto the porch and exchanged greetings with Rebekah, turn. I hug them, then hold my daughter, as lush as a fresh peach, at arm's length.

"The babymoon looks good on you, darling. Thank you so much for the flowers and the note. They meant everything." I look at Luke and Griffin. "Now, what have you crafty three done?"

Luke, who seems thrilled with Crewtopia, has brought two cases of the Oregon Pinot Gris that I love for the wedding or for *whenever*. Whenever comes after dinner for Parker, Rebekah, and Luke. We've built a bonfire and circled the chairs. Sitting between Luke and Parker, I watch the light play over the faces of all those I love. The twins, happy to be included, hold cups of cocoa with two hands, but Mile's face is perplexed. "So Luke is Caro's dad, but Granddare is not his wife."

"That's right," says his wise mother, again answering no more than her child has asked.

Miles smiles. "Hey! Now Jimi and me *and Caroline* all get a dad!"

We all laugh, Caroline and I misty-eyed.

Parker says, "Why don't you guys take Lucie for a walk when you finish your cocoa?"

"I'm finished now," Jimi answers, slugging his down.

"Me too!" Miles says. And they're off, negotiating over who gets to hold her leash and when.

I turn and survey the three conspirators. "How did this lovely surprise come to be?"

Griffin grins. "All Caroline has talked about is *Luke this, Luke that.*" Flush rises in Caroline's cheeks. "When the babymoon came up, I knew there was only one place to take her."

I almost strangle on my cocoa. "You went to *Clingman Falls?*"

"We did."

"Did you take the train?" They laugh.

"We did."

Luke twists his mouth to one side and nods. "They found The Hermit the same way you did." I am stunned. Mute.

"The minute I saw him, I knew," Caroline says.

"Same," Luke says, already picking up on millennial vernacular.

Caroline looks from Luke to me. "We'd already been emailing and texting before that. He knew I wanted to come." Luke nods. My eyes meet Rebekah's. She's as rapt as I am. "Luke rented us a darling bed and breakfast suite in town."

"Just *darling*," Griff says. Caroline gives him a swat.

She goes on. "He was the best tour guide! But we spent most of our time up at his beautiful cabin, talking for hours." Her lips tremble. "And . . . getting to know each other." Luke takes her hand and pins it in the crook of his arm. "And he cooks! Like really well." I close my eyes as wistful images from my time at Luke's parade behind my lids.

"Luke has great taste in music," Griff says to Parker. "You should see his collection."

I open my eyes as Luke shifts in his chair, releasing Caroline's hand and giving it a pat. He sets his wineglass on the arm of his chair and leans forward, his big hands between his knees. "Enough about me. But Rebekah and Parker, I would like to give you a wedding gift. A honeymoon—if you haven't already made plans—two weeks at the cabin. Maybe in the spring when the scenery is the prettiest? Or whenever you'd like. You can check out my album collection," he adds with a grin. "Oh, and I won't be there."

My heart misses a beat. *Where will you be?* "If Dare will have me, I'll rent us a cabin out here." As Parker and Rebekah rush to thank him, my mind turns inward. *But what happens with you and me between now and then? What about the winter?*

Luke sips his wine and winks at me. I manage a smile. "Sounds lovely to me."

"Consider it done," Luke says to Parker. We'll discuss dates?"

"Awesome." Parker puts his arm around Rebekah and they touch foreheads.

"Pinch me," she says close to his lips.

"Later," he promises, then whispers something to her. Lucie and the boys trot back to the fire and climb into their laps. "How would Squeak One and Squeak Two like to camp out in the pup tent tonight?

"You cannot be serious," Jimi says. Miles straddles Parker's lap and grabs his face between his hands. "Heck yeah, we'd love it!"

"Then let's go get the camping gear from the shed."

I call to Parker, "Hey, Parkie!" He turns. I blow him a thank-you kiss, and he catches it in a fist. I whisper close to Luke's ear, giving his lobe a little nip with my teeth. "Guess who gets to sleep in my bed?" I jump up before he can answer. "Oh, my word! I need to go put on fresh sheets!"

"Leave them be. I want to roll around in your smell. Sheets will be the last thing on your mind."

Parker's parents, the Randalls, arrive the day before the wedding. Parker booked them an Airbnb in town. Their southern Alabama accents make Parker's pale in comparison. Harriet Randall is a tiny wren of a woman, heavily perfumed, while Jerry is tall like Parker with his same carroty hair and a booming jokey voice. "You know, we live in L.A. too," he says, elbowing Griffin. "Lower Alabama." He chuckles merrily. But his voice snuffs out when Parker introduces his parents to Rebekah and the twins. Hope and Jerry exchange a look that two people who have been prepared—in this case for dark skin—but are nevertheless uncomfortable do. Undaunted, Rebekah graciously invites them into the house for tea. *There will be no drama here,* her eyes dictate to the rest of us.

The morning of the wedding, the guys haul the furniture and firepit from the front yard and stack them by the shed. The twins—practically vibrating with excitement and underfoot—are tasked with raking the bonfire remains and summer detritus from beneath the trees. The table and chair rental truck surges up the drive. Men begin arranging chairs and tables for a small reception. I send Rebekah to take a nap. Then I supervise the setup and fasten the flowers we made to the chairs.

An hour later, another vehicle turns into the drive but then makes a loop. *Someone's gotten lost.* But the streamlined white van begins *backing* down the drive. I stand, baffled, shielding my eyes against the sun and watching as Rebekah comes down the steps, freshly bathed and scented in her bathrobe. "Who in the world is this?" I ask. She smiles enigmatically.

Henri St. Martin steps from the van. *What the hell?*

Rebekah produces a purple tulip from behind her back and hands it to me. *Forgiveness.*

Henri says hello and opens the back doors of the van just as the boys trot up.

"The wedding cake!" Miles says. "A ginormous one!"

I stand like one of Luke's sculptures while Henri slowly eases the confection onto a table spread with a white cloth.

"Stay back, fellas," Rebekah warns them. She looks at me. "I told Henri I was getting married when I saw him at the market, and he insisted on making the finest cake west of L.A. as his gift to Parker and me."

I gape at Henri, thinking of the all the butter that must be in the frosting. I find my voice. "It certainly is gorgeous. Merci beaucoup, Henri." I break the head off the tulip close to the stem and poke it into the buttonhole on the lapel of his chef's coat. "We will return to the market for bread soon."

Jimi and Miles, resplendent in small gray tuxedos, their happy faces wreathed by close-trimmed silky afros, walk their mother along the grassy aisle. Rebecca's hair is braided in a beautiful updo and twined with blush-colored flowers that match her gown, a column of blush silk. Harriet Randall's admiring sigh drifts amongst a host of other happy ooohs and ahhs, and I'm happy the Randalls made peace with their son's choice of mate.

They begin with vows of their own. "Parker," Rebekah softly says, "God made the two of us into a wedding quilt stitched from the finest fabric and sprinkled with stars. But he must have realized how unfair it was to put so much magic in one piece and split it into two. How else is it that, when you breathe, my own lungs fill with your energy, your loving, life-giving air?" She smiles. "Though it took a while for both of us to see the truth, we were meant to be pieced back together. I dedicate my half of the quilt to you for the rest of my life."

As sniffles rise into the trees, I stand behind Rebekah and glance at the small gathering: Luke, at whom I tremulously smile; the boys' teacher and her partner; a flock of Rebekah's music students and their parents; our neighbors; Griffin's colleagues; a handful of Parker's friends from L.A; and Lucie, who repeatedly sits and scratches at her bow tie with a hind foot.

Rebekah hands her bouquet to me, and Parker takes his bride's hands. "Rebekah, you are my World Series." The congregation laughs, but Parker takes no notice. His eyes roam Rebecca's face, her lovely hair. "How someone as elegant and wise and talented as you could fall in love with me and give me your heart—or half the quilt—is a mystery I'll never understand. But I dedicate my heart," he says, touching his chest with one hand, "to you for the rest of my days. I will be safe with you at our home plate."

When the ceremony concludes with applause, the couple process, followed by Mom, Griff, and me. Rebekah and her students prepare to perform for us while sweet congratulations are bestowed. Wine and sparkling apple juice flows with the music of Mozart. The refreshments are nibbled, the cake sliced and ravished. Later, when the guests have trickled away, the Randalls, who will head back to their L.A. in the morning, say their goodnights.

Only the crew remains, seated around a large table, the guys with their ties undone and looking sexy. "Let's get this party started," says the bride. Parker springs up to put music on in the house. Lucie jumps into Luke's lap. He removes her itchy bow tie, then goes inside and reappears with a tray: two bottles of Dom Perignon, sparkling apple juice for the boys and Caroline, Griffin, and me, and a collection of mismatched glasses from the kitchen.

Luke and I pour the drinks. Griffin, as best man, stands and raises his glass. "May I propose a toast to the best friends and family one could ever have? We were thrilled when your relationship ripened into love. May that love be an example to all who know you. To Rebekah and Parker."

We raise our glasses. "To Rebekah and Parker."

The twins dissolve into merry laughter, swept up in this unprecedented adult activity. Parker asks if he might propose a toast. "To Jimi and Miles. Boys, your mother and I love you to the moon and back. Now that we are married, I am going to officially adopt you as my sons." He searches both pairs of their round brown eyes. "That is, if you will have me as your forever dad."

When they look up solemnly at Parker and say "We do" in tandem, there are as many tears as there are spills of laughter at their cuteness.

Luke gets to his feet. "I'd like to propose a toast." *How precious is this man? How I love him.* "First, to the stunning bride and handsome groom. May you always be as happy as you are this moment." Rebekah pins a grin to Parker's mouth. "Second, to all of you for your gracious hospitality. And to Dare O'Day, the love of my life, lovelier now than at eighteen." He nods at Caroline. "I don't mean to steal your thunder here, but several days ago, I asked my daughter for her mother's hand in marriage." Nobody moves. "Caroline honored me by saying yes." He hikes up a tux pant leg and takes a knee next to my chair. "Dare, will *you* say yes? Will you marry me?"

My world splits apart. As I whisper "Yes," it comes back together again, and everything is renewed. The others are mere white noise, though they applaud and hoot their approval. I pull him to me for the first long kiss of the night. Rebekah and Parker have their first dance. But nothing at this moment is more important than Luke's mouth on mine.

Two days later, Luke and I are settled into the same Airbnb that Parker rented for his parents. I have bought more white sage and rose water and rid the place of the lingering odor of Harriet's perfume. Our lovemaking seems urgent and new.

But our wedding date is casually discussed, the details unimportant. We haven't even discussed rings. We have all the time in the world. Luke will stay on with me in Topanga through the baby's birth and Christmas and then go back to tend to some foundry work, check on the gallery. Parker and Griffin have begun tricking out the shed for a temporary bedroom for the boys so that Rebekah and Parker can have their privacy. I wonder where in the world they will store all the things already out there. The twins are exultant but miffed that Rebekah insists on setting their old baby monitor out there. I suspect Lucie will be forwarding her address to the new room as well.

Jimi turns the kitchen calendar over to the last month of the year. He jabs a jubilant finger at the square for the twentieth. "Here's the day the baby comes!" December chill blasts its way in. But Caroline, who swears she's as big as the chicken coop, has three fans going in her room all the time. Griffin takes to spending nights next to her in a wool sleeping bag. Like a new bride tending her hearth, Rebekah has been quilting like crazy. She'll sell her year's collection when the Topanga outdoor market becomes the holiday market this weekend. The boys practice writing the last name *Randall* every night. The day Parker, Rebekah, and the boys leave family court as a quartet of Randalls, we celebrate with cake and ice cream.

When the boys take off to play, it occurs to me that the time is right for discussing the intentional community piece with the crew. "May I talk with you for a few minutes?" Concern traces Caroline's brow. "It's about the article I wrote for the *Journal*," I say, patting her hand and reassuring my girl.

Griffin runs a hand through his curls. "Damn, Dare, I'm sorry. Caroline and I read it and thought it was terrific." He looks at Caroline, who grimaces.

"Mom, I'm sorry too. We forgot to get back with you."

"It's fine. Of course. You've had so much going on. I wasn't fishing for compliments, though they're nice to hear, but I needed to know that none of you felt . . . exposed in any way by the article." They exchange looks, shaking their heads, their mouths pursing.

"No problem," Griff says. "There are lots of successful communities, especially in SoCal. It could be based on any of them."

"And as the population grows and ages and healthcare concerns change, providing readers with creative ways of sharing our spaces and supporting each other is what it's all about," my bright girl says.

"I would be interested in the article as someone unfamiliar with the concept," Luke puts in.

I flop back against my chair with relief. "So we have a consensus?"

Parker grins and sticks out his hand, palm down. The rest of us pile ours on top. "It would have been cool, though, if you'd said that a famous baseball player lived there."

One afternoon, two weeks before her due date, Caroline abruptly begins having intense contractions. Griff, Rebekah, and I are at home, the boys staying late at school for chess. Even though they planned for a hospital delivery, Griff declares he's not fighting L.A. traffic trying to get to the hospital only for Caroline to have the baby in the Jeep. He's pacing with his phone, poised to call an ambulance, when Rebekah suggests calling the midwife first to check Caroline for dilation. "Oh yeah, okay. But I need to let Dr. B know." Griff makes the call. While we wait for Kristie to arrive, I buzz Seraphina. She swears she predicted my call and will be on the first plane. "In the meantime, don't let Caroline look at the moon." She ends the call.

"Caroline, Seraphina says not to look at the moon."

She smiles and shakes her head. "*Well, if Seraphina* says so, there must be something to it."

Rebekah attends Caroline as she gets comfy: brushing her teeth, using the bathroom, getting into a fresh nightgown and into bed. As far as I know, Caroline hasn't fretted over giving birth. But I sit on the edge of her bed and ask how she's feeling. "I've had some menstrual-like cramps all day, but that's normal. I didn't realize I was in labor."

Rebekah says, "Your yoga's going to be super beneficial." She looks at me. "Especially if this goes as fast as it looks like it will." Caroline resituates her head on her pillow and lies with her palms up, inviting fresh energy as another contraction hardens her belly. I check my watch as she slowly inhales through her nose and then pauses before slowly exhaling through her mouth. Fewer than four minutes have passed since the last.

Caroline suddenly pipes up. "My water just broke." Griffin pales beneath his tan and goes to get clean towels. We help Caroline scoot onto them.

Kristie, who must have let herself in the house, pops her head in the door and greets us. Dropping her bag, she tents a blanket over Caroline's knees, pulls a pair of gloves from the pocket of an aqua smock, and stretches them onto her hands. "I'm going to check you for dilation."

Griff kneels beside the bed and whispers something to Caroline. He takes her face in his hands and plants little kisses all over it so tenderly that I have to look away. Another contraction slices through Caroline. She inhales through her nose, pauses, exhales through her mouth. Four minutes again.

"Let's see what we have here, Caroline. Are you doing your organized breathing? Push out the tension from your head to your toes. Okay," she says stripping off the gloves. I grab the trash can and hold it up so she can drop them in. "You're eight centimeters dilated, well into transition." She smiles. "Your baby's coming this afternoon."

The gravity of the room increases. Caroline continues breathing like a champ. "Let your breathing relax your shoulders and chest now. That's it. Great job," Kristie says. I want so badly to know what Caroline is thinking, but she is deep inside herself now with her baby, nurturing it already. "Move your focus down to your abdomen, your hips." Caroline's breathing is deeper now, her eyes tightly closed. Kristie looks at me. "Your face is tensing. Okay if Griffin or your mom massages it?" Caroline nods rapidly. Griff nods at me, giving me the honor. A new contraction hits three minutes later, this one lasting sixty seconds.

Gingerly, I climb on the bed and rub light, slow circles on her temples, her brow, her jawline. Her face relaxes beneath my hands. "Thanks, Mom," she murmurs as another contraction homes in three minutes later and lasts ninety seconds. Caroline changes her breathing pattern at Kristie's direction, a series of shallow breaths followed by one long deep cleansing one, and focuses on relaxing each part of her body in turn.

I sit back on the floor, my back against the wall, breathing along with her. On the other side, Griff leans on the bed and murmurs to her. Naturally, he and I adapt our breathing to hers, changing patterns when she does. I give him a reassuring smile.

For two hours, we keep this up. Kristie asks Rebekah for some ice to moisten Caroline's mouth. The contractions are coming in one-to-two-minute intervals now, punctuated by Rebekah pounding ice with a mallet in the kitchen, and lasting much longer. Caroline gratefully mouths crushed ice, then breathes on but complains of back pain.

"The baby's moving down," Kristie says, "pressing on your sacrum. That pressure is normal and will help you push more efficiently when it's time."

"It's time!" Caroline says, her brow popping with sweat that runs down the sides of her face. She clutches the sheets, her arms shaking.

"Focus your mind on moving the baby down and out," Kristie says. "When you feel the need to push, take a deep breath and slowly release it while you bear down."

"I need a *drishti*, something to focus on," Caroline insists. "I had a picture packed for the hospital." Kristie pulls on a new pair of gloves and turns to rest her chin on her shoulder, surveying the room.

"How about the poster over your bed?"

"No, I need Mom. I want Mom's face."

I rise on legs I'm not sure will hold me up but manage to move next to the midwife where Caroline can see me. I smile and nod at my panting and blowing child, steeling myself not to cry. Her green eyes fasten on mine.

Kristie looks up at Griffin. "The baby's *almost* out. Move down next to me?"

Griffin slides his arm beneath Caroline's shoulders and holds her, helping her rise higher on her pillow. "Baby," he says to her, "you know I'd walk through hell wearing gasoline underwear for you, but I just can't watch."

Caroline lets out a long whoop of laughter and release. "Here we go," Kristie says, catching a messy bundle in her hands and laying it face down on Caroline's abdomen, rubbing its bag with a towel until it squalls. Turning it over, she calls to Caroline and Griffin. "It's a girl! Just beautiful."

My heart is so full, I need to loosen my bra.

Seraphina arrives the next day, cooing and fussing over the baby and Caroline in Spanish. She presents the baby with a pink onesie printed with CARIÑO EL SEGUNDO on the front. Caroline stares at her. "I love it, but how did you know to get pink?"

"I saw it in the moon. You know. In the village where I grew up, women are taught to read the moon for revelations."

The next day, Caroline's milk comes in. Griffin can't seem to take his eyes off her enormous breasts. "How long do we have to wait to make love again," I hear him ask her.

The Panakises are on their way from Hawaii. Griff and Caroline are waiting to reveal the baby's name until they arrive so that they'll feel more a part of things. The twins are smitten with the six-pound baby, especially her caper-sized toes. "Are we like her uncles?" Miles asks at the dinner table.

"No, you're like her cousins," Griff says, winking at Rebekah. "And she's gonna think you're the coolest ever."

Sallie and Corbin Panakis arrive and are thoughtful enough to stop in Santa Monica and bring a takeout dinner for the whole of us: huge pans of moussaka, bread, and Greek salad. We sit out around the firepit in chairs, the boys and Parker on quilts. Corbin is exactly what I expected: a commanding figure with dark hair cropped in a military cut. Sallie is tall, slim, and very quiet.

At dinner, Griff's father asks Luke and me—before the entire gathering—to help persuade Caroline and Griffin to marry for the sake of the child. Acid rises in my esophagus. "They need a stable relationship and a safer, more traditional home."

Caroline and Griff have planned a sweet baby-naming ceremony after dinner. I'll not let Corbin ruin it. For a moment, I watch Caroline and Griffin, who are oblivious, making goo-goo eyes at each other and the baby, and itch to fling Corbin a scathing retort. I look at Luke, who closes his eyes and nods. I sit tall. "Caroline and Griffin are intelligent adults. Whether or not they marry or live in a circus wagon is their business, not ours." Seraphina bounces her fists on her knees and gives me a yass-girl smirk.

Sallie's cheeks blaze as she lays a hand on her husband's forearm. "Let's talk later," she says sweetly.

Griffin hops up and claps. "Are we ready?" He asks the twins to distribute tiny candles he ordered from a church supply company to each of us. I watch Miles hand a candle to Corbin. *Can't you see that Crewtopia grows not only vegetables and flowers but finer things like this precious little boy?* Caroline, Rebekah, and I have prepared readings. When it's my turn, I smile and look intently at the Panakises as I quote words from Mother Teresa, including "You will teach them to live, but they will not live your life... the print of the way you taught will always remain," while Luke, as the maternal grandfather, holds the baby. Caroline lights her candle at the firepit. She passes the flame to my candle, and the light moves from person to person, creating a magical circle of love. I pray the spark of disapproval that Corbin has introduced in the midst of our joy will be drenched.

When everyone's candle is lit, Caroline begins to speak, her eyes outshining her candle. "Flowers are special to my mother and me, as well as was a woman who we wish could be here tonight. I name this child Poppy Taft Panakis."

Griffin adds, "She will be Poppy." He smiles at his father. "Poppy Panakis."

Chapter Twenty-Four

Caroline

On Poppy's due date, Mom and I stroll through the Topanga Canyon holiday market, arm in arm. Poppy's securely swaddled against my chest, wearing a bite-sized, hand-knit baby reindeer cap. I feel so proud of my lovely baby and appreciate each compliment she receives. "How about this new bro bonding thing? Griff, Luke, and Parker heading out to cut down a tree? Think they'll come back beating their chests with this massive fir we can't get through the door?"

Mom laughs. "I love it. I hope it becomes a tradition."

James's Taylor's "Have Yourself a Merry Little Christmas" tinkles down to us from speakers at the corners of the big white tent. As Mom examines natural wreaths, my head reels with the far-reaching and ambitious decisions my father made. He's keeping the beautiful cabin in Clingman Falls as a second home, a place that any of us can use as a getaway. He and Mom will live in the rental cabin in Topanga until he finds land far enough out to operate a foundry but close enough to Crewtopia to be near the family. In confidence, he asked me if I thought Griff and Parker would be receptive to letting him help them build an addition onto the bungalow at Crewtopia with more beds and baths. Poppy will need a room of her own. And if Seraphina read the moon right, there may be more babies. I wonder if they'll be mine and Griff's or Rebekah and Parker's. Maybe both?

Mom and I stop and buy a plus grande chocolate bûche de Noël from Henri and wish him Merry Christmas. A young woman selling fresh jams does a double take at Mom. "Didn't I see your picture in *The New Yorker*? The piece on intentional communities?"

Mom almost manages to suppress the grin that spreads across

her face. "Yes. I authored the piece. Hello. I'm Dare O'Day. Did you enjoy the read?"

"I loved it. We just started a community up near Trippet Ranch. You helped validate—man, for *thousands* of people—the rewards of the life." She laughs wryly. "Especially for parents who don't get it." Mom thanks her and buys a dozen jars of strawberry lavender jam to send as gifts.

A woman selling vintage crèches tilts her head as though sizing us up. "Are you sisters or mother and daughter? I mean you look so much alike, even your mannerisms."

"She's my mother," I say proudly. "Though we're only eighteen years apart."

The woman smiles. "So you've always been close?"

Mom and I exchange a nostalgic smile. "We've had our issues," she says, answering for us, "but have come to a good place."

"Well, Merry Christmas to you both," the woman replies warmly.

"You too," I say with a smile as Mom and I drift to the next booth.

As James Taylor sings the part where he wonders if in a year we'll be together, Mom reaches out to stroke one of Poppy's peach-soft cheeks. "Wouldn't it be wonderful if Taffy could be here with us? We'd be four generations."

"It would." I wonder if Mom's thinking as I am of the joyful Christmastimes we forfeited before arriving at this good place. Though we weren't aware of it at the time, Taffy started each of us on our paths toward reconciliation, first with lessons of hard work, perseverance, and independence, and then of wisdom and forgiveness. "Mom, I found the list of values you wrote on a Post-it when you first came here: honesty, forgiveness, and renewal."

"You did? I wondered what happened to that."

"I figured out what you were up to when you brought me chrysanthemums for honesty. And that's why I gave you the tulips for forgiveness."

Mom halts and reaches out to rub tiny circles on the baby's back. "Guess we didn't get around to renewal. Maybe this little flower here is our symbol for new beginnings." I blink around tears of happiness and fulfillment.

"Happy holidays," says the next vendor, an artisan of stained glass suncatchers.

We return the greeting. "Mom, look! A sunflower."

"OMG," she says, taking a piece from the woman's quickly outthrust hand.

"Adoration, loyalty, and strength," we murmur at the same time.

Mom holds it up to the twinkle lights encircling the display. "I think I'll send it to Seraphina for her loyalty and love for the three of us," she says, including Poppy with a fond glance. "To hang in Taffy's kitchen window overlooking the garden."

"Yass! It'll pay homage to the love of the earth and flowers that Taffy instilled in us." I think for a minute as I survey the collection. "You don't happen to have a hyacinth, do you?"

The woman beams, turning to her display. "I do indeed."

Mom stills. "Caroline. Renewal." Our eyes and futures lock together in that moment.

The woman beams and hands me a pretty purple and green piece. "You gals *sure* speak the language of flowers."

Mom and I exchange a grin as the woman wraps the suncatcher in Christmas tissue. "I'm getting this one for you, darling, for Poppy's room," she says.

The vendor quickly looks up. "Did you say *Poppy*?"

I pat my baby's bottom through the snuggly. "Yes, my daughter's name is Poppy."

"You know, I *had* a poppy, but it may have sold. Let me check a box. One moment." Mom clutches my arm and I hold my breath as a flash of red appears. "Here we are. The last one."

"Mom, I'm getting that for you." I stumble over my words to get them out. "For peace. For . . . the security and unconditional love our Poppy will know all her life. From her parents. And *grandparents*. And the legacy she'll pass on to her own children." We exchange a hug from which neither of us seems willing to let go until we're laughing and wiping our eyes on a burp cloth before paying for the gifts. The vendor holds out a festive bag, in which she's placed our treasures.

"Merry Christmas to your beautiful family."

"And to yours," I say with a shiver as a gust of bright cold air falls around us. I blow through fisted hands and recheck Poppy's swaddling. "Let's get some cocoa."

"Oooh, let's, with lots of gooey marshmallows."

I hoot a laugh. Poppy startles, awakens, and peers solemnly up at me with eyes that are already greening. I kiss her button nose. "We'll toast to Taffy's eccentricities. And how she taught us it's okay to be who we are."

Mom's Guatemalan market basket is heavy, though her personal assets are lighter. She has sold her Foxfield home to Seraphina and Jumbo Aronoff for one dollar.

I can't wait to take Poppy to Taffy's garden, to watch my little flower toddle through the others, to watch her face light as it tips to meet the sunflowers.

The End

Acknowledgments

This manuscript just felt like the one. The truest women's fiction. The novel for which I would stop the insanity of querying and submissions and become an indie author. The story for which I created Evocative Publishing LLC. For inspiring and holding my hand through that entrepreneurial endeavor, I thank my friend, the savvy visionary and innovative writer Kristina Parro.

I see so much of my former critique partner Elizabeth Parman's suggestions in the pages of *Topanga Canyon*.

A big thank you to my copy editor, formatter, and friend, the perspicacious and kind Julie Klein.

I must thank the members of the Women's Fiction Writers Association, who supported and helped me learn the elements of the craft, especially Christine Adler, Angela Shupe, and Laurie Batzel. And *mille mercis* to those who have furthered my branding by helping make *The Evocative Author Podcast* a reality: Dan Blank, Greg Ketchum, and my growing roster of amazing and supportive guest authors. #authorssupportingauthors is real!

To the amazing boss women business leaders who have helped me grow a Greenville readership by promoting this novel and inviting me to hold special signing events: Ashley Warlick and June Wilcox of M. Judson's Booksellers, and Naomi Horne and Jodie Reece of Wisteria Spa.

To the essential longtime champion family and friends: Mary and Rob Sumner, Susan Beth and Bob Purifico, Lisa Stanford, Joan S. Stanford, Lina DiMora, Lynne Niva, Betts Lofton, Andi Defelice, Deb Ketchum, Genna Fable, Alice Vargo, Theresa Jackson, Sheila Athens, Nancy Dettor, Sharron Buyer, Anne Chambers, Kelly Bowie, Vicki Bell, and Mary Tillson.

And to my "crew," who made me feel like the real deal from the start. Porter and Olivia, you are this writer's raison d'être.

Made in the USA
Columbia, SC
12 May 2025